STAR-CROSSED
Betas

THE NORTHERN SHIFTERS
BOOK 1

EMORY WINTERS

This book was self-edited. Please email author.emorywinters@gmail.com if you would like to report any typos or errors.

Cover designed by Emory Winters with cover artwork from Darin @thewellnessartist.

Copyright © 2024 by Emory Winters

All rights reserved.

No portion of this book may be reproduced in any form (with the exception of quotes and exerts on social media) without written permission from the publisher or author except as permitted by UK copyright law.

This is a work of fiction. Unless otherwise indicated, all the names, characters, businesses, places, events and incidents in this book are either the product of the author's imagination or used in a fictitious manner. Any resemblance to actual persons, living or dead, or actual events is purely coincidental. The use of any real company and/or product names is for literary effect only. All other trademarks and copyrights are the property of their respective owners.

ISBN – 978-1-7390946-1-4

BLURB

Connor:- Ending up in an arranged marriage with the man who ripped my heart out of my chest and put it through a blender—was not on my bingo card this year. Yet what did I expect when I made the most clichéd mistake of falling in love with the son of the enemy pack? If we don't find a way to coexist and build a pack together, we're in breach of the peace agreement.
But how do you forgive the unforgivable?

Phoenix:- Regret should be the title of my memoir. One secret spilt to the wrong person toppled my life like a house of cards. I'm desperate for Connor to forgive me, but too much is at stake if I tell him the truth about why I betrayed him. How are we supposed to build a life together on a land filled with bitter-sweet memories? The last pack on this land died in a series of fires fifty years ago.
I only hope that Connor's fiery temper doesn't lead us to the same fate.

CONTENT ADVISORY

Some of the content warnings I've included contain spoilers, so I have put them at the back of the book. Star-crossed Betas is not a dark book, but I would rather you be safe than sorry.

This book is for an 18+ audience and includes explicit on-page sex scenes between two consenting adults. Enjoy ;)

Please note that Star-crossed Betas is based in the UK and is written using British English, so there may be the odd word or phrase you're unfamiliar with. I have listed a few below:

- Joggers/jogging bottoms = Sweatpants

- Footy/Football = Soccer

- Joiner = Carpenter/woodworker

- Quid = £1

- Car boot/boot = Trunk

- Bum = Bottom

- Pissed = Drunk or Angry

- Mardy = Annoyed

DEDICATION

For everyone who's into the wine and not the label.

CONTENTS

Meet the Packs   1
Prologue   3
Part I
1. One   7
2. Two   16
3. Three   24
4. Four   31
5. Five   41
6. Six   53
7. Seven   63
8. Eight   73
9. Nine   85
10. Ten   98
11. Eleven   108
12. Twelve   117
13. Thirteen   126
14. Fourteen   134
15. Fifteen   142

16. Sixteen	155
17. Seventeen	160
18. Eighteen	170

Part II

19. Nineteen	178
20. Twenty	186
21. Twenty-one	197
22. Twenty-two	205
23. Twenty-three	216
24. Twenty-four	227
25. Twenty-five	238
26. Twenty-six	252
27. Twenty-seven	263
28. Twenty-eight	270
29. Twenty-nine	278
30. Thirty	293
31. Thirty-one	302
Epilogue	311
Coming next...	321
Acknowledgements	322
About the author	325
Content Warnings	327

MEET THE PACKS

THE LAKE DISTRICT PACK

Alpha Juliette Campbell (Phoenix's mother)
Malcolm Campbell (Phoenix's father)
Jasper Campbell (Phoenix's older brother)
Phoenix Campbell
Alfie Campbell (Phoenix's younger brother)
Jade Campbell (Jasper's wife)
Henry Campbell (Jasper and Jade's son)
Alice Graham (Phoenix's best friend)
Milo Graham (Alice's brother)

THE PEAK DISTRICT PACK

Alpha Sean Kelly (Connor's father)
Cara Kelly (Connor's mother – deceased)
Samuel Kelly (Connor's older brother)
Connor Kelly
Niamh Kelly (Connor's twin sister)
Mikey Kelly (Connor's cousin)
Karl Kelly (Connor's uncle)

William Locke (Connor's best friend)
Orla McNamara (Connor's great grandmother and pack witch)

THE NORTHUMBRIA PACK

Alpha David Eastwood
Margot Eastwood
Calvin Eastwood
Benjy Eastwood
Iris Eastwood
Oliver Armstrong
Nina Fenwick (pack witch)

OTHER KEY CHARACTERS

Noah McNamara (Connor's cousin and a witch)
Natasha Richardson (witch)

PROLOGUE

The horrible sensation dredges up an old memory I had long forgotten. I was only a child, maybe eight years old at the time. I had woken up in the middle of the night, unable to move a muscle or make a noise. Silent tears soaked my cheeks as I hoped and wished my dad would come and find me and make the awful feeling of being locked in my mind go away.

The next morning, when I had reawoken, this time to the sun shining through the gaps in my jungle-themed curtains, it felt like nothing more than a bad dream. The nightmare had faded into the recesses of my mind, and this was the first time I'd thought of that night since.

This feels almost the same but different. It's worse somehow that I can open my eyes and look around the room, but my muscles are frozen in place.

In my periphery, the flames are spreading along the carpet, licking at the hem of the curtains, hundreds of fiery tongues eating through the fabric rapidly. Too rapidly. My eyes close instinctively, the thick, relentless smoke making them red-raw.

If I'm lucky, the smoke will kill me before the fire does. Bile rises up my oesophagus at the thought of being awake when the flames engulf me. I've never considered myself to be particularly morbid, rarely dwelling on how I might eventually die. In contrast, I currently find myself evaluating and ranking what kind of death would be preferable over another. In the face of being burned alive, I can confirm that I would take most of the alternatives right about now.

Except maybe a death involving a deadly spider—I really hate spiders.

With nothing to do but lie here and wait for it all to be over, my overactive brain won't switch off. I find myself praying the authorities discover my body before he does. Nobody should have to find their loved one's charred remains in the bed they shared together.

Part of me regrets that we argued earlier, and he's pissed off with me, but that's why I'm alone while he's out running off his bad temper. I've also never been so grateful for his short fuse because, although it won't be fun to die here by myself, it would be a hundred times worse to watch him suffer by my side. He'll be furious with me for dying before him, but I'm grateful he'll have a long life ahead of him.

When I reopen my eyes, the curtains are fully ablaze. The bedroom window makes a loud cracking noise, shattering from the intense heat. I try to take deep breaths, inhaling as much of the smoke as I can, willing it to end my life before the fire does. My chest rattles when I cough, and my eyes burn and water furiously.

Closing my eyes once more, I decide it's probably best to keep them that way. All I can do is wait and see what takes me first—the smoke or the flames.

PART 1

ONE
MARCH 2022 - PRESENT DAY

PHOENIX CAMPBELL

The tension is so palpable it's like a living, breathing beast sucking the air out of the room. I'm pretty sure outer space would be a less hostile environment. My older brother, Jasper, grips my knee to still my incessant leg bouncing.

God forbid the son of an Alpha show any sign of weakness.

The six of us have been sitting around this large oak table in some tiny village in Yorkshire for over seven hours. My mum, and also my Alpha, Juliette Campbell, sits poised without a hair out of place. Her honey-blonde locks are long but tied back into a ponytail today, making her face look more severe than usual.

"I'm sure you can appreciate that given the scandal *your* daughter caused during our last attempt at this, we need some assurances that there is a sufficient deterrent in place to prevent history from repeating itself," my mum says to the other Alpha across from her. Her voice is firm and doesn't waver despite this being the fifth time she's said precisely this in so many words.

Alpha Kelly is opposite her—in every sense of the word. His hair is almost as fiery red as his daughter Niamh's, except for the smattering of grey starting to appear near his temples.

Where my mum has been educated within an inch of her life and holds three degrees plus a PhD, Alpha Kelly probably never finished high school and has made his living as a roofer. His face is weathered, but the wrinkles around his eyes and mouth show a man who has laughed and smiled for most of his life.

"As I've already said, I understand your concern. But surely you can appreciate I'm never gonna sign somethin' leavin' us solely responsible should anythin' prevent this weddin' goin' ahead. I've agreed to keep Connor confined to his room until the weddin' takes place, and I think that's more than reasonable." Alpha Kelly sounds exasperated, his Northern Irish accent getting stronger as he grows increasingly frustrated.

Heat crawls up my neck and along my cheeks with embarrassment. The implication that the only way Connor will go through with marrying me is if he's kept prisoner until the big day is humiliating. When I glance up from the scuff mark I've been staring at on the table, I almost flinch at the expression on Connor's face.

His piercing green eyes, once filled with affection for me, are absent of anything but venom. Where his hair used to be shaggy and unruly, he has it trimmed short now, only a bit of length on top. It makes him look older, emphasising his sharp features. I hate the physical reminder that an entire year has passed since I last laid eyes on him.

His intense gaze used to set me on fire from the inside out, but now it makes my heart feel like it's pumping ice through my veins. I've never feared Connor, but today, I fear what he could say or do out of retribution. I'm not even worried about the harm it could cause *me* but the irreparable harm it could cause *us*. Connor doesn't forgive others easily but is even less inclined to forgive himself.

I suppose I should be grateful; this time last year, his twin sister Niamh was sitting across from me. Day to his night. Where Niamh is sunshine personified, Connor is a storm. I have nothing against Niamh; she's beautiful with her fiery red hair, freckled nose and dimpled cheeks, but I've only ever been interested in the boy she shares those green eyes with. After twelve months of absolutely no communication, I'd sooner be on the receiving end of his withering glare and snarky remarks than return to the radio silence.

Today marks the second attempt at forming a peace agreement between our two packs. Back in 1972, a series of arson attacks led to the deaths of every single wolf shifter in the Yorkshire Dales pack. It's one of the worst tragedies in our recent history. My great-grandfather, who was Alpha at the time, accused the then Alpha of the Peak District pack of being behind the attacks, and they, in turn, accused us. With zero evidence, let alone forensic evidence, both packs came to the logical conclusion to begin a war with one another.

A year ago, my mum and Alpha Kelly sat down to hash out a peace agreement to put an end to the turf war. The main component was I married Alpha Kelly's daughter, Niamh, and for us to build a pack together in Yorkshire. A day or two before the wedding was due to take place, much to my relief, Niamh ran off and married her childhood best friend, Will Locke.

The next twelve months saw an increase in trespassing and violence between the two packs, so that brings us to today, peace agreement 2.0.

Sighing deeply, I psyche myself up for what I'm about to propose. Both Alpha's heads snap towards me at the sound of my interruption. The impulse to bear my neck is strong, but I clench my teeth until the need fades to the back of my mind.

"Might I suggest a solution that doesn't involve anyone being held hostage? What if we skip the engagement?" I keep my head down in submission while waiting for them to respond.

"If you haven't noticed, *Phoenix*, we've spent the last seven hours sittin' around this table with this *engagement* as the sole item on the agenda," Connor snaps back. I hate how he says my name like it's poison on his tongue, yet his familiar Mancunian accent makes my heart ache at the memory of its absence.

"You misunderstand me. I'm proposing we sign the agreement and have the binding ceremony for the marriage on the same day. We can still have the wedding party next Saturday as planned, but we'd make it official in advance." I manage to speak clearly despite my heart trying to beat its way out of my chest. As I lift my gaze to Connor's, I'm met with a brief slack-jawed expression before he swiftly schools it back to his preferred scowl of indifference.

"Looks like all the money you threw at the boy's education paid off; that's not a bad idea." Alpha Kelly's tone is baiting my mother. However, given she makes no secret of our pack's wealth and the fact she spends a considerable amount of it on private tutors for every member, Alpha Kelly is barking up the wrong tree—pun fitting but not intended.

My mum looks over at me before she responds. I hate how much I preen at the pride in her eyes.

"I agree with my son. I suggest we meet back here tomorrow to sign the agreement. Jasper will contact Calvin Eastwood to officiate the marriage with Nina Fenwick to assist in the binding ceremony." I'm glad it's Calvin who will be leading the ceremony. He comes across as quite stoic and serious, but he has a soothing presence I know I'll be grateful for tomorrow. As the eldest son of Alpha Eastwood, Calvin is well suited to his future as Alpha of the Northumbria pack. I've never met their pack witch, Nina. But our pack doesn't have a witch so I'm curious as to what she might be like.

"I would also propose that during the week between the official ceremony and the wedding party, Phoenix and Connor spend half the week residing with us in the Lake District and half the week residing in the Peak District before they take up residence in Yorkshire. It will give us time to sort out more permanent accommodations for them." My mum presents her 'proposal' as more of a non-negotiable statement.

Alpha Kelly looks to his second in command, Sam, his eldest son and Alpha heir, who dips his chin in agreement. When he moves his gaze to Connor, the thick tension that has been an additional guest here today swirls around the room suffocatingly. Eventually, Connor submits, bearing his neck to his Alpha.

"Agreed. We'll meet back here tomorrow at noon then." My mum merely nods in response, stands, and puts her hand out for Alpha Kelly to shake. He mirrors her, shaking her hand firmly and bringing the meeting to a close.

Our fate is sealed.

As we file out of the room, nothing more is said. The atmosphere would lead you to believe we are heading for the gallows rather than matrimony.

When we leave the house, I walk briskly towards the tree line, not hesitating to strip once I'm out of sight. Shoving my clothes into my backpack, I shift quickly, scooping up my bag with my mouth before I set off running.

I was nine years old when I first shifted, a reasonably average age. It took so much concentration to manage it back then, yet now it often feels as though I've shifted as soon as the thought has crossed my mind. It doesn't hurt exactly, but it's an odd sensation. Similar to the feeling you get after a big workout, your muscles are sore and aching, but it kind of feels good at the same time. Satisfying—like you've finally scratched an itch you couldn't reach all day.

Needing to burn up some of the pent-up energy from sitting around in a tense room all day, I run swiftly through the woods. My paws pound against the damp ground as I weave in and out of the trees.

Around three-quarters of an hour later, I slow down as I approach the familiar cottage. The beautiful stone house in Kendal sits on the very edge of our pack's territory. The property has been in my family for generations. Although it isn't the home my family usually resides in, it's one of my favourite places to stay.

The scents of our land—fresh water with earthy undertones—fill my senses, and I suddenly have to swallow a lump in my throat. It's only just hitting me that this land I've called home my entire life won't belong to me anymore. In a week, I'll be living in Yorkshire, trying to build a new life there.

Before I can get too caught up in my thoughts, I'm assaulted by a small timber wolf bursting through the front door. My younger brother Alfie is fourteen, and as a late shifter, the novelty hasn't worn off yet.

Although his fur is similar in colour to mine, when he's in his human form, he's the spitting image of Jasper. They both take after our mum with honey-blonde hair, pale blue eyes and porcelain skin. I, on the other hand, am the double of our dad, tall and broad with olive skin, chestnut brown hair and brown eyes.

I've always been especially close with my dad; he's a pure beta, same as me. Jasper is an Alpha-beta, which essentially makes him the Alpha heir. My younger brother Alfie is a beta but has a dormant Alpha gene, so he'll probably always be a beta.

Our mum has been grooming Jasper to take over for as long as I can remember, and I was often overlooked as a result. I think my dad must have seen it too, because he always made an effort to spend extra time with me.

"Nix. Mum. Alpha Mum. Where's Jasper? All Safe?" Alfie sends his jumbled thoughts through the pack bond.

"Jasper's safe. He's gone to get Calvin. Shift back, Alf," I reply, before returning to my human form and throwing on my clothes from my bag.

Standing in the doorway is my dad; he smiles at me softly and squeezes the back of my neck as I walk through the front door. He smells of old leather and *home*.

The cottage is toasty inside; my parents' housekeeper, Claire, has lit the fire and prepared dinner. Claire joined us from a pack in Cornwall when I was still a toddler. She was originally our nanny but became the housekeeper once the three of us were enrolled in school. We all gather around the table to eat. She's made lasagne with garlic bread—one of my favourite meals.

"Thanks, Claire. You're the best," I say to her as I serve up an exorbitant amount of food onto my plate.

"You're welcome, love." She smiles at me over her shoulder while clearing up the kitchen. My parents are both reticent through dinner. Still, Alfie compensates for the silence by yammering on about his latest D&D campaign.

After scoffing down a ridiculous amount of food, I try to make my excuses and head to bed. My thoughts are scattered, anxiety swirling in my gut, and I desperately need some time alone.

"Can I speak to you privately before you go to bed, Nix?" my mum asks. I nod and then follow her into the study when she gets up.

I love this study; it's small and cosy, the walls lined with old, musty-smelling books. In one section is over a hundred books detailing the history of our pack since its inception in 1845. I've always loved history and learning about the way of life back when my ancestors settled on this land all those years ago. I suppose it's really no surprise that I chose to become a history teacher.

The weathered, red chesterfield armchair squeaks slightly as I sit, and my mum leans against the windowsill opposite me.

"Don't tell your dad, will you," she says, lighting a long, thin menthol cigarette. I snicker, knowing my dad will smell it immediately from the other room. She takes a long pull and then blows out the smoke from the corner of her mouth through the ajar window.

"I wanted you to know that as your Alpha and as your mum," she tacks on 'mum' like this fact is an afterthought. "I am incredibly proud of you for the sacrifice you're making to ensure the future safety of our pack," she says; her little speech is somewhat stilted and not particularly heartfelt. My shoulders droop, and I nod in response. I'm not entirely sure what I'm supposed to say to that.

She's made it very clear what limited choice I have in my own future. This is the woman who tried to forbid me from studying history at Uni, declaring I should be getting myself an engineering degree instead. I don't have a mathematical bone in my body, so I never understood where the idea came from other than it being Jasper's chosen career path.

"You seem... less resistant this time around?" She phrases it as a question, and my back stiffens in response. The memories of the arguments from a year ago flood my mind. Things were said and done during that time that she can never take back.

"Yes, well, a lot has changed in the last year," I reply, being purposefully vague.

"Indeed it has. You've grown up a lot. It's a shame, in some ways, you won't get the opportunity to be a beta for your brother. You would have made an excellent right-hand man." I can't help but bristle at her words. I'm not ashamed to be a beta; honestly, most of the time, I'm grateful I'll never have any part in leading a pack. Still, I know my mother, and I know she views me as inferior for it.

"I should get some sleep. Big day tomorrow and all," I say, waiting for her nod of dismissal before I leave the room.

"Goodnight, Phoenix."

TWO
June 2017 – Five Years Ago

CONNOR KELLY

Usually, I love running with my pack, especially with my twin sister, Niamh. I kind of hate to admit it, but she's also my best friend. We even had our first shifts on the same night, shortly after our eighth birthday, which is super rare.

Today, though, I need some space.

Tomorrow marks seven years since our mum passed away. Nobody knows exactly why she ended up so far beyond our territory. Mum told my da she was off to do border checks, and when she never came home, he tracked her scent.

Da found her right where I'm standing, in the Forest of Bowland, which is neutral territory. She'd been caught in a bear trap. We don't have bears here, and the traps have been illegal since the eighteen hundreds. My da spent years trying to get to the bottom of it, and it felt as if he lost a part of himself in the process.

He and my mum were mates. They met when they were eighteen and knew it through scent alone. My mum used to tell me my da smelled like a fine vintage leather jacket and *trouble*. He would wink at her and say, 'Aye, but I'm your brand of trouble'.

TWO

Seven years on, and my chest still aches to think of her. She's the reason I fell in love with books. No matter what was going on in our lives and how busy everyone got, my mum would sit down each night and read to each of us. I'm pretty sure I still read so much because I like the idea of her looking down on me and feeling proud. I'm probably well past the age I should be seeking my dead mother's approval, but it is what it is. Reading feels like it tethers me somehow to her memory.

I try to outrun my melancholy thoughts. It's best not to stop in this particular forest. Sometimes omegas live here. Omegas are wolf shifters that, for whatever reason, have ended up without a pack. If they don't join another pack quickly enough, they get stuck in their wolf form and eventually become feral. They usually keep to themselves, but they can suddenly become violent if you accidentally encroach on what they consider their territory.

It rained heavily this morning, so the forest bed is bouncy under my paws, and everything smells more intense than usual. The air has been sticky for weeks, and there's nothing quite like the crisp smell after the rain has cut through the humidity.

As we head into the summer months, all the foliage is luscious green, and the smell of rabbits and birds fills my nose. Before I realise how far I've run, I find myself right on the edge of the forest; slightly further on is Ingleton, which is right on the cusp of the Yorkshire Dales territory—the territory I'm forbidden to set foot on without my Alpha's permission.

My pack's territory is one of the largest in the UK. We're a split pack, so beyond our territory in England, which spans from Liverpool through Manchester and up to the Peak District, we also have land in Mourne, Northern Ireland. My da travels back to Mourne as much as possible, but with the ongoing turf war with the Campbell pack, he can't be there as much as he'd like.

My da was born into the Belfast pack but was expelled at eighteen because he was an Alpha-beta, and the Alpha saw him as a threat. That's how he and my mum met. He petitioned to join the Peak District pack, and since the Alpha had no heirs, he took a chance on my da. I think it's partly why he has hardly any interest in the turf discourse with the Campbells; he essentially inherited this war.

A few of the families in our pack have some strongly held views regarding us holding our ground in the dispute, having lost close friends and family in the skirmishes. They also happen to be the families with the deepest pockets, so my da can't exactly afford to alienate them.

A secret I've never told anyone, not even Niamh, is that something within the Yorkshire territory has always called to me. If I run without thinking, I always find myself here. Sometimes, I have dreams of pounding my paws across the North Yorkshire Moors, surrounded by endless land covered in heather. Maybe it's only because it's forbidden, perhaps it's a delayed rebellious streak, but something deep within me whispers it's more than that.

My pace slows as I near Ingleton, I shouldn't go beyond here, but my blood sings for me to go a little further. Since the sun is still shining, I take a break and curl up under a tree for a nap. It's pretty far off the beaten track, so the chances of coming across a human here are low. As the sun travels across the sky, I'm no longer in the shade and stretch out, enjoying the way my dark fur absorbs the heat. Half dozing and half keeping an ear out in case anyone approaches, I try to push thoughts of my mum to the back of my mind.

❖❖ ・◆・ ❖❖

Peeking one eye open, I notice the sun is long gone, and the sky is dark, lit up only by a sliver of the moon. Peering over my shoulder in the direction of home, I know I should start making my way back. The anonymity of the darkness makes me feel sort of bold, though.

I pad slowly in the direction of the Yorkshire territory, but when I step over the border, instead of the adrenaline rush I anticipated from being somewhere forbidden, a wave of calm washes over me. It's so quiet out here, with only the sounds of insects rustling and crickets buzzing, reminding you the woods are still filled with life.

As I near Ingleton Falls, I catch the scent of something unlike anything I've ever smelled before. It's damp earth and lavender, only amplified. Without thinking, I'm tracking the scent with my nose to the ground—I don't think I could stop myself even if I wanted to.

The sound of the waterfall reaches my ears, and I stop dead in my tracks. Someone is swimming in the pool beneath the falls. He's naked and looks so at ease, drifting through the water. Staying as still and silent as possible, I watch him from afar.

He must sense my gaze because he turns around and faces me suddenly. I'm hidden in the treeline, and a human wouldn't be able to see me, but he can; he's a wolf shifter, same as me.

My heart beats fiercely in my chest, common sense telling me I should back away and run safely back to my own territory, but a yearning curiosity has me placing one paw in front of the other. As I make my way closer to the water's edge, he shifts into his wolf form and approaches me with a look of trepidation.

His fur is chestnut brown, but his ears and paws are closer to a shade of honey. He lowers his head in submission, letting me know he means no harm, so I do the same. As we get closer, I take another deep inhale. I'm engulfed by the seductive scent I'd been following earlier. Damp earth and lavender—it's him. The scent settles something deep inside me, a scent that says *home*.

A scent that says *mine*.

I'm startled by my own thoughts; I've never smelled anyone who made my teeth ache with the need to claim. Even if I'm not quite ready to admit it to myself, I know what that scent means.

He comes closer, sniffing my neck. Whatever he smells on me seems to appease him because he lets out a happy whine before gesturing with his head for me to follow him into the water. Because we aren't part of the same pack, we don't have bonds to send thoughts through while we're in our wolf forms.

Once we're both in the deepest part of the water, we shift back at the same time.

Wordlessly, we appraise each other; he has olive skin and a slight t-shirt tan. His large, soft brown eyes are warm and welcoming, and his hair is short on the sides with a mop of messy brown waves on top. His full, pillowy lips are distracting, and I can't help but think he might be the most beautiful boy I've ever seen. I offer him a shy smile, and he returns it enthusiastically.

"You're not an omega," he says to me. I can't tell if he means it as a question or a statement. His voice is deep but gentle. Sturdy almost. The sound lights up all the synapses in my brain, and it takes me a moment to respond.

"No, I'm not. I'm a beta like you." I can smell it on him. Where an Alpha's scent is like iron, betas smell kind of woodsy, like an old oak tree. Omegas can be scented from a mile away, sickly sweet like toffee apples sold on bonfire night.

"There's no pack on this territory, and you aren't from the Eastwood pack." He phrases it as if he's trying to work out a maths problem. For a second, I'm relieved, thinking this must mean he belongs to the Northumbria pack. I don't know many people from that pack, so it wouldn't be surprising for me not to recognise him. Northumbria is the Switzerland of wolf packs in the North of England.

"No, I'm not part of the Eastwood pack," I say, not wanting to disclose too much.

"Neither am I…"

Bollocks.

I should have known. He sounds posh—pronounces all his t's.

In a panic, my brain starts coming up with all sorts of ridiculous ideas. I almost tell him I'm from a pack in Scotland. Thankfully, he saves me from myself.

"How about I don't tell you what pack I belong to, and you don't tell me what pack you belong to?" he suggests, giving me an out I am definitely going to fucking take.

"Ahh, plausible deniability." I offer him a smirk to bring some levity to the situation. The truth is we both know the other belongs on opposing sides of a territory war. An ember of guilt sparks to life in my stomach, though, as I realise that while he knows I'm part of the Kelly pack, he doesn't know I'm the Alpha's son.

"How old are you?" he asks, interrupting my spiralling thoughts.

"Nineteen, you?"

"Twenty. I was going to ask you your name, but you probably can't tell me that." He sounds bummed by that fact, and something within those soft brown eyes of his has me wanting to offer him a sliver of myself.

"How about you call me Cee?"

"Is it what your friends call you?" His furrowed brow suggests he doesn't like that prospect for some reason.

"Nope, nobody else calls me Cee." He seems to mull it over briefly before flashing me a smile.

"Cool. You can call me Fee then," he says, sounding pleased by this solution.

"Does anyone else call you Fee?"

"Nope. Cee and Fee. It can be our secret," he says, shooting me a look that's all mischief. I can't help the grin spreading over my face at that idea, I've never really had a secret before, and I'm already feeling quite protective of this one.

We swim together under the moonlight in companionable silence, with only the sounds of the waterfall in the background. It's peaceful in a way I've never experienced before. With a twin sister, an older brother and who knows how many cousins, peace and quiet in my family is hard to come by.

"Do you come here often?" I ask, breaking the silence. Ugh, blush warms my cheeks when I realise it sounds like the world's most clichéd chat-up line.

"I bet you say that to all the wolves." He winks at me playfully. "But nope," he says, popping the 'p'. "I'm thinking I might start making it a regular thing, though. In fact, I'll probably be ready for another swim next Sunday night." Relief and excitement simultaneously battle inside me, and I feel fourteen again, having my first crush.

"What a coincidence; I might be here for a swim next Sunday night, too." His big grin is infectious, and I don't hold back my own.

Fee lies on his back, floating along the water's surface, flicking his toes to make tiny splashes. He's naked like me, and his dick is soft, floating from side to side as he moves gently through the water. His chest and abs are defined in a way that suggests he works out a lot. My body is slimmer than his but is built mainly from genetics and the manual labour of my joinery work.

TWO

Growing up in a wolf pack leaves you relatively immune to nudity. Still, I find myself paying more attention to Fee's naked form than I usually would. As my gaze works its way up to Fee's face, I realise I've been caught looking for a little too long. His eyes sparkle with humour, and my face heats.

"Enjoying the view?" he asks, and I roll my eyes at him.

"I was thinkin' you must spend a lot of time in the gym to look like that." He lets out a deep, throaty laugh in response.

"Sorry to disappoint, but I'm not a gym rat. I just play a lot of rugby. I play for my uni team, my local team, and I help coach an under twelve's team." I'm surprised, although it does explain those thick thighs. Coaches kids' rugby? Did he have to be a fucking saint too?

"Now would be a good time to start listin' your faults, or I'm gonna think I'm in a fever dream."

"Hmmm. Well, I'm a duvet hog. When I shower, I leave my dirty clothes in the corner of the bathroom and ermm... I also sing to myself—constantly. Is that enough to keep you going?" His eyes glitter with amusement as he ticks each incriminating item off on his fingers.

"Yes, thanks. You're totally disgustin' now," I deadpan, and it earns me another of his deep throaty laughs. I'm a thief in the night, stealing them to replay later.

As the sun begins to rise, lighting the sky with a warm glow, I begin the run back home. My mind is buzzing with excitement as I fly through the air. Bright smiles and deep brown eyes consume my thoughts, and I wonder briefly if I should tell Niamh about my mystery waterfall man. In the end, though, I decide that for now, I'd quite like to keep him all to myself.

THREE
July 2017 - Five Years Ago

PHOENIX CAMPBELL

Cee is standing under the waterfall's spray with his eyes closed, letting the water cascade over his shoulders. He looks like a fallen angel, a frankly unreasonably sexy fallen angel sent here to tempt me into doing some very ungodly things to him. His usual tousled raven-black hair is plastered to his face, and the moonlight bounces off his sharp cheekbones and jaw, only adding to his enigmatic presence.

His pale, milky-white skin is entirely flawless. Wolf shifters generally have unblemished skin, considering we usually heal quicker than we can scar—but Cee's skin looks like it was cut from marble. This is the fifth week in a row we've met here, and my fingers are itching to touch him.

I think he flirts with me sometimes? But I'm so embarrassingly into him that I'm worried I'm reading into it. Cee's mossy green eyes, lined with thick dark lashes, sparkle with mirth when he catches me staring at him; I don't even bother to look remorseful.

Cee gracefully wades through the water towards me. He's so lithe and agile that even though I've seen him in his wolf form several times, I sometimes half expect him to shift into a sleek, black panther. He strikes me as someone who always lands on his feet and would most definitely scratch your eyes out if you cornered him. He pauses a few feet away from me, and a shiver runs down my spine as his gaze rakes over my body.

We do this sometimes; stare at each other as though we aren't entirely sure this isn't a mirage, and if we look away, the other will suddenly disperse like smoke into the ether. A light breeze in the air bathes me in his intoxicating scent of lightning and heather. Cee smells like a storm brewing, and I can't help but think that might be telling.

A part of me knows no good can come of getting so close to someone in the enemy pack, but I think it would take nothing short of a direct Alpha Order to keep me away.

I've only been on the receiving end of one once before. I was a pup and kept sneaking out to swim in the lake near our home. My brother Jasper snitched on me to Mum, and she Alpha Ordered that I only go when there was adult supervision. Being the precocious little pup I was, I figured out that if there were human adults in the vicinity when I went swimming, I could get around the Order that way. When she eventually caught me *again*, she was livid. I suspect she learned to make her Orders substantially more watertight after that.

"Let's play a game," Cee declares, cutting through my reminiscent thoughts. His eyes are all mischief.

"Okay... what game do you want to play?" I ask.

"I'm thinkin' Truth or Dare?" I can feel my Adam's apple bob as I swallow a large gulp of air. The last time I played Truth or Dare, I kissed my best friend Alice's brother, Milo. I'd been quite drunk, and the kiss was wet, sloppy and frankly—best forgotten.

"If we play Truth or Dare, I think we should still keep some truths off the table." I raise an eyebrow at him in question.

"Okay, how about Truth or Dare, but the truths can't include any identifying questions?" he proposes.

"Deal, your idea to play so your turn first, Truth or Dare?"

"Truth," Cee says with a glint in his eye. Biting the bullet, I ask the question that's been on the tip of my tongue since the day we met.

"Do you have a boyfriend or girlfriend?" I ask, holding his gaze so I don't look as nervous as I feel.

"Definitely no girlfriend, I don't generally swing that way..." He pauses, knowing full well why I asked, but I force myself to wait for him to finish answering the question even though my stomach is doing somersaults in anticipation. "And no boyfriend either. You?" he finally answers, and I let out a breath, a weight lifted off my chest.

"Nice try. That's not how the game works unless you want to waste your turn asking me the same question?" I give him a teasing look, and he splashes water at me.

"Fine, Truth or Dare?"

"Truth."

"Hmmm....." He hesitates as if he's thinking fastidiously about his question. "Have you ever thought about kissin' me?" His question catches me off guard; I wasn't expecting him to be quite so direct. His eyes hold mine, though, not faltering even for a second. Swallowing loudly even to my own ears, I take a deep breath.

"Yes, I thought about kissing you the day we met. Honestly, I've probably thought about it more than I should have since." Okay, so maybe my 'truth' borders on oversharing, but it's out there now.

"Interestin'." His smile becomes smug.

"Interesting? All you have to say to that is, 'interesting'?"

"Yes, very interestin'," he says, full-on smirking at me. I huff in response, splashing him with water again. Cee lets out an evil cackle at my expense.

"Wanker." I try to keep a straight face, but I'm fighting back a smile as I say it.

After I've gathered myself, I ask, "Truth or Dare?"

"Dare." He steps closer to me while answering. The air between us is charged with tension as I gather my courage.

"I dare you to kiss me how *you've* pictured it." My stomach is filled with butterflies as I wait for his response.

"I never said *I'd* pictured it." He tilts his head playfully.

"Well then, I guess if you've never pictured it, then you don't need to kiss me," I counter, calling his bluff.

His tongue darts out and licks his bottom lip lightly before he tugs it between his teeth in a way that makes my dick twitch below the surface of the water. The heated look in his eyes makes me feel akin to prey when I've only ever been a predator.

He glides towards me, closing the final distance between us. Standing so near, I have to tilt my chin to look down into his eyes. He's several inches shorter than me; I'd guess five foot ten to my six foot two. His pupils are completely blown out, almost eclipsing his mossy green irises.

With one hand, he reaches up, cupping the side of my face, and the other squeezes the back of my neck, tugging my face down to him. My pulse is a loud heartbeat in my ears, and I'm worried if he nudges his hips any closer to me, it's going to be very obvious quite how into this I am.

He pauses for a moment, the briefest look of vulnerability flashing across his eyes; if I'd blinked, I would have missed it. He comes across so confident, but I think maybe some of that is for show. Not wanting him to doubt even for a second how much I want this, I lean down and press my lips to his.

We kiss tentatively at first, tasting each other and gently exploring. Still, it lights up every nerve ending in my body. When his tongue tangles with mine, I release an uncontainable groan into his mouth, and he deepens the kiss in response. I'm insatiable; I could keep doing this for hours and never tire of it. The hunger in my belly is unlike anything I've ever experienced before.

My hands wander down his chest, and I brush my thumb gently over his hard nipple. A small gasp escapes his mouth in response. My hands roam all over his body, seeking to touch him everywhere at once. My brain catalogues every minuscule sound he makes; the breath he sucks in when I gently brush my fingertips down his rib cage and the small whimper when I dig my fingernails into his strong, muscled back.

Our mouths are feverish, stoking the fire building inside us. When I'm so close to the edge that a light breeze on my cock could make me come, I pull away and gaze down at him as I try to catch my breath.

We're both panting as though we've been running for our lives, and Cee's lips look pink, swollen, and devourable. I feel like I've been struck by lightning, and a small hysterical laugh bubbles out of me at the irony. I knew that lightning scent of his spelled trouble. My skin feels so overheated I half expect steam to start rising from the water's surface, and it takes me longer than it should to get my heart rate to return to its steady beat.

Cee appears to get his bearings back much quicker than I do. He tips his head to the sky, where the moon now sits low. His voice is raspier than usual when he speaks.

"I better head back," he says, sounding disappointed to be bringing the night to a close. The thought pleases me more than it should. With a deep sigh, he turns, making his way back out of the water. Before he gets too far, I grab his wrist, pulling him back into me to kiss his soft pink lips one last time. We say goodbye for another week. Seven days never seemed very long to me before, but each week since I met Cee, seems to drag on for an eternity.

"Goodnight, Cee," I whisper into his slightly parted mouth.

"Night, Fee," he replies before walking out of the water. I catch a brief glimpse of the sexy dimples at the bottom of his back before he shifts. Despite Cee being several inches shorter than me, his wolf form is enormous and domineering. His fur isn't quite as dark as his jet-black hair, more of a charcoal shade of grey.

Cee's large body blends into the dark treeline, but I spot two big green eyes looking back at me before he sets off to run home. I rub the heel of my palm into my chest, not understanding why I feel the loss of him so acutely.

"Get a grip," I tell myself, shaking my head to try and knock some sense into my brain.

I've no idea what the time is when I finally make it home, but I close my bedroom door as stealthily as possible behind me, and I nearly jump out of my skin.

"Fuck." I whisper shout. "You almost scared me half to death," I say quietly to Jasper. He's leaning against my window in the dark room.

"Where have you been?" he asks me in a low voice. Jasper and his wife Jade have been staying here while their house gets renovated, and I've come to realise I definitely love my brother with more distance between us than a paper-thin wall.

"None of your business, Jas. Why are you even awake?" I reply, my buzz from earlier dissipating in an instant. He steps towards me, and I step back, trying to give him a wide enough birth so he doesn't scent another wolf on me.

"This is the third week in a row I've heard you sneaking out. I thought following you was probably a step too far, so I resorted to waiting up for you. Where have you been? Or should I ask who have you been with? I can smell them all over you." I roll my eyes in response.

"Jas, you're my brother, not my keeper. Go back to bed," I say firmly.

"If Mum finds out where you've been going, I won't be able to help you." I try to keep my heart rate as even as possible because Jasper will be even more suspicious if he hears it beating erratically. For a moment, I worry he knows who I've been with. Even by wolf standards, Jas has the ears of a bat and the nose of a bloodhound, but there's no way he could know that if he's telling the truth about not following me.

"I know. I would never ask you to defend me. Go back to bed." He walks towards me and grips me by the back of my neck, pressing his forehead against mine.

"You know I'm only looking out for you, right?"

"I know." I let out a sigh.

"Go take a shower, Nix; you smell like sexual frustration." He cackles as I open my bedroom door and shove him out.

"Fuck off," I whisper, trying to ignore the heat flooding my cheeks because he's not wrong.

FOUR
March 2022 - Present Day

CONNOR KELLY

For a brief moment when I wake up, it's just another familiar day of standard abject misery. That's until the memories from yesterday come flooding back to assault my mind.

No, today is a day that definitely comes under the category of, *maybe if I claw my own skin off, I won't have to go through with it*, kind of day. Unfortunately, I'm certain that on this occasion, my da would drag my skinless body around that table and have me sign the agreement with my own blood if necessary.

The sound of Niamh stomping up the staircase like a baby elephant pulls me out of my spiralling thoughts. *Please don't be up here to talk to me*, I say to myself internally right before there's a loud knock on the bedroom door.

We're staying in my crotchety Uncle Karl's farmhouse in Marsden; it's on the very edge of our territory. Thankfully, Karl should be out herding the cows by now. I ignore the knock, knowing fine well Niamh will burst through the door in less than five seconds, regardless of an invitation.

"One of these days, dear sister of mine, you're gonna walk in on somethin' you don't want to witness," I say as she appears on cue.

"When we were fourteen, I could literally hear your loud, gross pubescent thoughts when we were shifted. I've never been able to look at Kieron Cooper the same way since. What's another item on the agenda for my future therapist," she says brightly.

My face flushes with embarrassment. Kieron was my first boyfriend; we went out for roughly six months as teenagers. He preoccupied most of my thoughts at the time, and they often leaked out when I was in my wolf form.

Niamh's mind, on the other hand, has always been a steel trap, so I've got nothing on her. Thankfully, by the time I'd met Phoenix, I'd learned to lock those thoughts away.

"Why are you so chipper today? It's annoying." I shoot her my best scowl with the scant energy I can muster.

"Well, *dear brother of mine*, my disgraced husband is out herding cows to avoid running into our father. My twin brother is about to marry his ex-boyfriend and *my* ex-fiancé. Frankly, Eastenders has nothing on our family drama, and if we don't laugh, we'll cry, Con, so buck up; you're getting married today."

"When you put it that way, you make it seem almost unreasonable that I'm contemplating launching myself out of the window."

"You and I both know that if you do that, the worst that'll happen is a broken leg, and I don't think you need to make today any more painful than it's already going to be. Now get dressed; you need to look hot for the ol' ball and chain."

"No," I say, shaking my head at her.

"No, you won't get dressed? Or no, I'm not allowed to refer to Phoenix as your ol' ball and chain?"

"The latter," I confirm. "I'll get dressed; today is gonna be humiliatin' enough without addin' nudity into the mix."

FOUR

"Nice, that's the positive attitude we know and love you for, Con." She winks at me and starts dragging clothes from the wardrobe on the room's far wall. I let out the deepest sigh of my life.

Fee and I—I mean *Phoenix* and I—stand side by side at one end of the room while my da and Alpha Campbell put the final signatures on the peace agreement.

"You look good," Phoenix says softly under his breath, still looking straight ahead.

"I figured I'd dress to match the mood of the day," I reply sarcastically. I'm dressed in black from head to toe because I am, in fact, petty as fuck.

I don't return the compliment. It's actually rude of him to look this good. The navy blue suit he's wearing is tailored to him perfectly and complements his olive complexion in a way that should be illegal.

"It's good you finally got to put the suit you bought for marrying my sister to use; it would have been a shame for it to have gone to waste." I'm aiming for snarky, but the hurt in my voice is evident. Phoenix opens his mouth and closes it again, clearly thinking better of what he was going to say before clenching his jaw so tight it would take a crowbar to prise it back open.

I have a natural gift for making bad situations worse. Apparently, I've decided it's not enough for this day to obliterate what's left of my own shredded heart; I need to inflict some extra damage on him to even the playing field.

With the paperwork finalised, we file out of the house and into the garden, resembling a funeral procession. I knew my outfit choice would really complement the day's sombre atmosphere.

The marriage ceremony is small today. Quite the opposite to the circus show the public wedding next weekend will be. Phoenix and I stand opposite each other in front of Calvin Eastwood underneath a wicker archway with white flowers weaved into it. Obnoxiously romantic for the circumstances, in my opinion.

Calvin is extremely tall and as broad as his dad, Alpha David Eastwood. Alpha Eastwood is adored by everyone in the region. His parents moved to England from Jamaica shortly before he was born, fleeing their pack for reasons similar to my da's. He's known for being approachable with a great sense of humour, and he's clearly raised his son to follow in his footsteps. Calvin must be nearing six foot five; his brown skin is lighter than his dad's since his mum is white. He has a calming presence I'm grateful for today.

His younger sister, Jade, is one of the witnesses today. She's married to Phoenix's brother Jasper, and their baby son, Henry, is sleeping in a sling cocooned against her chest.

Our respective Alphas stand close by, and I get a pang of envy at seeing Phoenix's mum standing there when mine remains frozen in the past, existing only in memories.

The other witnesses on Phoenix's side include his dad and younger brother Alfie. On my side, there's Sam, Niamh and Will. As far as I know, the latter are the only people who know the whole truth of this catastrophe. I imagine that for them, this is not dissimilar to watching a car crash; you know it'll be grim, but morbid curiosity wins out, and you can't quite bring yourself to look the other way.

I've not been paying attention to what Calvin's been saying, mainly focusing my eyes on the trees behind Phoenix. As I shift my gaze, I glance at him, and I'm shocked to see those familiar soft brown eyes filled with

FOUR

so much hurt that if I had to speak right now, I think I'd choke on the words.

A niggle of regret stirs in my stomach over lashing out at him earlier. Still, I remind myself of his betrayal and the self-righteousness I've cloaked myself in for the past year, extinguishes any remaining embers of guilt.

Calvin's voice uttering the vows we have to repeat back sounds distant, as though I'm listening from underwater.

Phoenix squares his shoulders, rallying for battle.

"I, Phoenix Frederick Campbell, promise you, Connor Liam Kelly, to honour and protect you, place your life above my own, and care for and cherish you until death parts us." His eyes are glassy and filled with so much love and regret it pierces a small hole in my armour.

How am I supposed to stand by my resolve to hate him forever when he looks at me like that?

Now it's my turn. I take a deep breath and silently beg my voice not to quiver, giving me away. Because I'm not completely deluded, I'm well aware this farce of a marriage will wreck me irrevocably.

"I, Connor Liam Kelly, promise you, Phoenix Frederick Campbell, to honour and protect you, place your life above my own, to care for and cherish you—" My voice cracks on the word *cherish,* and I swallow a large gulp of air before continuing, "—until death parts us." My eyes burn, remembering the hours I used to spend dreaming of the day Phoenix and I would stand in front of our families and be able to claim each other out in the open.

Be careful what you fucking wish for.

"You may now kiss," Calvin says and my stomach drops. I'm not entirely sure how I managed to forget this fairly significant part of a wedding ceremony. We both hesitate, staring at each other wide-eyed.

His gaze flickers to everyone watching, but I can tell from his expression that he's leaving the choice to me. I give him a barely-there nod, and we meet in the middle. It's chaste, a featherlight brush of his lips against mine, but it wakes up something inside me that I've worked hard to bury. Part of me wants to wipe my lips with the back of my hand, to try and undo the last thirty seconds, but it's too late. The endless memories of countless kisses are tattooed on my lips. Permanent. Irreversible.

With everyone seemingly oblivious to my internal crisis, Nina Fenwick replaces Calvin and stands between us. Nina is tall and slender, with smooth, dark brown skin and a bright, playful smile.

"Today's binding ceremony is slightly different to normal," she explains. "While I'll be binding the two of you together in matrimony, I'll also be binding you to this land."

Well fuck, that sounds both potentially painful and concerning.

"Don't look so worried, love," she says, squeezing my shoulder as you would console a child.

Firstly, we tackle the part I'm familiar with. I watch as she pulls something from the pocket of her maroon blazer. A knife. The sun glints off the sharp metal blade as she unsheathes it.

Nina uses it to slice a shallow cut across our right palms and then presses our cut hands together. I have to hide my physical reaction to feeling his skin on mine for the first time in a year. A strong wind could knock me off my feet, and yet, the pull I've been ignoring for so long finally fades away. Nina cocoons our joined hands in between her own before closing her eyes.

"This binding is a magical manifestation of the marriage ceremony your family has witnessed here today. Your blood will recognise each other as kin and pack until the seal is broken by death or other means.

FOUR

The magic binding you represents a new family being formed and will solidify your bond."

A sizzle of electricity sparks to life between our joined palms, travelling into my bloodstream and disembarking in my heart. I squeeze my eyes shut, trying to ignore the deeply buried emotions being stirred awake in my chest.

The binding ceremony itself existed prior to marriage in wolf shifter packs. It was a way to form a closer bond between shifters who weren't true mates. Over the years, wolf shifters became more acclimated to human customs, and it became necessary for them to get married to access more mundane things, such as inheriting their partner's pension after death. Nowadays, most wolf shifters who are true mates will exchange the mating bite and have a human marriage, whereas wolf shifters who aren't mates will take part in the binding ceremony and a human marriage.

I look down at the palm of my hand, where the cut has already disappeared.

"It has been over a hundred years since a new pack has been bound to a territory in England. It's a privilege to witness and participate in what will be a landmark moment in wolf shifter history today. When you're ready, I'll talk you through each step of the ritual," Nina says.

I'm not convinced I'll ever be ready, and I'm not entirely sure what's about to take place. This suddenly feels too last minute for something so monumental.

"This time, Connor, you'll make a slightly deeper cut across Phoenix's left palm, and he will do the same to you. It'll be easier if you both kneel as you do it so the blood can spill to the ground before the cuts heal."

We both kneel on the cold, unforgiving ground, and she joins us. I don't enjoy cutting Phoenix's hand as much as I anticipated. Once again, we join our palms and keep them close to the ground. I watch as the crimson liquid mixes together and runs down our wrists in rivulets before the droplets escape and are soaked up by the earth below.

Nina doesn't touch us this time, her hands hovering over the top of ours.

"As the joined familial blood of Connor and Phoenix is absorbed by the Yorkshire land, this territory has a pack once more. Please both place your palms on the ground."

My eyes go wide as my bleeding hand adheres to the earth as though it has its own magnetic force pulling me down. I glance at Phoenix to see if he looks as stunned as I feel, but his expression is calmly focused on Nina.

"You are bound to this land, and the land is bound to you. May your pack and the Yorkshire territory go forth and bask in a symbiotic and enduring relationship." When Nina finishes speaking, the sensation ebbs away, and I'm able to lift my hand back up. Across my left palm is a very faint silver scar. I've never had a scar before, and I can't seem to tear my eyes away, fascinated by it.

When I eventually look up, Phoenix's brow is furrowed, looking at me in confusion. I stand up abruptly, dropping my hand and dusting off some dry mud from my knees.

"Congratulations," Nina says conspiratorially before walking off and joining our guests, who have begun chatting amongst themselves.

⊷⋙⋅⋅✦⋅⋅⋘⊷

After everyone has left, I slide down the wall of the small reception room where we had our 'celebratory' meal with our families. Sitting on the floor with my legs outstretched, the wall is cool against my back, and I thunk my head against it.

FOUR

I've lost track of how many panic attacks I've had over the years as I would spiral, fretting over what would happen if the truth about Phoenix and me ever got out. He joins me on the floor, leaving enough of a gap between us so we're not touching.

I hate that gap.

And yet, if he'd sat closer, I would have shuffled away and created the gap myself, so all rational thought has clearly left the building.

I'm sitting on the floor next to my *husband*. My husband, who coincidentally is my ex-boyfriend.

Over the years we were together, Phoenix would periodically get frustrated from all the hiding and declare we should run away together. I would always nip those ideas in the bud because I knew that if I chose him, I'd lose everyone else. After seeing the chasm my mum's death created, I couldn't put my family through another loss.

Of all the scenarios I obsessively played out in my mind, though, our families viewing our relationship as a potential way to bring peace between the two packs never even crossed my mind.

A hysterical cackle bubbles out of me, and suddenly, I can't stop. My eyes water from laughing so hard as I lament over the cruel irony of it all.

"This was not on the list of reactions I anticipated today," Phoenix says as I try to calm myself down. "What's so funny?" he asks, nudging his foot against mine. It takes me a moment to gather myself enough to answer coherently.

"It's just the absurdity of it all. I spent most of my adult life worried someone would discover us. And now, a year since we broke up, those same people we were hiding from have forced us to get hitched."

"Well, when you put it that way..." Phoenix says before a deep, throaty laugh escapes him. "Fuck it, may as well laugh about it." He sets me off again, and we're both sitting, shoulders shaking at the ludicrousness that is our life.

After we've both calmed down, I move to stand up, but Phoenix reaches out and grabs my forearm, twisting me to face him. I rolled up the sleeves of my shirt earlier, and his fingers press into my bare skin. I'm so overly aware of the point of contact; it's like a brand being burned into me.

"For the record, though, nobody forced me, *this time*," he says seriously.

"It's not as if either of us had much choice in the matter either," I reply.

Once I'm standing, I reach out on autopilot to help him up. He looks at my hand, momentarily assessing whether it's some kind of trap—not that I can really blame him—but he takes it and stands. There's a brief moment where neither of us drops the other's hand, and I see his thoughts and emotions play out across his face. He gently lets go, and it seems to pain him to do so.

My hand feels cold and empty, which is familiar now; it's been cold and empty for the past year.

FIVE
September 2017 - Five Years Ago

PHOENIX CAMPBELL

I can't help but wince as Alfie takes a rough tackle on the pitch. He's a good player for his age, but he's overdue a growth spurt, and his scrawny frame isn't built for taking hard tackles yet.

We're nearing the end of the season, and it's cold where I'm standing on the sidelines. My breath lingers in the air like a puff of smoke as I breathe out. I'm not training today; only coaching the under-twelve team my younger brother plays for. Keeping an eye on my stopwatch, I blow my whistle to let the kids know the drill is over.

They all sprint over to their water bottles the second they register the noise. Their arms, legs and even their faces are thoroughly caked in mud from practising tackles.

"Two more drills, and then it's home time, boys," I shout as I walk over to explain. Alfie stands off to one side, slightly away from the group. He loves to play, but he's never quite figured out how to interact with them all.

It doesn't help when you already *know* you're different. I remember that feeling all too well. Eventually, I learned over time to put the wolf shifter in me to the back of my mind so I could be part of the group, but a divide always remained. With only a handful of exceptions, people high up in government/ police, humans who have married into a wolf pack, and the few who find out by accident, there will always be an *us* and *them*. Some shifters believe we should go public, but the reality is that it will always be too dangerous. The likelihood of us being hunted or captured is too high risk.

"Come on, the sooner we get started, the sooner you can grab a shower and warm up."

When practice is over, the boys run off towards the outbuilding where the changing rooms are. Alfie stays behind to help me pick up the various equipment dotted around the field. While I think it's partly because he has to wait to catch a lift home with me anyway, it's also because he's struggling with where he fits into the team.

"Why don't you go and get changed with the others? I'll come find you when I'm done," I suggest. He shakes his head.

"No, it's okay. I want to help."

"It's hard to make friends with your teammates if you always avoid them off the field, Alf."

"They don't want to be my friend."

"You don't know that; you need to at least try."

"I do know that. I heard Johnny and Fletch last weekend saying the only reason I'm on the team is because I'm your brother," he says it matter of factly as though it's not somewhat soul-destroying to hear your teammates talking about you that way behind your back.

It's under-twelve rugby in the Lake District; there is no criteria to make this team. Alfie could be related to the local drug dealers, and he'd still get a spot. We aren't picky. But Alfie is a wolf; he might not have had his first shift yet, but it won't be long now. He's fast and slippery with shifter eyesight and quick reactions. Once he builds his confidence, he'll be showing up little shits like Johnny and Fletch.

Maybe 'little shits' is a bit harsh to say about children, but if they're going to be nasty to my baby brother, they'll be doing hill sprints next weekend.

With all the equipment put away into the storage room, Alfie finally heads to the showers, just as most of the boys are heading out to meet their parents to go home.

I check my phone. Barely past eleven am. Only approximately twelve more hours until I get to see Cee... I don't know what's wrong with me. My skin feels like it's pulled taught around my body, and it only relaxes again once I'm in his vicinity. By every Sunday, I'm vibrating with need. How embarrassing. But he's like water in the desert, and I can't seem to get enough.

⋅⋙⋅⋅✦⋅⋅⋘⋅

The beginning of Autumn has brought a significant drop in temperature and, thus, an abrupt end to my late-night swims. The pair of jeans I packed to change into are sitting on the ground next to me, but I decide to enjoy the warmth of my wolf form a while longer since Cee hasn't turned up yet.

Resting my head against a large mossy rock, I watch the waterfall, which is flowing more enthusiastically after a large spell of rain earlier in the week. My nose twitches, somehow scenting him before I even hear him approach. The hairs on my neck stand on end, and I can feel his eyes on me. The sound of leaves crunching on the ground is followed by a large grey furry head rubbing against my shoulder.

Cee has a pair of blue denim shorts clutched between his teeth and dangling from either side of his muzzle. He drops them on the ground with my clothes.

We both usually shift right away because we can't speak to each other when we're in our wolf forms, but I'm comfortable and warm at present, so I'm not in such a hurry.

I'm also not feeling especially chatty today. I've recently started the final year of my history degree, and I got into a massive argument with my mum this afternoon about applying to do my teacher training next year. Apparently, going into teaching would be 'a waste of such a great education' —cue the eye-roll. Having become accustomed to my mother being largely disinterested in me in favour of helicopter parenting Jasper, I'm not enjoying the sudden turn of her attention.

Cee pads around to face me, nuzzling his snout into the fur of my neck. I take in a deep inhale, letting his scent fill my senses. Calm washes over me, and his presence settles the agitated mood I've been in for most of the day.

Feeling more myself all of a sudden, I lick his face playfully in lieu of being able to kiss him. His eyes pin me with a look that suggests he's less than impressed. He leans back on his haunches before leaping at me, knocking me to the ground and pinning me there. His tongue assaults my face, licking and slobbering all over me in retaliation.

We roll around on the ground for a while, play fighting. I love seeing this side of Cee. Sometimes, when we're in our wolf forms, we feel like the purest version of ourselves.

Once we're both panting for breath, Cee pads over to a nearby tree and curls up underneath it. I follow suit, and by unspoken agreement, we take a nap, enjoying the warmth of our furry bodies wrapped around each other.

When I wake up a short while later, Cee still snores softly, his large head resting on my shoulder. I shift back and try to extricate myself carefully. My skin breaks out in goosebumps at the sudden cold temperature, and I walk quickly to where we left our clothes when we got here.

After I've tugged on my jeans, I take Cee his shorts. One of his big green eyes peaks open, side-eyeing me when I shake his shoulder gently to wake him. His dark fur is soft and warm under my hand but is suddenly replaced by skin as he shifts back. I reach out and attempt to tame where his shaggy dark hair is in disarray.

"Your shorts," I say, holding them out. With a grunt, he pulls them on, still looking cosy and dazed from his nap. He thunks his head against my bare chest and takes a deep inhale, sighing contentedly.

"Hey, Fee," he mumbles into me.

Cupping his face with my palms, I tip his head back and kiss his pillowy lips softly. He lets out a dainty whimpering sound that makes me melt into a puddle of goo.

I regret not bringing a hoodie because the tree bark is digging into me uncomfortably where my back leans against it. Still, mild discomfort is a small price to pay with Cee sitting between my legs, his head resting on my chest.

We've both been quiet tonight, but it's not awkward. Sometimes, having company while I process my thoughts is comforting. He's been playing with the fingers on my left hand for the past ten minutes and using his fingertips to make swirling patterns on my palm, making me a little ticklish.

"So... I was thinkin'," he says quietly, interrupting the silence. "What if somethin' came up, and I couldn't make it here to meet you?"

Confused at first, a seed of worry plants itself in the pit of my stomach. Is he trying to tell me he doesn't want to come and meet me anymore?

"Ugh, stop."

"Stop what?" I ask, bewildered.

"Stop overthinkin'. I don't think I'm gettin' my point across very well." He huffs, sounding exasperated, but I can't quite tell if it's with me or him.

"Okay, why don't you try to articulate what you mean? And I'll try not to overthink. Deal?"

"What I meant was, we've had a pretty lucky run. What if one of these days, somethin' comes up, and we can't make it here on a Sunday night?" He swivels to face me, kneeling between my legs. I tilt my head to the side, trying to figure out what he's attempting to say in his very roundabout way.

I've come to learn this is quite typical of Cee. He beats around the bush for a while when he's nervous or shy before eventually getting to the point. I think I can reasonably guess what he's aiming for, and I'm not sure why I didn't think of it sooner.

"Cee?" I ask, smirking at him.

"Yeah?"

"Would you maybe want my phone number?"

"I suppose that's one solution, yeah." He huffs.

"Yes, Cee, of course you can have my number; what an excellent idea," I reply condescendingly.

"In case nobody has ever told you before, you're very annoyin' when you look all smug," he says, looking all cute and scowly.

"I have two brothers. I'm told on a daily basis how annoying my face is, don't worry about it." I boop him on the nose to wind him up a bit more. "You're pretty cute when you're grumpy with me."

"I must be cute all the time then because you're very infuriatin'." He pouts at me, and I can't help but kiss him.

FIVE

The kiss heats up quickly. We're breathless when we pull apart, and I have to reach into my jeans to readjust myself. He looks down at my crotch, pleased with his efforts.

Cee returns to sitting with his head against my chest while we endeavour to simmer back down. This is easier said than done, though, because his back is providing just enough pressure against my dick to stop my erection from waning. I attempt to think unsexy thoughts. The great Irish potato famine was between 1845 and 1852. WWI started in 1914 and ended in 1918. WWII began in 1939 and ended in 1945. The first wolf shifters to settle in England came over with the Vikings in 739.

My dick finally gets the picture and admits defeat.

Cee keeps fidgeting, which usually indicates that he's overthinking something.

"What's on your mind?"

"I hate it when you do that," he says with a slight chuckle.

"No, you don't. We'd never discuss anything if I didn't squeeze it out of you." I squeeze his body between my legs for emphasis, and he laughs some more.

It probably says a lot about my current state of blue balls that I'm reasonably confident I could get off to the sound of Cee's laughter; it's deep and unreserved like sunshine bursting through a gap in the clouds. It's quickly become one of my favourite sounds in the world.

"D'you ever think about sex?" he asks shyly.

"Probably seventy-five percent of my day," I answer him honestly.

"Great, love that for you." His voice is laced with sarcasm.

"I'm young and horny. I think about sex a lot. What's wrong with that?" I laugh, and he mumbles something under his breath. "What was that?"

"For someone who thinks about it a lot, you've never tried to have sex with *me*."

I spin him to face me. His neck, all the way to the tips of his ears, is a bright shade of pink.

"You didn't ask me who is starring in all these x-rated sexy thoughts of mine."

"Oh yeah?" he asks, sounding a little less embarrassed.

"For quite a few months, there's been this one recurring co-star—"

"—Super hot co-star," he interrupts me, seeming to have regained his momentarily lost confidence.

"My apologies. There's this one recurring, *super hot* co-star I can't keep my mind off."

"He sounds very intriguing; go on..."

"Well, he's got jet black hair that refuses to be tamed, bright green eyes I frequently get lost in, the softest skin I've ever touched, and he's got the sweetest pink lips that I regularly imagine wrapped around my..." I let the end of the sentence hang in the air between us.

"Wrapped around your what?" he asks when I don't continue, his breaths sounding uneven and his skin flushed.

"The key to holding an audience captive is to always leave them wanting more," I whisper into his ear.

"Maybe if you told me what those lips were wrapped around, I might do it," he says into my parted mouth.

Holy shit.

"You might?"

"I might... if you ask me nicely." He smirks.

Moving quickly, I wrestle him to the ground so he's laid on his back, and I'm hovering over the top of him, hands on either side of his head.

"Babe, what I wouldn't give to have those sweet pink lips wrapped around my cock," I say like I'm reciting terrible poetry. He swallows loudly, and my eyes track where his Adam's apple bobs in his throat. Without breaking eye contact, he reaches down and pops open the button on my jeans.

"That was a statement, not a question, but I'll let it slide." Cee licks his bottom lip as he pulls down my zipper. I'm not sure when I got hard again, but as he reaches into my jeans to palm my erection, I let out a small gasp. I'm not wearing any underwear, so his hand is warm against my naked skin.

I whimper embarrassingly when he removes his hand.

In a flash of movement, Cee catches me off guard, gripping my shoulders and shoving me so he's on top of me, straddling my thighs. His soft lips pepper my jaw and neck with feather-light kisses. As he works his way lower, he takes my nipple into his mouth and sucks before flicking his tongue against the now-hard bud. An involuntary moan slips from between my lips.

"Jesus, your mouth is amazing," I tell him. His wide eyes, dilated with lust, peer up at me through dark lashes.

Cee tugs on the waistband of my jeans, and I help him pull them off, exposing me to the cool air.

Leaning back on my elbows, I watch in awe as he kisses and licks my inner thighs, grazing his teeth on the soft skin and making me shiver. Ignoring my cock, which is throbbing and leaking beads of precum, he laps gently at my balls. When he takes them into his mouth and sucks, my hips buck off the ground, reflexively seeking more friction.

Putting an end to his teasing, Cee finally sucks on the tip of my cock, tasting me for the first time. He makes an 'mm' sound that vibrates against me, and it takes a herculean effort not to thrust into his mouth.

I briefly wonder if this is his first blowjob, but the thought instantly gets washed away when he lowers his head, taking my entire length into the back of his throat. Definitely not his first time, then. He sucks me down enthusiastically, his saliva making it wet and sloppy but so completely perfect.

"Holy shit, Cee, I don't think I'm gonna last very long," I garble.

Swirling his tongue around the tip in a way that makes my eyes roll into the back of my head, he uses his hand to stroke up and down my shaft in a quick rhythm. Cee's grip isn't quite as firm as I'd do it myself, but my orgasm is gradually building in the base of my spine regardless.

I card my fingers through his hair, tugging gently so he looks up at me.

And that turned out to be a mistake.

The sight of his swollen, rosy lips wrapped around me with those big eyes gazing up in adoration is my undoing. I worry I'm coming embarrassingly fast for a moment, but I realise it really doesn't matter. Cee makes me feel safe in a way I've never experienced before. Like I can show up as I am without expectations.

"Babe, if you don't pull off, I'm gonna come in your mouth," I gasp out in warning. Undeterred, he takes me all the way to the root, swallowing and groaning around me. I mutter some expletives as my release shoots down his throat. I've never come so hard in my life, and I think I possibly blacked out there for a second. All my nerve endings are on fire, and I can't tell if I'm tensing all over or entirely boneless.

Cee sits up, wiping saliva and cum that's dribbling from the corners of his mouth. He smiles shyly, and I can't help but pull him into a searing kiss at the sight of his puffy, pink lips. Tasting myself on his tongue is heady and wakes up some primal part of my brain, declaring he belongs to me now.

"Wow," I say, completely at a loss for more eloquent words. "Take these off." I tug on the end of Cee's shorts. He shakes his head, and a deep, crimson blush blooms across his cheekbones. "Why not? I want to taste you too." Cee covers his face with his hands and mumbles into them. "What?" I ask again, pulling at his wrists and dragging them away from his face.

"Please don't make me say it."

"Don't make you say what? Oh…" It's then I spot a slightly damp patch on his denim shorts. "Damn, that's actually a lot hotter than it ought to be."

"How is that hot?" he asks, still sounding mortified with his hands returning to cover his face.

"You were so into blowing me that you came; that's hot," I declare, and I mean it. "Take these off anyway."

"Ugh, no. What's the point?" He's laughing now, at least.

"We're young, and I can think of some creative ways to get you hard again so I get my turn," I say, grinning. He shakes his head despairingly, but he takes his shorts off before blanketing my body with his and burying his face into my neck.

"I'm embarrassed."

"Don't be. Not with me; you don't ever have to be embarrassed with me. Sometimes, during sex, funny things happen, and if we can't laugh, then we probably shouldn't be doing it," I say, stroking a hand down his back.

And because it's there, and I can, I pinch his bum cheek. I can't help but laugh as he lets out a tiny squark of indignation.

Something about Cee makes me want to wrap him up like a burrito, hide him away in my room so nobody can go near him and keep him all to myself forever. I wonder briefly if this is what love feels like? Fortunately, I still have just enough good sense to keep the thought to myself.

I'm pretty sure saying 'I love you' right after someone gives you a blow job is a big faux pas.

SIX
December 2017 - Five Years Ago

CONNOR KELLY

Tonight is the night, and it's going to be romantic as fuck.

Well, I hope it will be. Since October, we changed our meeting spot to this abandoned barn so we don't freeze our bollocks off. There are also some stacks of hay in here that are much more comfortable than the frozen ground outside.

The hinges on the barn door creak loudly as Fee's large, brown furry head nudges it open. His eyes dart around the room, immediately seeking me out, and my stomach flutters. Fee's wolf form is slightly smaller than mine, but his brown fur is long and puffs out, making him appear bigger. My gaze is locked in place as I watch his fur and bulky frame shrink away, leaving him standing before me, naked and smiling.

"You brought things," he says right away. It's a particularly bitter winter, so he quickly puts on some joggers.

"I just thought maybe a gas lamp and some blankets would make it less resembling of the set of a horror film," I reply, more defensively than is warranted.

"You're cute." He grins and walks towards me, planting a kiss on my lips. "What else have you got in that little backpack of yours?" he asks teasingly.

"Erm, like, stuff, you know, just in case, stuff." He arches an eyebrow at me questioningly.

"Ahh, just in case stuff, that very specific kind of stuff, I know exactly what you mean."

I can feel my face heating, and his eyes light up the second he notices. Damn my face for always giving me away.

"You're blushing. I was only messing around, but now your face is that colour; I'm going to need you to show me what's in the bag." I can't help the scowl on my face; this was meant to be romantic, and he's ruining it.

"If you're gonna be a prick about it, I can guarantee you won't need anything I have in this bag," I snap. He furrows his brow like he does whenever he tries to decipher one of my outbursts. I try desperately to bury all my mushy feelings that keep threatening to spill out.

"I'm sorry, babe, I didn't mean to poke the bear. I was just curious." He at least has the decency to sound contrite.

"I'm not a bear; I'm a fuckin' wolf," I mutter under my breath.

"The cutest fucking wolf I've ever seen." He pushes me back down onto the blanket, settling between my legs and kisses me leisurely, as though we have all the time in the world.

I've always had a short temper; thankfully, Fee never seems to take it personally. Even if I get irritated and snap at him, he laughs it off, and a minute later, he's over it. I hate apologising, so I appreciate how quickly he lets things go.

Somewhat regretting getting stroppy with Fee over the contents of my bag, I want to get the night back on track.

"Um, Fee?" I ask between kisses. "Have you ever had sex before?" I try to sound casual.

"Huh...? Erm, we've had sex quite a bit, so I'm kinda worried you don't seem to remember it. Have you hit your head on something?" He holds my face, pretending to inspect it for bumps and scrapes.

"Ugh, you know what I mean."

"Are you sure you want to know this?"

"Yeah." I nod, vehemently.

"Fine. Roughly two years ago, I got pretty hammered at my brother's wedding and slept with a bridesmaid. She was from a different pack, so it seemed a good idea at the time. My brother disagreed since she was his new sister-in-law. Honestly, I don't even remember it very well." Fee gets a dusting of colour on his cheeks at the confession.

"So, you've never had sex with a guy before then?" I blurt out.

"Not anal, if that's what you mean. I've done other stuff. Why the sudden twenty questions about my sexual history anyway?" he asks before the penny drops. "Oh shit, that's what's in the bag, isn't it?" Fee says in a rush before going to grab the aforementioned bag from the ground next to us.

"I don't have anal in my backpack, no," I reply, being difficult on purpose.

"Got the good stuff, too," he says, inspecting the label of the lube he found in the front pocket.

My face feels so hot it must be crimson. Why is this so embarrassing? We sixty-nined right in this very spot a week ago, so I've no idea why I'm suddenly getting shy about this.

He gently kisses the tip of my nose, then looks around at the pile of blankets and the gas lamp that's creating a soft glow.

"Baby, I can't believe you did all this," he says softly.

"I've, um, never done this before, but I've read about it, and I thought maybe we could try it?" My voice comes out a few octaves too high, betraying my nerves.

"I've thought about it a lot too, anal, I mean," Fee says, and relief washes over me.

"You have?"

"Mhmm. When you planned this, did you, erm... picture yourself on the giving or receiving end?" Fee asks, sounding as nervous as I am, which makes me feel better. Like we're in this together, and it helps me find some of my confidence.

"I thought maybe at first you could try fuckin' me, but if you don't want to, we don't have to—I'll just blow you."

"'I'll just blow you'—way to woo a guy," he says teasingly. "I've read about it too, you know..." I arch my eyebrow at him. "Fine, I watched some gay porn—for research purposes. I knew if we ever did this, that I wanted to make it good for you."

I can't help but laugh, and it breaks some of the tension. I believe him, though. Above all else, I know Fee will put his all into making it good for me.

"What if, well. What if, um, there's... you know...?"

Fuck me, why can't I get my words out.

"I can honestly say I've no idea what you're asking me, but if there's something worrying you, you don't need to be embarrassed to talk to me about it, okay?" I take a deep breath.

"Um. What if there's, like, shit?" I can see him fighting the urge to snicker because he doesn't want to offend me, but with the words finally spoken, I can't help the laugh that slips out, and all I do is set him off.

Gathering himself, he says, "Look, there could be some shit, yes. But think of it this way, if I come knocking on your front door, and you answer, I can't exactly act surprised by that, can I? If you get what I'm saying…" I snort out even more laughter at his analogy, but it does ease some of my concerns, and how he puts me at ease makes my heart swell.

"You really missed a great opportunity for a back door joke there." Fee shakes his head at me, but he's grinning.

Deciding the time for talking is over, I reach up and pull Fee's face down to mine and kiss him hard. The anticipation of what we're going to do has me tenting my joggers, and when he grinds against me, I groan into his mouth.

We break apart the kiss just long enough to pull our bottoms off. With neither of us wearing underwear, we're suddenly exposed to the cold air until Fee blankets me, settling back between my legs. His hard cock rubs against my own, but it's not enough.

Fee nips and licks along my jaw and down my neck as I thrust my hips, trying to seek out more friction. Trailing kisses down my body, he sucks on my nipple, making my back arch in response.

"I love this," he says, running his finger along the trail of hair between my belly button and pubes. I don't have a lot of body hair, but it's dark and contrasts with my pale white skin.

I'm not as vocal as Fee is during sex, but I love the way he seems to speak without even realising it. Telling me exactly what he enjoys and how good everything feels, reassuring the parts of my brain that worry I'm getting all of this wrong.

When I hear him uncap the lube, I lean onto my elbows to watch him. He coats his index finger and rubs it over my rim.

"Can I?" he asks, his voice deep and gravelly.

"Yeah, but go slow, okay?"

He nods, and if I wasn't so keyed up, I'd laugh at the serious expression on his face. He pushes his finger into me carefully, and I wince. It doesn't hurt exactly, but it does feel odd, and I suddenly regret not trying this part by myself in the privacy of my bedroom.

"Is this okay?"

"Yeah, feels weird, but it's okay."

The new and strange intrusion causes my dick to soften. Noticing, Fee leans forward and takes me into his mouth. I harden immediately on his tongue, and it successfully distracts me from the finger working its way in and out of me.

"Fuck, okay. I can take more now." Fee pulls his mouth off me and adds more lube to his fingers. He returns to licking up and down my cock slowly before there's a slight pressure of two fingers pressing in. I'm surprised to find it feels better than with only one. With Fee's warm, wet mouth wrapped around me, I welcome the way his fingers stretch me open, and I can't help but moan.

When he crooks his fingers, precisely brushing over an unfamiliar spot, every nerve ending in my body lights up like a Christmas tree. My hips move reflexively until I'm riding his fingers, every self-conscious feeling I have flying out of the window. Crawling up my body to kiss me, I whimper at the empty sensation when he removes his fingers. The kiss is wet and sloppy, and I'm so turned on my skin feels like it's on fire.

"Are you ready?" he asks between kisses.

"Yeah, I think so. Please."

"So polite." He smirks at me and I smack him on the chest.

My irritation is quickly forgotten as I watch him pour lube onto his cock, which looks bigger all of a sudden. I can't help but gulp at the prospect of it having to fit inside me. I try to swallow my nerves, but Fee must see it written all over my face.

"I'll go really slow, and if it doesn't feel good, we'll stop, okay?" I nod and try to relax, knowing it'll go smoother if I'm not tense. "Lift up a sec."

I do as I'm told, and Fee tucks one of the spare folded blankets under my hips. Wrapping his hand around my cock with a firm grip, he starts stroking me, torturously slow. I try to breathe out when his tip pushes against the tight ring of muscle. He continues, pushing in slowly, and I bear down until he's fully seated inside me.

"Are you okay?" Fee asks, searching my face for any signs of discomfort. Beyond a bit of an initial sting, I'm surprised by how good it feels. The sensation of being so full is satisfying in a way I hadn't expected.

"Yeah. Feels good, actually. Better than I thought," I say breathily. Fee looks down at where we're joined and tugs his full bottom lip between his teeth.

"Babe, you have no idea how hot this looks. Is it weird if I take a photo to show you?" I almost say yes because that does sound hot, and I *would* love to see it, but then he pulls out ever so slightly before pushing all the way back in again, and I can't think of anything at all.

"Maybe next time; I really need you to fuck me now, or I might actually implode," I gasp out.

"Sorry, my bad." His big hands push my thighs back, and I hook one leg over his shoulder and the other around his waist as he bends down to kiss me, folding me in half.

Fee moves in and out of me, slowly at first, all the way out, before plunging back in and making me moan. Using the leg wrapped around his waist, I pull him closer, encouraging him to go faster until the sounds of skin slapping against skin fill the near-empty barn.

I reach a hand down between us to stroke myself, but he leans back, dropping my legs down and bats my hand out of the way so he can take over.

Pouring the lube over my cock, Fee starts jerking me off in time with his thrusting hips. My orgasm quickly starts to build at the base of my spine. The way he rubs his thumb over the head of my dick, exactly the way I like it, is driving me wild.

Fee overwhelms me in the best way, his cock stretching and filling me, his hand wrapped around me. When I look up at him, his usually soft brown eyes are dark with desire. Affection and adoration feel like birds trapped in the cage of my chest, desperate to escape through the three words we've yet to say out loud.

What did I do to deserve him?

"You look so bloody beautiful laid out for me, taking me so good."

And that does it.

All the muscles in my body seem to tense and release at once, followed by jets of cum spraying from my cock, all over Fee's hand and my stomach. My skin tingles and the tremors from my orgasm seem to keep vibrating through me as he continues to fuck into me.

Fee stares down at the mess of cum on my abs and then grips my thighs, pounding into me hard for several thrusts before his rhythm stutters.

"Fuck. Holy shit. Fuck. I'm gonna come," he says right as his cock pulsates, filling me up. I revel in the feel of his warm release inside me. I love knowing it was *my* body that made him come. I'm suddenly grateful that we don't have to use condoms since we can't catch STIs or any human diseases.

He collapses on top of me in a heap, breathing heavily, and I press a kiss to his shoulder. I'd never put a considerable amount of thought into how I wanted to have sex for the first time, but I'm not disappointed. I can't help the smile that spreads across my face as I'm blanketed by a hot and sweaty, sexed-out Fee. This was perfect, and I wouldn't change a thing.

Thankfully, I thought far enough ahead to pack some baby wipes. We clean up the best we can before settling back under the blankets.

I'm curled into Fee's side, my fingertips playing with the light dusting of hair on his chest and completely content. We're both blissed out and for the first time since I can remember, my thoughts are quiet.

Until they're suddenly not so quiet.

"I think I know who you are," I whisper, no longer wanting there to be unspoken secrets between us.

"What do you mean?"

"Fee... it's short for Phoenix, isn't it? Phoenix Campbell?"

"Yes, yeah." He sighs and squeezes me with the arm wrapped around me. "Does this change things?" he asks, sounding worried.

"Not really. Don't you wanna know who I am?"

He kisses the top of my head.

"I know who you are, Connor Kelly."

I'm not sure why I'm surprised, but I am. I'd guessed who he was a while ago, but the mention of his brother's wedding basically confirmed it.

Jasper Campbell marrying Jade Eastwood was all anyone could talk about a few years ago.

"How d'you know?" I ask, not annoyed, just curious.

He takes a moment before replying, "A couple of weeks ago, you mentioned having a twin. How many wolf shifter twins have you heard of?" I laugh because I hadn't even realised I'd let that slip. Twins amongst wolf shifters are beyond rare. "I've met your dad before; there's not much of a resemblance."

"No, Niamh and Sam take after him. I look like our mum."

"I'm sorry you lost your mum. I can't imagine what that must have been like." I almost reply with the usual 'it was a long time ago', but I don't feel like lying to Fee.

"I still miss her a lot. I think she would've liked you," I tell him honestly. My mum had a wicked sense of humour and would have warmed to him immediately. It's oddly comforting to know that.

"She wouldn't have threatened to beat me off with a stick if I broke her son's heart, then?"

I snort a laugh.

"Probably that too. She was fierce; Niamh is the same way." Fee rolls on top of me and starts peppering kisses all over my face.

"If she was fierce, it sounds as if you're a lot like her, too." I hold his face still, cupping his cheeks with the palms of my hands, and gaze into his big brown eyes, which are so open that I don't think he could hide something from me if he tried.

"I love you," I say, realising I can feel it in every fibre of my being. Fee's eyes get a mischievous glint in them before he replies.

"One good dicking was all it took for you to fall madly in love with me?" I can't fight the laugh that bursts out of me, but I pinch his side in retaliation regardless. "Ow!"

"Way to ruin the fuckin' moment, dickhead."

"I love you too, Connor Kelly."

And even though I knew it because Fee showed me in all the ways that count, it still warms my heart to hear. Sometime in the last six months, it seems Fee burrowed under my skin and made a home in my heart—and I wouldn't have it any other way.

SEVEN
March 2022 – Present Day

CONNOR KELLY

After the small ceremony, Phoenix and I head towards the treeline. The branches are still bare, but the tiny daisies beginning to bloom in the grass show spring is right around the corner. I strip down quickly so I can shift and burn off some of the pent-up anxiety pumping around my nervous system. My insides feel raw and exposed, and I desperately want to get to wherever we're staying tonight so I can lock myself away in the dark.

I'm calmer as a wolf; all my swirling thoughts slow down and become easier to manage and process. Phoenix pads towards me on all fours; he walks slowly, his head bowed slightly in submission.

"Cee. Follow me. I'll show you my home. Please follow me. I missed you." The stream of thoughts startle me; it never even occurred to me that the ceremony would create a pack bond between us. A jumbled rush of emotions crashes into me at the thought of a tangible bond between us, but I can't deal with that right now. I nod at him again without responding, knowing he'll sense my messy feelings down the bond and not wanting to reveal so much of myself to him.

He sets off running, and I easily match his pace; a stubborn part of me is unwilling to follow from behind, so I stay on his right-hand side, hearing nothing but the rhythmic *thud thud thud* of our paws hitting the ground as we run.

"Are we alone tonight?" I brave sending the thought after we've been running for almost an hour. Anxiety over potentially spending even more of the day around strangers overcomes my desire to give Phoenix the silent treatment.

"Just us tonight. Wedding night," he replies.

I falter at his thoughts and stumble over a large tree root, tumbling over my front paws. If I were in my human form, I would not be able to hide the blush on my face. I've never been so grateful for my dark grey fur.

Phoenix slows down and nudges my face with his own, checking I'm okay.

"Didn't mean it that way. Family tradition. We'll stay in my home, not my family home."

I right myself as his thoughts come tumbling into my mind; there's an amusement behind them, clearly finding it funny where my thoughts went when I heard 'wedding night'. I should probably be more embarrassed than I am. But given Phoenix has witnessed almost every single one of my most raw and vulnerable moments, it seems a pointless endeavour.

We keep running until we reach what appears to be a small farmhouse on a hillside overlooking a lake. It's weird stepping foot on Campbell territory; I always assumed I'd sense I didn't belong, yet there's no denying the beauty and calm here. The sun is setting in the sky, making the clouds glow in stunning shades of orange and pink.

I pause at the gate, taking in my surroundings. Phoenix's home is a small, slatestone cottage with a sheltered veranda added on. It blends in beautifully with the landscape, and I can't quite believe I'm really here.

Phoenix must have shifted back quickly because he's already wearing low-slung jeans with a big rip in the knee, not the kind you buy ripped, the kind that are soft and torn from being well-worn. He walks towards me, holding out a pair of running shorts. I take them from his hand with my mouth, and he turns so his back is to me while I shift back and put them on.

"You saw me naked the day we met. Turnin' away to preserve my modesty seems somewhat redundant, don't you think?" He swivels back to face me, his shoulders drooping as though he's carrying the weight of the world on them.

"Today was hard, Cee. I don't have it in me to spend the rest of tonight in a verbal sparring match with you." He sighs deeply, sounding more exhausted than I've ever known him to be. I don't think he even looked this tired during his teacher training year.

"It's Connor, not Cee," I reply like an arsehole. I can hear how petty and unreasonable I'm being, but I can't stop the word vomit from pouring out of my mouth. The need to get the last word in always overtaking any fucking common sense I possess.

Stomping ahead of him like the overgrown toddler I'm emanating today, I go full steam ahead, up the steps and onto the porch and then turn the door handle—the locked door handle. I huff irritably while waiting for Phoenix to catch up. He nudges a plant pot by the front door with his bare foot and retrieves a key from underneath.

Once he's unlocked the front door, he lets me walk in ahead of him, and I can't fight the overwhelming urge to sniff the air around me. Phoenix's scent is embedded into his home, and it gives my chest an unwelcome ache. Unable to help myself, I run my hands over the furniture, needing to add my own scent into the mix.

It's not very different from the pictures he showed me when he first moved in. It must have been around two years ago. It's fully furnished and has obviously benefited from a lick of paint. Most of the walls are a neutral cream colour, but the far wall is a deep navy blue, and a comfy-looking, large, dark green sofa pushes up against it. There's a wood-burning stove with a bookshelf to the right. I run my hands over the spines of the books, fighting a small smile at the endless history books. At least that hasn't changed.

"If you like any of the furniture, we can bring it to the new place. Or if you'd rather bring your own furniture, that's fine too. Or we can get new stuff," Phoenix rambles.

"I don't have any furniture. Bring whatever you want." Phoenix's brow scrunches in a confused expression. Still, I don't elaborate on why I no longer have any of my own. It's embarrassing, and I'd rather he didn't find out.

"It's a nice place. I suppose you wouldn't have wanted to bring your new wife—sorry, I mean my *sister*—to an ugly home," I lash out at him again.

"Stop," he says firmly, "You know she was never going to live here, so just stop, okay?"

"Where am I sleeping?" I ask, ignoring his reply.

"There's only one bed." Because, of course, there is. I assess the sofa to decide whether it's big enough for me to sleep on, and I quickly deduce that it most definitely is not. Sighing in defeat, all the fight drains out of me like a deflating balloon.

"Fine, lead the way," I say quietly.

We manoeuvre around each other carefully, taking turns to shower and get ready for bed with minimal interaction.

Settling into bed, we're both lying on our backs, side by side but not touching. Our breathing sounds loud and harsh in the silent room. I'm bone tired, but my whole body is wired and alert to the fact Phoenix is lying *right* there. It could be minutes, or it could be hours later when Phoenix breaks the silence.

"Connor? Are you still awake?" he whispers. I take a minute... I know I told him to call me Connor, but now he actually is—I *hate* it.

"Mm."

"This is weird, isn't it?"

"You'll have to be more specific; everythin' about this day has been weird." He goes silent again, and I wonder if he's fallen asleep.

"Of all the times I spent picturing the day you'd finally be in my home, lying next to me in my bed, I... I never pictured this," he chokes out the last part.

My eyes burn as I try to hold back the tears which have been threatening to spill all day. If I say anything out loud at the moment, I'm very much in danger of sobbing, and once I start, I'm not sure if I'll be able to stop.

Maybe it's the emotional day I've had or the lateness of the hour, but I reach out my pinky finger and brush it against his hand, interlocking it with his. It's not much, but right now, it's the best I can do, a tiny little olive branch to let him know, *me too*.

❖❖ ⋅ ❖ ⋅ ❖❖

PHOENIX CAMPBELL

I scrub my hand over my face as I wake up and take in my surroundings. I'm in my own bedroom, but my left arm is completely numb. As I dip my chin, I'm suddenly reminded of why. Cee is curled around me, using my bicep as his pillow; his arm wrapped around my waist and his thigh thrown over mine.

Taking a deep breath, I let the scent of lightning and heather fill my senses. I allow myself to enjoy the brief tranquillity while it lasts. It's been over a year since I woke up to this, but as much as I want to cling to the moment, I know as soon as he wakes up, the spell will be broken. I have just enough self-preservation to discern I can't handle the inevitable rejection. I don't want to witness the moment he realises his unconscious mind sought comfort in *me,* and he immediately pulls away. Untangling myself from his heavy limbs, I move slowly and carefully so as not to disturb him and head downstairs to make some coffee.

As I scoop coffee grounds into the filter in the top of the machine, I can't help but dwell on how I ended up in this mess. The toilet flushes upstairs and the hot water pipes begin to squeal, alerting me to the fact Cee is awake.

If someone had told me a year ago that one day, Cee would be in *my* house, having spent the night sleeping in *my* bed, as *my* husband, I would have probably cried with relief. It's hard to feel that at present, though. It's a cruel irony he's finally here, existing in my space, and yet he despises me. I laugh, but it's ugly and bitter.

"I think laughin' to yourself might be one of the first signs of madness." Cee's voice startles me. I must have been entirely in a world of my own not to hear him walking down my creaky staircase.

"It occurred to me I don't know how you take your coffee, four years together, and I've no idea if you take milk or sugar; how bizarre is that?" I'm trying to hold back the laugh because even to my own ears, I sound slightly hysterical. I remove the full jug of coffee from the machine, enjoying the bitter aroma that fills the kitchen.

"If you had to guess, how do you think I take my coffee?" he asks.

This feels like a test.

"I'd guess you take it with a splash of milk and maybe one sugar?"

"You'd think that by now, I'd be less surprised you'd get it right on the first try," he snorts. "It's as if you know me or somethin'."

I'm relieved, as though somehow passing this stupid coffee test is a good omen. I think I needed the reminder that while we'll never know every single thing about each other, he's right, I *do* know him.

I whip up a quick breakfast of scrambled eggs on toast, and we sit opposite each other at my tiny kitchen table, eating and sipping coffee.

"What's the lake your house overlooks?" Cee asks.

"It's Lake Coniston."

"Does your family live near here?" I'm so on edge around him at the moment that I find myself looking for the trap in anything he asks me.

"Um, not too far. My parents and Alf live north of here in Glenridding, which is on the edge of Ullswater. Jasper, Jade, and Henry live East near Windermere. The rest of the pack are pretty spread out." He pauses before responding.

"You have a beautiful home."

"Yeah, it's nice. It's not very big, but it suited since it was only me here."

"You know, you don't have to leave your home behind," Cee says.

"What do you mean? Of course I do? We can't live on this land," I reply, confused.

"What I mean is, although we'll have to have a house in Yorkshire, the agreement never stated we had to live there all the time."

"No... the agreement states we have to start building a pack on the Yorkshire territory. I'm not sure how you think we'll do that if we don't even live on the land. Why would you even want to live here instead?"

"I never said *I* would live here instead." The penny drops.

"And there it is," I say, exasperated.

"There what is?"

I theatrically look at the non-existent watch on my wrist.

"Less than twenty-four hours. I'm actually kind of impressed it only took you this long to come up with an out." I can feel my nostrils flare in anger. Running a hand through my hair, I tug at the roots in frustration, the slight sting momentarily distracting me.

"You honestly thought that after everythin' that's happened, we'd sign on the dotted line and live happily ever after in Yorkshire? I've always known you were an optimist, Phoenix, but I didn't have you pegged as completely delusional. This whole *thing*," he gesticulates his hand between us, "Is a sham. It's nothin' more than a very fragile peace agreement. It's not exactly a love marriage," he chokes out the word love as though it's a dirty word.

"If we can't make this work, *Connor*, I can promise you that a lack of love won't be our downfall. It's never been hard to love you; living with you, however, when you're so pig-headedly determined to act like a vicious little cat, it's another matter entirely." My voice is raised, and I'm white-knuckling the fork in my left hand. He looks stunned; I've only ever lost my temper once, in the entirety of our relationship, but I've lost every shred of the control I can usually keep a tight lid on. Cee knows how to get under my skin, unlike anybody else, not even my brothers.

"I am *not* a vicious little cat," he snips back. Grabbing his plate, he scrapes the remnants of food into the bin before dumping it into the sink and storming out of the house. A blur of dark fur flashes past the window as he sets off running down the hillside.

"Excellent work, Nix. You really kept a level head there." I sigh, shaking my head. "And now you're talking to yourself; that's a healthy sign, I'm sure."

Cee becomes a tiny grey dot in the distance. It's rare to witness someone both figuratively and literally running away from their own feelings.

※ · · ◆ · · ※

After I've done the washing up, made the bed, and cleaned the already spotless bathroom, I grab my laptop and start the marking I've been avoiding. It's the Easter Holidays, so I have almost two full weeks off work before I'm back to reality.

Cee's words from earlier play on a loop in my head, confirming all my fears over him having one foot out the door. When I return to work after the holidays, I'm due to tell the Headteacher at my school I won't be continuing to work there from September. Suddenly, the idea of starting a new job in a new town, while Cee searches for the nearest exit, fills me with dread.

It doesn't take long before the boredom of reading the same answers to the same questions makes me want to smash my head against the table. There's still no sign of Cee. It's crisp but sunny outside; spring finally making an appearance.

Grabbing a book I keep picking up and putting down on the wolf packs of Scandinavia, I sit on the veranda outside, waiting to see if Cee will even bother coming back.

I haven't been reading long when the weather takes a sudden turn for the worse and the heavens open up. Thick sheets of rain pour from the sky relentlessly. Fortunately, the veranda has a roof, so I can enjoy the white noise of the heavy rain from my dry and comfortable chair.

As I finish a chapter on the Ulberg pack in Norway, the oldest known wolf pack in history, I lift my head in time to see a large, soaking wet, grey wolf leaping over the gate and landing on the path with a loud thud. Cee stalks towards me with a surprisingly impish expression, his tongue lolling out.

"You are not going in the house like that; you'll make the whole place smell of wet dog," I say to him sternly. He tilts his head and there's a playfulness to his eyes I've not seen in a long, long while. He continues to prowl towards me slowly, like I'm prey he's trying not to spook. I stand up from where I was sitting and block the doorway. Leaping suddenly, he pins me to the floor before licking up the side of my face and getting my clothes all wet from his damp fur.

"Ughhhh, you are disgusting," I say while laughing. One thing to know about Cee, though, is he'd sooner choke on his own tongue than apologise out loud; this right here has always been his way. He's always found it easier to be in his wolf form when he's all up in his feelings.

He lies down on top of me, his deadweight knocking the breath from my lungs. His head rests on my sternum, and those deep green eyes of his tell me everything he'll never say out loud.

"I know, Connor, I know," I say to him, and he lets out a low, unhappy whine. "You want me to call you Cee again?" He yips his agreement. I bring my hand up to scratch behind his ear, and he pushes his head into the touch. I know this moment won't last, but I think the only way I'll survive the times he pulls away and lashes out, is to remain present in these soft moments. I need to fill up my cup with these, albeit brief but tender interactions and hope they don't remain too few and far between.

EIGHT
February 2018 – Four Years Ago

CONNOR KELLY

Me: Free tonight?

Fee: Got a family dinner. You ok?

Me: Yeh, all good. Just thought I'd check on the off chance.

Fee: Hmm… what you not telling me?

Me: How do you do that even over text?

Fee: Skillz. Now spill.

Me: It's really not a big deal, still on for Sunday night?

Fee: Shit, it's your birthday or something, isn't it?

Me: It's Niamh's birthday.

Fee: You're twins knobhead -_-

Me: Can't believe you called me a knobhead on my birthday :o

Fee: 2am, barn?

Fee: PS Happy Birthday… to your sister ;)

Fee: Just kidding. Don't be mad. See you tonight then?

Me: You sure you can get away?

Fee: I'll make it work babe, see you later birthday boy xx

I arrive at the barn at ten minutes to two. A few weeks ago, I stashed a bag here with some warm clothes and blankets because even with wolf heat, it's pretty fucking cold. On my run here, the ground had already frosted over, crunching beneath my paws.

As is routine now, I spread the blankets over the hay on the ground and wait for Fee to get here. I'm scrolling through my phone when Fee's big chestnut head pokes through the door. I chuck some joggers and a hoodie at him, and he shifts back in time to catch them in his hands.

"In lieu of an actual birthday present, because *someone* didn't tell me the date, my presence will have to do as a temporary gift," Fee announces.

"What if we make it my only gift? I don't need anythin'."

"Oh, okay, in that case, I'll save the birthday blow job for next year," he says, looking smug.

"Let's not get ahead of ourselves. I wouldn't want to, you know, take away your opportunity to suck my dick when you've clearly put a lot of thought into it," I say, unsuccessfully holding back a big grin.

"Always ready to fall on your sword, aren't you, babe?" He winks at me.

"More like always ready to fall on your sword." Blanketing me with his big body, we both crack up. The sound of his rumbling laughter, bursting freely from his chest, makes my stomach do somersaults.

Shuffling out from underneath Fee's deadweight, I sit with my back to the wall. Fee eventually arranges himself, so he's straddling my thighs, and we're face to face.

"Happy birthday, baby," he says before licking up the side of my face.

"Ugh, gross." I wipe his saliva off my cheek with my sleeve. "You clearly need to keep your mouth occupied." I waggle my eyebrows suggestively. He seems to contemplate it, looking down at my crotch before responding.

"I was thinking..." he says.

"Don't strain yourself." My response earns me a *lord give me strength* look.

"As I was saying, I was thinking since it's your birthday, I could try and bottom for you?" He speaks quickly, obviously nervous about the idea. Digging my fingertips into the peachy flesh of his bum, I pull him closer towards me so our lips are almost brushing.

"As much as I think the idea of bein' inside you is very fuckin' hot, I don't think you really want that, do you?" I ask gently. A dark blush spreads over his cheekbones.

"Maybe. How can I know for sure when I haven't tried it yet?"

"Fee, I once stuck a finger in there mid-blowjob, and you said it felt like you needed a shit. It clearly didn't do it for you, and my dick is quite a progression from my index finger," I reply, chuckling at his determined expression. "I love you, I love that you wanna do this for me, but I don't want you to do somethin' you don't really wanna do. Especially not as some gesture for my birthday. If you couldn't tell by the copious orgasms, I am a very big fan of you fuckin' me." I plant a soft kiss on his lips, and he lets out a little huff.

"I know, I just worry sometimes." He looks down as though he's embarrassed, and my heart rate picks up. I didn't realise there was something to be worried about. Frankly, out of the two of us, I generally assumed I'd be the one doing the majority of the worrying.

"What's on your mind?" The few seconds it takes for him to reply feels like the longest pause in the history of pauses.

"It probably sounds stupid. I just don't want you to wake up one day and realise being with me isn't worth all the hassle." I open my mouth to tell him that's not even a possibility, but he holds up his hand and continues. "What if you meet someone vers so you don't always have to bottom, and they're not related to enemy number one, so you can be with them out in the open?" He looks at me with those big, soft brown eyes that I'm a total goner for. I take a moment to gather my thoughts and work out exactly what I want to say.

"I love havin' you all to myself. I'm a twin, I've shared everythin' my whole life, and I like that you're only mine. Seeing you is always the best part of my week. Nobody makes me laugh like you do; nobody makes me feel as safe as you do. Honestly, I really hope one day, things change enough that we can claim each other in public. If need be, we'll be the ones to make that change. I'm not worried I'm missin' out on anythin'. Everythin' we've ever done has felt good for me, so maybe ask me before you start makin' wild assumptions about whether I'm satisfied, okay? I'm not goin' anywhere."

"Okay." He nods.

"Great, so where did we end up landing on the whole, you givin' me a blow job then?" I say teasingly, trying to lighten the mood.

EIGHT

An hour or so later, we're both lying on our sides, facing each other under a blanket. Fee's fingers make gentle patterns on my naked back.

"Hey, when's your birthday?" I ask. His hand abruptly stills on my back. Burying his face in the crook of my neck, he mumbles against my skin. "What was that?"

"September 26th..." Fee repeats loud enough for me to hear this time but keeps his face hidden.

"You little shit," I shove him lightly so I can see the sheepish look on his face.

"I forgot?"

"Mhmm. Sure you did. I guess I owe you a blowjob then." He glances down at his spent dick.

"Maybe give me half an hour first?" We both crack up laughing before I return to smushing my face into the light dusting of hair that covers Fee's chest.

"Did you mean it when you said you'd want to claim me in public one day?" Fee asks over the top of my head. I shuffle a bit so I can see his face.

"Of course I meant it. Don't you want that one day?"

"Every time we're together, my teeth ache with the need to mark you. Sometimes, I wonder if we went ahead and mated, our families wouldn't have a choice but to eventually get over it." I'm shocked by what he's suggesting because there's a high possibility we'd both end up expelled from our packs if we mated without permission. But it's also more complicated than that, and I know I need to come clean.

"There's somethin' I need to tell you, but I need you to fully hear me out before you react, okay?" I ask him.

"Okay...you're starting to freak me out; what is it?" I take a deep breath, and I really hope he loves me enough to get past this.

"So you know my best friend, Will? I'm sure I've mentioned him before." He nods slowly. "Uhm, we're sort of promised to each other," I blurt out.

"You're what?" Fee raises his voice slightly and sits up. I move to mirror his position, keeping us face-to-face while I try to explain. His eyes are wide with shock.

"Just hear me out, okay, please?" I beg him.

"Have you been engaged to someone else the entire time we've been together?"

"We're not exactly engaged, it's complicated. I promise I'm not cheatin' on you, and I'm not cheatin' on him. You know how my pack doesn't have much money? Well, Will's family does. He has four parents. Both his mums and his dads were mated, so they had Will together. One of Will's mums is from old money, and all four of them are big on status. They joined our pack when Will was eight, and he's been best mates with me and Niamh since then.

"Nothin' has *ever* happened between us, not even a kiss, but when we were sixteen, money got really tight, and Will's mums agreed to give the pack a pretty hefty lump sum of money, but only if my da promised me to Will. They really wanted their son to marry into the Alpha's family. I didn't get any say in it at the time, and I've never intended to go through with it, I promise. I just haven't found a way out of it yet." Fee looks shell-shocked by my revelation, and I can't say I blame him.

"When are you meant to marry him?" he asks in a choked voice.

"Once we're both twenty-one, but I'll find a way out of it by then," I promise, and I mean it. I know I'll never feel that way toward Will. "I love you—only you. I really hope you believe me." I reach out and cup his cheek with my hand, using my thumb to wipe a tear that's slipped free of the soft, brown lashes framing his soulful eyes.

"That's a lot to process," he whispers.

"I know. I wanna give you time, but please don't give up on me?" I ask, my own eyes welling up.

"I don't think I could give up on you if I tried," he says with a sniff and a tentative smile.

"I'm all yours, Fee; if you try to run, I'll track you down and stick to you like a limpet." This earns me a small chuckle from him, breaking some of the tension.

"Yeah? Get over here and limpet me then." I waste no time crawling onto him and wrapping my arms and legs tight around him, and when he hugs me back, a weight has been lifted. I know this isn't fixed by any means, but keeping this secret from Fee has been eating away at me, and it's a relief to have it all out in the open.

"I want you to know that if things were different, I would mate with you in a heartbeat. But right now, if we went behind my da's back, I'd be cut off from the whole pack, including my family. We've already lost our mum; I can't do that to them," I say, hoping he understands.

"I know. I just wish it was different. It's so stupid we have to keep this a secret because fifty years ago, two Alphas fell out over something, with zero proof, might I add," Fee says, exasperated. "I hate that you're promised to someone else." He sounds deflated.

"I'm sorry. I know it's fucked up. But we'll get there one day—I know we will." I try to reassure him. "Our brothers will be Alphas one day; maybe we start laying the groundwork with them for some kind of long-term peace agreement to be put in place when they take over?" I suggest.

"I started having those conversations with Jasper back in July." He sighs deeply, but I don't reply because there's nothing to say. So much of this is beyond our control.

My obnoxious phone alarm wakes me up at nine am the following day. I didn't get home until five, and I'm grateful to my past self for booking today off work.

I jump in the shower before heading downstairs because the more attached I get to Fee, the more paranoid I become about us getting caught. Whenever I see him, I stop by a small stone house with an outside tap on my way home. In the winter months especially, I can't say I particularly enjoy blasting myself with icy cold water. Still, it's better than risking anyone from my pack catching his scent on me. The second morning shower is more of an extra precaution, even going so far as to use some horrendous mint shower gel that makes my balls sting and my eyes water, but it seems to do the trick.

When I walk into the kitchen, I make a beeline for the kettle. Our house is an old Victorian terrace. On the bottom floor is an open-plan kitchen with a large farmhouse-style dining table.

Up one floor is Da's study and the living room, which is where I find my brother and sister, coffee in hand. Niamh peers up at me from the book she's reading; she's curled up on the sofa under a blanket.

"Mornin', Con, taken today off?"

"Yeah, figured I had the days to use up, earned myself a post-birthday lazy day," I reply, smiling at her. Niamh has been my best friend my whole life; the guilt of lying to her by omission has been eating away at me these last few months. I can feel the distance between us like an ocean of my own making.

"Same. I'm already bored, though. There's a Van Gogh exhibition in Manchester today if you fancy it?" I hate that she feels she has to ask because six months ago, she would have just demanded I go with her.

EIGHT

"Sure, what about you, Sammy?" I ask my older brother, who's sitting in the armchair on his laptop.

"Huh?" he replies.

"Me and Niamh are gonna head to Manchester for the Van Gogh exhibit if you wanna join?" I'm really hoping he says yes because I'm pretty sure a whole day of only Niamh and me and the truth will erupt from me like lava from Vesuvius.

"Oh, no can do. We found a Campbell wolf on our land last night, so dealing with the fallout today," he answers, sounding both distracted and frustrated. My heart rate spikes and my palms are sweaty as I panic over whether it could be Fee. Could he have followed me here for some reason? I need to calm my nerves before he or Niamh notices.

"That's annoyin'. Who was it?" I ask, trying to sound nonchalant, but I can sense Niamh's eyes boring into the back of my head.

"Some fifteen-year-old pup gettin' too big for their boots, I think," he replies, and my shoulders sag in relief. Definitely not Fee—thank fuck.

I'm sitting on the other end of the sofa to Niamh, scrolling on my phone when Sam leaves the house, the front door slamming loudly behind him. I wait a few minutes to ensure he's not forgotten anything.

"Sammy sounded pretty exhausted by the whole Campbell wolf being on our land thing, don't you think?" I ask Niamh, and she puts her book down on her lap.

"Yeah, I suppose so. Probably feels like puttin' out a bunch of pointless fires."

"Do you reckon when he's Alpha, maybe he'll attempt to bring an end to the conflict?"

"Doubtful. Da's been grooming him to take over as Alpha his whole life, leading a turf war included," she says. My stomach twists painfully. That wasn't the answer I wanted to hear.

Five minutes later, I realise Niamh is still staring at me; I can tell she's building herself up to interrogation. I have a feeling that when she realises I've texted Will to hang out with us today, she isn't gonna be happy. Not that she doesn't love Will, but she'll see it for what it is—an avoidance tactic.

"Con, I know you're hidin' something from me." Straight to the point, that's Niamh.

"Oh yeah, what am I hidin' from you?" I try to keep my voice even.

"Don't treat me like I'm thick. What I was going to say was, I'm assuming there's a good reason why you haven't told me because you've never kept secrets from me before." I swallow loudly. "But I need to know if I should be worried?" she asks, eyes shining with concern for me. Ugh, I feel utterly rotten for making her worry. I can't tell her the truth, but I can't lie either.

"It's for the best you don't know, okay? But you don't need to worry, I promise." It's a half-lie. If she knew the truth, she would definitely be worried.

"Okay," she says, putting a surprisingly quick end to what I expected would turn into an inquisition. "I'll let Will know he can hang out with us today then." She's smiling now.

"He's such a snitch; he texted you?" I say accusingly.

"Of course he did. What? You think because he's your future husband, he's always on your side? Will would probably stab you if I asked him to." She's got a smug look on her face. I'm relieved we seem to be back to normal, but her reminder about Will has my stomach in knots. I can't help but picture Fee's face as I broke the news to him last night.

"Thanks, that's very reassurin'," I say sarcastically.

"And then he ran into my knife," she replies in a bad American accent.

"He ran into my knife, ten times," I add on with an equally terrible impression. "You should really spend less time watching Chicago; it always leaves you a bit too stabby for my liking." We're both laughing, and I forgot how much I missed this. It occurs to me that if my relationship with Fee is going to continue—and I really hope it does—I have to find a way to stop the secrecy from driving a wedge between me and my family.

Standing in front of *Bedroom in Arles* at the Van Gogh exhibit, Will comes over and rests his head against my shoulder. I wrap my arm around him instinctively, but I feel a pang of guilt in my gut. Wolf shifters are tactile in nature, and Will is especially. I've never really thought twice about it, but now I wonder if I'd be doing this if Fee was here? Not that he can be here, but still.

How would I feel if he had his arm wrapped around someone else?

Pretty feral if I'm being completely honest with myself.

Dropping my arm from his shoulder, I step away and search for Niamh, who went looking for a bathroom around ten minutes ago. My attempt at putting some physical distance between us clearly goes unnoticed by him since he catches up to me in a second and puts his hand in mine.

"Thanks for inviting me today," he says, squeezing my hand. The statement reminds me of how little time I've been spending with him and Niamh recently. The three of us have been inseparable for most of our lives, but I've been pulling away from both of them.

"You don't need to thank me. I'm glad you could come," I reply, returning the squeeze of his fingers before untangling them and letting go. He smiles brightly at that, his soft rosy lips stretched wide around straight white teeth.

Will is objectively beautiful; he has curly blonde hair that always seems to fall just right and big blue eyes with full lips. Plenty of people dismiss him as nothing more than a pretty face, but he's also super intelligent and fiercely loyal. Sometimes I wonder, if it weren't for Fee, would I have fallen for Will eventually? He wouldn't be hard to love that way.

I don't, though; it scares me sometimes how much I love Fee. In many respects, my life would be simpler if we'd never met, but the thought of never knowing him makes a cold sweat trickle down my back. When I look at Will, all I see is one of my oldest and closest friends, who I will probably hurt when I find a way out of this arrangement. But my heart belongs to a big, brawny, soft-hearted boy in the Lake District, and there's nothing I can do about it.

NINE
MARCH 2022 - PRESENT DAY

PHOENIX CAMPBELL

My stomach drops as we step into the drawing room of my parents' house. Jade's sister, Iris, sips red wine as my dad talks her ear off by the fireplace. I have no idea why my mother invited Iris to this, of all dinners.

For the past couple of days, there's been a tentative peace between the two of us. We've only got this one dinner to get through with my family before we head to the Peak District tomorrow.

Cee manages not to flinch as I gently press my hand to his lower back, nudging him out of the doorway. Jasper wanders over to us with a sleepy-looking Henry resting on his hip.

"Look who it is, Hen. You want a cuddle from Uncle Nix?" Jasper says to his son in a sing-song voice. Henry seems to debate it for a moment before reaching out his chubby little hands to me. He rests his heavy head on my shoulder and settles back down again. I might be biased, but I have the cutest nephew *ever*. His skin is quite fair, similar to Jasper's, but he has tight black ringlet hair just like his mum's, and his dark lashes frame big brown eyes that always look remarkably thoughtful for a toddler.

Before I get a chance to ask Jasper what Iris is doing here, my mum appears behind me. She runs a hand affectionately over Henry's head before asking us all to make our way into the dining room for dinner.

Starters have just been served when Jade joins us at the table, having put Henry down to sleep. My mum, as Alpha, sits at the head of the table. My dad, Cee, and I are on one side, and Alfie, Jasper, Jade, and Iris sit opposite us.

A painfully uncomfortable knot forms in my stomach. Other than the highly unlikely scenario that Iris happened to be visiting Jade and Jas when this dinner was organised, I can't think of a single *good* reason why my mother would have invited her tonight.

We make it through the first course relatively unscathed, with nothing more than inane small talk. Things start to take a turn as we wait for Claire, their housekeeper, to serve the main course.

"I hear Alice Graham is thinking of leaving us," my mum says.

"What? Where did you hear that?" I ask. Alice is my best friend, and while I know she's not particularly happy in this pack after everything that went down last year, she's never mentioned leaving.

"She's been spending significant time with the Eastwood pack, isn't that right, Iris?"

"I wouldn't say so. She visits her cousin, Oliver, fairly frequently, but since the rest of his family are human, they haven't spent much time around anyone in the pack, except for maybe Calvin," Iris replies. I'm grateful she's not throwing Alice under the bus.

"Calvin, as in the future Alpha of your pack?" My mum's tone is baiting as if she's trying to catch Iris in a lie.

"Calvin, as in mine and Jade's older brother, and Oliver's best friend." Iris' firm response brokers no room to continue the conversation—she's braver than I am when it comes to my mother. I suppose she benefits from my mum not being her Alpha.

The awkward silence that follows is brief because Claire appears with large plates of food. Mum has clearly gone into full *show-off* mode with sirloin steaks and lobster tails. Cee's eyes go wide when the dish is placed before him. A wave of embarrassment washes over me because while it may appear my mum has pulled out all the stops for a special guest, this is just another way for her to flaunt our pack's wealth.

I'm chewing on a mouthful of steak when my mother decides to start the one conversation I was dreading.

"It's such a pleasure to have you with us this evening, Iris. It feels as though we've hardly seen you since you and Nix broke up." Iris' face goes scarlet red, and I pinch the bridge of my nose, wincing. Cee is white-knuckling the cutlery in his hands and glaring a hole into his dinner plate. While I don't want to give my mum the satisfaction of knowing she's caused a rift, I also really don't want him to think I have a secret ex-girlfriend.

"Mum, Connor is right there; what a weird thing to bring up," Jasper says. He thinks he's helping, but he's kind of not.

"Will you come and speak to me outside for a minute?" I whisper into Cee's ear.

"We're in the middle of dinner," he replies through gritted teeth.

Great, he's definitely pissed off.

"I need to speak to Connor privately; we'll be back in a moment."

"Phoenix, you will not be so rude as to get up in the middle of dinner," my mother retorts as though we're dining with royalty, and it's not just a room of mostly my own relatives.

"Is that an order?" I ask, and she visibly blanches.

"Of course not."

"Right. Okay then. We'll be back in a moment." I grab Cee by the arm and pull him out into the hallway. It's still not private enough for wolf shifter hearing, so I tug him further down the hall into the downstairs guest bathroom.

CONNOR KELLY

My mind is still reeling as Phoenix pulls me into what appears to be a guest bathroom. What's with rich people and their overabundance of bathrooms? How posh do you have to be before the idea of sharing a porcelain throne becomes scandalous?

Anyway, I digress; back to the issue at hand.

Phoenix has an ex.

Either he omitted to tell me that when we were younger, or he dated her in the year we spent apart. I feel physically sick at the idea of him with someone else. In the year we were separated, Phoenix never stopped reaching out. Was I naive to think that meant he hadn't moved on? It's not like *I* didn't try to. The first six months after we broke up, I was barely going through the motions, dragging myself to work and back, hardly seeing or speaking to anyone.

Was he with her then?

This was a mistake. This whole marriage is a mistake. I can't protect my heart when he's literally *everywhere*.

"Stop, please stop spiralling, and let me explain. I'm begging you." Fee's back is to the door, but he's giving me space like he knows I'll scratch if he comes too close.

"What's to explain? We're just havin' dinner with your ex-girlfriend. Nothin' weird about that. Out of interest, though, did you wait a whole forty-eight hours after we broke up before you got back out there?"

"What? No. She was never my girlfriend, and it was long before I'd ever even met you."

"Oh, so you were just fuckin' her and invitin' her around for family dinners, then? Sounds an awful lot like a girlfriend, Phoenix," I snap at him.

"I told you that when I was eighteen, I got really drunk at Jasper and Jade's wedding, and I slept with Iris. My mum overheard me and Jas fighting over it. He was pissed off with me, and my mum asked me to go on a couple of dates with her so there wouldn't be a rift between our packs.

"We went on no more than five dates, purely to get our families off our backs, and then we've hardly crossed paths since. We never even slept together again, I promise. I didn't go into all the details with you back then, but I didn't lie. We were never together. I don't know why my mum made it sound as though we were." He lets out a breath, and his big brown eyes plead with me to trust him.

I keep clenching my fists at my side, I have all the adrenaline from being ready to fight with him, but I believe him.

I think his mum is a total bitch—but I *do* believe him.

"You promise?" My voice comes out all weak and shaky. I hate how much I need the reassurance.

"I promise. Do you want to leave? We can leave. We *should* leave," he rambles on.

"No. We should stay." I stalk towards him and grab his face between my palms, pulling him so his lips crash against mine. I kiss him aggressively, tugging on his full bottom lip with my teeth until it's rosy and swollen. I mean for the kiss to be brief, but the taste of him is addictive. My body remembers precisely how good it feels, and my brain struggles to remind me why this is such a terrible idea. My fingers tug at his wavy brown hair, mussing it up, and I rub my lightly stubbled cheek along his jaw and neck.

When I eventually pull away, I'm panting for breath, and so is he. He shakes his head like he's trying to get his brain back into gear.

"We should go back in there and finish dinner. Wouldn't wanna be rude," I say, not remotely hiding the smirk on my face. Phoenix smiles and rolls his eyes at me.

"You sure you don't want to pee on me while you're at it?" he asks.

"No. I think that'll do," I gesture at the mess I've made of his hair and rumpled shirt.

When we return to the dining room, everyone immediately stops their conversation as we retake our seats. There's a faint blush along Fee's cheekbones, but we both pick up our cutlery and finish our meal as though the interruption never happened.

Dessert is homemade profiteroles, and I hate to admit it, but they're amazing. I could have eaten ten portions of them.

Once dinner is finally over, we're invited to stay for another round of drinks, but I'm grateful when Fee makes our excuses.

On the drive back to Fee's house, my mind wanders to the heated kiss in the bathroom, and I start to harden in my jeans. Subtly, although evidently not subtly enough, I try to cover the evidence with my hand. Fee glances over and snickers at me.

"Fuck off," I say, without any real bite behind the words.

※ ※ ※

"Ugh," I groan. I feel like I've only been asleep for twenty minutes when there's loud knocking on the front door. Since we've both been woken up, neither of us can pretend we haven't spent the night a tangle of limbs, with me using Fee's chest as a pillow.

NINE

Fee lets go of me and tugs on some jogging bottoms before going to see what all the noise is about. Right before I burrow back under the duvet and go back to sleep, I hear Jasper downstairs. Overhearing the mention of Sam and Niamh's names, I drag myself out of bed.

I pull on Fee's t-shirt from the floor for no other reason than the fact it's at least thirty inches closer than mine. It is *not* because it smells of him. When I trudge down the stairs, Fee silently hands me a mug of hot coffee.

"Thanks."

"Your brother and sister are on the edge of our land. They're here to escort the two of you to the Peak District territory. Their presence has a few members of our pack getting twitchy, so it'd be better if you went to meet them sooner rather than later," Jasper explains. I had no idea we were being escorted; it seems drastic for two fully grown shifters to need escorting across neutral land, but whatever.

Once we've each filled a duffel bag with our things, we go outside and shift, scooping up our bags with our mouths and heading to where Jasper told us we'd find my siblings.

I've been living with Niamh for the past year, and we rarely spend more than a day apart, so after the weirdness of the last few days, I'm excited to see her. When I spot her and Sam in the distance, I speed up, bounding towards them as fast as possible.

"Niamh?" I try to send the thought down the bond but can't find it. Where is it? *"Niamh?? Niamh?! Sam??"* My heartbeat speeds up. Why can't they hear me? I slow down my approach as my brain tries to catch up. Fee tilts his large head at me with a confused expression.

"What's wrong?" he asks, and it's only then I realise why I can't communicate with them.

They aren't my pack anymore.

When I'm close enough to see Niamh's face, I can see the realisation dawn on her. She lets out a low whine, and I drop my bag, unable to fight the pained sound that escapes me in response. Niamh's been by my side almost every single day of my life; I never thought there'd be a day we weren't pack anymore, and my chest cracks open at the sudden loss.

"I can't communicate with them anymore. The bond is gone," I explain to Fee.

He must be able to sense my distress because he leans close, pressing his head into my neck and nuzzling me.

I might not be able to talk to her through the pack bond any longer, but she's still my twin and my best friend, so I walk up to her and rub my face into her fiery red fur. I always used to joke that Niamh wasn't actually a wolf shifter but rather a giant fox shifter instead.

We press our heads together and allow the feelings of sadness at what we've lost. Sam comes over and joins us. Fee steps back, collecting my abandoned bag and letting me have this moment with them.

When we eventually make it to Will and Niamh's house, the place I've called home up until now, we don't even reach the front door before Will comes bounding out with a big grin. Right before he launches his arms around my neck, Phoenix steps in front of me and growls. I roll my eyes, but I can't deny the bit of satisfaction I get from him being territorial over me. Especially after I basically rubbed my scent all over him in his parents' guest bathroom during dinner.

Will's cheeks pinken in embarrassment, we've always been very affectionate with each other, and I don't want him to feel shitty. I nudge Fee out of the way and press my muzzle against Will's chest. He strokes the fur on my forehead before reaching around to scratch behind my ears, exactly where I like it. Fee growls again when I let out a satisfied sigh, and Will drops his hand. Fee presses up against my side and bumps his shoulder into mine.

"*Want to piss on me while you're at it?*" I ask down the bond, repeating his words from last night.

"*Yeah, I wouldn't mind, actually.*"

He pretends to cock his leg like he's going to pee on me, so I knock into him while he's off balance. I have him pinned to the ground, and he tilts his head in a surprising act of submission that pleases me more than it should.

"*Come on. Let's shift and act a bit more civilised.*"

We all shift back and throw on some clothes before heading inside. The five of us occupy too much room in the small kitchen we've gathered in. Sam is taller than I am and much broader; he looks more like Niamh with his auburn hair and the dusting of freckles covering his nose. It's at odds with his demeanour, which always comes across as severe. He's a big softy, really, but our da has spent his entire life preparing him to take over as Alpha, and the pressure has meant he's serious more often than he's not. I've never envied the burden and responsibility that was put on his shoulders at such a young age.

"Sorry. I was rude to you outside," Fee says, extending his hand out to Will, who shakes it and looks fairly bewildered.

"Um. No problem. I wasn't trying to… erm… step on your toes or anything. Sorry," Will stammers out. Sam and Niamh both look faintly amused by the exchange.

"Has my good little house husband prepared dinner for my arrival home?" Niamh says, winking. Will lets out an irritated huff before replying.

"Till death do us part is going to come around sooner than planned if you keep calling me that. But yes, there's a pie in the oven; it should be ready in around twenty minutes." In spite of the fact Niamh and Will are in a platonic marriage, thanks to yours truly, they're a bit of a power couple. Will is halfway through his second training year as a junior doctor, and Niamh is a solicitor in employment law.

"Thanks, hubby." Niamh plasters a big kiss on his rosy cheek. "Can I get anyone a drink, tea? Coffee? Beer? Jägerbomb?" In unison, we all make a disgusted sound at the mention of the latter. Sam leaves then to go see Da, presumably to report back that Phoenix and I were retrieved from Campbell land unscathed.

PHOENIX CAMPBELL

After we finished lunch, Will excused himself to bed since he's currently on night shifts. Niamh left shortly after, heading to a meeting in the office that afternoon.

As Cee and I make our way into the living room, we're alone for the first time since we woke up. I feel an odd sense of relief and dread.

Cee sticks on some *Parks & Rec*, presumably to give us some privacy from wolf shifter hearing. We sit side by side on the small, grey two-seater sofa. Our thighs are touching, and I daren't move a muscle in case he notices and retreats away from me.

"What's wrong?" he asks, breaking the heavy silence between us since we sat down.

"Nothing," I reply, unable to find the words I really want to ask but probably don't want the answer to.

"Mm. Seems like nothin'. Everythin' from the tense shoulders to the grimace on your face really screams 'nothing' is wrong." I sigh and then twist on the sofa to face him.

"There's nothing romantic between Will and Niamh, is there?" I ask. He looks surprised at the question but shakes his head. "Have you and he...? I mean, you've been living with him for the past year." The pie we had for lunch threatens to re-appear at the thought, but I need to know.

When he looks away from me, my heart is in my throat.

"We weren't together anymore, Phoenix," he whispers. Even though I suspected as much deep down, the confirmation hurts even more than I anticipated.

My mind is assaulted with visions of him and Will in bed together. Him and Will kissing and cuddling.

I think I might be sick.

"Have you been together this past year? Am I... am I in the way of something?" I can't stop the tremble in my voice. I didn't realise how much hope I was holding onto that this could be our second chance until right this moment.

"No. It wasn't like that. It was one night, we were both drunk, and it was a mistake for both of us. But you don't get to be mad, okay? We broke up because you agreed to marry my sister. I didn't owe you anything after that," he replies, his voice firm. I nod and bite down on my lip hard, trying to fight the tears threatening to spill. A part of me is relieved that he and Will aren't a thing, but I can't move past the images of Will having a piece of Cee that only I ever had. When I try to blink away the tears, one drops down onto my cheek. I quickly look the other way and wipe it off with my hand but I know he saw.

"When?" I ask, praying my voice will hold steady enough.

"A couple months after."

"June?" I ask, already suspecting the worst.

"Yeah."

"When in June?" He doesn't reply, and my stomach drops out again. I know it's not totally rational because it's my fault he doesn't know the entire story, but I suddenly feel furious. Of all the days he chose to move on, our anniversary? Really? Did he do it to spite me and hurt me? "So when I texted you that day, begging you to talk to me, you ignored me because you were with him?"

"I was hurtin' that day, and no good would have come from answerin' your texts. We got drunk to take my mind off it, and I took comfort from a friend. Don't turn it into somethin' it wasn't." His words cause some of my anger to dissipate. Still, the part of me that always felt slightly insecure about his relationship with Will isn't so easily appeased.

"You were practically engaged to him the entire time we were together. Did you have feelings for him all along?"

"You know that I didn't."

"Do I? Because you weren't in a hurry to call off the engagement to him, were you?" Suddenly, the idea of him and Will together that way has me re-framing our entire relationship. Was I the idiot that thought we'd end up together? If the engagement to Niamh hadn't occurred, would he have left me for Will eventually anyway?

"Fuck you, Phoenix. Don't twist that now. From the day we met to the day you left me, I was loyal and faithful to you, and you know it. Don't you dare turn this around on me. And don't you dare take any of this out on Will, okay? He's not in the wrong here." He stands up and storms over to the window with his back to me.

'The day you left me,' the reminder that my decision to keep Cee in the dark about why I couldn't call off the engagement to his sister, sits like lead in my stomach. He slept with Will because he didn't know the truth, and the reason he didn't know the truth was because I kept it from him. It's all my fault, yet if I tell him the truth now, it will only make things worse.

Unable to fight them off any longer, the tears track down my cheeks. My breath hitches loudly as I try to stifle a sob. I'm surprised when Cee comes over and tugs me to stand up. He pulls my face onto his shoulder and wraps his arms around me. I don't deserve for him to comfort me, but I don't have it in me to walk away. As I silently cry into his black cotton t-shirt, he cards his fingers through my hair.

"You get to be upset, but you don't get to be mad at me," he says quietly. He's completely right, I probably don't even deserve to feel this devastated, but I can't control that.

"I know, I'm sorry," I whisper before an embarrassing hiccup escapes me.

TEN
March 2022 - Present Day

CONNOR KELLY

I take a deep breath, and I'm overwhelmed by his painfully familiar scent—lavender and damp earth. Fee's breathing is slow and steady, so I'm pretty sure he's still asleep. I try to keep my own breathing even so I don't wake him up and cut this moment short. My subconscious seeks him out when we're sleeping, and I always wake up curled up into his side, his arm wrapped around me, keeping me as close as possible.

It makes me ache.

Falling for Fee was probably the easiest thing I ever did; I don't even remember the day it happened, but suddenly, he was buried deep under my skin.

Fee said he needed some space after yesterday's heavy chat about Will and me, so he went to bed early. Ergo, I spent the rest of the evening ruminating obsessively over whether I did the right thing in telling him. I told myself I was honest with him because I don't like keeping secrets, but a part of me wonders if I told him because I wanted him to hurt a little bit, too.

Truthfully, I do regret sleeping with Will, not because of Fee, but because I hurt my friend. Will still had feelings for me, and I knew that. He was the last person I had any business rebounding with.

TEN

I had no idea heartbreak could hurt that much. Those first few weeks after we broke up, I couldn't even sleep alone. Niamh stayed with me every night and held me while I cried myself to sleep. It's a bit humiliating to recall if I'm honest. After a few months, when the ache of it all hadn't really subsided, I realised it was probably a pain I needed to learn to live with.

So, I went through the motions.

I got up out of bed every day, ate three meals, went to work while avoiding talking to my cousin, Mikey, all day. And I plastered a smile onto my face when I caught anyone looking my way for too long.

It's been over a year since I told Fee I hated him. I wish I did hate him; this might hurt less if it were true. This marriage is splitting me in half.

I still love him.

I'm not so delusional that I can't admit that to myself, even if I refuse to say it out loud. But I can't trust him; I've never been good at trusting people, but I trusted Fee with every fibre of my being, and I'm not sure I can ever forgive him for betraying me.

How do we build a pack on these lands when I'm always looking over my shoulder, waiting for him to pick the Campbell pack over this one, over me? I guess that's the crux of it; when he was backed into a corner and had to choose between me and his pack, he chose them.

I suspect Fee views this marriage as a second chance for us, but I resent it.

It took almost the entire time we were apart for me to barely begin learning how to live a full life with part of my heart missing. To learn to live, not just survive, with my soul always yearning and pining for my mate who was only a hundred miles away.

I went on a few dates, nobody blew me away. I didn't even sleep with any of them, but I was making small steps to moving on. I could see there was light at the end of the tunnel, even if it felt a long way off still. To be thrown into a marriage, forced to spend every day with the person I've spent countless hours trying to get over, feels cruel.

Fee starts to stir, so I begin to untangle myself before those big brown eyes of his start knocking down any more of my defences.

I head to the bathroom and take a piss and a shower. As I stand under the spray of water, it takes me back to all those times under the waterfall with Fee. Fuck, I'm way too sentimental today. Shaking my head, I try to clear my mind of past memories and turn off the water. I must have been taking my time in here because there's a soft knock on the bathroom door.

"You almost done? I'm going to piss myself in about thirty seconds," he says through the door.

"One sec," I call back. I grab my towel and wrap it around my waist before opening the door. "All yours."

"Thanks," he mumbles, rushing into the bathroom behind me.

Downstairs in the kitchen, Niamh is sitting at the small round dining table in the corner with her laptop open and a ring binder.

"Mornin', sunshine, sleep okay?" she asks, sounding far too upbeat for this early in the day.

"Uhuh," I grunt.

"Coffee is fresh," she says, pointing to the side in the kitchen. I fill two mugs and pass one to Phoenix when he appears in the doorway.

"Oh, thank you," he says, giving me a timid smile. Thankfully, Will isn't back from his night shift. They've yet to cross paths, but I suspect when it happens, it will be awkward as fuck.

"No problem."

"Look how cute and domestic you two are," Niamh says, looking gleeful.

TEN

"Fuck off," I reply succinctly, and she just snorts.

"What are you working on?" Phoenix asks, nodding at the laptop in front of her.

"Sorting out the final seating plan for the wedding reception."

"Sorry, we've contributed literally nothing to these wedding plans," he says sheepishly.

"Planning this wedding is basically my redemption for, you know, ruining the last one." Phoenix chokes on his coffee.

"Wow, you're really blunt." He laughs awkwardly, and she cackles like a cartoon witch.

"You two ready for the big day on Saturday?" she asks once she's composed herself.

"Feels a bit redundant, given we're already married," I reply.

"I guess it's probably not so much about us. It'll be the first time a large number of both packs are in the same place and not at each other's throats," Phoenix says, ever the diplomat.

"That we hope," I add darkly.

We're at the venue for a rehearsal ahead of the wedding in two days. It's part of a converted castle; the inside shows the exposed stone walls and beautiful wooden beams adorn the ceiling. It's not the kind of venue my family could usually afford; however, Phoenix's parents agreed to foot the bill, and I can't deny the place is stunning.

I'm not entirely sure why I'm required to practise walking in a straight line and standing in one spot, but when I raised this point with Niamh, she smacked me upside the head.

"So, we need to decide who's walking who and in what order," Niamh announces.

"What do most people do?" I ask.

"I don't know what it's like in the Campbell pack, but in ours, each groom is usually walked down the aisle by their parents or, in your case—parent," she replies.

"I thought maybe Connor and I could walk down the aisle together," Phoenix suggests.

"Is that how your pack usually does it?" she asks him curiously. I hold my breath to fight the sting in my eyes.

"No, not traditionally. Just an idea. This way, neither of the Alphas can argue over who goes first, etcetera," he says. That's not the reason he suggested it, though it does make sense. He's looking at me to confirm, but my voice will betray me, so I nod in agreement.

One summer a couple of years ago, we were at the top of Whernside, lying under the moon and stars. I asked Fee if he thought we'd ever be mated, and he told me he'd mate me and marry me in a heartbeat if I gave him the word. I couldn't hide the smile on my face at the surety in his words. I never had to guess how Fee felt about things; you could just ask, and he'd spill everything as though it never even occurred to him to protect his heart or feelings from me.

"What do you think our weddin' will be like?" I asked him.

"I think it will be small and intimate, and we'll walk down the aisle together, starting our marriage as equals. Fuck tradition!"

"Wow, not that you've thought about it much or anythin'."

"Not at all." He smirked at me.

"I like that idea, not so much all the attention, but I don't think it'd be so bad with you by my side."

"Always," he said, squeezing my hand in his.

The memory crushes my heart in a vice. He must read it on my face because he subtly shuffles closer and hooks his pinky through mine,

TEN

giving it a small tug in solidarity. Before he can let go, and trying not to overthink it, I put my hand in his and interlace our fingers. He looks down at our joined hands with a sad smile on his face. It's like I can see the same memory running through his mind. Niamh looks over and notices, too, but I raise an eyebrow at her, daring her to bring it up. She smiles knowingly but continues.

"Great, I love that idea, and logistically, it's easier. So, all the family members will already be sitting in the first few rows. Calvin will stand at the front, and then when the music starts, the two of you will walk in together.

"Phoenix, you'll be on the left. Con, you'll be on the right, all sound good?" she asks. We both grunt yes in agreement. "Perfect, at the end of the ceremony, you'll walk back down the aisle together, and then both of you, plus immediate family, will head off for photographs, and the guests will make their way over to the reception, capiche?" I can't help but think that I don't particularly want photographic evidence of the day, but I'm pretty sure I'm just along for the ride at this point.

"Sure," I agree, sounding defeated, and Fee nods.

"Okay, you're both dismissed for the time being. Keep your phone close in case I think of anything else, though. Please, thank you and goodbye," Niamh says, not waiting for us to reply before she's skipped off to deal with the next item on her agenda.

I let out a deep sigh and drop Phoenix's hand as we head out of the front door and into the unusually sunny March day. My hand feels cold and empty; I'm itching to reach out again, but today, holding hands feels like the gateway drug of affection.

⟫ ⋅⋅✦⋅⋅ ⟪

PHOENIX CAMPBELL

My stomach flutters with nerves as we pull up to Cee's dad's house. It's a large red brick terraced property somewhere south of Manchester. Niamh explained how the entire row of houses is owned by pack members. It's a culdesac with direct access to some woodland at the end, pretty ideal way of keeping shifters out of sight of humans so close to a big city.

Will is driving, and he seems almost as nervous as I am. As far as I'm aware, Cee hasn't told Will I know what happened between them. To be honest, I've been trying to forget it myself. It's torture watching every single interaction they have, looking to see if there's anything more there than friendship. The wedding is tomorrow, and then we'll be alone in Yorkshire, and as apprehensive as I am about that, I think I'll need it for the sake of my sanity. Will parks the car on the street outside, and we all spill out of his burnt-orange SEAT.

Niamh opens the front door without knocking, and there's a lot of noise coming from deep within the house. Cee takes my coat to hang it up, then leads the way through the hall and down some stairs, where we enter a large kitchen dining room bustling with people. Cee's brother Sam is standing over a sizeable range cooker, stirring a giant pot of something that smells amazing. Alpha Kelly is sitting at the dining table playing some kind of card game with a few people who look close to his age. He looks up and grins at us as we walk into the room.

"Right on time to watch me steal both your dads' money," he shouts over to presumably Will. He smiles in response, but it looks a touch forced. Niamh explained yesterday how Alpha Kelly really lost his shit with them for getting married last year, and although she claims her dad is both quick to anger and quick to move on from it, Will is still wary of him.

"Clear the table, tea's ready," Sam announces, and everyone busies themselves. He places the large pot—which I can now see is a chilli—and a massive tray of baked potatoes onto the table. Niamh starts handing out plates and cutlery, and everyone dives in. I'm kind of taken aback; this is so far out of the realm of *my* family dinners that I'm not entirely sure what to do with myself.

"Here, gotta be quick, or these greedy fuckers'll eat it all," Cee says, smiling and placing a potato onto my plate. The volume dials down while everyone is busy devouring the delicious food, and there's a laid-back atmosphere in the room I didn't expect.

"Nervous for the big day tomorrow, lads?" Alpha Kelly asks as Will and Niamh start clearing away the empty dishes.

"A little," I reply. "But it feels sort of odd since we're already married."

"Mm. You've settled into it faster than I thought. Wouldn't have guessed you were practically strangers a week ago," he says, his eyes sparkling knowingly. Too knowingly.

"Well, when you spend twenty-four hours a day with someone for a week, you get to know each other pretty quick," Cee interrupts, and Niamh abruptly changes the subject. My neck sweats a little when I feel Alpha Kelly's eyes still on me.

Fortunately, he's easily distracted by Sam and Niamh arguing over last weekend's footy results, and the rest of the evening is relatively uneventful.

⠀⠀⠀⠀⠀⠀⠀⠀⠀⠀⠀⠀⠀⠀⠀⠀⠀⠀⤻⠀⠀⠀⠀⠀⠀⠀⠀⠀⠀⠀⠀⠀⠀⠀⠀⠀⠀⠀⠀

Later that night, we're both lying next to each other in bed, not touching, just side by side, and the silence is so suffocating that it permeates the room. I think the weight of the spectacle that tomorrow will be, lies heavily on both of us. Cee's breathing is even, but I think he's as wide awake as I am. It must be the early hours of the morning.

"I know this isn't how either of us imagined our wedding to be," I whisper, breaking the silence. "I know you still hate me," I add, even quieter, "But there's still nobody else I would ever want to do life with." Connor's breath hitches and I turn onto my side to face him. Seeing the silent tears run down his smooth, pale cheeks, I can't help but tentatively reach out with my thumb to wipe them away. He looks into my eyes, and a sob escapes him.

"Can I hold you?" I ask gently. I see the moment all the fight drains out of him, and he nods his head ever so faintly. I pull him into me, and he buries his face into my neck, taking a deep breath. I wrap my arms tightly around him and put my thigh over his hip so there's no space at all between us.

My heart breaks even more as he cries in my arms, but I think he needs to let it all out. If I can hold him as he falls apart for a short while, offer him some comfort in all this, it's the least I can do for him. I rub my hand up and down his back until, eventually, he relaxes, and his breathing starts to even out.

"This wouldn't hurt so much if I actually hated you," he says, his voice muffled against my neck. He pulls his face away slightly, and his eyes are red and puffy, but he's as beautiful as ever. I don't expect it when he softly presses his lips to mine; it's gentle, and there's no heat behind it, but it's painfully familiar.

I promise myself if I really do get a second chance with him, I'll do better. I'll never be the reason he's sobbing in my arms again. Planting a chaste kiss against his forehead, I squeeze him tightly. Nothing more is said, but somehow, the air has been cleared a little. Tomorrow won't be easy, but maybe it won't be a total disaster either.

ELEVEN

December 2018 - Four Years Ago

PHOENIX CAMPBELL

Me: Merry Christmas babe, miss you! xx

Cee: It's Christmas Eve

Me: It's now past midnight so it's Christmas day!

Cee: Yes but when you sent the message, it was 11:59pm

Me: I hope Santa brings you a lump of coal for being a shit.

Cee: MERRY CHRISTMAS FEE!!!!!

Me: Grrrrrr I hate you

Cee: No you don't, you love me ;)

Me: It's a good job you're pretty -_-

Cee: And to think, I thought it was my mad BJ skills that won you over ;)

> **Me:** You'll have to remind me :p Going to sleep before Santa gets here, night xxx

> **Cee:** Hope you've been a good boy this year ;) Night xxxxxxxxx

"Who ya texting?"

"Jesus Christ, Alf, thought you were asleep," I whisper shout at my younger brother.

We're staying at the family cottage in Kendal for Christmas, so I'm sleeping on a pull-out bed on the floor in his room because Jasper and Jade are sleeping in the room I used to share with Jas.

"I was trying to sleep, but then I kept hearing you giggling down there," he replies.

"I wasn't giggling, and it's Alice. Santa won't visit if you're awake," I tell him. I make a mental note to text her because then it feels less of a lie.

Alice is my best friend and neighbour, we've known each other since we were pups. She doesn't know who Cee is specifically, but she does know I've been seeing someone in secret, and she covers for me sometimes.

"Charlotte told me Santa isn't real."

How did I go from a quick Merry Christmas text to my boyfriend to having to choose whether or not to kill my ten-year-old brother's Christmas spirit? As future Alpha, Jasper can field this one.

"Maybe you should ask Jas about it tomorrow. He's very clever; he'll know," I whisper back. "But it's probably best to go to sleep just in case, you know?"

Alfie lets out a little hmm, like he's debating the merit of my suggestion.

"Yeah, okay. Night, Nix," he says before rolling over. I may not have a visit from Santa to look forward to, but I can't wait to see Jasper try to dodge Alfie's line of questioning tomorrow. I shoot a quick Merry Christmas text off to Alice and try to get some sleep myself.

<hr />

"You ever going to tell me who your mystery man is?" Alice asks down the pack bond. We're both in our wolf forms so we can head to our respective New Year's Eve plans.

"Are you going to tell me which Eastwood sibling you're going to meet tonight?" I ask back without answering her question.

This whole situation has worked out pretty sweet for me this year. A couple of weeks ago, Alice started hooking up with one of the Eastwoods, I'm guessing it's Benjy because he's our age, but she won't tell me. I'm pretty sure the only reason she's keeping it a secret is because she's salty I won't tell her who Cee is. We told our families we'll spend New Year's Eve together, so we're meeting back here tomorrow morning.

"I'll tell when you tell," she replies. See? Salty.

"I'll tell you one day." This is my stock answer to this question now, and I'm not lying. I will tell her one day; I'll tell everyone one day. I know I'm only twenty-two, but Cee is it for me, and I know we'll find a way to be together out in the open eventually.

I'm an hour early when I get to the abandoned barn where Cee and I meet. Plenty of time for what I have planned. I carried a big duffel bag in my mouth the entire way here so I'd have everything I needed. I start by hanging a pack of battery-powered fairy lights along the top of the wall in the corner. The hay we use to cushion the ground is scattered from the last time we were here, so I set to work spreading it more evenly before laying out two thick blankets over the top.

We found this barn last autumn; there's never been anyone else's scent here, so we assume it's probably sitting on some unused land. There was a particularly bad storm in November, though, that ripped off some of the roof shingles. Fortunately, we were able to patch it up. Okay, so it was mostly Cee—he's an actual joiner—I just passed him the tools when he asked for them.

The final touch for my New Year's plans is the bottle of champagne I nabbed from my parents' cellar and two plastic wine glasses. Laying them in the centre of the blanket, I step back to admire my handiwork. It looks pretty cute, if I do say so myself.

Around six months ago, Cee made us a joint playlist we could both add songs to. It's basically half songs I enjoy and half songs he adds to try to annoy me. Joke's on him, though, because I love me some Whitney Houston. I'm connecting my tiny portable speaker to my phone when I hear the gentle *thud, thud, thud,* of heavy paws in the distance.

A few minutes later, Cee's big furry grey head pokes through the door; he nudges it wider and walks inside before he shifts back.

"You did all this?" he asks, taking in my surprise. I grin at him in response and make grabby hands, beckoning him to hurry up and cuddle me. "One sec, let me throw some joggers on," he says, reaching into his rucksack.

"I mean, don't feel you have to because I'll probably just take them right off."

"Exactly, and who am I to deny you the opportunity to strip me naked." He winks at me as he pulls the joggers on; they hang loose on his waist, and I accidentally let out a needy whine.

"Get over here and kiss me. I haven't seen you in a bajillion years." Cee laughs at me but makes his way over and straddles my thighs. Holding my face in his palms, he presses his lips to mine in a kiss far too chaste for my liking.

"Two weeks, actually," he says between kisses.

"Precisely, two *whole* weeks. I'm surprised you even recognise me," I reply before I grab him by the hips and flip us so he's lying under me.

Our mouths crash together, his tongue pressing against mine, and he pulls my bottom lip between his teeth. This is the kiss I wanted. A loud, embarrassing moan slips free, and I'm way too on edge already.

Cee tugs my t-shirt up, and I help him pull it off over my head quickly before our mouths are fused together again. I grind my hips against him; our erections rubbing together is amazing, but it's not enough.

I need to feel his skin against my skin.

I pull my joggers off with an unnecessary degree of urgency. It might be December, but my skin is burning so hot I can hardly bear it.

"I told you not to bother putting these on," I tell him as I tug his bottoms off.

"Fine, you were right. Now hurry up," he says, sounding needy. I love it when he gets this way.

"Hold on a minute... Did Connor Kelly just say I'm right? I'm going to need you to repeat that." He lets out an unimpressed huff and glares up at me indignantly until a sly smile crosses his lips.

"I was gonna suggest you lie back while I ride you, but if you'd prefer I repeat myself, I can do that instead." I think my brain sort of reboots over the mental image.

"Have I ever told you you're never wrong? Like you're the rightest right person I've ever known?" I say before I go back to kissing him.

"That's what I thought," he replies breathlessly.

Slowly making my way down his body, I pause to flick my tongue over his hard nipples, which never fails to get a sexy little gasp out of him. Settling on my front, I kiss and lick the soft, milky skin of his inner thighs. As I graze my teeth against the delicate skin, he shivers beneath me. Unable to help myself, I give him one long lick from the base of his cock to the tip and then push his knees back, exposing his hole to me.

"Hold your legs back." He does as I ask immediately, and this slightly submissive side of him never fails to make me as hard as a rock. I blow gently over his tight, pink hole, and it flutters. Watching how his body responds to me never gets old.

He whimpers as I press my tongue lightly over his rim. I gradually increase the pressure, tasting him thoroughly and loving the feel of him softening from my ministrations. He tastes so good, musky and something else so uniquely *him*.

"Fuck... I need..." he stutters.

"What do you need?" I ask between licks.

"I dunno, I just need," he mumbles incoherently, and I chuckle.

Grabbing the bottle of lube I packed, I coat two fingers in the silky liquid. His hole is already relaxed from my tongue, so I press two slick fingers into him easily.

"Is this okay?" I ask. I'm hypnotised as I watch my fingers move in and out of him. When he starts to move his hips, seeking out more, I crook my fingers to brush against his prostate.

"Fuck. Yeah, more than okay," he says, writhing and moaning. The way he comes undone for me is one of the most beautiful things I've ever seen. His brow is sweaty, and his chest and neck are flushed a dusky pink. I lick a bead of sweat from his Adam's apple and gently nip at his jaw.

"Stop, fuck. I'm too close. I'm ready; lie down," he says before gripping my shoulders and pushing me down onto the blanket.

He straddles my hips and grabs the lube, coating my cock. As he strokes the liquid up and down my shaft, I scrunch my eyes closed and try to think unsexy thoughts because I'm dangerously close to erupting.

Note to self—don't go quite so long without having a wank.

I can't look away as he goes up onto his knees, preparing to take me. I hold the base of my dick still and line it up before he sinks down onto me. The pressure around my cock as it squeezes through the two rings of muscle is almost too much, and I grab his hips to hold him still for a moment when he's fully seated.

After a few deep breaths, I'm not quite so on edge anymore, and I use my hands to guide Cee's hips up. He takes the greenlight to undulate up and down my length, slowly at first, as he adjusts. His own cock is hard and leaking precum; I swipe my thumb over it and bring it to my lips to taste him. He watches me intently as I lick my thumb clean, and his eyes darken with desire. Leaning down, he kisses me, tasting himself on my tongue. My fingertips dig into the fleshy part of his bum, and I'm frustrated there's no physical way to have him as close to me as I'd like.

Sometimes, sex with Cee feels like all my filthy fantasies come true. But he's water slipping through my fingers I can never quite hold onto, no matter how hard I try. He moans loudly when I bend my knees and thrust my hips up to meet him, pumping myself up into the tight warmth of his arse. I'm frenzied, fucking him harder and harder, completely out of my mind. My ears are filled with the sounds of skin slapping against skin and loud, blissful moans. Both of us chasing our release and enjoying how amazing our bodies feel joined together.

"Fuck, fuck, fuck, fuck, fuck," he gasps, and suddenly he's vibrating on top of me, ropes of his cum shooting out of his cock and coating my abs.

The combination of watching him come without even touching himself and the way his orgasm causes the muscles in his arse to constrict around me has me following him into ecstasy like a freight train. My hips surge up as I pull him down onto me as hard as I can, feeling my cum fill his hole. My whole body shakes, and I grunt when he clenches, milking every last drop out of me.

He flops down onto me like a dead weight, pressing his face into the crook of my sweaty neck, and I wrap my arms and legs tightly around him. I wonder briefly if you can be addicted to a person? If so, I think I might be addicted to Connor; it's been a year and a half and every day, I want him more and more.

"Happy New Year," I say softly. Cee starts laughing, which causes my very over-sensitive and softening dick to slip out of him. He lifts himself up so his face hovers over mine and kisses me gently.

"I love you, even if you're a bit ridiculous," he tells me. I grin up at him because I never tire of hearing those three words.

"I'm going to just ignore that last bit. I love you too, babe."

And then I squish him in my arms as hard as I can.

"Bitter-sweet, memories, that's all I'm taking with me…" I sing into my plastic cup, pretending it's a microphone. We've finished the champagne, and I've taken to serenading Cee with all the ballads he's been adding to our joint playlist.

"How can you not even remotely sing in tune?" he asks, lying on the blanket and laughing hysterically. I'm not actually a terrible singer, but making Cee laugh so hard he snorts has become one of my favourite pastimes, so I do what needs to be done and sing *very* off-key.

"I'll have you know my mother says I have the voice of an angel," I tell him.

"Then your mother is either tone-deaf or a liar," he replies with the biggest smile on his face.

"How very dare you." I chuck my empty cup to the side and dive on top of him, tickling his ribs until he's begging me to stop with tears running down his cheeks.

⋙ ⋅⋄⋅ ⋘

We eventually curled up under a blanket, and I fucked him again—slowly. Laid on our sides, I took him from behind, and if I was the type of person to say things like 'make love,' that probably would have been it. Neither of us desperate to get off, just enjoying being close and connected with my arms wrapped around him, kissing every bit of skin I could reach.

It's the early hours of the morning now, and Cee is fast asleep. He's tucked up in my arms, breathing deeply. I'm totally exhausted and should probably try to sleep for a while, too, but I want to enjoy the moment. Sometimes, it feels as if our entire relationship is built on a foundation of stolen moments. I only hope they're strong enough to withstand our inevitably turbulent future.

I worry it's not sustainable, though. How long can we keep this a secret from everyone? How long until someone finds out?

For now, though, I let the current take me. I press a soft kiss against his temple and tug him in closer, breathing in his scent—*heather and lightning*—until all the tension and worries fade into the background, and I'm just here with him warm and safe in my arms.

TWELVE
AUGUST 2019 - THREE YEARS AGO

CONNOR KELLY

When I arrive at Ingleton Falls, the sun is setting, lighting up the sky with a hundred shades of pink and orange. There's a pool that's shallow around the edges but deep enough to swim where the waterfall feeds into it at the centre. It was twenty-seven degrees today, so I'm looking forward to cooling down in the water.

I dump my rucksack in a small cave running along the pool's edge. It's early enough that someone could still wander by here, so I throw on some swimming shorts to avoid offending any human sensibilities.

The shallow water is warm from the sun bearing down on it all day, but it's cooler and refreshing as I get deeper. Swimming under the spray of the waterfall, I let the cascading falls pound down onto my shoulders; it feels good on my sore muscles from being in the workshop all day.

I finally finished my joinery apprenticeship last month, so at least I'm earning a proper wage from the long days. The workshop owner is a friend of my da's, and he's offered to keep me on, but I really want to go into building bespoke furniture. My cousin Mikey has been a joiner for the last five years, and we've discussed starting our own business once I have more money saved.

It's Fee's birthday in a few weeks, and I've been working after hours, making two wooden figurines that match us in our wolf forms. They aren't very big, but getting the details perfectly right is taking me forever. I'm pretty sure he'll love them, though, so it'll be worth all the swearing and the splinters.

"Oi, why do you have clothes on?" Fee asks, rudely interrupting my waterfall shoulder massage. He walks towards me, buck naked, looking affronted by my swim shorts.

"It was just after nine when I got here; I didn't fancy gettin' arrested for flashin'," I answer, swimming closer to him. He makes a disgruntled 'hmph' noise and crosses his arms over his chest. It's dark now, and I don't think anyone will come by here, so I strip off under the surface and throw them at him. My sodden shorts make a slapping sound against his forearm as he catches them midair before chucking them to the side as though their existence offends him. A laugh bubbles out of me at his ridiculousness. He wades further in, closing the distance.

"Much better," he says, smiling. Grabbing my waist, he pulls me the rest of the way into him. My foot slips on the slimy stones, and I stumble a little, but Fee's firm hands keep me in place as he brings his lips down to mine.

Fee has the softest, pillowy lips I've ever kissed, and I can't help but nibble them. He moans in response, digging his fingers into my hips as his tongue seeks out mine. I press my whole body into him. Sometimes, I have this overwhelming feeling, like it's impossible to get as close to him as I need to. I want to crawl inside him and never leave, but I keep those thoughts to myself; they'd sound kinda creepy voiced out loud.

We're both hard, and our stiff cocks press together, seeking out any friction as we kiss and pant into each other's mouths. We glide into the deeper part of the pool. Fee is still standing, but I wrap my legs around his waist, and he places his hands under my bum to hold me in place. He backs into the waterfall, and the heavy spray interrupts the kiss momentarily.

"I missed you," I mumble against his lips.

Over two years of clandestine meetups after dark, once a week if we're lucky, less than that when anyone starts to get suspicious. Before he has a chance to reply, he stiffens under my hands, his muscles coiled tight. When I look up at him, his eyes are wide, like he's seen a ghost. It takes me a second to realise he's looking behind me towards the water's edge. He drops my legs but still holds me close—protectively.

I can't easily break out of Fee's grip, so I turn my head to see what he's looking at. Bile rises in my throat as I start to panic. My heart is a steel drum pounding in my chest. Standing eerily still and silent by the edge of the water is a wolf—and not one I recognise. They're average in size, with colouring similar to a husky, all white at the front with light grey dusting all along their back.

For a moment, I'm frozen in place, then suddenly, time speeds up, and too many thoughts are tumbling through my mind at once. Who is this, and what pack do they belong to? Could they be an omega? No, their scent is beta. I'm not on my territory. I'm not safe here! Fee isn't safe here!

He finally drops his hold on me, and his shoulders sag. I don't understand; we should be shifting. We need to be able to defend ourselves because this wolf looks angry. Nothing in their posture is submissive, and if a fight breaks out here, of all places, there will be too many questions I can't answer. Fee and I will be outed, and we aren't ready yet. Fee turns to look at me, and my stomach drops when we make eye contact.

Those eyes of his—always so open and expressive—are telling me everything I need to know. Regret. He knows this wolf. This is a wolf from his pack.

He looks guilty. Why does he look guilty? Has he told someone about us? Did he know he was being followed? None of this makes sense.

We've kept this secret for two years; why now? Before I even consciously make the decision, I've shifted to my wolf form in the water. I can scent better like this; the stranger is female. I'm much larger than she is, but she makes no signs of submission, so I bare my teeth at her and growl defensively.

"Cee, listen to me. It's okay, I promise it's okay," Fee tells me, tugging at the fur around my neck. "Cee, please shift back so we can talk. You're safe. I wouldn't lie to you." He looks at me pleadingly, but I shake my head and keep my eyes trained on the other wolf.

I won't shift back until she does.

"Shit," he mutters under his breath. He moves to walk out of the water towards her, but I whip my tail out, forcing him behind me. I don't know what's happening here, but he's still *mine*. He lets out a sigh of frustration. "Alice, next to the big rock over there is my bag, there's a t-shirt in there. Shift back, please, so we can talk," he says to the other wolf.

Alice? His best friend, Alice? Why is she here, and why does she know about us? How did she find us here if she's from the Lake District pack? She pauses for a second and then lets out a huffing sound before making her way over towards Fee's bag. When she returns from behind the large rock, she's shifted.

Alice is small, maybe five foot one or five foot two. She's wearing Fee's t-shirt, which resembles a dress on her, cutting off around her mid-thigh. Her hair is a silvery blonde, long and pin straight, falling almost to her waist. She's beautiful, and the sight of her in my boyfriend's t-shirt causes an involuntary growl to rumble from my chest.

This time, when Fee tries to walk out of the water, I don't stop him, but I do follow closely behind. Alice holds out a pair of shorts for him, and he pulls them on quickly.

"What are you doing here?" he asks.

"I could ask you the same thing, what the fuck, Nix? Who is that?" she replies, pointing a finger at me.

Nix? It must be what his friends and family call him, and the thought makes me suddenly feel like an outsider.

"Did you follow me here?" They both seem to be answering questions with questions.

"Yes, I followed you here. I thought you were hooking up with some human I could rib you about, but that's definitely not a human," she answers, raising her voice. I snarl at the insinuation I'm just some guy Fee is fucking.

"Enough, Alice. I know I owe you some answers, but you won't get them if you talk about him that way," he says firmly. With a voice like that, you'd almost believe he could be an Alpha one day. "You're alone?" he asks, and she nods.

Fee turns towards me, lifting his hands to cup my face; he tugs gently on one of my ears to make me face him. "Cee, I didn't know I was being followed. You have to believe me, okay? Please shift back so we can all talk. I promise you're safe." His usual playful eyes are serious now.

I pad towards the small cave where I left my bag earlier and shift. After I've put on some athletic shorts, I return to where Fee and Alice are standing in suffocating silence. My neck tingles, warning me I'm unprotected around wolves from an enemy pack, reminding me I'm outnumbered. Fee meets me partway, pressing a brief kiss to my lips and holding my hand tightly as if I'll bolt if he doesn't.

"Alice, you have to promise me, you can't tell anyone, please?" he implores her. She stares at where our fingers are interlaced.

"Tell me that isn't who I think it is," she says to him as though I'm not standing right there.

"Alice, this is Connor, my *boyfriend.* Connor, this is my best friend Alice...right?" He phrases it like he's not sure he'll still be able to call her that after this particular revelation, and my heart pangs in empathy for him.

"How long?" she asks. He swallows loudly.

"Just over two years." She gasps at his admission, and her eyes fill with emotion.

"You lied to me," she says welling up. "Last winter, I asked you so many times who you were meeting in secret, and you fobbed me off, telling me it was a meaningless hookup." Her words stab me in the chest.

A meaningless hookup? I try to drop Fee's hand, but he holds on tight, his knuckles turning white.

"I did, I lied. I'm sorry you found out this way, but it was safer for you not to know. Because now I have to beg you to keep this secret for me, keep this secret from the pack and from your Alpha, and I never wanted to put you in that position." He reaches towards her with his other hand and rubs a thumb gently across her delicate wrist.

"I won't tell anyone," she whispers and the breath I'd been holding whooshes out of me.

"Thank you," I manage to croak out, speaking finally.

"Two years, Nix? What exactly is this?" she asks Fee but gestures between the two of us. Fee looks at me, silently asking my permission to tell the truth, and I nod. At this point, honesty seems to be our best bet for keeping this between the three of us.

"We're together, Alice. He's my boyfriend and I love him. I had to lie to keep us safe, so please don't hold it against me because all this secrecy is eating me alive as it is, and I can't lose you." A tear has sprung free from his eye and runs down his cheek. I give his hand a squeeze in support. They both turn my way as I clear my throat.

"He's tellin' the truth; if he wasn't Phoenix Campbell and I wasn't Connor Kelly, we'd be mated by now," I tell Alice sincerely.

Hearing Fee admit how much it tears him apart to keep up this lie is a painful reminder of how much it costs us to be together. I know we tend to avoid difficult conversations because we get to see so little of each other. The last thing we want to do when we're together is argue or upset each other, but I know in my gut it's not entirely healthy. If I gave the go-ahead, I know Fee would have us come out, and we'd face the consequences together, but I'm not even close to ready for that. I take a deep breath and hope his best friend knowing the truth buys me some more time.

I pull out the blue chequered picnic blanket I packed and lie it on the ground for the three of us to sit on. Alice looks small and sad, sitting cross-legged on the very edge of the blanket.

"You remind me a lot of my twin, Niamh," I tell her. "She comes across all feisty and fiery, but it's a bit of a front; she just feels everythin' really deeply. Can I give you a hug? You look like you could do with one," I ask. Her eyes are still glassy, and she lets out a little sniffle but nods. I scooch beside her and wrap my arms around her shoulders, bringing her to my side. She's tense for a second, and then I feel her let out a deep breath as she relaxes.

We sit there quietly for a moment, processing what's happened tonight. Having spent the past couple of years worrying over what would happen if anyone found out about me and Fee, there's some relief from getting caught and the world not crumbling around us. I know it could have been much worse; Alice catching us isn't the same as if Sam or Jasper, or god forbid, our Alphas, had found us.

I'm also kind of happy; meeting Alice gives me a tiny window into Fee's world I never get a glimpse of. He talks about his friends and family a lot, but having a real tangible person right here sitting next to me is different. Alice has known Fee since they were pups, and I hope now the secret's out, I might get the opportunity to get to know her.

The calm that had settled in the air between us is abruptly disturbed by Fee barrelling into us. He knocks us both onto our backs, and his broad shoulders and arms are like a dead weight. He's going to actually squish poor Alice if he's not careful.

"Get off me, you big oaf." Her voice is muffled from being trapped under him.

"I felt left out," he says with a sulky pout and makes no attempt to move. I shuffle out from under him, causing him to plop down in between us. He's acting playful, but I know he's looking for reassurance that we will all be okay—*us* as well as him and Alice.

I pull my shorts down and shift quickly to save Alice from an eyeful. Nudging Fee with my nose to do the same, he follows suit, with Alice shifting a few seconds after him.

Fee's big, warm, furry body lies down between us. I'm bigger than he is when we're in our wolf forms, so I curl around his back. Alice lets out a slight whine before snuggling into his front. Once we're all settled, it isn't long before I can hear a rumbling purr from Fee's chest.

He needed this.

Even though the idea of anyone discovering us scares the living daylights out of me, I'm not sorry that Alice followed him tonight. I can't help but wonder, though, how long it will be until he needs everyone else to know. Walking away from Fee is out of the question now, but I'm not ready to give up my pack and my family either. And the truth is, if we come out—it's a choice I'll be forced to make.

THIRTEEN
December 2020 - Two Years Ago

PHOENIX CAMPBELL

"Fuck, I missed you," Cee says right before grabbing my face and pulling me into a heated kiss. I can't help but groan at the feel of his soft, warm mouth on mine. His tongue licks at the seam of my lips, and I open up to let him taste me fully.

It's been three weeks since we last saw each other; between work and other commitments, we haven't been able to get away, and it's the longest we've been apart since we met. It's also why our rendezvous spot is somewhat higher risk than usual. We're only roughly a mile out from my pack's territory, but I was going to crawl out of my skin if I didn't see him soon.

We're both naked despite the cold, having shifted the second we got here. I grab the back of Cee's thighs, lifting him so his legs wrap around my waist. I walk forward a few steps until his back is against a tree, our mouths still fused together.

"Lube?" I ask. He shakes his head.

"I couldn't grab anythin' before I set off. I have max two hours before I need to be back home in time to get to the airport." Lowering Cee so he's back to his feet, I kneel on the ground in between his legs and take his swollen cock into my mouth, swallowing him down quickly.

THIRTEEN

We're going to have to improvise.

I groan at the scent and taste of him. Clean and masculine. Gripping his hips, I relax my throat and let him fuck into my mouth. As my hands roam up and down his legs, I enjoy the feel of where his coarse, dark leg hair softens the higher up I go. My eyes water a little, and saliva escapes the corners of my mouth.

We usually take our time, but the older we get, the more it seems life gets in the way of us actually being able to see each other, and tonight we're both desperate. It doesn't take long before Cee's thighs are shaking under my hands, and I know he's close. Our eyes lock as I gaze up at him; his piercing green eyes never fail to take my breath away. As he reaches to pinch his nipple hard, I start jerking him off with my hand so only the tip is in my mouth.

"Fuck, I'm gonna come," he warns. Spurts of his release hit my tongue, and I have to fight the urge to swallow it down. When I'm sure I've got his entire load in my mouth, I stand up and spin him around. He puts his hands out to brace himself against the tree and arches his back slightly, presenting himself to me.

Cee's back is covered in scratches from where the bark cut into it, but his usually flawless skin is already healing. He shivers and moans as I scratch my blunt nails up his back. I desperately want to tell him how hot he looks and how badly I want him, but I can't speak yet. Dribbling some of his cum onto my fingers, I press them inside his hole and stretch him just enough that I won't hurt him. Spitting out the rest of his load into my hand, I coat my cock in it and rub some over his rim before pushing my length into him. Wrapping my arm around his chest, I tug him so his back is flush against my torso. The way his snug, warm hole grips my cock is unreal.

"Holy shit, I've missed you. Missed this," I mumble into his ear now I can finally speak.

"I think. That's the longest. You've ever gone. Without talking. During sex," he says, his sentence broken up by me thrusting into him—hard.

Placing a hand against the tree in front of us, I pound into him ruthlessly. My other hand grips his hip so hard I'd leave a bruise if he were human. I almost wish it *would* bruise. Some evidence we were here, and we did this. I want to see it on his skin and cover him in marks.

I have to turn my face away from him because I'm overwhelmed with the urge to bite down on his neck and really leave my mark—a permanent one. My teeth ache with the need. My orgasm is building quickly, taking me right to the edge of spilling inside him—and then I hear it.

Thud, thud, thud.

"Is that?" he asks, looking over his shoulder at me, his eyes widening in panic.

"Shit! I think so. Shift and hide." In the blink of an eye, his grey wolf form is a blur in the opposite direction, and he dives into the large overgrowth. I shift too, but before I can run and meet whichever wolf is heading our way, they're already approaching.

"What are you doing out here?" my dad asks as he enters the small clearing.

"Couldn't sleep. Went for a run," I reply, trying to get my heart rate to slow down. The only thing currently in my favour is the wind blowing my scent away from him. *"How come you're out?"* I ask. I was certain he and my mum were asleep when I snuck out.

"Your mum has extra patrols out since the announcement." The announcement being that Jasper and Jade are expecting a baby. Our pack has seen a rapid decline in pups being born in the past ten years. The

fact Jasper's baby is most likely to carry on the Alpha line has everyone on edge until they're born. Our pack is one of the few where the title of Alpha has remained in the same family for over twenty generations. *"It's not safe for you to be out running at night, off our land. I'm heading back. Coming?"* my dad asks. I fight the urge to look over my shoulder towards where Cee is hiding and just nod my head at him.

I follow my dad back to the cottage, trying to keep enough distance between us so he doesn't scent Cee on me. When the skies suddenly open up, and we're hit by heavy rain, I've never been so grateful in my life. I'll still need to scrub myself down in the shower, but at least this will lessen Cee's scent all over me.

CONNOR KELLY

Fuck, fuck, fuck! That was way too close. We were thinking with our dicks and almost got caught. Maybe we did get caught, for all I know. I've no idea who the wolf was and whether they could scent me on Fee. I run home as fast as I can. I need to get to my phone so I can speak to Fee and find out what happened.

I shift back at the downstairs entrance to the block of flats I live in. Fortunately, they're all owned by a wolf in my pack, and he changed the locks so all the doors are opened with a code instead of a key.

Keys are particularly annoying when you're shifting back and forth. I type in the code, and the main door opens. I leg it up the stairs two at a time, feeling the cold air against my naked body and immensely grateful I run at a very high temperature. When I buzz in the second code to get into my flat, I immediately dive across the room to check my phone.

> **Fee:** I'm so sorry. It was my dad but I don't think he scented you. Are you ok?

I let out a sigh of relief and take deep breaths to get my heart rate to slow down. It's okay, we're okay. Nobody found out. We have to be more careful, *but nobody found out*.

> **Me:** I just got home. Are you still awake?

> **Fee:** Yeah. I wish I could call you. When can I see you?

> **Me:** I get back from NI on 4th Jan. Working through to the 9th but could see you that night? Don't have to be anywhere on 10th.

> **Fee:** I've got a match on morning of 10th but fuck it, I'll make it work. I miss you so much, we can't keep on like this :(xx

> **Me:** You're right, I miss you too. Will find a way to see you more. I'll take on less work or something. I love you

> **Fee:** You know it's not only about how much you work. We'll talk properly when you get back xxx

We'll talk properly when you get back? That cannot be fucking good. We've been together for three and a half years, but the past year has been the most challenging.

I went into business with my cousin Mikey, and we've had to work some intense hours to get it off the ground. I've frequently been working seven days a week, and we've been lucky if we've had more than two or three hours together before one of us needs to get home again. I know it's not sustainable, but I don't know how to fix it.

> **Me:** We're okay though aren't we? You're not leaving me?

My heart pounds, and I feel sick. Ugh, I sound so insecure, and I hate it. In the past six months especially, Fee has been talking more about wanting us to come out to our packs, and I'm worried my time is running out. I haven't even told my da yet that I won't be marrying Will. I don't even breathe while I watch the bubble at the bottom of the screen as Fee types.

> **Fee:** We're obviously not ok babe. We never see each other, I can't even call you right now because my family could hear. But no, I'm not leaving you. I love you and I'll always love you. We just need to come up with a better plan xx

My breath whooshes out of me in relief. He's not leaving me. I've no idea how I'm going to fix this, but I will. Fee moves into his own place soon; at least then, we can call and video chat without risking anyone overhearing. It'll help bridge the gap when we're apart. It has to.

> **Me:** I love you. I promise we'll come up with something xx

> **Me:** Why was your dad out btw?

> **Fee:** Mum has been organising extra patrols. Was going to tell you tonight actually, Jas and Jade are expecting, new baby Alpha heir incoming xx

> **Me:** Wow. You're gonna be an uncle, makes you sound old lol

> **Fee:** The idea of little Alfie being an uncle is funnier. He'll be thirteen when the baby is born xx

> **Niamh:** Setting off now, will be there in twenty x

Bollocks.

> **Me:** Gtg. Twenty mins to shower and pack. I'll text you when I land?

> **Fee:** Yep, have a safe flight babe xxx

"Why do I always have to have the middle seat?" Niamh whinges.

"Because you're practically a hobbit," Sam points out.

"I'm five foot five!"

"Exactly."

The cabin crew stands in the aisle and begins their demonstration of how to fasten a seat belt. I can't help but think if someone is unable to figure that out and dies as a result, it's merely natural selection.

I dig out my noise-cancelling headphones from my rucksack and stick some music on to block out the noise of Niamh and Sam bickering. I haven't slept in over thirty-six hours, and I'm starting to feel nauseated. When I press shuffle on the playlist I created for me and Fee a few years ago, 'The Time of My Life' from the Dirty Dancing soundtrack comes on. I have to turn my face toward the window to hide the smile that spreads over my face at the memory.

One night last summer, Alice joined us at Ingleton Falls. Fee wanted to try doing the lift from dirty dancing, but Alice kept freaking out at the top. In the end, he coaxed me into doing it, and we managed it on the first attempt. We didn't have a speaker with us, but Fee insisted on singing (very badly) at the top of his lungs. On the third attempt, he almost dropped me because I couldn't stop laughing long enough to hold the position. As soon as I got home that night, I added the song to the playlist.

Nobody has ever made me laugh like Fee does. The fond memory only adds to my determination to do better for him. I can't lose him.

Sam, Niamh and I are spending just over a week with our grandparents in Northern Ireland, which will give me plenty of time to figure out how to make all of this better again. We love each other; we've made this work for years. This is just a rough patch we need to work through, I'm sure of it.

FOURTEEN
January 2021 - One Year Ago

CONNOR KELLY

"**M**other fucker!" I shout loudly enough to startle my cousin.

"You better not be bleedin' on that fuckin' table, Con," Mikey yells from the other side of our workshop.

When we opened our business building bespoke furniture a year ago, we set up shop in a small industrial estate in north Manchester. It's not a huge space because we didn't want high overheads when we were starting out.

I turn off the bench saw I was using and look down at the piece of wood I'd been attempting to cut through; there is definitely a *lot* of blood on it. For fuck's sake. Looks like I'll be starting over on this one.

My hand is throbbing where the jagged blade cut through the muscle, and my eyes are watering profusely.

"Thanks for the concern. I almost lost my fuckin' hand," I gasp, wincing at the pain. I take some deep breaths and count to ten, squeezing my eyes shut.

"Ouch, how'd you manage that?" Mikey asks when he wanders over to inspect the damage.

"The blade caught on an edge, and the wood kicked," I tell him through gritted teeth.

FOURTEEN

"Bet you're glad you're not a human right about now," he says, looking at the tissue in my hand knitting back together. He's not wrong; I definitely appreciate the sped-up healing time, but it still fucking hurts like a bitch.

My head is in the clouds today, and if I wasn't a shifter, I'd be on my way to a hospital. I managed to cut a jagged slice through the fleshy part of my hand between my thumb and forefinger. Thankfully my left hand. Still, it looks gory as fuck.

"Come on, let's have a brew while your hand heals up," he suggests, slapping me on the back.

We put in a small kitchenette when we set up in the workshop, but it only has a kettle, a microwave, and a mini fridge. I plonk myself down on the sofa nearby while Mikey puts the kettle on.

"Not like you to be so distracted, what's up?" he asks.

To be honest, I'm not entirely sure what's wrong. I think it's a build-up of all these different things in my life that are completely out of my control. I've seen Fee once since I got back from Northern Ireland, but we only had a couple of hours, and neither of us wanted to ruin it by bringing up heavy shit. Lately, it feels as if we never have enough time to sort through anything.

I can't exactly tell Mikey my head is fucked because I hardly get to see my boyfriend—the one nobody knows about.

"My da and Will's parents are pushing for us to set a date for the weddin' again, and I'm *sooo* not ready." I let out a sigh.

"Not ready or haven't figured out a way to get out of it yet?"

Will and I were supposed to get married when we turned twenty-one. I'm twenty-four next month, and he's twenty-four this summer, so I've been postponing it for several years, and the pressure from our families is mounting.

"No comment," I reply. Mikey knows I don't want to marry Will, but he's big on 'you do what you have to do for the good of the pack,' so I avoid bringing it up with him too often. The gash on my hand has finally stopped bleeding, and I watch the top layer of skin going pink.

"Will's one of the prettiest guys I've ever met and one of your best friends; I don't see why you're so put out over the match." As if that's all that's required to commit your entire life to someone.

"Yeah, he's pretty, but I don't see him that way; we're just pals. I'm only ever going to view him as a friend. I don't understand why everyone is so focused on me and Will when Sam is the Alpha heir with no intentions to settle down." I know I sound stroppy, and I don't mean to throw Sam under the bus, but I am *so* over this constant debate.

"You and I both know nobody can tell a future Alpha who they're gonna marry. That stubborn Alpha gene of his would have him swearin' to never settle down if anyone pushed it," Mikey says, snickering.

"And my Alpha gene? Why can't I use the same excuse?" I ask, getting exasperated.

"Yours is dormant. You're just stubborn because you're a Kelly. You'll get over it," he says dismissively, and I huff in annoyance.

"Yeah, well, Sam might want to get a move on. Campbells will have another Alpha heir soon, and our line ends with Sammy." I'm hoping if my family starts focusing on getting Sam to settle down, they'll be less livid when I finally call things off with Will.

"What do you mean?" he asks curiously.

"Apparently Jasper and Jade Campbell are expecting. New baby Alpha en route," I tell him. I really hope he doesn't push where I got this information from because I can't exactly tell him the truth.

"Fuck. Really? If you don't marry Will, the pack is gonna be broke without his family's money and with a new Alpha on the way; it won't be long before their pack is stronger than ours, too. Does your da know?"

He's reacting to this news with much more vehemence than I expected.

"No, I don't think he does, anyway," I answer. Knowing that since I haven't told him, it's highly unlikely he would have found out elsewhere. Guilt niggles me; maybe this is something I should have kept to myself.

"Good, that's good. Probably best not to tell him right away," he says distractedly. He's acting really strange which is saying something because Mikey is a bit unpredictable at the best of times.

"Why's that good?" I ask, but Mikey gets up and leaves the room like he didn't even hear me.

My hand only has a rapidly fading pink scar on it now, thank fuck for quick healing since I'll have to plane the tabletop again, and hope my blood hasn't soaked into it. Finishing the dregs of my brew, I dump the mug in the sink. I really need to crack on if I still want to finish early today since I promised to go and meet Niamh and Will at the pub after work.

※

My work boots stick to the grubby floor, and the smell of stale beer assaults my senses. When I spot a group of builders standing around the bar, I no longer feel bad for being so dusty and not changing out of my work clothes. The Fox & Hound is busy with the after-work rush, but I spot Will at a booth in the corner.

"You are my best mate in the whole world," I tell him, picking up the pint of Amstel on the table and taking a large sip. There's a bottle of red wine and two glasses in front of him, but no sign of Niamh yet. I dry my hand on my trousers from the condensation on the glass.

"I'm your only friend that isn't related to you," he replies, arching an eyebrow.

"Touché." I slide into the seat opposite him.

"How's your day been?"

"I almost took my thumb off with a bench saw, so I've had better days. You?"

"Shit, are you okay?" He grabs my hand and inspects it for damage, rubbing a thumb over the faint pink scar. It feels like a strangely intimate gesture. It makes my stomach flip, and not in a good way. Will has always been tactile—wolves, in general, are—but I'm now distinctly aware of the fact he thinks I'm single and that I'll marry him one day, so I pull my hand back.

"Hurt like a bitch, but it's fine now. What's new with you? Where's Niamh?" I ask, grasping for a subject change.

"Umm. Actually, I texted her and asked if she could join us a bit later because I needed to discuss something with you."

Oh fuck, I have a really horrible feeling about this. I look towards the pub door, genuinely considering making a run for it, but I know that's not an option.

Probably best to get this over with.

"Oh yeah... What's up?" I ask, trying to sound nonchalant.

"I was having dinner at my mums' house last night, and your dad turned up. They got into an argument over there not being a wedding date set yet, and he told me we have until the end of this week to pick a date and that the date we choose better be in a year ending twenty-one..." Will stares into his wine glass as he talks, and I take a large gulp of my lager.

FOURTEEN

If my da's demanding this all of a sudden, it has to be because the pack is broke. Will's parents promised him a lot of money, but most of it only after Will and I tie the knot.

"Ignore him; he's such a prick. We're only twenty-three. What's the big rush?" I reply, even though I know there's no ignoring my da about this anymore; he's our Alpha, after all.

"Con, I think we should maybe set a date." He looks up at me and tugs on his earlobe, which has always been Will's nervous tell. In fairness, I haven't always been the most cooperative where these discussions are concerned, so his apprehension is understandable. It still seems pretty fucked up to me that at age sixteen, our parents made this decision for us, and now I'm the arsehole for not wanting to go through with it. Sometimes, I really wish Will would speak up and point out how ridiculous this engagement is so it doesn't always fall on me.

"We can't get married just so some money will change hands. Don't you wanna find your mate one day? Fall in love and build a life with someone?" I ask, desperate for him to put an end to all of this.

"I know you don't see me that way, but maybe you could? Maybe if we tried and went on a date or something?" He sounds so hopeful, but I feel sick to my stomach. I want to scream out that I already belong to someone else, but I can't, and my heart aches with it.

"Will, you're my best mate, but I can't, okay? I'm sorry, but I just can't." I down the last of my drink. "I gotta go. I forgot somethin' at the workshop. Tell Niamh I'll call her later." I don't even give him a chance to respond before I make my way out of the front door.

When I round the corner of the pub, I end up bent over at the waist, hands resting on my knees as I try to catch a full breath. My throat feels tight and raw, like it's closing and not enough air can get through to fill my lungs. My chest is tight, and my palms sweat despite the cold temperature. I try to steady my breathing, but every breath is too fast, and too shallow, and not enough. When my vision starts going spotty, I begin to panic even more. Suddenly, two firm hands grip my shoulders.

"Breathe in through your nose and out through your mouth for me, okay?" Will's voice is soft but firm, and I try to do as he says. "Good, now tell me five things you can see." I try to blink the black spots out of my vision to see what's around me.

"Um. Your Converse, a glass bottle, graffiti, my hands, the pavement." I manage to get the words out around my laboured breathing.

"Great, you're doing good, Con. Now, four things you can touch."

"My trousers, the wall, the ground... Your hands." My chest feels less restricted, like the rope that was wrapped around me finally has some slack.

"Three things you can hear."

"Your voice, traffic, my voice," I say softly, eventually calming down. "I'm okay now, thank you. Sorry. Fuck. I'm such a mess. You shouldn't have followed me out here." Will lets go of my shoulders and moves to lean against the wall next to me.

"Well, I'm glad I followed you out here. I didn't even know you had anxiety, Con. Have you had panic attacks before?" I can tell he's trying to hide it, but I can hear the hurt over me keeping this from him. Let's add it to the list of reasons I'm a terrible friend.

"Only in the past year, not many," I answer quietly.

"Will you come back inside? We don't have to talk about it," he offers.

"Yeah, okay. I'll be in in a minute. I just need to make a quick call." Will seems to consider whether I'm using it as an excuse to make a run for it, but he must see how much I don't have the energy to lie to him at present and ultimately nods before heading back inside.

My hands shake as I pull my phone out of my pocket.

FOURTEEN

"Hey, you're through to Phoenix Campbell's voicemail. Leave a message, and I'll get back to you."

"Hey Fee. I just needed to hear your voice. Can I see you tonight? I really need to see you. I love you."

My phone buzzes with an incoming call as soon as I disconnect.

"Hey babe, I was driving and forgot to connect to the car. Everything okay?" I swallow the lump in my throat.

"I really need to see you. Can I see you tonight?"

"Yeah, I can see you tonight. Are you okay though? You don't sound okay. Where are you?"

"I'm fine, I promise. I'm at the pub having a drink with Will and Niamh."

"Okay. I'm driving home from work, but I'm free all evening. Text me a time?"

"Yep, will do. Gotta go, Niamh's just spotted me. I'll text you. Bye."

"Okay, love you. Bye."

"What's wrong?" Niamh asks the second she reaches me. "And don't say 'nothing'." I let out a deep sigh before answering.

"Fine. Not nothin', but I don't wanna talk about it. Will's inside. Can we just hang out and drink beer and pretend?"

"Did Will already speak to you about Da?" I nod in response. "Okay then, tonight we can pretend. But you're going to have to come clean to me at some point, Con. Whatever it is, it's eating you alive." With one last pitying look, she turns and enters the pub, going in search of Will.

"I know," I whisper before following.

FIFTEEN
March 2021 - One Year Ago

PHOENIX CAMPBELL

> **Cee:** How soon can you meet me? It's urgent.

> **Me:** I'm at work, I don't have a class last period though so I can probably get out by 2:30? What's wrong? xx

> **Cee:** Can't tell you in a text. I'll be at the barn from 3

> **Me:** Are you ok tho? You're freaking me out?

> **Cee:** I'm ok, I promise.

Well, that's ominous. It's almost the end of lunch now, and at least I only have my year elevens to go. I'd been planning to stay late today because I'm drowning in marking, but it's safe to say I won't be able to concentrate on anything until I've spoken to Cee.

Things have been better between us these last few weeks. We're still definitely overdue some serious conversations, but with him taking on less weekend work, we've finally been able to steal more than a few hours together at a time.

Since I moved into my new house a month ago, we both live alone now, so we've been able to have video calls most nights before bed. I didn't even realise how much I needed the extra contact until I had it. Hearing him talk about his day and what he's been building—in his own voice—has brought us closer somehow.

I'm trying not to get too panicked by his texts because Cee does have a slight habit of blowing things out of proportion. I don't want to stress myself out if it turns out to be nothing too serious.

An hour and a half later, I make my excuses to my department head to duck out early. My last class of the day was not particularly effective in distracting me because we were doing mock exams.

It's raining heavily when I leave the school building, so I make a dash for it to the teacher's car park. Still, my clothes are soaked through by the time I dive into my Jeep. I shoot Cee a quick text to let him know I'm on my way and turn my windscreen wipers on as I reverse out of my spot.

It takes me around forty minutes driving to get off the territory. Spotting a passing place further up ahead, I dump my car there for now since I haven't passed anyone for a while.

The sky rumbles with thunder and a flash of lightning cracks through the dark clouds. After I'm undressed, I stuff my clothes into my backpack. Shifting quickly, I pick up my bag with my teeth and start running in the direction of the barn. I can get there faster in my wolf form than in my car, and the dreadful weather will help keep me out of sight of anyone braving a walk today. Most humans who see a wolf shifter in the distance tend to tell themselves they've just seen a large dog, but we try to keep out of sight as much as possible.

Running through the trees usually calms my mind, but my thoughts are spiralling over what Cee could possibly have to tell me that he can only say face-to-face. Having spent most of the afternoon telling myself it's probably nothing, my stomach is churning with worry as I get closer to the barn.

Cee explained to me a few weeks ago how his dad was really starting to pressure him and Will to set a date, but he promised he would find a way out of it. What if he couldn't do it? What if a date has been set? There's no way I could sit back and watch him marry someone else.

What if he's decided he's never going to leave his pack, so he needs to leave me instead?

Maybe I've been pushing too hard for us to be together in the open, and now he thinks he has to make his choice before he's ready. But I can't see why he'd need to discuss that with this level of urgency.

Truthfully, I'd rather spend the rest of my life in the dark with Cee than not have him at all. These have been the best few years of my life. When I'm around him, I get to laugh and be silly. When I'm at home or with my pack, I'm the Alpha's son, and everyone expects me to always be responsible and serious. If Cee wants to talk in person, then it can't be too late, right?

I'm out of breath and panting by the time I nudge the barn door open with my head. I don't think I've ever run that fast in my life.

Cee's already here; he looks cosy in an oversized hoodie of mine and some grey jogging bottoms. He wouldn't be wearing my clothes if he was breaking up with me, would he? As his eyes meet mine, though, my stomach drops. His eyes are red-rimmed and puffy. He looks devastated.

I shift quickly and run towards him.

"I'm so sorry. I fucked up," he chokes out, handing me a pair of shorts and a hoodie to shove on.

"Why are you sorry? Don't be sorry. Whatever it is, we'll work through it," I tell him desperately.

"You need to get Jasper and Jade to a safe place and not tell anyone where they are, not until the baby comes." His fingers dig into the flesh on my arms as he speaks.

"What are you talking about? What have Jasper and Jade got to do with us?" I ask him frantically. He really needs to tell me what's going on before I implode.

"This isn't about us, Fee. I didn't know it would lead to this. If I'd known, I never would have said a word. I need you to believe me!"

"Said a word about what? I need you to take a deep breath, baby. Calm down and tell me what's going on." He tries to take some deep breaths, but they keep hitching on a sob. I've never seen him like this before. Using the sleeve of my jumper, I wipe some snot from under his nose, waiting for him to calm down enough to explain.

"A few weeks ago, I told Mikey Jade was pregnant. You remember I told you I almost took my thumb off with the bench saw?" I nod, recalling it well because he'd called me out of the blue later that day, saying he needed to see me—he'd seemed so exhausted and, well, sad. "It was that day, and I wasn't thinkin' straight. He kept badgering me about Will, and I wanted to change the subject, but I had no idea it would lead to this. I... I had no idea. I didn't think..." Fresh tears stream down his cheeks, and my lunch sits like lead in my stomach.

"Lead to what?"

"Niamh overheard Mikey and some of his friends talkin'. She said they were plannin' something to make it look like Jade died in an accident. They think if a new Campbell Alpha is born, we'll be at a disadvantage. Everyone knows the pack is almost broke, and Sam doesn't have a mate. My da's gettin' older, and people are starting to panic over the pack's future."

My mind whirls, trying to process too much information at once. Before I can unpack everything else, I need to make sure my family is kept safe.

"I need to go," I tell him calmly, uncurling his fingers where they're digging into my skin.

"Niamh is telling my da, right now. He'll put a stop to it." His voice wavers, and I can't help but think he only hopes that's the case. I certainly can't risk the safety of my family on his dad, *hopefully* putting a stop to this. I need to go and warn them. How do I warn them, and leave Cee out of it? "I'm so sorry," he tells me again.

"Don't be. It's my fault."

"How could any of this possibly be your fault?" He tries to reach out for me again, but I take a step back, and he looks crushed. His fingers flex as though he doesn't know what to do with them if he can't touch me.

"I shouldn't have told you about the baby. My pack trusted me, and I betrayed them when I told you. It's my fault, and I need to go." I can't stop the cold from leaching into my voice, but I need to leave and warn my family before I can break down.

"What do you mean? I'm your boyfriend, you should be able to tell me things. I fucked up, I know I fucked up, but I'm going to fix this, okay? Let me fix this." His voice is pleading with me, but I'm angry with him, and I need to leave before I say something I'll regret. He needs to let me go.

"You've done enough. If there's anything else I need to know, text me. I have to put my pack first for once."

Why would he have told his cousin? I always assumed everything we talked about stayed between us. As soon as we both came clean about who we were, I honestly didn't even filter what I said around him, and he didn't seem to around me. I knew how dire his pack's financial situation was, but I never would have told anyone, not even Alice.

What else has he told them?

As easily as the snap of a twig, the trust is broken. I feel embarrassed and foolish for trusting him so implicitly. I thought it was an unspoken rule that the things I told him when we were alone were said in confidence. He clearly didn't see it that way.

⋙ ⋅⋄⋅ ⋘

When I make it back to my car, I call my mum, giving her a brief run-down so she can get Jas and Jade somewhere safe quickly. By the time I've pulled my clothes back on, she's sent me a text with an address. It's a safe house that's vaguely familiar. It's right in the heart of our territory, deep in Whinlatter Forest, up in the mountains near Keswick. My Satnav says it'll take roughly an hour and a half to get there. It's only late afternoon, but the sky is a dark grey, and the rain is still heavy. The weather reflects my current situation poignantly.

As I drive up to the chalet-style property, I see Jas's beat-up Land Rover parked on the driveway. After pulling my Jeep up behind him, I make a quick dash for the front door, trying not to get drenched through for the third time today.

They must have got here considerably faster than I did since Jas already has a fire going and is pacing a hole in the carpet. Jade looks surprisingly unphased; she's curled up under a blanket, watching *Schitt's Creek*. She gives me a soft smile and pauses her show as I toe off my shoes, and Jas raises his eyebrow at me in question.

"Sit, and I'll explain what I can." Jade lifts her feet so Jasper can sit on the sofa next to her, and I plonk myself down in the armchair facing them.

The entire drive over here, I debated what exactly to tell them. As hurt and angry as I am with Cee for telling his cousin something I thought I told him in confidence, I know he never in a million years would have seen this as a possible outcome. I know I need to put my pack and my family first, but I also need to find a way to protect him too. I'm not going to throw away almost four years over one horrible mistake.

I can't lie to myself, though; there is a paranoid part of my brain that has me questioning everything I've ever told him. For so long, I've assumed everything we talk about stays between the two of us, like some unwritten rule, and suddenly I don't know for certain if that's the case.

Have I had the measure of what's between us all wrong?

I know Connor loves me, but he's also made it clear his family comes first, and I think I've been choosing to ignore that. And now my family is in danger because I always hear what I want to hear rather than the truth.

"I'm trying not to freak out here, Nix, but I really need you to start talking," Jas says.

"Sorry. My head's all over the place," I reply.

Taking a deep breath, I explain as best I can while keeping Cee's identity a secret. I tell them I've been seeing a girl from a Scottish pack in secret but that it's over now. Taking responsibility for my part in this, I admit I told them about the baby and apologise for thinking they would keep it a secret but that I did trust them.

It's a struggle to contain my anger towards Cee because I should have been able to trust him. After almost four years together, trust and love were all we had. With that broken, what's left?

Where my tale gets a bit dicey is when I try to explain how they were close with someone from the Kelly pack, overheard the plot against Jade, and warned me as soon as they found out.

Jade nods her head and absently strokes a hand over her baby bump while Jasper sits with his brow furrowed.

"Who is *she*?" His eyes narrow in suspicion, and I don't miss how he emphasises the word she.

"I can't tell you, okay? But it's over. I don't expect you to understand, but I need you to believe I have a good reason for not telling you who it is."

My stomach lurches when I say it's over. Is it over? I don't know how we'll move past this, but I get a very real searing pain in my chest when I even contemplate not being with Cee anymore.

"I'm so sorry, Jade; this is all my fault."

"You weren't to know, love. Honestly, I can't help but think nobody was. Alpha Kelly couldn't have even known."

"What makes you say that?"

"Tensions between us and his pack are the same as they've always been, but he has a good relationship with my dad's pack in Northumbria. He wouldn't risk that. And honestly, I know his pack is enemy number one to you guys, but he's a good friend of my parents, and he's always seemed like a good man to me."

Her explanation makes sense, and I feel some relief wash over me. I'm smart enough to understand I've been raised with a very biased view of Alpha Kelly and his pack. I can't imagine anyone horrible could have raised Connor to be the way he is, though. When I met with Cee earlier, Niamh was already telling their dad about it all, so it feels safe to assume Jade will be out of danger for the time being.

> **Cee:** I'm so sorry. Can I call you?

> **Cee:** My da is dealing with Mikey, nothing bad is going to happen to Jade, I promise.

> **Cee:** Please don't shut me out. I know I fucked up but I love you.

> **Cee:** I understand if you need some time, but please tell me you're ok?

I had left my phone in the car while I was talking to Jasper and Jade; I hadn't meant to leave him stressed out. When I step back into the house, Jasper is ending a call.

"Any news?" I ask.

"That was Mum. She's spoken to Alpha Kelly, and they're meeting tomorrow. She says there's no immediate threat, but for Jade to stay here with at least one of us until everything has been ironed out." I nod and let out a deep breath.

"I'm meant to be coaching this weekend; I can come straight back after, though."

"It's fine. I can be here and work from home next week if need be." I decide then that I'll come back afterwards and stay here regardless. I owe it to them after causing all this mess.

As I watch Jasper sit back down on the sofa, resting a hand protectively over Jade's bump, I wander down the hallway to one of the guest rooms to give them some space.

> **Me:** I can't call you but I'm ok. I love you, but I need to make my family a priority right now. Give me some time to process all this x

When I see the message go immediately from 'delivered' to 'read', I almost laugh. Three little dots appear within seconds.

> **Cee:** I understand. I love you. I'll wait to hear from you x

I sigh, because if Cee does, in fact, wait to hear from me, I'll be extremely surprised. It actually pisses me off how much I tip-toe around him when he needs space, and yet if he's anxious, I have to provide all the reassurance required. Sometimes, I wish I got to be the unreasonable one. I want him to learn that I get to have space too when I need it. And I think I need it? I'm honestly not sure if I'm asking for space because it's what I think I *should* need, what I *do* need, or if there's a part of me that's punishing him for letting me down. It's probably a combination of all three.

I hate how even when I'm angry with him, he's the person I want to comfort me. He's the person I want a hug from and the person I want to vent to. The person I want to reassure me it's all going to be okay.

After what feels like ten hours of marking but was probably closer to three, I hear the front door open and my dad's voice echoing from the hallway. I head out of my room to say hello. He's got a big shopping bag in each hand that I take from him to go and put away in the kitchen. I take a quick glance into the bags to see what I'll be cooking for us tonight. Chicken thighs, potatoes, and some root vegetables. I'll probably roast it all.

"Are you staying for dinner?" I ask him as I walk back into the lounge. He shakes his head.

"No can do. Just popping by with supplies. I need to pick up Alfie from his rugby practice," he explains. Alfie has aged out of the team I coach, so now my dad has to ferry him around.

My dad follows as I go back into the kitchen to prepare dinner and shuts the door behind him.

"How're you holding up?"

"Shouldn't you be asking Jasper and Jade that question? It's my fault, after all." He gives me his soft dad eyes. The ones that never fail to make me well up if I'm already feeling like shit.

"Nobody thinks this is your fault, son. Maybe it's time we finally put this feud to bed. Some good can come of this."

"Mum blames me." I press my palms into my eyes, trying to get rid of the tears before they fall. It's embarrassing how at twenty-four, I still care this much about getting my mum's approval. My dad pulls me into a hug and squeezes me tight.

"Don't tell her I said this, but your mum isn't always right. She was raised to be an Alpha, and sometimes she forgets to be a mother first," he says quietly before letting me go. I fight the urge to scoff at his use of the word 'sometimes'. I don't think she's ever put being a mother before being an Alpha.

<hr />

Over the course of the next week, it's basically Groundhog Day. I get up early to make the long commute to work, teach my classes and then come back to the safe house to spend the evenings with Jasper and Jade. Jade seems reasonably content, but Jasper gets progressively agitated as the week goes on.

Every evening, my mum calls, and we get the same update. She's been meeting with Alpha Kelly every day, and they're coming up with some sort of peace agreement to put an end to this. I should be relieved, but my chest is tight with anxiety.

I didn't speak to Cee for a few days, but then I realised the 'space' I'd been asking for wasn't really making me feel any better. We agreed that for the time being, we'll talk, just not about what's happening with our packs. It's mostly small talk, telling each other how our work day went, but the somewhat tense contact feels better than none at all.

As I'm chopping carrots and celery to make a bolognese for dinner, I spot Jas pacing in the hallway, so I pop my head out.

"What's up?" His head shoots up at the sound of my voice.

"Mum called. She says she needs me to join her for the meeting with Alpha Kelly tomorrow, but she didn't tell me any more. Something feels off, though," he explains, and the inner turmoil I've felt over these 'peace talks' makes my heart rate spike.

"It makes sense for you to be there. You're the next Alpha, after all." He nods but looks no less unsettled. "Why don't you go out for a run? Just being in the same house as you is making me tense. I'll be here with Jade." For a moment, he looks like he's going to argue with me on it, but he knows it's for the best that he lets off some steam. Jas rarely sits still for longer than five minutes; a week inside the house is like trapping him in a tiny hamster cage.

❖ ❖ ❖

The following day is a Sunday; rugby training is cancelled because the field we use has flooded, so I get a lie-in. By the time I get up to make coffee and breakfast, Jasper has already left for the meeting.

Jade and I enjoy a full English breakfast courtesy of my dad stopping by with more groceries yesterday, and once we've eaten, I clear up the dishes.

I manage to kill a few hours with more marking, then making lunch, and then with nothing else to do and no word from Jasper or my mum, I join Jade in the living room while she binge-watches the latest series of *Always Sunny*. I keep checking my phone even though it's on vibrate, as though through sheer will alone, I'll receive a message from my brother.

On the hundredth time of checking, I notice my phone isn't connected to the wifi, and there's no signal here, so I wouldn't have received anything anyway. I quickly reconnect and get two messages through immediately.

> **Jas:** I'm really sorry Nix, I'll explain properly when I get home but this isn't what I wanted for you.

> **Cee:** Please, you can't go through with it. I'm begging you Fee, please don't do this!

Don't go through with what?

SIXTEEN
MARCH 2021 – ONE YEAR AGO

CONNOR KELLY

I don't know why I'm even here. He signed the agreement. He has promised to marry my sister. I wish I hadn't agreed to meet him here; this barn holds too many memories. This is where we had sex for the first time. Where we said I love you for the first time. I suppose it's a fitting venue for getting my heart broken for the first time, too.

When Niamh came home a few days ago looking alarmingly pale, she dropped the biggest bombshell of my life on me. In the wake of hearing about the plot against Jade and the baby, instead of retaliating, Alpha Campbell met with my da, and they decided enough was enough.

They had meetings every day for over a week, putting together an agreement to put an end to this asinine turf war. The hours I must have spent over these last four years, wishing for this very moment, desperate for peace between our packs so Fee and I could finally be together out in the open. And now, that same peace agreement I've longed for is what will break us apart for good.

Phoenix and Niamh are engaged.

The wedding is set to take place in a few days, and then they'll move to the Yorkshire territory and start to build a pack of their own. If this goes ahead, not only will I lose the love of my life, I'll lose my twin sister too.

She won't be part of our pack anymore, and I definitely can't stomach watching her build a life with the man who was supposed to be mine.

When I shift and open up the plastic storage box we keep spare clothes in, I choke up seeing Fee's big threadbare uni hoodie I always wear. I bypass it and dig out one of my old jumpers from the bottom. Next, I shove on some jogging bottoms; at this point, I have no idea who they belong to because we've been sharing these clothes for years.

Fucking years.

Sinking to my knees, I couldn't stop the heaving sobs that escape me if I tried. I'm still hiccuping and covered in snot when Fee pads into the barn on all fours. He looks into the box and picks up his uni hoodie with his mouth, dropping it into my lap and nudging me with his head.

"It's yours," I whisper. Fee shifts and dresses in silence.

"It's your favourite, you have it," he says softly, sitting down opposite me.

"Don't. Give me. This. Hoodie like. It's some. Consolation prize." I should be embarrassed by the way my sobs interrupt every other word, but I'm too exhausted and too broken to care.

Fee leans forward and uses a t-shirt from the box to wipe the snot and tears off my face before discarding it behind him.

"When did you last sleep?" he asks, rubbing his thumbs under my puffy eyes and along my cheekbones. His hand drifts down, and he tugs my lip from between my teeth where I've been chewing on it. "Please don't hurt yourself, baby," he whispers, pulling me into his lap and wrapping his arms around me. My breathing keeps stuttering as I try to gain some composure. He presses a soft kiss to my lips, but it's over before it even registers.

What if that's the last kiss we ever share, and I was too wrecked to even take in the moment?

"P—please. Don't go through with it," I beg, even though I've already asked him a million times.

"Babe, I need you to really listen to what I'm going to tell you. Listen to the actual words, okay?" I nod.

"I *have* to marry Niamh. I have *no* choice in whether I go through with this or not. Do you hear what I'm saying?" He speaks slowly, as though I lack speech comprehension. Condescending prick.

I hear precisely what he's saying.

I scramble off his lap. Apparently, I have just enough remaining dignity to stop continuing to embarrass myself.

"Yes, *Phoenix*, I hear what you're sayin'. You're breakin' up with me and marryin' my fuckin' sister. Do you know how disgustin' that is?" I start pacing because I can't stay still for this.

"Right. So you didn't listen to what I said at all then. I'm not breaking up with you, but I *have* to marry your sister." He keeps looking at me like I'm being purposefully difficult, and it's only adding fuel to my fire.

"Oh, how fuckin' generous of you, *Phoenix*. I get to be your side piece while you run off into the sunset with my TWIN!" I shout in exasperation because I don't understand how he can say all this to me, knowing he's ripping my heart to shreds.

"Can you stop saying my name like it's some kind of disease? I'm not asking you to be my side piece. For fuck's sake, you aren't listening to me. Can't you tell Niamh the truth? Surely she wouldn't go through with it if she knew?" He has some audacity to put this on Niamh when she's the innocent party in all of this.

"I've fuckin' told her, okay? I told her as soon as I found out, but if she backs out of this, she'll be shunned from our pack. I can't ask her to give up everythin' for me. You told me you'd run away with me if you could,

I know I said I couldn't do it, but I can. I will. I'll leave with you today, but please don't marry my sister. I won't survive that," I plead with him.

I rescind my previous statement. No dignity left whatsoever.

Fee lets out a resigned sigh. He looks as exhausted as I feel. The dark shadows under his eyes make him appear suddenly much older. His jaw is covered in a thick stubble that hadn't filled out when we first met. A deep crinkle nestles between his eyebrows as he frowns at me. I have to fight the urge to smooth it out with my thumb.

"Don't say this now. I've waited years for you to say this. You can't say it now. Please hear me, unless Niamh calls off the wedding, I *have* to marry her. I love you, Cee, and I will always love you, but Niamh *has* to be the one to call this off." He sounds exasperated, but there's a finality to his words.

"I hear you. All this time, you told me if you had to choose between me and your pack, that you'd choose me, was a fuckin' lie. Hear *me* this time; if you go through with this, I will never forgive you." I choke on the words even though I mean them. There's no coming back from this.

"I have *never* lied to you, never. I don't have a choice. And let's not forget Will; where does your future husband fit into all of these plans you have for us?" He spits the words at me, and I've never heard him so angry. I'm oddly grateful for them because it's easier to be angry than broken. I'd sooner yell and scream at him than fall apart at his feet.

"Don't you fuckin' dare throw Will at me. I've never hidden that from you, and you've always known I wouldn't go through with it. My family have been on my case for years to set a date, and I've never even come close."

"You might not have set a date, but you never called it off either, did you? Maybe Will's been your safety net all along. You were right, I've asked you so many times to run away with me, and you always said no.

Obviously, I should have listened." I'm ready to launch into a defence, but he interrupts me. "Did you know I found him through your socials once? You're in half of his photos, and he looks at you like you hung the damn moon, Connor. I told myself it didn't matter because I trusted you, but maybe you've been stringing us both along."

Connor? He never calls me Connor.

I physically flinch at the words he throws at me, every single one landing like a dagger in my heart. I hardly even recognise the man in front of me. Where has my soft brown-eyed boy gone, and who is this stranger cutting me into pieces?

I feel as though he's ripped out my heart with his bare hands and is squeezing it tight, digging in with his fingernails to be sure to leave a scar. How fucking dare he try to make this my fault when he's going to marry my own sister. I wipe my eyes with my sleeve, and when I look at him, I can see the regret swimming in his eyes. He covers his hand with his mouth as though he can shove the words back in.

I hope he regrets this moment for the rest of his fucking life.

"I fuckin' hate you."

I shift so suddenly that the clothes tear right off my body, and I take off running. I need physical distance between us, and yet with every step I take away from him, the bond between us pulls taught. The bond between our souls that demands we be together—because bite or no bite, we're mates.

How do I get my brain to tell my soul that *my* mate is going to marry someone else? That *my* mate is going to marry my sister.

SEVENTEEN
March 2021 - One Year Ago

PHOENIX CAMPBELL

> **Me:** Can you meet me at the Kendal cottage asap? It's an emergency! x

> **Alice:** Are you there now?

> **Me:** No, I'm on my way

> **Alice:** See you there soon x

When Alice eventually arrives at the cottage, I'm already sitting on the floor of the study with every relevant book pulled off the shelves.

"Um, when you said it was an emergency, I wasn't picturing emergency studying," she says as she walks into the room.

"I have two days to find a way out of this, and I need your help."

"Two days to get out of what, exactly?" she asks.

I explain the peace agreement that my mum and Alpha Kelly have had me sign and how the main proponent of it is that Niamh and I get married.

"Holy shit. That's fucked up. Why can't you ask them to let you marry Connor instead?" She raises a valid point. However, it highlights an essential bit of information I've withheld from her since she discovered us.

"Because Connor has been promised to another member of his pack since he was sixteen years old," I say it quickly to rip the plaster off because I know this news will go down like a lead balloon.

"He's been engaged to someone else this entire time? Why didn't you tell me?"

"Not exactly. They were meant to get married when they both turned twenty-one, but Cee has been putting it off for years, and we always figured there would be time for him to find a way out of it," I tell her, sighing at the mess we've got ourselves into.

"Okay. Truth bomb to one side, you can't marry Connor's sister; not only is it gross as fuck, he's your mate, Nix. You have to tell your mum you can't go through with it. They'll find another solution," she says, like it's all so simple.

I try explaining why I can't do that, but I literally gag on the words. I need to take a different approach. Picking up the book I found earlier, I hand it over to her with the relevant page open.

"I need you to read this book and listen to exactly what I say. I *have* to go through with marrying Niamh. I do *not* have a choice, okay?" She raises an eyebrow at me but reads the page before her.

The book I've given her is a book on the Wolf Shifting Code from 1901; the page she's reading is on the laws pertaining to Alpha Orders. Alice audibly gasps when she reaches the relevant section, and my shoulders sag in relief that she's worked it out.

"She didn't?!" She looks furious. If she were a cartoon, steam would be exploding out of her ears in plumes. I physically cannot confirm or deny it, so I just stare at her pleadingly, needing her to understand my lack of any response for the admission it is.

"Oh my god—she did." Her words are hardly more than a whisper, and my relief is short-lived when I see the expression on her face. She looks devastated. I never wanted to burden her with this, but I can't do this on my own.

My mum showed up at the safe house shortly after I received those cryptic texts from Jasper and Cee. She asked me to take a walk with her, and regretfully, I did. She informed me she and Alpha Kelly had come to an agreement that would not only keep Jade and the baby safe, but would bring an end to the feud between our packs. The pit had formed in my stomach before she even told me what they'd agreed, my brain replaying the texts I'd already received on a loop.

She told me they'd agreed I will marry Alpha Kelly's daughter, Niamh. That once the ceremony has taken place, Niamh and I will move onto the Yorkshire territory and start to build our own pack there.

We got into a massive row. I was so livid I could hardly even see through the red mist of anger. It was probably the first time in my life I'd ever really stood up to her because she isn't just my mum—she's my Alpha. Being a pure beta, everything inside me screams for me to follow, to submit, to not break rank. But there was no way I could marry Niamh when I already knew her twin brother was my mate.

I had debated telling her about Connor right then, but I knew the risks to her finding out I had been lying by omission—for years. The party line of the pack had always been clear on one thing—no fraternising with members of the Kelly pack or risk expulsion. I had no doubt, that as her son, I would be used to set an example, familial bonds be damned.

My mum and I have never had the easiest relationship; I think she loves me deep down in her own way, but I've always been acutely aware that

I'm expendable to her. Jasper is the Alpha Heir, and I'm not even the Alpha spare because, as I said—I'm a pure beta. My mum had laid the guilt trip on thick, telling me it was a noble sacrifice to protect the future Alpha line of our pack. She told me I'd be doing my part to end the war and keep everyone safe.

When that didn't work, she tried telling me how beautiful Niamh was, how I'd be lucky to marry a woman as pretty as her, and I just felt sick to my stomach. And finally, when she realised I was still unconvinced, my mum did the unthinkable, the unforgivable.

She gave me an Alpha Order.

She Ordered me to go through with the marriage, and to top it off, Ordered me not to breathe a word of it. It seems she learned from her mistakes in that regard; it was watertight this time. The page Alice just read details the laws that were put in place to stop Alphas from doing precisely this.

Alpha Orders supposedly existed as a way to keep pack members united and safe. However, there are still Alphas who use their Orders to control and manipulate their pack. Amongst most packs, though, the general consensus is that there's very rarely an excuse for an Alpha to use their Order.

"Does Connor know?" Alice's question brings me back to the tangled web of issues at hand.

"No, I tried to explain the best I could, but he was too upset to hear what I was saying. Even if I could find a way to tell him, if I can't offer a solution, then what's the point?"

"The point is he wouldn't be out there thinking you're voluntarily marrying his twin sister? What the fuck, Nix? *I* could tell him. He must be wrecked by this." I sigh and press the heels of my palms into my exhausted eyes. Maybe if I press hard enough, I can erase the image of Cee's heartbroken expression from my mind.

"If *I* tell him or get *you* to tell him, he will out my mum. He's hot-headed, and he'll react before thinking of all the consequences."

"Would that be the worst thing? What she did is illegal. Shit like this is outlawed for good reason. She wouldn't have pulled this crap if you weren't her son. She shouldn't get away with this."

I understand Alice's outrage; I do. But it's more complicated than that.

"If it gets out what she's done, she'll be stripped of her title and expelled from the pack. My dad would then have to choose either to go with her, to stop her from becoming an omega, or to stay behind. Alfie is only thirteen years old. My mum isn't going to win Mother of the Year, but he needs both his parents. I can't be the reason he ends up being raised by his brothers. Jasper will be a father in a few months; he's not ready to suddenly become the Alpha of our pack. I love Connor, more than I can even express, but I can't ruin the entire lives of my family for him." When I look up, I see now that Alice understands the gravity of the situation. She reaches over and squeezes my shoulder before taking a deep breath.

"I guess we better read some books and find you a loophole then."

I'm so grateful for my best friend I could cry. Although that could also be the exhaustion, who knows. Her pragmatism gives me hope there may be a way out of this after all.

⋅⋙⋅⋄⋅⋘⋅

"So, in conclusion, there is no solution besides exposing your mum's crime," Alice says as she snaps the final book closed a few hours later. Fuck. There is nothing here to help. "Unless…"

"Unless what??" I ask, desperate for something. Anything.

"What if there was a spell to undo the Order?" Alice asks. It wasn't something I'd thought of. My pack hasn't had a witch for so long that we rarely turn to them for a solution.

"Who, though? If Nina Fenwick caught wind of this, she'd tell her Alpha."

"The only other witch I know is Orla McNamara, and you can't exactly ask her." Since Orla is the Kelly pack witch, she's a definite *no*, but that does give me another, potentially insane, idea...

"I wouldn't even know how to reach him, but if anyone knew a way out of this, it'd be Noah..."

"Noah?"

"Orla's great-grandson and Connor's cousin. He's always refused to become a pack witch, so he's a bit of a nomad. From what Cee's told me of him, he avoids getting mixed up in shifter business, so I doubt he'd spill." Alice nods thoughtfully in response.

"I'll give Nina a call, see if she has any contact details for him."

Alice returns to the study just as I've finished putting all the books back on the right shelves.

"Any luck?"

"She gave me a number that went straight to voicemail, but she said she visited him a week ago to pick up some ingredients, and she gave me the address."

"Where is it?"

"Got time for a road trip to Edinburgh?"

We pull up outside an old stone house around three hours later. It's only nine pm, but the curtains are closed, and the lights are all off downstairs.

As we get out of the car, we both tip our heads up and spot a light on upstairs, providing an ember of hope that Noah is home.

"It's warded," Alice says as she steps through the small iron gate ahead of me. Wards always leave a faint smell of burning rubber in the air, I scrunch my nose up as I pass through. By the time we've walked down the cobbled path, and my fist is raised to knock on the front door, it opens, and I have to do a double take. It's eerie how much he resembles Cee.

"What do you want?" he asks in a strong Northern Irish accent.

"Nina gave us your address, I'm Alice Graham, and this is Phoenix Campbell. We need some help, and we ran out of people to ask." Noah's gaze rakes assessingly over both of us. Faintly lit by the streetlamp outside, he's topless with two full sleeves of tattoos and more spread over his rib cage. He's slimmer than Cee, but their facial features are all the same sharp angles. They look more like brothers than cousins, but where Cee's eyes are a deep, mossy green, Noah's are a calculating, icy blue. Right when I think he's preparing to close the door in our faces, he steps back and gestures for us to come inside.

Alice walks in first, but we both stand to one side of the hallway, waiting for him to lead the way. He walks past us wordlessly, and we follow him into a kitchen at the back of the house. With the flick of his wrist, the ceiling lights come on, bathing the room in a soft yellow glow. He gestures for us to sit down at the rickety kitchen table but doesn't join us, instead choosing to lean against the counter with his arms crossed over his chest.

He must have shoved his jeans on in a hurry when he felt us come through his wards because his top button is undone, and he isn't wearing any underwear. Heat spreads across my cheeks when he catches me looking and raises an eyebrow at me.

"Colour me intrigued. What might two Campbell wolves possibly want from me?" he asks, breaking the awkward eye contact.

Before I begin to explain, there are loud footsteps on the staircase. A moment later, a guy—a human guy—around my age appears in the kitchen doorway in nothing but a very tight pair of white boxer briefs. Noah seems entirely unphased, but the guy blushes when he spots us sitting here.

"Shit. Sorry. I didn't realise anyone else was here. Should I, erm... go?" he asks Noah, looking over his shoulder towards the front door and back again. I try not to stare, but the guy is cute and has a pretty big hickey on his collarbone.

"No. Wait for me upstairs; I won't be long," Noah replies, returning his attention to us. The guy mutters something unintelligible but quickly retreats back to the bedroom. I can't help but shift in my seat at how incredibly awkward this is. "Go on then."

Right, the reason we're here.

"Will whatever we ask you stay between us?" His eyes narrow as he considers the question, but then he shrugs and nods for me to continue. I guess that's as good as I'm going to get.

"Do you know much about Alpha Orders?"

"Plenty."

"Do you know if there's any spell or any way of undoing an Alpha Order?" He tilts his head inquisitively as he considers the question before answering.

"No spell, no. To undo an Alpha Order, you have to strip them of their title by either expulsion from the pack or killing them. Alternatively, the Ordered wolf can leave their pack."

And with those words, my final sparks of hope are snuffed out. It's like a dam breaks inside me and I need to get out, need to be alone.

"We're sorry for barging in on you. Thanks for your help. We'll let you get back to... your friend," I ramble. Noah and Alice are both looking at me like I'm a ticking time bomb. I stand up abruptly and dash for the front door; it's like I can suddenly feel the walls closing in on me, and I need to be outside. As I begin to panic, it feels like my ears are filled with cotton wool, and I can distantly hear Alice saying goodbye to Noah.

Once we're back on the street and Noah's closed his front door, I bend forward with my hands on my knees and attempt to catch my breath. Alice stands next to me, stroking a soothing hand up and down my back as I try and get my shit together.

"I'm sorry, Nix. I really thought we'd find a way out of this," she says softly.

"Me too, Alice. Me too." I tip my head up to the sky, willing the tears that are threatening, to remain at bay.

<hr />

As I lie in my bed later that night, I ruminate over the options Noah gave me. I replay Cee's words from the other day, asking me to run away with him and wondering if he'd still be willing. He told me he hated me, but my gut tells me he was just lashing out and he didn't really mean it.

I immensely regret what I said to him about Will. Deep down, I wanted him to instinctively *know* I wouldn't have done any of this on purpose. I wanted him to give me the benefit of the doubt that more was going on here. But he didn't know, and I just dumped all my insecurities over Will in his lap at the worst possible moment. I've texted him several times apologising for what I said, but they've all sat on 'delivered'.

If Cee's right and Niamh isn't going to call off this wedding, then it looks as though I only have one option left. With my mind made up and a heavy heart, I set my alarm for the next morning. My dad and brothers will feel completely blindsided and betrayed, but it's the only choice I can live with.

Tomorrow, I'll go to Alpha Eastwood in Northumbria and beg if I have to. The only way out of this, without bringing everyone down with me, is to leave my pack and join another.

EIGHTEEN
MARCH 2021 – ONE YEAR AGO

CONNOR KELLY

My head is throbbing.

Partly due to the fact I've been lying in bed crying solidly for the past two hours and in part due to the half-empty bottle of tequila, I'm currently clutching like a teddy bear.

That's how Niamh finds me when she barges into her spare room.

After I got back home from seeing Fee last night, I lost my shit and trashed my flat. Losing all my control, I shifted inside. I couldn't think past the haze of anger, and I tore everything apart. I let the place off a friend of my da's, and I'm going to be in deep shit when they find out. Even the kitchen cupboards didn't survive my onslaught.

"You smell flammable. You can't fester in here forever," Niamh says as she pulls back the duvet I've been hiding under, exposing me to the cold air.

"Fuckin' watch me," I tell her, trying to snatch the covers back.

"As much as I love belligerent drunk Connor, I'm going to need you to start sobering up."

She shoves a take-out coffee cup under my nose. I'm half tempted to throw it across the room, but it does smell good, so I take a sip, glaring at her while I do it.

"Delightful," she mutters under her breath as she walks away with my tequila.

"Oi, give me that back."

"No."

"What possible benefit is there to me being sober right now? I tried it earlier, and I cried so hard I vommed. No, thank you," I say stubbornly.

"You're going to need to be clear-headed to fix this, Con," she says firmly.

"I already tried. I begged Fee not to go through with it, and he just kept saying he *had* to, like some sort of martyr."

"Yeah, well, Phoenix isn't the only one who needs to call off an engagement." She looks at me as though her patience is wearing thin with one eyebrow raised.

"What's even the point in calling things off with Will? Fee is gonna to marry you in a couple of days, so I may as well marry Will." My words slur from the haze of alcohol.

"I'm going to forgive you for saying that because you're obviously drunk and hurting right now. But Will is one of your best friends; he's been in love with you for the better part of fifteen years, and he deserves better than being your fallback guy. Drink the coffee because Will is on his way over, and we're going to find a way to fix this mess." Niamh's tone leaves no room for debate.

Part of me wants to deny Will is in love with me; I don't think he really is. Still, deep down, I do know he feels differently for me than I do for him. If it had been up to him, we'd have gone through with getting married by now, but it was always easier to ignore those niggling thoughts. Guilt eats at me for being so selfish, yet I can't seem to stop myself from lashing out at everyone around me.

By the time I've downed the coffee, some water, and had a shower, I can hear Will and Niamh talking downstairs. Unfortunately, I've sobered up enough to really start to dread having this conversation with him.

The argument with Fee has left me raw and exposed, and I don't want my best friend to hate me. Equally, I can't help but think if I'd been less of a coward and called things off with Will sooner, this engagement between Niamh and Fee might never have happened.

The three of us sit around Niamh's small wooden kitchen table with cups of tea. Will must have come straight from work because he's still wearing his scrubs. My life would be a lot easier if I did love him that way. Will has a heart of gold; he's hard-working, and he's loyal to a fault.

"What's going on, you guys?" he asks nervously, looking back and forth between Niamh and me.

"Go on," Niamh says, kicking me under the table.

I come clean about everything. All the way back to when Fee and I met, to us breaking up now. I try to explain why I kept it all a secret, and through it all, he never interrupts. When I've finished spilling my guts, I wait for him to say something, but when I look up from the tiny scratch on the tabletop I'd been staring at, he looks stunned.

"Did you know all along?" he asks Niamh, and I feel fucking awful at how betrayed he sounds.

"No. I found out a few days ago."

I wish he would yell at me or something. I'd rather he get mad than have to see the wrecked look on his face.

"I'm so sorry, Will. I don't expect you to forgive me, but I'm so sorry." And I mean it. Because all this time I've been telling myself Will just had a little crush on me, I've been lying to myself. I recognise the broken-hearted expression on his face because I've seen it in my own reflection.

EIGHTEEN

The sound of Niamh's chair scraping against the tiled floor echoes around the room as she gets up. She leans down and kisses me on the forehead.

"I love you, I'm here for you, and everything's going to be okay," she says softly to me. I look up at her, and she has her quietly determined face on. I'm not sure what she thinks she can do at this point, but I know my sister, and she won't quit until she's exhausted every avenue.

"Come on, Will. Let's take a walk." She squeezes his shoulder, and he stands up to leave.

"I'm so sorry, Will," I blurt out again before he makes it out of the door.

"Yeah, me too, Con."

In the past twenty-four hours, I've told my boyfriend I hate him, wrecked my house and broken my best friend's heart. To top it off, I've left Niamh to pick up the pieces, even though she's the one who has to marry a stranger in a couple of days. Even thinking of it makes my stomach churn. Enough is enough, though; I can't have a pity party forever. I down another pint of water and plug my phone in to charge.

When my phone finally turns back on, I ignore the incoming texts from Fee and text my da.

> **Me:** I need to talk to you urgently. Are you home?

I lie back on Niamh's spare bed, waiting for a reply. I know I told Fee it was down to him to put a stop to this, but I have to try. If I tell my da I've called things off with Will, he'll be angry, but maybe he'll consider making a change to this agreement. I can't sit back and do nothing anymore.

> **Da:** Down on the south border with Sam. Can it wait until the morning?

I sigh, feeling slightly defeated because I'd just psyched myself up to tell him tonight. Realistically, it won't make much difference if I tell him tonight or in the morning, though, so I reply and make plans to go round to his for breakfast.

I put *Parks & Rec* on in the background while I wait for Niamh to get home.

I must have fallen asleep. As I open my eyes, I register the sound of footsteps on the stairs. It's dark outside. A glance at my phone tells me it's four am.

A few seconds later, the bedroom door is being nudged open. I'm surprised to see Will toeing off his Converse and padding towards me. He peels back the duvet and climbs into the bed, curling into my side and resting his head on my chest. I've lost count of how many nights we used to spend like this. Back before I started putting so much distance between us.

"Are you drunk?" I ask. I'm pretty sure I can smell espresso martini, which is Will's weapon of choice.

"A lil' bit, yes."

"Are we going to be okay?" I whisper into his hair.

"Eventually," he says with a sigh. Will is a few inches shorter than me; he's quite slim and feels sort of delicate in my arms. I squeeze him a little tighter, unable to find the words but needing him to know that even though I've been a total dick, he still means so much to me.

"Niamh isn't going to marry Phoenix," he tells me before I can even form the words I want to say.

"What? What do you mean? Where is she?" I ask, my heart rate spiking. He pulls away slightly and leans on his elbow, looking down at me.

"She's on her way to your dad's to tell him. I said I'd come and tell you because there's some other things I need to say to you." I turn onto my side and mirror his position so we're face to face.

"Niamh is no longer eligible to marry Phoenix tomorrow. Because she's married to me."

"I'm sorry, what? How long was I asleep for? What do you mean she's married to you?" I ask incredulously. Have I had some shroom tea? Am I hallucinating?

"We went to Northumbria last night. Nina Fenwick performed the binding ceremony. We agreed to stay married for a year or two until things have calmed down, and then we'll get her to undo it."

My brain scrambles to try and comprehend what he's telling me. I'm not totally surprised Niamh would do this for me; for all the shit we give each other, we'd take a bullet for the other. But I don't understand why Will would do this. I stomped all over his heart yesterday. I'm reeling and can't seem to process what he's told me.

"I don't even know what to say. Why would you do this?" I ask.

"Okay, I'm going to say my piece, and then I'd prefer it if we put this to bed and never speak of it again, alright?" he asks. I don't think I have any right to do anything except agree.

"Okay," I promise.

He takes in a deep breath before speaking. "I married Niamh because I love you. I've spent an embarrassingly long time waiting for you to see me as someone other than your childhood best friend, but truthfully, you've never given me any indication that would ever happen. I thought if we finally got married, we'd get there eventually. But I've felt how you've kept me at arm's length for years now, and I chose to ignore it. I understand why you couldn't tell me about Phoenix, but I really wish you'd told me there was someone else. Even if you couldn't tell me who.

I love you enough that I can't sit by while you watch the love of your life marry your sister. I don't know what will happen next, but I do know Niamh will not be marrying Phoenix."

I lie there, shocked and stunned into silence, as I absorb what Will is saying. I'm not sure what I ever did to deserve so much love from my sister and best friend, but I know that I won't take it for granted ever again.

"I know it's not in the way you wish, and I know I've been such a shitty friend to you, but I need you to know that I do love you, and I will never forget this." I squeeze both arms tightly around him and pull him into my chest.

There aren't the words to convey what this means to me, so I just hold onto him tight. When he trembles in my embrace, his breath hitching a few times as he cries in my arms, I feel so fucking ashamed of myself. I kiss the top of his curly blonde head and try to be there for him as best as I can.

I'm not sure how long I lie with Will in my arms, but eventually, his breaths become steady and even, and I realise he's fallen asleep.

I'm so relieved Niamh and Phoenix won't be getting married anymore, but I'm not entirely sure where it leaves us. When crunch time hit, I chose Fee over my pack, but he didn't choose me back. I don't think I'll ever be able to move on from this, knowing that truth in my bones. I'll forever be grateful to Niamh and Will for this sacrifice, but it stings that it ever came to this.

All Fee needed to do was refuse to go through with the wedding, so why didn't he?

PART II
PRESENT DAY

Nineteen
March 2022

PHOENIX CAMPBELL

The wedding ceremony with both packs in attendance went by in a bit of a blur. It felt more robotic than the smaller one last week. Lots of being told to 'stand here' and 'walk over there'. We've finally finished posing for what must be the most awkward-looking wedding photos in the history of the world.

We're walking a few metres behind our families as they make their way over to where the reception is being held. I keep glancing at Cee from the corner of my eye as if he'll run ten miles in the opposite direction if I look away for too long.

"What?" he asks. "Have I got somethin' on my face?"

"No, nothing. Sorry," I mumble like a bumbling idiot. He huffs in response, and we continue to the venue in silence.

As we enter the main room, I can't help but wince at how loud it is. I quickly remember to plaster a smile on my face as people start coming over to congratulate us both. I'm eternally grateful when Connor snags two glasses of champagne from one of the servers as she walks past. He passes one to me, and I take a large gulp; Cee downs his in one.

NINETEEN

It's strange to only recognise around half of the attendees at your own wedding, but considering both packs seem to be mingling without any bloodshed, I'm counting this as a win.

❦

Next time someone asks me who my ideal dinner guests would be, dead or alive, I'm saying literally anyone except for the combination right here.

The large round table is covered with a crisp white tablecloth, and a floral/foliage arrangement decorates the centre. Shockingly, Cee and I are not the most awkward people at the table. I think Jasper and Jade might be in the middle of a fight because their smiles look forced for Henry's benefit. Sam is sitting on Jasper's other side, and I don't think they've exchanged a word the entire meal. And Sam has excused himself to go to the bathroom so many times it's getting kind of embarrassing. Niamh and Will are really carrying the burden of conversation, but I think even they might be reaching their limit.

With the dessert dishes cleared away, my mum gently taps a spoon against her champagne flute, and the room falls silent.

"I would like to thank you all, on behalf of my son, Phoenix, for joining us today at such short notice. I find I don't quite have the words to express how grateful I am to see the seeds of peace between our two packs being sewn here today.

"Most of us in this room have lost friends and family to this war, and while I know they will never be forgotten, I am hopeful that with the beginning of a new pack on these lands, all of the packs in the north can finally prosper with this feud put behind us. Let us all raise our glasses to Phoenix and Connor, whose sacrifices have united us today." She raises her glass, and our guests do the same.

"To Phoenix and Connor." The room is filled with clinking glasses as everyone toasts our 'union'.

Not to be outdone, Cee's dad stands up next.

"Twenty-five years ago, my late wife Cara and I were blessed with twins. We were awake in bed one night when they were a few weeks old, Cara feeding them and me just keeping her company. Little Sammy was fast asleep between us because I was a soft touch." He pauses, and our guests laugh softly. "Cara had just placed Niamh into my arms while she finished feeding Connor when she asked, 'Who do you think they'll be when they grow up?' Now, I will hold my hands up and say I responded like a man who didn't know any better and said, 'Whoever we raise them to be,' to which my lovely wife laughed so hard she woke the wee babes up." Everyone laughs at this, and when I glance at Cee, his eyes look glassy.

"So I asked her, 'If you're so clever, who do you think they'll be when they grow up?' and she says, 'I think they'll be kind and fierce, with big hearts just like their daddy, they'll be exactly who they're meant to be, and I can't wait to find out,'" Alpha Kelly's voice breaks. He takes a deep breath before continuing on. Cee's eyes are filled with unshed tears, and before I can think better of it, I reach for his hand under the table and squeeze. Anticipating rejection, I'm shocked when he grips my hand back and doesn't let go.

"Sadly, my sweet Cara never did get to see the wonderful people you've all turned out to be, but she wasn't wrong. My boy Connor is kind and fierce with a huge heart, and he turned out to be exactly who he was meant to be. I couldn't think of a better person to take on the responsibility of building this new pack, and I hope over time, the two of you will be able to grow a love like Cara and I. Welcome to our family, Phoenix, and take care of my boy."

"To love," he says, raising his glass in the air.

We unclasp our hands to join in the toast, and I find myself holding back tears of my own at Alpha Kelly's heartfelt speech. My chest aches at the fact Cee's mum never got to see him grow up to be the man he is today. Because even on his worst day, he's still my favourite person in the world.

When the reception is blessedly over, we stand by the doors, saying goodbye to the last few guests as they leave. I'm tired down to my bones, and I'm grateful this is all finally over. Niamh and Will are the last to leave, and my shoulders sag with relief from not having to be *on* anymore. When it's finally the two of us alone, Cee leans against the wall and closes his eyes.

"Home?" I ask. He lets out a deep breath before nodding.

By the time we make it to the dainty cottage we're renting in Pateley Bridge, we're both exhausted from the day we've had. We trudge upstairs and groan at the sight of all the unpacked boxes along the far wall of the bedroom.

"Is there bedding in any of these?" Cee asks. I don't want to admit my parents' housekeeper, Claire, packed up my house for me because I know he'll give me the *You're a pampered little prince* raised eyebrow.

"Yeah, I think they should be labelled. I'll help you look in a sec, need a piss," I tell him before I make a quick dash for the bathroom. When I walk back into the bedroom, my entire face heats with embarrassment.

"What the fuck is this?" Cee asks, waving a small purple dildo in the air. If there was ever a convenient time for the world to swallow me whole, now would be it. I totally forgot I had it, and the realisation Claire must have boxed it up for me only adds to my humiliation.

"I'm pretty sure you know what that is." I try to grab it from his hand so I can hide it away and pretend this never happened, but he takes a step back. I can't help but feel confused when I look into his eyes and see them blazing with anger. This is pretty mortifying, but why on earth would he be mad I own a dildo for fuck's sake?

"How soon after we broke up did you start fuckin' someone else?" My eyebrows scrunch as I become even more confused. He continues on undeterred, "Must be pretty serious if you bought a sex toy to fuck them with," he spits out the words at me. As my brain catches up to the frankly absurd accusation, I go from bewildered to pretty fucking pissed off very quickly.

"Why would I fuck someone else with a dildo when I have a dick to do that with?"

"Who is it?"

"Out of curiosity, do you warm up before you start jumping to conclusions, or do you just dive right in?" I ask, riling him up some more.

"Stop avoidin' the question. Are you gonna be fuckin' someone else while you're married to me?" The slight quiver in his voice and the vulnerable look in his eyes drains the short-lived fight right out of me. I hate that I always break before he does.

"I haven't fucked anyone else since the day I met you," I tell him, exasperated by this pointless and frankly embarrassing conversation.

"Then why do you have this?"

"Honestly, it's none of your business."

"Tell me anyway."

"Fine! Because you're such a fucking bossy bottom sometimes, I thought maybe one day, if I got used to it on my own, I could let you try and top me, okay? Are you happy now? Put the fucking dildo in the bin. I'd forgotten I had it anyway," I huff and start rummaging through the box for some bed sheets.

"No."

"What do you mean, 'no'?"

"Keep it."

"I don't want to keep it!"

"Well, I want you to keep it!"

"Why would you want me to keep it?!"

"Because picturin' you fuckin' yourself with a dildo for me, is makin' me hard as fuck. So keep it!"

I'm not sure who moves first, but we're suddenly chest to chest with our mouths crashing together. Cee's fisting my shirt, and I rip his open, buttons flying off in all directions. He bites down on my bottom lip—hard, and I can taste the coppery liquid on my tongue.

I take my shirt off, and Cee undoes my belt, mouths only parting momentarily to catch a breath. He shoves his hand into my boxers and wraps his hand around my already throbbing cock.

"Shit," I mutter as he squeezes tightly, dancing along that line between pain and pleasure. I shove him back onto the bare mattress and tug down his trousers, taking off his socks as I go. Ditching the last of my own clothes, I climb on top of him, grinding my erection against his. It's been so long, and the tension between us is pulled so tight that I don't expect either of us to last very long.

Our kisses remain aggressive, biting each other's lips until they're puffy and swollen. Pushing back Cee's knees, I expose him and press my tongue to his hole. He moans loudly as I lick and spit into him, getting him as wet as possible because god knows where the lube is. I reach my fingers up to his mouth so he can suck them. Once they're coated in his saliva, I press them both inside him slowly, waiting for him to adjust to the intrusion. He bears down, and my fingers sink deeper. I change the angle so they graze over his prostate, and he moans, as responsive as always. He moves his hips, and I lick around his rim while he fucks himself on my fingers.

"Fuck, I'm ready. Fuck me." He groans as I pull my fingers out. He doesn't need to tell me twice. I spit on his rim some more so it's wet enough and then use the precum leaking out of his tip to lube up my cock as best as I can. As I nudge my swollen tip into his hole, my eyes roll back at the intense pressure. I forgot how fucking amazing and tight he feels wrapped around me.

I slowly enter him, inch by inch, and he moans when my hips are flush with his arse. As I look down and watch where I'm fucking into him, I'm reminded of our first time. My mind was blown at how well he took me inside his body and how much he trusted me to make him feel good. When I pull out, he shuffles back on the mattress and turns onto his front, his forehead against his forearms, as he presents himself to me.

It stings that I know he's doing this to make it feel less intimate, but I'm currently far too desperate and horny to dwell on it. I can't help but bite my own lip at how sexy he looks with his back arched like that. Pressing my thumbs into the dimples at the bottom of his back and gripping his hips, I push back inside him.

"Fuck, right there. Yes." He gasps when I change the angle to peg his prostate with each jerk of my hips. My thrusts get faster, and Cee meets every single one, pushing back onto me. He feels so unbelievable that I'm battling to stop myself from coming before he does.

I reach around to jerk him off because I know I won't last much longer. The moment his release spills onto my hand and his hole clenches and pulsates around me, I'm a goner. He moans obscenely as my cock throbs inside him, filling him with my cum. My orgasm hits me so hard I think I even black out for a second.

As my limbs turn to jelly, I drop on top of him. We're both sweaty and breathing heavily. I'm too spaced out at present to think about what this means for us going forward, but it's safe to say a year apart hasn't dulled any of the passion between us.

I'm a bit lightheaded from all the champagne and could do with some water, but I don't want to move. I know as soon as I get up, the spell will be broken, and nothing has ever felt more right than having Connor's warm, soft, naked body under mine. Now, just to work out how to keep him here forever—because I'm not naive enough to believe a marriage certificate will be enough.

TWENTY
MARCH 2022

CONNOR KELLY

Fuck. This was a bad idea. This was a very bad idea. Probably one of the worst ideas I've had in a while, and that's saying something because most of the time, my life feels like a series of highly questionable decisions.

After our major lapse in judgment last night, Phoenix made the bed while I quickly washed up in the bathroom. Now, the sun is peeking through the curtains, and I'm lying still as a statue with Fee sprawled half on top of me, his morning wood digging into my hip. Having sex with him last night has cracked me wide open, and I'm suddenly exposed in a way that's making my skin itch.

There were times in the last year I tried to convince myself that sex with Fee wasn't all I'd made it out to be; I told myself I didn't know any better because he was my first and only. While he's no longer the only person I've had sex with, I know a connection like ours is rare. I think we could live five lifetimes and still want each other on that baser level. It's not only physical, though; it would be easier if it was. His soul speaks to mine, telling me I'm right where I'm supposed to be when I'm wrapped up in his arms, enveloped in his scent.

Damp earth, lavender, home and mine.

TWENTY

It's a slippery slope taking comfort in Fee's arms, though. He broke my heart once, and he could do it again. The sensible thing to do is to put some distance between us, both emotionally and physically. Starting by untangling myself from his heavy limbs.

Most of the shops in the small village we're living in will be shut today as it's a Sunday. I don't have a car here because Mikey and I share a work van, but I'm insured to drive third-party, and Phoenix's Jeep is just sitting out there on the drive. I pull up Maps on my phone; Leeds is only an hour's drive away. I could probably be there and back before he even wakes up.

Right as I pull up to Go Outdoors, somewhere between Leeds and Bradford, my phone pings, alerting me to a text message.

> **Do not text him:** Assuming you borrowed my car and we haven't been robbed?

I should probably change his contact information since we're married and living together and shit.

> **Me:** Yep, just me. Hope that's ok, I didn't want to wake you. Will only be an hour or so.

> **Do not text him:** No probs

As I step inside the shop, the smell of camping gear has me suddenly nostalgic for childhood holidays. I head straight for the section promising to provide me with a short-term solution to my 'physical distance' problem. I grab a double air mattress plus a sleeping bag from the shelves and make my way over to the tills.

I obviously can't sleep on an airbed forever. Nevertheless, I'm hoping it'll buy me enough time to figure out what to do where Phoenix Campbell is concerned.

"Do you have a discount card?" the guy at the checkout asks. 'Josh', his name tag says.

"No."

"It'd save you ten pound."

"Thanks, but I don't foresee a lot of camping in my future." He looks at the airbed and the sleeping bag and then back at me. While I appreciate my purchases might appear to contradict that statement, I didn't come to Go Outdoors on a Sunday morning to be judged by 'stoner Josh,' so I stare at him until he continues.

"That'll be a hundred and forty quid." Jeez, that's expensive for a piece of plastic and a glorified blanket.

As I walk back to the car, I give myself another pep talk, reminding myself this is for the best. I need space—physical space. Each night I spend in bed with him, my feelings start pouring out of me like a fountain. Good luck, *feelings*, because tonight I'll be in the spare bedroom with only my *own* limbs to contend with.

On the drive home, I give Niamh a call.

"Am I the problem? Is it me?" I ask her as soon as the call connects.

"Most people say 'Hello, how are you?' before they launch into an existential crisis on the phone.'"

"Hello, how are you?" I retort, my voice laced with sarcasm.

"I'm great, thank you for asking. You're on loudspeaker by the way. I'm helping Will pick out an outfit for his date tonight."

"Ooo. Who's the lucky guy, Will?"

TWENTY

Although wolf shifters are all fairly fluid where sexuality is concerned, he's only ever really been attracted to men. I'm similar to Will, whereas Phoenix has always been pretty evenly attracted to all genders.

Will and I had a rough few months after he and Niamh got married. He had moved into Niamh's place to keep up appearances, and I was living in their spare room after destroying my flat. I considered crashing with Sammy, but he didn't know the full story, and it seemed too exhausting to keep up the charade of being fine, day in and day out.

Unfortunately, I was the one person Will desperately needed space from, especially after the June drunken sex debacle. He was only trying to be a good friend because I'd been moping and feeling sorry for myself all day. Will had offered to take me out to get drunk and dance to take my mind off the fact it would have been my and Phoenix's anniversary. It worked for a little while; we both got totally wankered and stayed out until three am. When we got home to an empty house—Niamh was in London for work—we ended up in my bed together.

I was drunk and sad; Will was warm and familiar. The sex wasn't great. We were both too inebriated to be particularly co-ordinated and the fact I'd never topped anyone before—showed. As much as I'm almost a hundred percent sure the experience was as lacking for him as it was for me, it made things awkward and tense between us for a few months afterwards. Especially living under the same roof...

Will's voice interrupts my wandering thoughts. *"Nobody you know. I don't think anything will come of it; I just think it's time to put myself out there."* He sounds surprisingly cheerful about a date he's already decided doesn't have a future.

"Hold up, is this a date or a hookup, Will? Because the outfit I've picked out for you says 'let's watch a movie and a dry hump if you're lucky' not 'I'm a naughty little twink that likes to get railed into next Sunday', so which

is it???" Niamh asks Will, and I have to bite my lip to stop from howling with laughter down the phone.

"*Do you have an option for something in the middle? In the unlikely event he's the love of my life, I don't want to forever hear, 'Do you remember how on our first date you dressed like a sexy stripper?' but also, if he's not the love of my life, I would not say no to being railed into next Sunday,*" he replies.

"*I'm not a magician,*" she deadpans, and Will sighs loudly.

"Dark grey skinny jeans with my old Ramones t-shirt you criminally took scissors to and turned into a crop top," I suggest. "You'll look hot but not too *try hard*."

"*Lip-gloss or no lip-gloss?*" he asks.

"*No lip-gloss. Try the rosy-tinted lip balm,*" Niamh replies. "*Anyway, let's go back to talking about how you're the problem, Con.*"

"Right. Yes, that. So I did a stupid thing," I tell her. "Last night, me and Phoenix got into a slightly heated argument, and I may or may not have accidentally fucked my husband."

"*I'm pretty sure your husband was the one doing the fucking,*" Will snickers unnecessarily down the phone, and I blush at the memory of Phoenix ploughing me into the mattress last night.

"*Ew. I do not need that many details about my brother's sex life, William. But yeah, I can clearly see the problem. You and your husband, who you're madly in love with, had sex. Sounds awful. Are you okay??*" Niamh asks sarcastically.

"Not helpful. Everythin' is still such a big mess between us. Until a week ago, we hadn't spoken a word to each other in twelve months." I sigh.

"*That's not entirely accurate. Phoenix reached out to you plenty during that time; you were just too stubborn to answer the phone. So yes, in answer to your original question, you are the problem."* I'm suddenly not entirely sure why I called Niamh. The woman would jump in front of a bus for me, but she's never been inclined to tell me what I want to hear.

"I would like to go on record to say I agree with Niamh. You are the problem," Will chirps down the phone after her.

"So good talkin' to you guys. Gotta go. I'm drivin' through a giant tunnel. Probably won't be able to speak again for several months. PS, I hope your hookup has erectile dysfunction, Will." I shout down the phone. Right before I cut off the call, I hear Will saying that's the meanest thing I've ever said to him.

<hr />

When I get home, there's no sign of Phoenix in the house, so I make a start on unpacking the boxes stacked in the kitchen. The majority is Phoenix's stuff because most of my belongings didn't survive my bad temper last year.

After I've unpacked the kitchen and living room, I head upstairs and shuffle my boxes into the currently empty spare bedroom. Pushing them up against the far wall to deal with later, I grab today's purchases from the boot of the car to set up my temporary bedroom furniture.

By the time Phoenix gets home, it's tea time, and he quickly starts clattering around in the kitchen.

"Thanks for sorting out the boxes," he says as I walk into the room.

"No problem. Where were you today?" I ask, even though I know it's not really any of my business.

"I look after Henry for a few hours most Sundays so Jasper and Jade can get some time alone. And yes, I'm pretty sure it's as gross as it sounds." He winces, and I let out a chuckle in response.

"Oh shit, sorry, you needed your car, didn't you?" I say as soon as I realise.

"No, it's fine. I enjoyed the run; helped clear my head. We've absolutely no food in the house, by the way. Do you want to order in?" he asks and takes out his phone, I assume to see where will deliver.

"Sure, you pick."

"Damn, looks like there's only Indian that delivers. I think this pizza place might do collection, though."

"I'm good with Indian if you are?" I ask. He frowns at me in confusion.

"What are you talking about? You don't like Indian food."

"When have I ever said I don't like Indian food?"

"Literally any time I ever picked up food for us, you'd say 'just not a curry'," he fairly points out. My cheeks flush as I remember my reasoning.

"Oh yeah, erm…Well, I do. So we can order it."

"Explain, please," he says, looking at me like I've been withholding pertinent information from him all this time.

"Or…I could not. And you could just order the food?" I ask hopefully. His arched eyebrow tells me we will not be eating until I explain this very minor miscommunication. This is not the kind of chat you want to be having before your tea.

"I bottom…" I say slowly, hoping he understands my meaning without forcing me to elaborate. His cheeks go pink at the statement, and I wish I didn't find that so cute. He coughs to clear his throat.

"I'm aware… I was there. What's your point?" he asks me in a way that someone who has only ever topped would ask. I sigh, knowing I'm going to have to spell this out.

"Well, Phoenix, if you're going to have someone's dick in your arse, it's usually best not to have a load of spicy food beforehand. Comprende?" Now his whole face is blushing, and it's hard not to laugh.

"Oh." His eyes widen in recognition.

"Yeah, oh. Now, can we order the food?"

"Why didn't you ever tell me? It seems like something I should have known." He looks genuinely put out that I haven't mentioned this to him before. We were always pretty open about anything related to sex, but I never felt the need to go into detail regarding how I went about preparing myself beforehand.

"It wasn't as if I was keepin' it a secret. I kind of assumed you knew."

He still looks as though he's trying to solve a mental crossword, but thankfully, he doesn't say anything else and gets on with the task at hand.

Tea is fairly painless, and we stick on some *Always Sunny In Philadelphia* to kill some time before bed. We haven't mentioned a word about last night, which I'm grateful for because I'm no clearer on where my head is at. After 'Dennis Looks Like a Registered Sex Offender' finishes, I tell Phoenix I'm beat and head up to bed.

It doesn't take me very long to really start regretting all my life choices. I'm lying on my uncomfortable air bed, and it squeaks whenever I move. When Phoenix walks up the stairs a short while later, after he's walked into the master bedroom and found it and the bathroom empty, I hear him call out my name in the hallway.

"In here," I say, just loud enough for him to hear. A few seconds later, he opens the door to the spare room and stares at me. His eyebrows bunch together in confusion.

"Why are you in here?" he asks, and I hold in a breath; this isn't going to go down well.

"After last night, I thought some space would be good."

"Space?"

"Yeah, space."

"While you sleep?"

"Mhmm."

"Mister Uses-me-as-a-human-pillow, needs 'space' while he sleeps?" I don't dignify that with a response, mostly because I don't have one. He has a point, but I'd sooner set myself on fire than admit that fact. "Is that where you went first thing this morning? To buy this thing?" He looks at the airbed like it's a giant cockroach.

"I had some errands to run anyway, and I thought I'd pick this up while I was out." I sit up on the bed and pick at a non-existent hangnail on my thumb.

"Oh yeah, what other errands?" he asks, immediately zoning in on the lie. Damn him for being a walking polygraph test.

"You know, just...like...stuff," I reply, ever so smoothly. I hope nobody ever interrogates me because, apparently, I do not hold up well under pressure. And by pressure, just Fee marginally narrowing his eyes at me. "Fine. Okay. I didn't have any errands. I can't think clearly when you're so close all the time, and as evidenced by last night, bad things happen when we don't think clearly."

"Bad things?" His voice cracks, and he looks like I kicked his puppy. Or maybe he's the kicked puppy. Either way, a puppy has been kicked by my big mouth. If I could stuff the words back into my face, I would.

"I didn't mean—"

"Fuck you for saying that," he interrupts me. There's no real anger behind his words, which is so much worse. He looks fucking gutted.

I am such a dick.

He turns and makes his way back to our bedroom before I can even find the words to apologise.

I lie back down and toss and turn a few times, but this horrible rubber bed makes so much noise I have to lie as still as a corpse if I have any hope of falling asleep tonight. Guilt gnaws away at me until I can't take it anymore.

I partially shift so I can use a claw to pop a hole in the mattress. The mattress that now represents everything I hate about myself. It's a very loaded mattress.

When I walk into our bedroom, Fee appears to be a big lump under the duvet with his back to me. I can hear from his breathing that he's still awake, though.

Lifting the covers on my side, I get under them and shuffle up behind him. I tug on his shoulder lightly, pulling him to lie on his back, and when I look down at him, he's glaring up at me angrily.

I have the really unfortunate and extremely inappropriate urge to laugh all of a sudden. Why is it that the moment you think about how awful it would be to laugh, one instantly tries to bubble out of you? Barely managing to stifle it, I stroke a hand over the light brown stubble across his cheek. I can feel his jaw pulsate with how tightly he's clenching his teeth. It's kind of sexy if I'm being honest, but I digress.

Bending down, I kiss the corner of his mouth, but he doesn't budge, and he doesn't say a word.

Looks as though I'll have to actually use my words. Yuck.

"I'm sorry, Fee, please forgive me?" I whisper into the near-silent room. He opens his mouth and closes it again without saying anything, so I try again. "It wasn't a bad thing, I shouldn't have said that. I've never regretted having sex with you, ever. I'm sorry I said it," I tell him sincerely.

To myself, I silently add that I'll stop punishing him now. It's not as though I've suddenly forgiven him for everything, but I don't want to keep hurting him. Honestly, it hurts me too. Fee wordlessly turns back onto his side, and right before I can retreat to my side of the bed and give him some space, he reaches back and pulls my arm so it's resting over his waist. Taking the hint, I wrap myself around the curve of his back. Resting the palm of my hand on his warm stomach, I gently stroke over the soft hair there with my thumb until I hear his breathing even out, telling me he's drifted off to sleep.

TWENTY-ONE
May 2022

CONNOR KELLY

It turns out Phoenix didn't get the memo about the truce. I honestly didn't know he had it in him.

There is a land called passive aggressiva, and Fee is their king. He has usurped me of my throne.

I am not a morning person. One of the only things that makes me a functional human being before nine am is coffee. But once again, when I step into our small kitchen just minutes after Phoenix has left for work, I find myself staring at the empty coffee pot in defeat.

Today marks six weeks. Six weeks since Phoenix switched from making coffee for two to coffee for one. I tried calling him out on it, but he claimed it was because he wasn't sure what time I'd be up.

He's a liar who lies.

To top it off, it's dirty from when he used it, so not only do I have to make my own pot, I have to clean it first. I'm not one to get overly metaphorical, but fuck me, if this empty, dirty coffee pot hasn't come to symbolise the state of our relationship.

I scrub it clean, more aggressively than necessary. Once it's on, I glare at it while the brown liquid that promises to wake me up drips down from the filter into the cup.

This guy! This fucking guy! To confirm my theory Fee is, in fact, being a petty little miscreant, I decided to get up just a couple of minutes after him this morning. Our house has absolutely zero soundproofing qualities, topped with wolf shifter hearing, so I know he fucking heard that I was up.

"Thanks for making enough for two," I say sarcastically as he pours the perfect amount of coffee for one person into his mug. Did he fucking measure the water first? He's certainly precise with his vindictive behaviour.

"You're not usually up."

"Mhmm. You'd think your ears would have informed you otherwise."

"It's just coffee. I'll make another pot if it's that important to you."

"Don't strain yourself," I mutter as I make my way to the offending kitchen appliance. Fee looks like he's going to acknowledge the snarky remark, but instead, he gets up from his chair, pours his coffee into a travel mug and leaves the house without another word.

I thunk my head against the cupboard door several times and groan.

Fuck! I'm running late. Where are all my clean clothes? I saw Fee put the washing on two days ago!

I'm meant to be meeting Niamh and Will for drinks in ten minutes but my only pair of black jeans that aren't totally scruffy are nowhere to be found.

"Fee?" I yell down. He was sitting in the living room the last time I checked. No answer.

I stomp down the stairs to see where he's gone, but he's disappeared off somewhere. Fucking great.

Upon returning to the bedroom, I empty out the laundry basket onto the floor. I try to take deep breaths and count to ten when I realise that only my dirty laundry remains. He separated his clothes from mine and washed them. Like we're fucking roommates.

Logically, I'm aware that I'm partly to blame for the mess we're in now. But Fee doesn't get to make our whole life together miserable because I fucked up once. If he hadn't agreed to marry Niamh we wouldn't be in this mess in the first place. So, fuck him.

Flinging open his wardrobe, I grab his favourite pair of dark blue jeans and one of his nice black leather belts for good measure. I have a smaller waist than him, after all.

"Fine, dick head. You want to only wash your own clothes? I guess we'll be sharing a wardrobe now," I mutter to myself.

I quickly shoot off a text to Niamh with an updated ETA, spritz a little aftershave on my neck and leave as quickly as possible. I need to get fucking drunk tonight.

⇢⇢ ·◆· ⇠⇠

Mission accomplished. I don't remember exactly how much I drank last night, but guessing by my cotton mouth and the fact I'm on the verge of tears from the loud crashing that's coming from downstairs, I'm going to assume a lot.

Once I've brushed my teeth and thrown on some joggers, I go in search of water and paracetamol.

"What, in the fiery pits of hell, are you doin' right now? It's a fuckin' Sunday mornin'," I spit at Fee, who appears to be bashing all of our pots and pans together for no fucking good reason.

"I'm cleaning," he says like I'm the one acting deranged here.

"Most people clean with a sponge. I'm not sure bashin' the pans together is gonna give you the result you're lookin' for." Unless his intention is for my head to explode so my brain matter sprays the wall, then I suppose he's right on track.

"Where were you last night?" he asks. I'm surprised by his sudden change of subject; this might be the first question he's asked me in weeks.

"I went for dinner and drinks with Niamh and Will."

"Nice. You and Will famously make good choices when you've had too much to drink."

"Mhmm. We drank so much that we actually fucked on the dinner table. Turns out I'm an exhibitionist at heart. My twin sister being right there was a little awkward, but we made it work!" A tiny little part of my brain tells me that was not the right thing to say. But I'm hungover. And he's bashing pans. A man can only take so much.

Fee narrows his eyes at me, and I'm ready for the fight. My head might be throbbing, but I'll ignore it if we're finally going to have this out.

But no.

He drops the pan in the sink, grabs his car key off the side and leaves.

I want to punch something.

I don't, though.

❖❖ ❖ ❖ ❖❖

It's a Friday night, but I told Sammy I'd help him fit a bathroom in his new house tomorrow, so I went to bed early. I also went to bed alone.

Fee went out at around eight pm wearing his nice jeans and a dark green polo that fitted him sinfully.

He didn't say where he was going, and I'd have rather swallowed my own tongue than ask him. Hasn't prevented me from obsessing about it, though.

After what feels like several hours spent tossing and turning, I finally fall asleep, only to be woken up about an hour later.

A quick glance at my phone tells me it's three in the morning. The front door slams shut. The tap runs in the kitchen. Then he clambers up the stairs, before stumbling gracefully into the wall.

When he literally crashes into the bedroom, I turn on the bedside light. He squints at the light and tries to cover his eyes with the back of his hand.

"Go back to sleep," he mumbles as he face-plants onto the bed, fully dressed, still with his shoes on.

I sigh.

Tossing back the duvet, I get out of bed and begin undressing my barely conscious husband.

"W'you doin'?" he asks but makes no moves to assist me.

"Puttin' your drunk arse to bed." Once he's down to a t-shirt and boxers, I manage to wrangle the duvet and cover him up. I grab some painkillers and a glass of water from the bathroom and put them on his bedside table.

Fee snores like a freight train next to me, and I lie there wide awake, wondering if it's ever going to get better or if this is just our life now. The last two months have really started to wear on me. At first, I thought I just needed to wait it out until he got over it. Fee always gets over it. But not this time. I'm on eggshells around him now.

Fee rolls over, throwing an arm around my waist, and I hold my breath. Apart from occasionally reaching out for me in his sleep, Fee hasn't touched me in weeks. And I'm not talking about sex. I mean, not even a shoulder nudge, and I'm ready to burst out of my skin.

Wolf shifters are tactile, and the need for touch is as strong as the need to run for miles and miles. Scrunching my eyes closed, I try to fight the swell of emotion at the fact the only time my husband will come within a metre of me is when he's unconscious. Knowing it's largely my own fault, doesn't make it hurt any less.

I'm still wide awake when my alarm goes off a few hours later, and Fee doesn't stir at the noise.

※

"Um, are you home for tea tomorrow night?" I ask Fee almost a week later.

He looks slightly suspicious but says, "Hadn't made any other plans, why?"

"Niamh and Will are coming over for dinner. I was going to make lasagne—your favourite." I'm not beyond bribery to get him to spend time with me, even if he is determined to be Frosty the Snowman.

"Sure, okay." It's the enthusiasm that warms my heart, I swear.

※

"Damn, this is actually really good," Niamh says as we tuck into the lasagne I made.

"Thanks, tried a new recipe."

"Ooo, whose is it? Delia Smith's?" Will asks, and I immediately regret opening up this line of questioning. My cheeks pinken.

"Um. No. Actually, it's a family friend of Phoenix's."

"It is?" Fee asks, sounding surprised. I just nod. "You got the recipe from Claire?"

"Yep. It's no big deal," I reply, nudging a piece of garlic bread on my plate with the prongs of my fork.

"When?"

"A few days ago." His face scrunches up in confusion, but he doesn't say anything else. Something about his total apathetic response to the fact I had to speak to his fucking horrible mother to get hold of Claire for this recipe makes me see red.

I'm sick of the empty coffee pots.

I'm sick of separate laundry.

I'm sick of all of this.

When I reach over to get more lasagne, I 'accidentally' drop some in his lap.

"Ooops."

"Shit, that's hot," he says. I should feel bad. But I don't.

"Sorry, they're your favourite jeans too. That must be super annoyin'."

"It's fine. They'll wash," he says through gritted teeth.

"It's understandable if you're annoyed; I'd be annoyed if it were me."

"Wouldn't take much," he mutters. Before I can offer a snarky reply, Niamh kicks me under the table.

"Will, oh my god. Tell them about the potato patient," Niamh blurts out. Will looks from her to me, unsure.

"Oh, erm, yes. Funny story. I'm working in A&E at the moment, and we had a patient come in with a potato in his rectum. Claimed he'd been gardening naked, and somehow, it had got stuck up there. We couldn't get it out, so he had to go to surgery. The next day I asked how it had gone. The surgeon was like, 'I don't think he did that gardening somehow.' I was like, obviously, but why not? He goes, 'Because the potato we removed was completely peeled.'"

Niamh snorts a fake laugh, having heard the story before. Fee offers a tight smile. I would ordinarily find the story hilarious, but not right now. Nothing feels very funny right now.

"Wow. Tough crowd. That story has really been killing it lately," Will mumbles. "Maybe I didn't tell it right?"

"Sorry... I got distracted," I reply.

Once the world's most awkward dinner comes to a close, I walk Niamh and Will out to their car while Fee cleans up.

"I say this with love, but do not ever make me sit through a dinner like that again. Jesus. I almost stabbed myself with a fork because a night in the hospital would have been less painful than that,' Niamh says, pointing in the direction of the house with her thumb.

"Same here. And I literally just came from there," Will agrees.

"What are you going to do to fix this? You can't live like this forever," Niamh says, and I groan.

"I know." I dig my fingertips into my eye socket. "I've tried all sorts. I might have to do something drastic. Like a romantic gesture. How disgustin'." Niamh just pats me on the back.

"Let's not arrange another dinner like this until you've tried that. I do love you, just not that much." I snicker and press a kiss to her temple. I give Will a hug, and they both get into his car and drive off.

Before I head back inside, I tilt my head up to the sky. It's a rare, totally clear night, and the longer I look, the more stars appear. I take a few steadying deep breaths, rallying to return to my house of silent hostility.

TWENTY-TWO
June 2022

CONNOR KELLY

Things are...civil. We're being very cordial.

It's awful.

It's been about a month since the world's most awkward dinner with my sister and Will and around three months since the night of the stupid airbed incident. Combined with finding out about me and Will, it seems that's what finally tipped Fee over the edge. I managed to break the most patient man to have ever lived.

We share a bed every night, falling asleep as far apart as possible before inevitably waking up tangled together and then pretending it didn't happen. We go to work during the day, although I use the term loosely. After everything that went down last year, I couldn't work with Mikey anymore, so I let him buy my half of the business. Up until a month and a half ago, I'd been taking on ad hoc joinery jobs to keep me ticking over. At the moment, I spend most of my days working on a project I'm trying to keep a secret from Fee for as long as possible.

> **Me:** Centuries.Shorter.Forgives. 1pm?

My stomach flutters with butterflies, and my hands clam up while I stare at the text message, waiting and watching as it turns from 'delivered' to 'read'. Three dots appear and then disappear. And they're back...

Fee: Ok

How anticlimactic. At least it wasn't a no.

Back when we first met, if we wanted to meet somewhere other than the usual spot, we'd use What3words to send a location. I was hoping my text might soften him up a little, but his blunt response says otherwise. I can't blame him, though. Phoenix reached out with so many olive branches, and for the most part, I beat him over the head with them. Now, it's my turn to try and make things right. I just hope it's not too late.

It's a warm Saturday with a clear blue sky, so it's busier than I'd have preferred. To give us a modicum of privacy, I've laid the picnic blanket on a grassy patch above the waterfall, where it's quieter. It's five minutes past one, and waiting for Fee to get here is making me antsy. I can't seem to sit still.

What if he thinks this is the most pathetic idea ever?

Before I get a chance to totally spiral, pack everything away and pretend this never happened, I spot Fee walking towards me.

He looks really fucking good. The slightly longer scruff on his face suits him. Makes him look older and more rugged. He's wearing a well-worn pair of denim shorts he's had for as long as I've known him and a white T-shirt a size too small and a tad transparent—not that I'm complaining. He clearly caught me checking him out because when I look up at him, his right eyebrow is arched.

"What's all this?" he asks, gesturing to the blanket and the food I've laid out.

"A picnic?" I'm not sure why I phrase it as a question. It's clearly a fucking picnic. He doesn't respond to my stupid answer, so I plough on, "Um. Since it's five years ago today we met, I thought it might be nice to…erm…do something," I stammer out.

Someone punch me in the face, I beg you.

"I know what day it is," is all he says in response.

"You remembered?"

"Of course I remembered." His words are clipped, and he sounds angry I'd assume otherwise. Anger I can work with. It's certainly a step up from the past few months of apathy.

"Well, you were gone when I woke up this morning, and I didn't hear from you, so I figured you'd maybe not realised the date."

"I didn't forget. I also didn't forget last year, you know when I called you and texted you, and you didn't reply? When you went and got pissed and slept with Will?"

Ouch. My gesture is rapidly backfiring, and I'm not sure how to claw my way back.

"Why did you come then? You obviously knew why I asked you here today."

"Because you asked me to. Because even though I'm pissed off with you, if you ask me to come, I'll come."

DO NOT LAUGH. I roll my lips between my teeth, and my eyes water at the gargantuan effort to not say the words.

"You're dying to say 'that's what he said,' aren't you?"

I silently nod my head.

"I'm glad you came," I reply, and we both crack up. Some of the tension between us melts away, and a tiny blossom of hope blooms in my stomach.

Fee inspects the sandwich I pass him, and his eyes gentle when he sees I made his favourite, pastrami, pickle and mustard on seeded bread. I get a muttered thank you, and I'm taking it as a win.

"What did you think when you first met me?" I ask Fee as we eat our sandwiches. He raises an eyebrow at me.

"Fishing for compliments?" he asks, and I snort a laugh.

"No. I was just thinkin' about the first time we met, and I wondered if you remember it the same way," I tell him honestly. Recalling the memory with only my own perspective feels like half of the story is missing.

"I know what you mean." He looks thoughtfully toward the spot where we first met. "Weirdly, I remember your scent hitting me for the first time more than seeing you. I was minding my own business, enjoying a late-night swim, and then suddenly, all I could smell was heather and lightning. I thought it was so bizarre how the air could be so still and calm yet smell so much like a storm brewing. And then there you were. I'd been so distracted by the smell I hadn't even heard you approach. It was strange because I remember thinking I'd never been hit with a scent even close to it, but at the same time, it was familiar, like home."

Well holy shit, if that isn't the most romantic fucking answer I've ever heard.

"Only you could make me fuckin' swoon while you're still pissed at me," I say, trying to lighten the moment a little.

"Yeah, well, we both know I was never very good at staying mad at you." He rolls his eyes, and I'm flooded with relief. I know everything isn't suddenly fixed, but I'm starting to feel we could be heading in the right direction.

"I'm pretty much countin' on it at this point," I reply, and he huffs out a laugh.

"Do you remember that time I tried to see if I could give you a blowjob underwater, and I accidentally breathed the water in and thought I was going to die?" Fee asks while he picks through the punnet of cherries. He hates eating fruit with even the slightest bruise on it, as if it's contaminated or something. I pass him a few I'd put to one side that appear to be completely smooth, saving the marginally damaged ones for myself. He gets a soft look in those brown eyes when he realises, and I feel oddly embarrassed. The cherries have stained his lips a rosy red, and it's very distracting. Especially paired with him reminiscing attempted blowjobs.

"Yeah, I remember. You panicked and almost bit my dick off. Was a long while before you were trusted with your teeth in that region again." We must have been no more than twenty or twenty-one at the time; a lot of our sexual exploits back then were us trying out random things we'd watched in porn.

Newsflash—rarely a good idea.

"Piss off, 'a long while'. You wanted a blowjob a week later." He laughs, and the sound reverberates through me. He's not wrong. I smile fondly at all the stupid shit we got up to back then, and I'm grateful Fee seems to be joining me on the nostalgia trip today.

After we've finished eating, Fee takes his t-shirt off and lies on his front to bathe in the sun. I don't even bother trying to stop myself from ogling the large expanse of beautiful olive skin since he's facing away from me. Is a back fetish a thing? His skin glistens where he's sweating slightly, and I want to lick him.

"Stop staring at me." His voice is muffled from where his face is tucked into the crook of his elbow.

"What makes you think I'm starin' at you?"

"I can feel your eyes boring into the back of my head."

"What can I say? The back of your head really does it for me." He snorts but then returns to his cat nap, and I return to admiring the view—of his back.

When the sun hides behind a wall of clouds, I begin packing away and stuff everything back into my rucksack. We walk together and head out of sight towards the trees.

"Race you back to the house?" Fee asks as we start to strip out of our clothes.

"What do I get when I beat you?"

"Usual prize applies? Not that you're likely to win," he says, and my blood pumps a little harder at the promise. I want to win because I'm competitive, but I'm not sure I can really lose either way here.

"Deal." We shake hands on it before shifting.

We've always been pretty close in speed, I'm bigger as a wolf than Fee is, but he definitely dodges obstacles better than I do. After around a mile of running, I'm marginally ahead of him, but he keeps nipping at my back legs with his teeth, trying to throw me off. He tries again, and his teeth nick me.

"Sneaky bastard, stop cheating." Even now it's strange to me that we can speak mind to mind. We've only been running together a few times since the ceremony, so I'm still getting used to it.

"Sorry. Mistook you for a little rabbit. You look like prey."

Behind the thoughts he sends me, I can sense his emotions. He's amused and impish at the moment, and I've missed this side of him. It's been odd seeing him so serious these past few months. It was as if the playful glint in his eyes had been extinguished, and I was the water that had doused the flame.

Hold up, did he just call me a little rabbit? Wanker! I whirl on him and pin him to the ground. I press my teeth to his jugular but don't bite down.

"Who are you calling a little rabbit? Who's prey now??"

Fee's tongue is lolling out of his mouth, making him look dopey and ridiculous. I shake my head at him and huff in amusement. He pushes up suddenly and flips us so I'm beneath him.

He distracted me with his goofy face!

I could probably get out if I wanted to, but he looks so pleased with himself I'm hesitant to move. I regret my decision immediately when he starts licking my face and slobbering all over me. The next thing I know, he's leaping off me to get a headstart back to the house. He's playing dirty today. Someone clearly wants the prize.

PHOENIX CAMPBELL

Cee gets home a few seconds after me and I'm crouched in front of the door, ready to pounce and feeling smug as anything. He rolls his eyes at me but doesn't seem too put out over losing.

Our house is set back away from the street, so we have a lot of privacy. We can't exactly have neighbours seeing us shift or wandering outside in the nude. He bows his head at me, acknowledging that I won this round, and I whine happily.

Despite my attempts to stay mad at him, I've had a pretty great day.

Cee shifts back and stands before me, completely naked and unabashed. With the sun bearing down on him, I can see a faint tan from where I assume he must have been doing some work outside lately. My gaze travels down his body. His smooth chest is more muscular, and his dusky pink nipples have a few hairs around them. Cee's never been especially hairy; he has a dark happy trail from his belly button down to his pubic hair, which he trims enough to keep it tidy. His cock, which had been soft when I started my perusal, begins to plump up.

"Do you want to claim your prize now, or later?" Cee asks me, his tongue darting out to wet his lips. "I'm not sucking your furry dick, Fee, so you better shift back." His eyes sparkle playfully as he stalks towards me.

I shift back, and I'm left kneeling on the doorstep by the time he reaches me. He cups my cheek in his palm and tugs on my bottom lip with his thumb. I laugh when I hear the satisfied rumbling noise in his chest. Despite the fact I know we've both always been content with our dynamic of me topping and him bottoming, I know he gets turned on by the submissive gesture. When I look up at his eyes, they're dark and full of a heated promise.

"Stand up," he says, and I do as asked, leaning against the front door. He takes my place and kneels on the welcome mat in front of me, placing feather-light kisses to my cock as it continues to stiffen. Somehow, there's nothing submissive about the way Connor kneels for me. His beautiful, stubborn face tells me he'll only ever give as much as he wants to.

His attention moves to my balls which he laps at before sucking one into his mouth and swirling his tongue around it in a way that makes my eyes roll into the back of my head. Holy shit, that's good. I haven't had his—or anybody's—mouth on me in so long that I forgot how incredible it feels.

"Fuck, you taste amazin'."

I look down at him while he strokes me leisurely. He plants gentle kisses to the crease of my groin; it's so attentive and loving it makes my heart squeeze a little. He shaved his stubble this morning, and it highlights his sharp features; his strong, masculine jaw and high cheekbones.

Dark hair flops over his forehead. He let it grow out some the past couple of months, making him look closer to how he did when we first met. Unable to keep my hands to myself, I push his hair back away from his face.

Damn, he's beautiful.

How was I supposed to ever move on from him after I'd had a taste of perfection?

I can't help but moan as his tongue licks up my length slowly, like he has all the time in the world and is just savouring the taste. As he takes me into his mouth, he gazes up at me through those thick, dark lashes, and I'm done for.

He sucks me and licks me with enthusiasm, looking completely wrecked. I definitely lucked out with Cee and how much he's always loved giving head. He really perfected his craft over the years we were together, and I was more than willing for him to practise on me all he wanted.

Cee groans with me in his mouth, and the vibrations around my cock feel incredible. He finally reaches between his legs and strokes himself. His tip is glistening with precum, showing me exactly how turned on he gets from sucking me.

When I hit the back of his throat, he gags for a moment before relaxing and swallowing around me.

Holy fucking shit.

"Oh, fuck you for that," I sputter at him, and he pulls his mouth off me.

"What?" he asks, like butter wouldn't melt. The glint in his eyes gives him away, though.

"How am I supposed to hold a grudge when you do the thing with your throat?" I say, sounding as desperate and horny as I feel.

"No idea what you mean," he replies before enveloping me in the wet warmth of his mouth again.

He hollows out his cheeks as he sucks me down, taking me deep into his throat and doing the exact thing he just feigned innocence over. I'd call him out on the lie, except nothing short of a nuclear bomb going off would get me to interrupt what he's doing right now.

I think even the postman could turn up, and the best I could offer would be an apology. He swallows again, and the feel of his throat contracting around me has me already close to coming. He can clearly tell I'm right on the edge because he increases his speed, sucking up and down my cock with precisely the right amount of pressure to ensure I lose any semblance of control.

My fingers rake through his hair, and I tug it lightly, just enough to sting in a way that makes him groan. I tighten my grip and start to gently thrust my hips.

"Shit, I'm so close. Why do you have to look so good with my cock in your mouth," I mutter—mostly to myself.

One final glance down at him, his tight grip around his own shaft moving faster and faster, the way his eyes roll when my dick hits the back of his throat with each thrust, and I lose the battle.

"Babe, I'm gonna come," I shout out before my release spills into his waiting mouth. I come so hard I'm pretty sure my soul just shot out of my dick, and I'm unsteady on my feet.

He spits my cum into his hand and uses it to jerk himself off frantically. There's something so wild and feral about it that has my cock trying to rally for a second round. It doesn't take long for his orgasm to build, and then he's shooting over his own hand and onto the welcome mat.

As we catch our breath, he stares down at where his hand is covered in the mix of our cum, and a satisfied smile spreads over his face.

"You called me 'babe'," he says, looking up at me, smug and happy. It might have been a momentary lapse in my judgement due to his enthusiastic blowjob, but even when I'm angry with him, even when he lashes out and hurts me, he's still mine. I never really thought he cared much about the term of endearment back when we were together, but it obviously meant more to him than I realised.

"Yeah, I called you 'babe'. Come here." I pull him up to his feet.

Swiping my thumb along his bottom lip, where there are still remnants of my cum, I kiss him. His lips are soft and familiar against my own; it's not a heated kiss, as we're both spent. It's a kiss that tastes a lot like a truce. I must be a masochist because it seems no matter how many times Connor swipes his claws at me, I always seem to end up crawling back for more.

I sigh deeply. I feel a strange mixture of resignation I can't seem to keep him at arm's length, and relief I no longer have to.

"Nothin' says 'welcome' like a cummy doormat," Cee says as we make our way inside.

TWENTY-THREE
July 2022

CONNOR KELLY

I can't help but grin like the Cheshire cat when I step into the kitchen. The coffee pot is still warm from when Fee made it, and there's enough coffee in it to fill my favourite bucket of a mug to the brim.

Although it's been several weeks since we made up, every morning that I come downstairs to find the coffee pot full, I'm flooded with relief. It's like a daily reminder that we're on the mend and we're going to be okay. Once I've added a splash of milk and half a sugar—I'm trying to cut down—I go in search of Fee in the living room.

"Mornin', love," I say, pecking a chaste kiss on his soft lips.

"Morning, babe. What do you want to do today?"

"I'm plannin' to spend so long on the sofa that I merge with it." Fee chuckles.

"Fine by me." And then we smile at each other like the disgustingly besotted fools we both are.

※

PHOENIX CAMPBELL

"Do you love it yet?" Cee asks, nudging my paperback with his sock-covered foot. I've just started reading *Wolfsong* after he spent two weeks telling me it might possibly be his new favourite book of all time. I'm not a huge fiction reader, but Cee loves his books, and when I read the ones he recommends, it seems to make him happy.

"I'm only three chapters in; give me an actual chance to read some of it first," I reply, pinching his big toe.

"Ouch! Fucker," he whines at me. "Kiss it better."

"You're so annoying. Get your foot out of my face, or I'll stop rubbing it." He quickly puts his foot back into my lap and wiggles his toes. I go back to pressing my thumb into the arch of his foot, and he makes this contented rumbling sound in his chest.

I've never known a wolf that's so cat-like. He's practically purring at me. I'm pretty content at the moment myself, though. I wouldn't say things with us are resolved by any stretch, but we've had a tentative peace for a good few weeks now.

We haven't had full-on sex yet because every time we head in that direction, I can hear Cee's voice in my head calling it a 'bad decision', and I backtrack. Apparently, my brain doesn't have the same negative associations with blowjobs and frotting, though, so it's not as if we haven't been having a good time.

It feels amazing to be back in a place where I can kiss him freely, and we exchange affection without a second thought. That said, we're still treading quite carefully around each other in every other regard. One of the things I always loved in our relationship was feeling like we could tell each other anything. I felt so safe and secure with him I didn't ever have to filter myself, and the last year and a half has left a mark on us both. I can tell we're both terrified of accidentally rocking the boat, so we stick to safe topics at all times, and it's starting to make me anxious.

Our marriage won't last if we don't find a way to communicate without coming to blows.

How is it we're now so bad at something we used to be so good at?

I move my hand up his leg and massage his calf muscle, earning me a satisfied little 'mmm' sound from his lips. Cee's reading an ARC of *Make Me Fall* on his Kindle, and it seems to be getting him a bit hot under the collar because he keeps having to adjust himself in his shorts.

"Would you ever get your dick pierced?" he asks, seemingly out of the blue. I move my hand to cover my dick protectively.

"Absolutely not. Do not get any ideas," I tell him, and he chuckles demonically. "Why do you ask?"

"One of the characters in my book has a Jacob's ladder. Sounds pretty hot."

"Good for him. I'm fairly sure fictional piercings hurt a lot less than real ones."

"Aw. Is the big bad wolf scared of a little needle?" he taunts me.

"Near my cock? Most definitely." Cee laughs and goes back to reading. This is how we've spent most of our Saturdays for the past few weeks. Except usually, we sit on a blanket in the garden. However, it's pissing it down today; can't beat a British summer...

A soft thud against the front door interrupts our comfortable silence, and we both suddenly turn to look at each other as if to confirm we heard the same thing. We've quite literally had nobody except Alice, Niamh and Will come to visit the past few weeks, and they all just let themselves in. We pull the same bewildered expression at each other as if to say, 'I'm not expecting anyone'. I tap Cee's leg gently so he'll lift his feet, and I head to the front door to investigate. The weather is still absolutely miserable, so I don't want to leave whoever is stuck out on our doorstep for too long.

As I open the front door, my eyes widen in shock when I'm met with a shifted wolf in front of me. His chocolate brown fur is soaking wet, and I can scent the tangy odour of blood on him immediately. His big dark eyes look at me pleadingly, and I reach my hand out to his nose so he can scent me.

"What's goin' on?" Cee asks as he approaches behind me.

"We need to get him inside, I'm not sure what's wrong, but he's definitely injured, so I don't think he can shift back."

"We won't hurt you, but we need to get you inside so we can take a look at where you're hurt, okay?" I say to the unknown wolf. He nods his head and makes a pained whimpering sound. To have made it to our house as wounded as he looks must have been a mission unto itself.

Between us, we manage to manoeuvre him into the kitchen where the floor is tiled so blood is less of an issue. Cee holds the wolf's face between his palms and calmly tells him he's safe with us; we will try and help. He slowly begins to apply light pressure down the wolf's back.

"Let me know when I reach somewhere that hurts, okay?" he asks, and the wolf nods. When he reaches the wolf's hind leg closest to him, he lets out an almighty great howl of anguish.

Shit, he must be really hurt.

We heal so fast as wolves the most likely thing is for a bone to have healed too quickly and be set in the wrong position. Breaking bones and re-setting them is no laughing matter, and I can't help but wince on his behalf.

"It's okay, you're gonna be okay. Are you injured anywhere else?" Cee asks, and the wolf shakes his head and whines.

"What should we do?" I ask Cee, who I'm grateful seems to be taking control of the situation.

"We need a witch."

I try calling Noah, but his voicemail informs me he's currently canoeing in Peru, of all places, and he won't have any signal for a few weeks. Next, I try Nina Fenwick; she's not a healer, but I hope she knows someone who can help.

Fortunately, she gives me the contact details of a witch on this territory, so things are starting to look up. I dial the number I've scribbled on a piece of paper and pray someone answers.

"Hi, is this Natasha Richardson?" I ask when the call connects.

"Who's asking?"

"Um, my name is Phoenix Campbell. I got your details from Nina Fenwick? She said you're a healer, and you live in Yorkshire?" There's silence for a beat, and I wonder if she heard me, but then she lets out a resigned sigh.

"Why do you need a healer?" she asks sceptically.

"I don't personally. We had a wolf show up on our doorstep. His scent is beta, so he should be able to shift back, but he can't. One of his back legs is injured, and he's covered in blood. We don't know who he is, and we don't know to what extent he's hurt, but it has to be pretty bad if he can't shift back," I explain, hoping to elicit some sympathy.

"He's definitely not part of your pack?" she asks, I'm not sure how that's relevant.

"No, he's not. We've never met him before."

"I can't come to you. You'll have to bring him to me." She rattles off an address in Malham Cove, and Cee and I just barely manage to bundle the wolf into the back of my car.

≫·•·≪

CONNOR KELLY

When I glance over at Fee, he's white-knuckling the steering wheel and driving well over the speed limit. The road we're currently on is pretty uneven, and the wolf in the back whimpers every few minutes. The Satnav says the drive will take around fifty-five minutes, but we'll be there in forty at this rate.

I reach over and gently squeeze Fee's thigh; tension is rolling off his shoulders in waves. It takes a lot for our kind to be injured this severely, and it doesn't look like an accident. I really hope this witch knows what she's doing because I don't think this will be a quick fix.

"We're almost there," I tell the strange wolf. I can't explain it, but I feel overwhelmingly protective of him. He's not pack; I've never met him before, and I've no idea who he is, but he sought us out to help him, and I feel responsible for him for some reason.

Fee turns left onto a long dirt road with thick conifer trees on either side, making it appear darker than it really is. The downpour of rain all day has made the ground muddy, and I'm grateful we have four-wheel drive. As we near the end of the driveway, a small thatched cottage comes into view. Fee pulls the car up as close to the gate as possible so we have less distance to carry the wolf.

The door to the cottage swings open as we're trying to get him out of the car, revealing a woman who I'm assuming is Natasha. She walks quickly along the garden path towards us and stares us down assessingly. She scrunches her nose like our scent offends her. She's quite small, around five foot three, with long, bone-straight blonde hair and sharp hazel eyes that could burn a hole through you.

"He can come inside. You two will have to wait out here," she says without any sort of greeting.

"He can't walk. We have to help him inside," Fee explains, although I think that fact is pretty evident after she watched us manhandle him out of the car. She narrows her eyes at us mistrustfully.

"You can help him inside, but then you have to leave," she retorts in a tone brokering no room for negotiation.

"We can't just leave him in there. We don't know you. At least one of us needs to stay," I try to reason with her.

"You said you don't know him, said he's not pack, what's it to you?"

"He's not pack, but he came to us for help, and we promised to keep him safe." She briefly seems to evaluate my response and then sniffs the air.

"Fine. The beta can stay inside and wait. Alpha-beta waits outside." She's making no sense.

"Who are you talking about? We're all betas," I say, getting impatient with her, considering we're carrying the weight of a very heavy and injured wolf right now.

"You're an Alpha-beta," she says, pointing a finger at me. "You can help bring him inside, but then you leave. The beta can wait inside." I still have no idea what she's talking about, but we don't have time to argue over semantics, so I agree and help Fee carry the wolf inside.

The stone path to her front door is narrow, with a wild, overgrown garden on either side. We're too wide for the space, and by the time we make it inside, I've got nettle stings all down my left leg and scratches covering my arm from the brambles.

The moment we're over the threshold, she steers us into a small room with a treatment bed in the centre. As soon as we place the wolf down, I'm ushered quickly back out of the house, and Fee is left to sit on a bench in the hallway outside.

Filled with adrenaline and worry, I spend the next hour pacing up and down the long driveway. When the rain begins to really pelt it down, though, I go and sit in the car. I'm restless, and my brain is firing off hundreds of questions I can't possibly get the answers to. Unable to concentrate on the book I stuffed in the glove compartment last week, I resort to playing sudoku on my phone. I try texting Fee, asking for updates, but I think he must have left his phone back at the house—we did leave in a hurry.

What feels like hours later, Fee finally re-appears. His eyes are wide, and his skin is drip white with beads of sweat along his brow. Judging by the awful sounds that came from the cottage, I dread to think of how bad it was inside. The entire time, my brain was screaming at me to go inside, to make sure they were both okay when they clearly weren't. I step out of the car to meet him.

"He's shifted back, but she's given him a heavy sedative, so he's still out cold," Fee tells me as he approaches.

He opens the boot of the car and starts rummaging through a duffel bag. Before I can open my mouth to ask what the witch did, Fee's low whisper interrupts me.

"I don't think our conversation is private. Let's talk when we get home." I raise my eyebrows in confusion and look back towards the cottage where Natasha is lurking in the doorway, obviously keeping an eye on us. Fee pulls out some gym shorts and a t-shirt and heads back towards the cottage.

"Can I come and help carry him back out?" I shout to Natasha.

"If you must," she replies before heading back inside.

Fee gets to work dressing the man on the table with his spare clothes. He looks quite tall, around six foot, with shoulder-length wavy red hair and a full beard. His skin is pale and freckled. Judging from looks alone,

I'd guess he came to us from a pack in Scotland. I can't help but speculate over what must have happened to him and how he ended up on *our* doorstep, of all places. Seeing him shifted back and no longer in pain eases some of my nerves.

"Did you find out anything about him?" I ask Fee.

"Nope. He was still screaming when he shifted back, so she put him to sleep. Don't even know his name." His soft brown eyes are sad and filled with concern and empathy for this strange wolf we appear to be taking under our wing.

"Okay. Let's get him home then."

With him safely strapped into the back of the car, I head back to the cottage to settle up with Natasha. Her home is not as *witchy* inside as I expected. I've only ever been inside one witch's house before, my great grandma Orla's place in Northern Ireland. She's ninety-eight now, and she's been our pack witch for almost seventy years. Her house is old and creaky, filled with trinkets and the sides are covered in jars of suspicious-looking substances. I always loved visiting her as a kid; I still carry my keys on a rabbit's foot keyring she gave to me for good luck when I was twelve.

Natasha's cottage is shockingly minimalist in comparison. Everything is... sterile, cleaned within an inch of its life, judging by the pungent smell of bleach lingering in the air. If it weren't for some scattered photo frames on the walls, you'd think it was a show home. I scan the pictures as I wait for her to finish writing out the invoice. One, in particular, stands out to me; Natasha must be only around five years old in the photo, but you can still tell it's her. She's standing between two women, who I'm guessing are her mother and grandmother, considering the resemblance.

I wonder briefly if they used to be pack witches for the Yorkshire territory. It's unusual to have a coven like this that's completely separate from a wolf pack.

"What made you think I'm an Alpha-beta?" I ask her, curiosity getting the better of me.

"Because you *are* an Alpha-beta," she replies, as though I'm wasting her time with asinine questions.

"I'm not, though. I'm just a beta with a dormant Alpha gene."

"Yeah, well, these lands have an annoying habit of waking things up that should be left well alone." I'm not sure what to do with her response. I still *feel* completely beta. I think I'd notice if I'd suddenly become an Alpha-beta; after all, my brother Sam is one.

"What does that even mean?"

"Here's your bill," she says, ignoring my question and handing me the piece of paper. Seven hundred quid—ouch. I quickly pull out my phone to do a bank transfer; once it's gone through, I show her the screen as proof and say goodbye. She doesn't respond, and I hear her locking her front door the second I'm outside.

On the drive back home, I mull over everything Natasha said, which was somehow both a lot, and not quite enough. Maybe I should speak to Sammy when I get home; he might know more about this. Fee and I barely exchange a word on the drive home. The ginger wolf shifter is still unconscious in the back, and Fee seems a bit shell-shocked by the whole ordeal.

As I'm fiddling with the invoice Natasha gave me, I spot some green writing on the back.

'You aren't safe on these lands.'

Weird.

Who isn't safe on these lands?

Is the note intended for me? Or for the runaway wolf in the back?

TWENTY-FOUR
August 2022

PHOENIX CAMPBELL

I see Archie flinch out of the corner of my eye when I accidentally drop a mug in the sink. It's been just over two weeks since he appeared on our doorstep, soaking wet and injured. When he eventually woke up the day after we took him to the witch, he told us his name was Archie, and he was from a pack in Scotland. Benjy, Alpha Eastwood's middle son, had told him about us. I don't know Benjy all that well, but I'm glad he knew we would be a safe place for Archie and that we'd protect him. We said he could stay with us as long as he needed, but when we asked him questions about what happened to him, he seemed to retreat into himself.

Whenever there's a loud noise, he recoils, and I really hate to contemplate what made him so skittish. Last weekend, we found him having a panic attack because he overheard us arguing. He couldn't hear what we were saying, just our raised voices, and we both felt so guilty afterwards.

In actual fact, we were only bickering over the fact one of Cee's favourite books had been made into a TV series. Apparently, my take that the TV show is actually better than the book was very controversial, and Cee practically gave me a TED Talk on the superior merits of the book. Since then, we've been careful to speak calmly and quietly when Archie's home.

"Sorry, didn't mean to make you jump." It's only him and me at home today. The school where I work has broken up for the six-week summer holidays, and while I'm enjoying the long break, I miss Cee when he's out at work all day. He's been working on some secret project these last few months, but he won't tell me what it is yet.

One thing we *have* learned about Archie is he's a big ol' computer nerd. He works for an IT company in software development, so once we managed to source a new laptop for him, he's been able to work remotely from home.

"It's okay. I'm sorry you and Connor both have to tip-toe around me. I'll be out of your hair soon," he says, and his voice makes my heart hurt a little.

"Hey, you're no bother at all. Like we said, you can stay here as long as you need," I tell him, and he nods, worrying his bottom lip between his teeth.

I sit opposite him at the little kitchen table; he's on his lunch break and eating a sandwich.

"I don't want to put any pressure on you at all if you're not ready, but you know you can talk to us about anything, right?" I try to sound reassuring.

"I know. Thanks. I actually just feel kind of humiliated by the whole thing," he replies with his soft Scottish accent. The guy should narrate audiobooks honestly; his voice is so gentle and soothing.

"A secret for a secret?" I ask, hoping if I open up, it might make it easier for him to. He looks hesitant but then agrees.

I explain my and Cee's actual backstory. How we met years ago and were together in secret for years. When I tell Archie about us breaking up a year and a half ago and how we essentially only spoke to each other again for the first time on our wedding day, Archie's eyes widen at my revelation. I probably should have checked with Cee before sharing it, but at this point, I don't think it really matters who knows.

"I'm kind of shocked, but also, that sort of makes a lot more sense," he says, laughing to himself.

"It does? What do you mean?"

"When Benjy told me about you two, he said the two of you were in an arranged marriage but also that you'd been engaged to his sister the year before?" he asks, and my face heats.

"Yeah, I sort of omitted that part," I say sheepishly. "It's not quite as bad as it sounds, and it's a much more convoluted story, but it's why we broke up." He nods in understanding.

"So yeah, over the past few weeks of spending time with the two of you, I thought, damn, they're very in love for two people who only met and got married four months ago." I laugh this time; it hadn't even crossed my mind how bizarre we must seem together from the outside.

"It was definitely rocky there for a while, but we're in a better place now," I say with a soft smile on my lips.

"My dad is Alpha Fraser." His eyes drop to the table as he leaves the statement hanging in the air between us.

Oh shit, I can't help but think things just got very complicated. I ask the question even though I'm not sure I want the answer.

"Is he why you're here?" He looks up at me, and his eyes are glassy. He doesn't answer, but he doesn't need to. It's all there in the look of fear and vulnerability on his face. "I'm so sorry. Can I give you a hug?" I ask, feeling completely useless.

He whispers, "Yes," quietly, so I get up and wrap my arms around him.

"You're safe here, you know? I know we aren't pack yet, but we can be. You don't ever have to go back," I tell him, and I mean every word of it. "Can I tell Connor what you told me?" I ask. Cee needs to know what the deal is if we take Archie into our pack. Thankfully, Archie agrees, and I squeeze him even tighter.

⋙ ⋅⋅♦⋅⋅ ⋘

"Fee? Phoenix?" Cee shouts when he walks through the front door.

"I'm upstairs!" I yell down to him.

"What are you doin'?"

"Wanking." I shout back.

The next thing I know, he's stampeding up the stairs and bursting through the bedroom door. Thank god Archie went out to the supermarket because Cee sounds like a herd of rhinos.

"Well, this is disappointin'," he says when he spots me fully clothed, standing in the corner of our bedroom.

"Why are you standin' there?"

"There was a humongous spider, and I managed to trap it under a glass, but now I don't know what to do with—Hey, what the hell is that?" I ask as soon as I spot the mini bundle of fur in his arms, distracting me from the eight-legged beast before me.

"Excuse me, he can hear you," he whisper shouts and pretends to cover its ears.

Cee plops the cat on our bed for a moment before retrieving the spider from under the glass and chucking it out the window. I make a 'bleurgh' noise at him having it in his bare hands. Gross.

Now the bedroom is safe once more, we join the cat on the bed, and Cee scoops him back up.

TWENTY-FOUR

"This is Magnus." The look of adoration in his eyes tells me everything I need to know.

It appears we now have a kitten.

"And where did Magnus come from?" I ask as I reach out to scritch under his tiny chin. I've never really been a cat person, but he does look pretty cute.

"When I was out workin' today, I could hear this little mewl, so obviously, I went to investigate."

"Obviously."

"The poor little guy was trapped under some wooden decking, and so I had to rescue him. Please say we can keep him?" He's giving me the puppy dog eyes. If I had any ability to ever say no to him, I'd probably point out we already have quite a lot on our plate before adding a kitten into the mix. However, I think I would have to prise Magnus out of Cee's cold, dead fingers to separate them. I may as well admit defeat.

Taking the kitten out of Cee's hands, I peer into his disproportionately big green eyes. I stifle a snort because it's not lost on me Cee has managed to find the kitten version of his wolf form with his almost black fur.

"Welcome to the family, Magnus," I say to him, and he lets out a tiny squeaky *meow*.

"Really? We can keep him?" Cee says as if he gave me any other option. I plop Magnus onto the bed so he can explore a little. His dark colouring is a stark contrast to the white bedsheets.

"What's another stray? We seem to be collecting them."

Cee launches himself at me and presses his lips to mine in a sloppy kiss.

"You are the best husband I've ever had." I burst out laughing.

"I'm the only husband you've ever had."

"And I think I'll keep you." He has a big, goofy grin on his face, and a kitten seems a small price to pay if it makes him this happy. "I love you, you know?" His voice is softer and more serious all of a sudden. I swallow down a small lump in my throat because we haven't properly said that to each other since we broke up over a year and a half ago.

"I know," I tell him, because I do. We still have a long way to go, but I see all the effort he's been putting in these last few months.

"I love you too. Always have. Always will," I say and kiss him gently. Our kiss gets more heated as our tongues meet, and Cee is straddling my legs in a way that is giving my dick all kinds of ideas. "We should probably calm down before we scar poor Magnus for life," I say with amusement. Cee's head rests against my shoulder, and he's panting a little. He looks over at Magnus, who's currently wrestling a cushion twice his size.

"I can't believe I brought a little cockblock into the house. What was I thinkin'?" Magnus accidentally topples himself over the edge of the bed. "Oh fuck. I'm so sorry, I didn't mean it!" Cee scrambles over to where Magnus fell and scoops him back up.

Half an hour later, and Magnus seems to have tired himself out. Cee is sitting next to me with the sleeping kitten on his lap; I'm not sure which of them is purring louder.

"So, I spoke to Archie today, and he kind of dropped a bit of a bombshell."

"He told you what happened?"

"Not exactly. He told me his dad is Alpha Fraser, and that's who he's running from."

"Fuck," Cee says, echoing my own thoughts exactly.

"I know I should have discussed it with you first, but I told him he could stay here and join our pack," I tell him, hoping I didn't fuck up.

"That's okay. You know I'd never send him back to that. I'm glad he felt he could talk to you."

"Speaking of... he kind of told me because I spilt the beans on us..." I really don't want to make waves, but I think it's best to be honest with him now so he doesn't find out later.

"What beans? We have beans?" he asks; his tone is playful, and it eases the knot in my stomach a little.

"I told him how we actually met like five years ago and that we used to be together," I explain, and he makes a 'hmm' sound. "Sorry if I overstepped. I just thought if I opened up, maybe he would feel he could too." Ugh, I feel bad for not checking with him first.

"That's okay. It's not like if the truth comes out now, it will really change much. Plus, I think it probably makes sense to tell anyone who joins our pack." I sigh in relief he's not mad over it. "We can't do this forever, you know," he adds, and I panic, my heart rate spiking all of a sudden.

"Can't do what?"

"Tip-toe around each other. Always scared the smallest argument will fracture everythin'."

He's right. Things have been good between us, but I'm always scared that if we have a disagreement over something, he'll run for the hills.

"I know it's my own fault, but I'm not goin' anywhere, okay? We'll inevitably have arguments sometimes, but I promise I don't have a foot out the door anymore." I'm grateful to him for saying it because I needed to hear it more than I knew.

My biggest fear is us finally getting back on track and building a life together, only for it to crumble like a house of cards at the first sign of trouble.

"Thank you for saying that." He squeezes my hand, and I let out a deep breath. "I'm not going anywhere either." I turn his hand over in mine and trace the silvery scar across his palm with my fingertip. It's been there since Nina performed the ceremony to bind us to the land. I look at my own unblemished hand and can't help but wonder why the ritual left him with a mark but not me. Either way, it's a nice reminder of what we're building here together, and it appears we have our first new pack member.

"Are you ready to go?" Cee asks.

"Do I look ready to go?" I've just stepped out of the bathroom with a towel wrapped around my waist.

"Could you at least pick up the pace a bit? I want to stop in on Archie before we go." Archie moved into a small flat nearby last week. We've given him a few days to get settled, but something about him brings out a protective streak a mile wide in Cee, and it's like he can't settle unless he knows we're both okay.

"How about you go downstairs, fill some bottles of water, and pack a few snacks? Then, by the time you're done, I'll be ready to go," I suggest.

"I've already done that."

"Okay... How about you go downstairs anyway because you're being annoying." He huffs, but at least he leaves.

Connor knocks softly three times on Archie's front door—he still startles easily.

"Oh, hey, you guys, I was just heading over to bring these." Archie is holding some Tupperware filled with brownies, and my mouth waters.

"Wow, they look good. The school holidays are almost over, so we're makin' the most of Fee's free time and headin' off to hike Pen-y-ghent. Fancy it?" Cee asks him as we follow him into his living room.

"That's okay. You two only just got your space back; you don't need a third wheel," Archie says. He smiles softly, and it's clear he'd like to come, but he's always worried about imposing.

"We've spent the last four days solidly together. At this point, you'd be doing us a favour by running interference," I try to reassure him, but he looks anxious.

"We're not in the middle of an argument or anythin', I'm just annoyin' Fee to death," Cee adds, managing to actually reassure him. I nod in agreement, he is very much annoying me to death today.

Archie seems to think about it for a second and then says, "Okay, nice. Gimme a minute, and I'll be ready."

Five minutes later, the three of us are piled into the Jeep and on our way. It's a beautiful sunny day, so all the windows are down, and Cee is playing DJ in the front passenger seat.

When we arrive at the car park in Horton in Ribblesdale, it's only nine-thirty in the morning, but it's still almost full. Cee grabs a rucksack from the back seat, and we wander past a tree decorated with hundreds of old hiking boots.

The first section of the hike is a pretty gradual incline, and there aren't too many people around.

"How're you settling into the new place?" Cee asks.

"Good, actually. The upstairs flat is empty, so it's nice and quiet," he replies. I hope when someone eventually moves in above him, they're not too loud because I imagine it would cause him a lot of stress otherwise. "How's Magnus?"

"Still a legend. Fee, show him the photo you took yesterday." I chuckle at the memory and dig my phone out of my pocket to show Archie. Cee had returned from a run in his wolf form and was sunbathing in the garden. Magnus climbed on top of him and took a nap on his back. Archie laughs softly at the photo.

"I now totally understand why you used to sit still for hours when he was asleep on you. He looked so cosy on me that I ended up staying in the garden until I was on the brink of starvation," Cee says in his usual hyperbolic way.

When we reach the section of the hike that's quite steep with a bit of scrambling involved, there's a slight bottleneck where the slower humans are taking a while, so we wait to one side and tuck into Archie's brownies.

"Oh damn. These are incredible," I exclaim. "You missed your calling as a baker, I swear." Archie smiles and then tucks the box back into his bag so we can carry on.

Despite the sunny day, the peak of Pen-y-ghent is incredibly windy. Cee keeps having to swipe his dark hair out of his eyes. Removing the rucksack from his shoulder, he digs out two beers and pops the caps on them both before handing one to Archie.

"I'm fine, you brought those for you both, I'm good," Archie says, trying to pass the beer back.

"It's tradition, and I can share one with Fee. It's also lukewarm and tastes like piss, so I wouldn't thank me either," Cee replies. He takes a large sip, winces and then passes the beer over to me.

"Wow, that's really bad." Archie laughs. "Why is this a tradition?"

"Well, years ago, when we used to meet up in secret, it was almost always in the middle of the night. During the summer, we started doing all these local hikes in the dark, and I'd steal a couple of my brother Sammy's cheap beers to have at the top. In hindsight, rich boy over here should probably have been in charge of the beverages, but alas, tradition now dictates that piss water beer is to be drunk at the peak," Cee explains, and Archie nods with a smile twitching the corner of his lips. I hand the bottle back to Cee, who downs the rest before shuddering in disgust.

"Um, do you guys mind if we take a picture? I never really got to have friends to do things like this with...before," Archie asks, his gaze down on the ground. My heart breaks a little for him. It took a lot for him to ask that question, and I'm so proud of him.

"Of course! New tradition, pisswater beers and a selfie at the top?" I grab my phone to take the photo, the wind has all of our hair flying in every direction and our cheeks rosy pink, but we all have big grins on our faces and joy dancing in our eyes. The first photo of our little Yorkshire Pack.

TWENTY-FIVE
SEPTEMBER 2022

CONNOR KELLY

My face is sweating. I haven't exerted myself—at all—so why is my face betraying me like this?

I'm so self-conscious of the fact I gave a pretty abysmal impression when I had dinner with Fee's family a few months ago that I'm a hot mess right now.

It's Fee's twenty-sixth birthday today, so Archie, Alice, Jade and his brothers are coming over for dinner tonight. In a rare moment of kiss-assery, I offered to cook, and now I'm on the verge of breaking out in hives in case I fuck it all up.

"What time is everyone gettin' here?" I ask Fee for the tenth time today.

"Half six, the same time as when you last asked." I think his patience is wearing thin.

"Right. Sorry. Why is the house so fuckin' hot?" I say, tugging my collar away from my neck.

"It's not hot. You're just getting yourself worked up over nothing." I glare at him, but he rolls his eyes in response. "It's my birthday. You aren't allowed to scowl at me." I plaster a fake smile onto my face and crinkle my eyes sarcastically.

"Better?" I ask. He walks towards me from the bedroom doorway, where he's been watching me try on every combination of clothing I own. His palms cup my face, and he kisses me briefly.

"Why are you so nervous anyway? You've already met them."

"I was too busy actin' like a bitter hag to really care what they thought of me. Now I have this horrible bitchy voice in my head tellin' me they'll hate me forever, and then eventually you'll be like, 'hmm, maybe they have a point,' and then you'll also hate me forever. And then how awkward will it be to be married and livin' together when you hate me?" I take a deep breath after speaking at a hundred miles per hour. Fee only laughs at me.

"I'm not saying they'll hate you because I really don't think they will. But even if they do, I don't need their approval. I love you, Alice loves you; anyone who spends any lengthy amount of time with you loves you, too."

"Ahh, so you're saying nobody likes me right away. I grow on people. Like a tumour."

"Yes, that's exactly what I said. Just be yourself, babe. But maybe don't mention tumours over dinner."

"'Be myself,' 'don't mention tumours,' why don't you hand me a self-help book while you're at it," I say, letting out a disgruntled huff.

"And after they've all left, I'm going to bring you back in here, take my time undressing you, tease you until you forget your own name. And then I'm going to fuck you into the mattress."

My jaw drops, and I must resemble a goldfish.

Fee and I haven't fucked since our wedding night fiasco six months ago. We've done pretty much everything else *but* that, and now I'm nervous about this, too. He gently grips my chin between his thumb and index finger and presses his lips to mine in a quick but passionate kiss.

"Great, now I'm hard. Thanks for that," I say, adjusting myself so I'm not tenting my trousers. Thank fuck for boxer briefs with a tight waistband.

"Bet you aren't thinking about my family anymore, though?" He winks at me, looking far too pleased with himself.

※

Our dining table sits to the side of the living room by the front window; it's not really equipped to seat seven people, so it's a bit of a squeeze this evening. Most of our guests are sitting enjoying a glass of wine while Archie and I dish everything up in the kitchen. I've cooked slow-roasted duck legs in a red wine jus with creamy mashed potatoes and green beans because, apparently, I'm a total brown noser.

"Wow. I lived here for weeks, and you never cooked anything this fancy," Archie says, eyeing up the food. He's right, I think the fanciest meal he got from me was bangers and mash, but I squawk indignantly anyway.

"You're Scottish. Your people eat deep-fried Mars bars," I point out, and he chuckles under his breath. Ever since he opened up to Fee and officially joined our pack, he's slowly but surely become more relaxed around us. I was worried he might be nervous around strangers tonight, but he seems to be taking it all in stride so far.

PHOENIX CAMPBELL

"That was delicious. Thanks, Connor," Jade says as she and Jasper start clearing the plates away.

"Glad you enjoyed it," he replies, blushing at the compliment. The food really was delicious. It's funny to think that after so many years together, I thought I knew everything about him, yet the secrecy of our relationship left certain stones unturned. It wasn't until we started living together that I had any idea Cee could cook. It was a very pleasant surprise.

In the past few weeks, he even started making extra portions so I could take leftovers for lunch. In typical Cee fashion, he never mentioned it; I just opened the fridge one morning, and there was some Tupperware with a Post-it note with my name on it. I figured he'd made too much, but every morning, I open the fridge, and there's my lunch.

I know I never stopped loving him, but these past few months, he's reminded me of why I fell for him in the first place. He loves quietly, but in a way that makes me feel cherished and cared for. He buys my favourite shampoo when he sees I'm running low, he rubs my shoulders when he knows I've had a stressful day, and he mended a hole in my flannel shirt the other day because he knows it's my favourite.

I think it's all the little things compounded that have made me realise I'm ready for us to have sex again. We aren't in the same place we were at six months ago, and I'm finally ready for us to move forward.

"Hey Fee, could you come into the kitchen for a moment?" Cee calls from the doorway to the kitchen.

"Fee?" Jasper mouths to me. Everyone except Cee has only ever called me Phoenix or Nix for short; it hadn't really crossed my mind anyone would notice.

"One sec," I tell Jas, and then I head into the kitchen to see what Cee is after. "What's up?"

"We don't own enough bowls." Cee looks wide-eyed and panicked—over bowls...

"Okay... Can't we use the side plates instead?"

"We only have six side plates."

"What if we use six bowls, and I'll use a side plate?"

"That will look ridiculous. I knew how many people were coming. Why didn't I buy more bowls?" he asks, sounding quite hysterical.

"Because we rarely have more than two guests at a time, so buying more bowls for one dinner is excessive," I point out.

"You are no help. Shoo," he says, shoving me back out of the kitchen. I love him, but he is ludicrous sometimes.

After we've all stuffed ourselves with the birthday cake Alice made (Cee eating his portion on a side plate—the horror!), we all settle into the living room. It turns out Cee's apprehension was unwarranted. The whole evening has been lovely, and it's been nice spending some quality time with my family.

We only have one large sofa and an armchair in the living room, so Cee is sitting on the floor between my legs. I'm playing with his hair, running my fingers through the soft strands, and he leans into the touch. Magnus seems to have befriended Alice and is curled up on her lap, purring away to my right. Jas keeps giving me curious glances, and I'm not sure what that's about.

"Who wants to re-watch Twilight and mock it mercilessly?" Cee asks everyone in the room. He gets an enthusiastic "Yes" from Alice and Jade. Archie just smiles and says, "Sure," while Alfie groans.

"Can't we watch the latest Jurassic World film?" Alfie suggests, hopefully. He's met with a resounding no from the rest of the room.

"As fun as that sounds," Jas says sarcastically, "I'm going to steal the birthday boy for a walk." I get a pit in my stomach because Jas is acting strange.

"Okay, sure," I agree, knowing I need to hear what he has to say because it's already putting me on edge.

"Want us to wait and start the film when you get back?" Cee asks.

TWENTY-FIVE

"Nah, it's okay. You guys go ahead," I reply and kiss the top of his head as I get up.

"I'm just gonna call my parents quickly to make sure Henry settled alright," Jade says to Jasper before giving him a peck on the cheek as she leaves the room.

The weather is fairly mild for late September, but I think it would most definitely be too cold for a late-night walk if we were human. We head down the garden path in silence, and then I lead us towards a footpath that starts across the road. It's a clear night with only a crescent moon, and this far away from any city lights, the stars shine brightly in the sky. It's stunning, and I wish I could take a photo that would do it justice.

"So, why the ominous walk?" I ask nervously after a few minutes. Jas takes a deep breath and then blows it out.

"It's him, isn't it?"

"You'll need to be more specific. What is who?"

"Years ago, when Jade and I were getting our house renovated, we were living at Mum and Dad's for a few months, and you used to sneak out, sometimes all night. You were going to meet Connor, weren't you?" I'm not sure what I was expecting from this conversation, but it wasn't this. I can't even fathom why he'd be thinking back to then; it was so long ago.

"Erm..." I stumble over my words, not sure how to answer this. There seems little point in lying, but I feel as if anything I say will give him more questions than answers. Sighing, I answer him honestly, "Yes. It was him. What on earth made you guess that after all this time?"

"Wow." He blinks at me, wide-eyed. "I kind of figured, but hearing you say it is just... Wow." We walk further down the footpath in silence as he gathers his thoughts. "At first, I thought it was strange how comfortable the two of you seemed so quickly. Then tonight, he kept calling you 'Fee,' like he'd been saying it forever. And his scent has always been so familiar, but I could never quite place from when or where. I assumed I must have crossed paths with him before, and it all sort of clicked tonight." Sometimes, Jas seems like he can't see what's under his own nose, and other times, I'm blown away by how perceptive he is. I exhale a deep breath. It's a lot to explain.

I go with the truth, and I tell him almost everything; how we met, how we were together for almost four years, how we broke up when I got engaged to Niamh, and how we didn't speak again until the day before we got married.

"Why did you agree to marry Niamh? You obviously love him. I don't get why you wouldn't just refuse. They could have found another way."

I debate answering this part honestly. With the Order passed, I can speak about it without gagging on the words, but I don't want to cause a rift. Nevertheless, I also need to know this isn't something Jas will ever do to someone when he becomes Alpha.

"My Alpha Ordered it. I didn't have a choice. Connor still doesn't know." I confess quietly, as though my mum could be hiding around the corner and hear me. I know I've dropped a bombshell on him.

"Mum did fucking, what?" he asks.

"You heard me correctly, Jas." I sigh.

"What the fuck? She broke the law? She violated the pack bond. How could she do that? She's the one who taught me I should *never* do that." Jasper's voice is raised in anger. I don't blame him, but it makes me feel raw to hash it all out again.

"I know, okay? I know. But it's in the past, and we can't change it. I need you to keep this to yourself, though," I plead with him.

"Fuck. How are things okay with you and Connor if he doesn't even know?"

"I think, in his own way, he's forgiven me for it. He cut off all contact with me for a year. Then he spent a week being pretty vicious and horrible to me. And over the last six months, we've sort of just slowly ended up in a better place."

It's the first time I've really acknowledged to myself how huge it is that Cee has forgiven me when he thinks I was going to voluntarily marry his twin sister. I've thought of telling him the truth plenty of times since we got back together, but it feels like picking at a scab that will inevitably get infected, and things are so good between us at the moment.

"Damn. He's a better man than I am. I don't think I'd have moved past that."

"Yeah, I'm very lucky. It got ugly there for a while, but now I'm married to my best friend, so it's hard to be too upset about how we got here," I say with a small smile playing on my lips, remembering how Cee worried himself sick over making a good impression on my family tonight.

"I'm glad you're happy, but I think you should tell him the truth," Jas replies. I'm surprised by the suggestion, given what's at stake if this gets out.

"Why? Surely, the fewer people who know about this, the better."

"I know it came from a good place, but I honestly don't think you had the right to keep that from him. If all that shit had gone down, and I'd only known half the facts, it would have driven me insane, trying to piece it all together." I can feel myself getting defensive, but I don't want to argue. I really don't see what good it would do to tell Cee now, even if I can feel the truth to Jasper's words. I can't go back in time and tell him at a point where knowing could have eased some of his pain. What's done is done. "I didn't say that to make you feel guilty. Most of the time, though, an ugly truth is better than a pretty lie."

He wraps his arm around my shoulder and gives it a squeeze. I don't even know what to say to that. Since we're having a heart-to-heart, I brace myself and ask him something that's been nagging at me for a while.

"Are *you* happy?"

"Sure. Why wouldn't I be?"

"Things with you and Jade have seemed a bit strained ever since the wedding. I thought maybe you'd had a fight that day, but things have felt weird between the two of you ever since. You know you can talk to me, right?" Jasper sighs but doesn't reply right away. We keep walking along the path in silence for a few minutes.

"Things are... complicated. Cee's your mate, isn't he?" he asks, the abrupt topic change, taking me by surprise.

"Yeah, we haven't completed the bond or anything, but he is. Always knew he was, to be honest. Jade isn't yours, is she?"

"No. But we always knew that. I love her, though, more than anything." A sympathetic pit forms in my stomach for my brother.

He's come across his mate, and it isn't his wife.

"Does she know?" He nods. "Do I know them?"

"I'm not really ready to talk about it. I made a commitment to Jade, and I've got Henry to think about." With no words to make the situation any better, I pause on the path and pull him into a hug.

❖❖ •❖• ❖❖

After everyone has gone home, I sneak up behind Cee as he finishes loading the dishwasher.

"Leave it until tomorrow. My plans require you to be in our bed," I whisper in his ear as I wrap my arms around his waist.

"Who am I to deny the birthday boy?" He smirks but turns to face me and wraps his arms around my neck, bringing my lips to his in a soft kiss.

I grab the backs of his thighs, and he wraps his legs around my waist as I carry him up the stairs koala style.

Lowering him onto the mattress, I start to fulfil my promise from earlier. Cee's chest rises and falls quickly, and he gets a pink blush on his cheeks as I slowly undress him. He starts unbuttoning his shirt, but I grab his wrists and pin them to the mattress above his head.

"Oi! Stop trying to unwrap my birthday present," I say playfully.

"How rude of me," he says breathily but with a hint of amusement. I finish unbuttoning his shirt and then undo his belt and trousers. As I pull them off him, I remove his socks and place a kiss on the arch of his foot. I watch as his skin breaks out in goosebumps in response. Palming his cock over his boxer briefs, I watch as a small wet patch appears where his precum seeps through.

As I pull off his underwear, I lick my lips at the sight of his full, hard cock. I gently kiss the tip, and Cee grips the sheets in his fists.

"Jesus, you look so hot laid out for me like this, my favourite dessert," I tell him and then lick a stripe up his shaft. Working my way up his body, I run my tongue along the divot between his abs. I kiss his neck, and my teeth ache to bite him at the juncture between his neck and shoulder.

To mark him so everyone knows he's mine.

When I make it to his mouth, I'm hungry for him. My tongue seeks out his, and I drag my teeth along his bottom lip, tugging on it. I could wax poetic about Cee's bottom lip; it's much fuller than his top and has a line in the centre that makes me want to bite it. The way they go rosy red after bruising kisses, and the way they stretch around me when he sucks my cock, is the stuff of my filthiest dreams.

As I make my way back down his body, I suck and nibble on his nipples until he's mumbling nonsense at me. Each time he tries to touch his cock, I move his hands back above his head. By the time I suck on the tip of his cock, swirling my tongue around the glans, he's writhing under me, and my own dick is aching for release.

CONNOR KELLY

He's trying to torture me.

I'm so turned on that my skin is a raging inferno, and I can hardly form the words I need to tell him to hurry the fuck up and fill me with his cock. He grips my thighs and pushes them back, exposing my hole, but only for a moment before he presses his tongue to me. I groan at the sensation; it's both too much and not enough. He continues to lick and push his tongue inside me, and I'm so overstimulated and desperate to come that a tear rolls down my cheek.

Fee grabs the lube from the bedside table and then pushes his slippery index finger inside me. He's kneeling on the floor with my arse pulled right to the edge of the bed, intently watching as his finger plunges in and out of me. Fee has always gotten off on watching any part of himself moving in and out of my hole. Back when we first started having sex, I used to get a bit self-conscious, but it's hard to feel that way at present when his pupils are blown wide with desire, and he looks at me like I'm the centre of his universe.

Once he's added more lube, a second finger joins the first, and he starts stretching me out. As usual, Fee is stubbornly more thorough than I can take when it comes to prepping me.

"Please, just fuck me already," I stammer, already feeling completely wrecked. I can't take the build-up anymore.

"No. We haven't done this in a long time. I'm going to make sure you're ready," Fee says, and his tone leaves no room for argument. I'm tempted to point out that with shifter healing, even if we went too fast,

I'd be healed before we even finished. However, the past would indicate he will not take that as a good enough reason, so I try to be patient—to be good for him.

I'm so fucking horny right now that I'm riding his fingers, desperate and pleading for more. Fee changes the angle so he's grazing his fingertips over my prostate, and my hips buck up off the bed.

"Fuck. Please hurry up. I'm gonna die if I don't come soon." The words spill out of my mouth in a garbled mess, but he adds a third finger, so I know we're almost there.

Once Fee's content I'm sufficiently prepped, he pours the lube onto his throbbing cock. He grabs a pillow, shoving it under my hips and pulls me to the edge of the mattress where he's standing. Lining his cock up with my hole, he slowly pushes inside me. I'm so aroused right now he thrusts all the way into me with ease.

I revel in the sensation of being so full. The way my rim stretches around him, and I can feel him everywhere. There's something peaceful about all my thoughts centring on how he's so deep inside me, filling me. Encompassing me entirely.

"Baby, you're so tight. Give me a second, or this is going to be over way too fast," Fee says, and he closes his eyes, taking deep breaths. I can't help but laugh at his look of concentration, causing me to clench around him. "Fuck, fuck, fuck. Don't do that," he groans. I tug on my cock gently, not enough to give me any real relief, but just enough friction to take the edge off. Fee looks down at where our bodies are joined and—fucking finally—starts moving.

He goes slow, pulling almost all the way out before sliding all the way back in again. It's sweet, sweet torture as the head of his dick pegs my prostate, and I shift my hips to try and seek out more of the sensation. Keeping the same angle so he hits me just right, his thrusts get faster and faster. I can feel the pressure building inside me, my orgasm close—too close.

"Fuck, I'm not gonna last long if you keep fuckin' me like this."

Fee pulls out and crawls onto the bed. He sits so his back is to the headboard with his legs stretched out in front of him.

"Ride me," he says, panting. I move quickly, straddling him backwards because I know he'll enjoy the view as I slide up and down his length. I ride him slowly at first, enjoying the change in sensation in this position. When I sink all the way to the base of his cock, I feel impossibly full. Fee grabs my hips, his fingertips digging in as he encourages me to ride him faster.

I moan loudly and grab the lube. Covering my cock in the slippery liquid, I jerk myself off—hard and fast. When Fee begins to thrust up into me, my orgasm builds quickly.

"Fuck, I'm gonna come. Don't stop," I tell him. Seconds later, every muscle in my body tenses before releasing, cum shooting out of me and covering my hand. My chest heaves, and my feet are tingling. All my nerves are firing like sparks of electricity forking in every direction underneath my skin.

As I return to earth, Fee is still pounding into me relentlessly; it's almost too much. I'm over sensitive from coming, but I can tell Fee's close, so I help tip him over the edge.

"I can't wait for you to fill me with your cum. I want to feel you dripping out of me all night," I say as I clench around him. His movements stutter, and then his cock is pulsating, his cum shooting deep inside me.

"Holy shit. Fuck," and some other garbled nonsense comes out of Fee's mouth as his orgasm slams into him.

He leans forward and kisses the back of my neck and shoulders, his tongue licking at the beads of sweat there. I feel sex drunk and groan as I lean forward, Fee's cock slipping out of me. He rubs his thumb over my rim, gently massaging it.

"I really love seeing my cum dripping out of you." I can sense his eyes on me. I bear down slightly so some more of it leaks out. I let out a gasp when he uses his fingers to push it back inside me again.

"Am I too old to have a new kink?" he asks.

I gasp, "I don't think so. What's your new kink?"

"This. I think I could keep playing with my cum in your hole all night." My cock perks up again at his words, and I turn to face him.

"Apparently, I'm also into that." We both laugh as he sees me getting hard again.

Eventually, Fee gets up and grabs a flannel from the bathroom. Something I've always loved about when we have sex is how he takes care of me afterwards. He wipes up my abs and chest before gently pressing the warm cloth to my rim. I make a contented 'mmm' sound at the feel of the warm water on my sensitive hole. Once he's cleaned me up, he chucks the flannel into the laundry basket and then climbs back into bed. Fee switches off the lamp on the bedside table, and I snuggle into his side, my head on his chest. I love listening to his heart beating rhythmically, reminding me this is all real.

"I'm sorry it took so long for me to be ready to do this again," he whispers before pressing a soft kiss to my head.

"Let's not be sorry anymore. Let's just love each other."

TWENTY-SIX
September 2022

CONNOR KELLY

"How come you're up so early?" Fee asks as he walks into the kitchen, where I'm nursing a cup of coffee. I'm not a morning person, and he's usually up long before me.

"Couldn't sleep. Kept havin' weird dreams." I sound like a small child, but I can't seem to shake the feeling that something isn't quite right.

"What about?"

"Dunno. Don't remember exactly; just have this horrible anxious feeling in my chest." I press the heel of my palm into my sternum trying to massage the sensation away.

"Maybe you ate something funny," Fee suggests.

"I'm anxious; I don't have fuckin' indigestion," I snap at him, and he deserves it. I might be grumpy from lack of sleep, but that is one of the stupidest things he's ever said. "I thought you were meant to be the smart one in this relationship."

"Sorry, sorry. That was unhelpful." He kisses my head on his way to the coffee pot.

"On this occasion, you may live to see another day." Although, I notice he doesn't disagree that he's the smarter of the two of us. Rude.

TWENTY-SIX

Fee left for work hours ago, but I still can't shake this nagging feeling something is wrong. I give Niamh a call to check on her and Will, which makes me feel somewhat better.

It's not raining for once, so I go for a walk to see if some fresh air will get me out of this funk. Wandering down to the village, I pop into the small local supermarket to pick up some milk and eggs since we're running low. I swear Fee eats a whole pack of eggs each day. He's a bottomless pit.

On my way home, I take a slight detour to pop in on Archie to see how he's getting on. We haven't seen him since Fee's birthday meal over a week ago.

I knock on Archie's front door and wait a few minutes, but he doesn't come to the door. That's odd; it's a Monday, and he's usually working from home. Pulling my phone out, I give him a call, but it goes straight to voicemail. I try Fee next.

"Hey, babe, what's up?" he asks when the call connects. I must have caught him during a free period.

"Hey, when did you last speak to Archie?" The ball of nerves in my stomach grows by the second.

"Erm, not sure. Let me check my phone, one sec." I wait while he faffs on the other end of the line. "Oh. Not since he was over at ours the weekend before last. How come?"

Dread claws at my insides. I can't pinpoint why because I know there are a million good reasons why he might not be home at the moment and not answering his phone, but something in my gut is screaming at me that this is bad.

"It's probably nothin'. I popped by his place, and he's not answerin'. Then I tried to call him, but it went straight to voicemail," I say, hoping

Fee will reassure me and point out how I'm overreacting. He hums thoughtfully.

"That's pretty unusual for him. You don't think anyone from his old pack could have tracked him here, do you?" That wasn't even something I'd considered, but now I can add it to my growing list of concerns. Great, love that for me.

"No idea. I know this probably sounds stupid, but I have a really horrible feelin' about this, Fee."

"It doesn't sound stupid. Sometimes, our instincts tell us things we can't see. His landlord is Mrs Jones. She lives next door. Why don't you ask for the spare key and check everything looks normal inside?" He suggests. It's a good idea, actually; I should have thought of it. At the very least, once I've seen everything is fine inside, I can stop jumping to conclusions.

I knock on the neighbour's house, and a woman who looks to be in her late eighties comes to the front door.

"Hi, I'm Connor. I'm a friend of Archie who's letting one of the flats next door."

"Hello, dear. Yes, lovely young man is Archie. How can I help you?" she says in a thick Yorkshire accent.

"I just wanted to check if you've seen him recently?" I ask, and I really hope she has.

"Let me have a think. Last Thursday, I think it was, he picked up some tea bags for me from the shops." I feel somewhat relieved. That was only four days ago. He's probably out for a walk or something.

"I'm sorry to bother you, but I haven't seen or heard from him and I'm a little worried. He's not answerin' when I knock, and he's usually workin' from home at this time. Is there any chance I can borrow your spare key to make sure he's okay?" She understandably takes a moment to consider. She doesn't know me, and I could be asking for the wrong reasons.

"I shouldn't, really, but he has mentioned you and your husband to me a few times and said you're good friends of his. Is it okay if I come with you?"

"Yes, of course." I'm not entirely sure what she thinks she could do to stop me if I was, in fact, here to ransack the place, but I appreciate she seems to have Archie's back.

Mrs Jones walks ahead of me to Archie's with the key in hand. She turns the key in the lock and opens the door, calling out Archie's name.

"Stop!" I tell her suddenly, pressing a hand to her shoulder to prevent her from going any further.

The second she opened the door, I could smell it.

Death.

I don't know what we'll find inside, but I know it won't be good.

"Sorry. Do you mind waitin' here for a moment while I check inside?" I ask, and I'm grateful when she agrees without too much fuss.

I hold my breath as I step inside the flat. Everything looks normal in the living room, and I can already tell the smell is coming from the bedroom.

I take a brief moment to look around at the home Archie has made for himself here in only a few short months. He doesn't have many belongings, but the flat came furnished. There are a few plants he bought when he and Fee went to the garden centre a few weeks ago—all perfectly tended to. On the windowsill sits a framed photograph of the three of us. We're all wide smiles and windswept hair at the top of Pen-y-ghent. My heart cracks at the memory; we were so sure that day was the start of something. The start of our new pack.

I'm hesitant to go into the bedroom. As if I can delay reality if I haven't seen it with my own eyes. I cast a final glance around and head towards the closed door.

Fuck, fuck, fuck, fuck, fuck.

I choke on a sob when I open the bedroom door.

Archie is lying on the bed. His head is at such an angle that his neck is clearly broken.

I promised to keep him safe. I let him down.

He's the first and only member of our pack, and I didn't keep him safe. I dig the heel of my palms into my stinging eyes, trying to keep my tears at bay until I've done what needs to be done.

Stepping closer, I spot the half-read paperback I'd loaned to him. My anguish quickly turns to fury as I ask myself who could possibly have wanted to harm a man as kind and gentle as Archie. The man who wouldn't even get up to fetch himself a drink of water if Magnus was curled up asleep on him. The man who came over every single week with a tray of baked goods just because. He'd obviously been dealt some shitty cards growing up, but he was making progress. Damn it, he was healing! Each time I saw him, he'd come out of his shell a tiny bit more.

"I promise I'll find out who did this to you, Archie. I'm so sorry," I whisper to his lifeless body.

I take a moment to gather myself before heading back to the entryway.

"I'm sorry, Mrs Jones, but I'm going to have to call the police. I found Archie in his room, but it looks like he passed away a few days ago," I explain as calmly as I can manage. She gasps and looks at me in total shock. I press my hand to her back, gently guiding her back towards her house. "Do you think you could make us both a cup of tea, and I'll contact the police?" I'm hoping if I give her something to do, she won't go into shock or anything. I also don't want her to overhear me on the phone.

"Oh god. I can't believe it. " She stumbles over her words but makes her way towards her kitchen.

"I'm just going to pop outside to make some phone calls," I tell her before ducking out.

"Did you find him?" Fee asks when he answers the call.

"Yes. He's gone, Fee. Someone's killed him." I can't even believe the words I'm saying are true.

"What? What the fuck? Why? Shit, I'm leaving work now. What can I do?"

"I'm not sure. I can't call the police, but his landlady knows, so it needs to at least *look* as if the police have been around to investigate. I could ask my da maybe, he'll have contact details for higher-ups at the police who know about us."

"Alice's cousin Oliver is a police detective in the North East. I'll try him first. Do you think it was someone from his pack?"

"Okay, yeah. Good idea. I don't see who else it could be. How long will you be?"

"Around forty minutes. Should I meet you there?"

"Yes, please. I love you," I add, needing him to know so badly right now.

"I love you too, baby. I'll be there with you soon."

I step back inside Mrs Jones' house. She's sitting at a small round table in her kitchen with a pot of tea and two tea cups in front of her. She looks up as I walk in and tries to pour the tea, but her frail hands keep shaking.

"Here, let me," I say, taking over. I add a big splash of milk to both cups, "Do you take any sugar?" I ask softly.

"Just one, please," she says barely above a whisper, sounding stunned. Using the little metal tongs in the pot, I pick up a sugar lump and stir it into her cup. We sit at the table in silence until my phone vibrates, alerting me to a new message.

> **Fee:** Spoken to Oliver. He'll be at Archie's flat in a few hours. I'm 30 minutes away xxx

PHOENIX CAMPBELL

Cee and I are in my car outside Archie's place after dropping Mrs Jones at her daughter's house about twenty minutes away. We're sitting in stunned silence as we wait for Oliver to arrive. Cee's head rests on my shoulder, and his hand is encased in mine. I haven't been in the flat; it might be selfish of me, but I don't want to remember Archie that way. He was quiet and kind, with a dry sense of humour once he was comfortable around you.

When Oliver shows up a few hours later in a BMW with blacked-out windows, I'm surprised to see Noah getting out of the passenger side. Cee and I make our way out of the car to greet them both.

"Hey, thanks for coming," I say to Oliver and introduce him to Cee. Noah steps forward and pulls his cousin into a hug.

"I didn't know you were coming," Cee mumbles into Noah's shoulder.

"Nina's away, so I'm minding her shop. Oliver explained what'd happened, so..." He gestures to himself as though his joining was the only forgone conclusion.

"In here?" Oliver asks, and Cee nods his head.

"We'll wait out here if that's okay." I pull Cee into my arms; he doesn't need to see his friend like that again.

Just over half an hour later, Noah appears first and explains Oliver will be here for a while, so we drive back to our cottage. I drop Oliver a text with our address to join us after he's done.

⇛ ✦ ⇚

Noah and I sit in the living room while Cee puts the kettle on. I offered to do it, but he said he needed to keep busy.

"That's Magnus," I tell Noah when our tiny black feline makes a home on his lap. "Connor found him abandoned, so now we have a cat." Noah nods, clearly knowing his cousin well enough to understand that I was getting a stray whether I liked it or not.

A few minutes later, Cee joins us in the living room and hands out cups of tea. He sits down on the carpeted floor at my feet, leaning against the backs of my legs. He tips his head back, and I run my fingers through his shaggy black hair. I can feel Noah's gaze on us, trying to make sense of our easy affection when, to the outside world, we're strangers in an arranged marriage. Right now, though, I can't bring myself to care. Cee needs this, and so do I. Need the reminder he's here and he's safe, solid beneath my hand.

Several hours have passed by the time there's a knock on the front door. Cee gets up to answer it before returning, with Oliver trudging in behind him. It must have started to rain because Oliver's blonde curls look a shade darker.

"Sorry I took so long. I had to speak to a friend of mine about running some of the forensics off the books."

"No problem. Can I get you anythin' to drink?" Cee asks.

"Sure. Coffee, please—milk, no sugar."

When Cee returns with another round of drinks, Oliver gets right to it.

"I've got someone who will come down later tonight to dust for prints and check for any DNA samples before I get a clean-up crew in."

"What'll happen to his body?" Cee asks.

"I can arrange for the body to be disposed of." Cee and I both flinch at the callous statement.

"No. We'll bury him and have a proper funeral. He deserves a real send-off by people who care about him," Cee says firmly. I grab his hand and interlace our fingers, nodding my agreement.

Oliver asks us some questions about who might have wanted to harm Archie. It's hard to comprehend anyone wanting to harm him, but we explain that he's the son of Alpha Fraser and how he came to us beaten up and injured back in July. I suppose that'll give him somewhere to start his enquiry.

"Do you two need to stay here tonight? We only have one spare room," I ask. Thankfully, we replaced the infamous airbed with a double when Archie first came to live here.

"I'll need to drive Noah back to the shop, I assume, but thanks."

"It's fine, stay. I can get myself home," Noah replies. Oliver has a confused expression on his face.

"Noah can teleport," Cee explains, and Noah snorts as though he disagrees with the description. It's news to me.

"You can?" Oliver and I ask incredulously at the same time.

"Mhmm." Noah doesn't elaborate.

"Shit, that's cool," I blurt out.

"It's convenient. And on that note..." Noah says, standing up to leave, "Let me know when you're visiting the Fraser pack, I'll come with you," the latter is directed at Oliver, whose eyes narrow in response, but he nods his agreement eventually.

⇝ ⋅⋅◆⋅⋅ ⇜

TWENTY-SIX

The following morning, I wake up to an empty bed. Opening the curtains, I'm met with a grey, drizzly day; Oliver's car isn't out there, so he must have left already. When I enter the kitchen, I find Cee on his hands and knees, scrubbing the skirting boards quite aggressively. He looks up at me, his big green eyes red-rimmed with sadness and exhaustion.

"Please don't ask if I'm okay."

"Did you sleep at all?" I ask instead. Cee doesn't reply, which gives me my answer. Unsure of what I could possibly do to help ease his pain, I grab a spare sponge from under the sink and join him on the kitchen floor, starting on the section he hasn't got to yet.

An hour later, the entire kitchen has been thoroughly deep cleaned within an inch of its life.

"We should do the living room next," Cee suggests, determined to run his exhausted body into the ground.

"No, enough now. Come with me," I say, taking his hand and tugging him back upstairs. I pull him into the bathroom and turn on the hot tap. As the tub fills, I add some bubble bath and salts to the water.

Wordlessly, I begin to undress him, taking my time. He lifts his arms to help me take his t-shirt off, and I plant a soft kiss over his heart. I tug down his jogging bottoms and boxers and gently kiss his hip bone. By the time I've removed his socks, the bath has enough water in it.

Cee climbs into the tub, and I quickly take off the athletic shorts I'd shoved on this morning. He scooches forward so I can slide into the bath behind him. I lather up the loofah and gently rub it in slow circles over his chest. I lift each of his arms to clean his underarms and then rinse the soap off. He sits forward slightly when I nudge him so I can massage the shampoo into his scalp and hair before rinsing it off.

While I leave the conditioner in his hair for a few minutes, I rub his shoulders, digging my thumbs into the knotted muscles, and he slowly begins to relax under my ministrations. Once he's all rinsed off, we get out of the bath and I grab a big, fluffy grey towel to dry him off with.

Back in the bedroom, I fetch us both a clean pair of boxers—whose is whose is anybody's guess at this point. But when I pull back the duvet, Cee shakes his head at me.

"I can't, Fee. Every time I close my eyes... I... I just see..."

"Come on, I have an idea." Connecting my phone to the bedside speaker, I put on the audiobook of *The Colour of Magic* by Terry Pratchett; it was one of Connor's favourites when he was younger. "You don't have to sleep, but you *do* need to rest. I'll stay right here, and if you can't sleep, listen to the book. But if you doze off, I'll be right here when you wake up. I won't go anywhere, I promise."

Cee curls up on his side, and I wrap myself around him, trying to cocoon him from all the awful shit in the world. He only manages to fight his exhaustion for a few minutes before he falls asleep in my arms.

TWENTY-SEVEN
OCTOBER 2022

PHOENIX CAMPBELL

We laid Archie's body to rest yesterday. Jasper, Alice, Niamh and Will joined Cee and me as we said our goodbyes. And Alice is staying with us for a few days. It's nice having her here; Alice lived next door to me for most of my life, and I've missed having her close by. She's currently lying on her front on the living room floor, trying to entice Magnus into chasing after a ball of tinfoil. Magnus seems less than impressed since he's already investigated the foil and is fully aware no food is contained within it. I never saw myself becoming a cat person, but I'm quite enamoured with this particular fluffball. I also love how he turns Cee into a total marshmallow.

"Where's Connor?" Alice asks. He was gone when we got home from a run in the woods.

"He's out working on some secret project he won't tell me about."

"Why's it a secret?"

"No idea; he won't tell me. He's been working on it for a few months; that's all I know."

"You are such a guy. I don't know a single woman who wouldn't have found out exactly what he's up to." Alice raises an eyebrow at me, silently asking permission to investigate this.

"Nope. Contain your nosiness. He'll let me know what it is when he's good and ready."

"Ugh. You're so annoyingly mature and reasonable. It's boring. What happened to the guy who spent years sleeping with the enemy in secret?" she asks, trying to bait me. I sigh.

"He ended up engaged to his boyfriend's sister and had enough drama to last a lifetime. Things with me and Connor are finally in a good place again, so I'm enjoying it while it lasts." I laugh lightly.

"Are you ever going to tell him what your mum did?" I groan because I just want to leave the past in the past, and everyone seems to insist on dragging it back up again.

"I thought about it not long after we got married. But then, eventually, we ended up sorting through things, and now it feels like I'd be picking at a gnarly scab. Also, Connor is hot-tempered. There's nothing to say he wouldn't lose his shit and end up outing my mum, and there's nothing to be gained from that."

What I don't tell her is how even though I genuinely believe it's for the best Cee doesn't know what my mum did; keeping the secret from him eats at me, especially since my conversation with Jasper last month. I can't help but think that when we started over with a clean slate, he should have known the real reason we ended up there in the first place.

"I want to join your pack," Alice says, and my jaw drops.

"What? But your parents? Your brother?" I ask, stammering and gobsmacked.

"I have family in your mum's pack. I have family in the Eastwood pack. But my best friend is in *this* pack." I swallow the lump in my throat. Alice is practically a sister to me at this point, and as much as I think it will cause some tension with my mum if she leaves, I can't deny I wouldn't love having her nearby again.

"Are you sure, though? Me and Connor don't currently have the greatest track record for pack members..." She gives me a wide-eyed look and smacks my shin closest to her.

"Jesus, Nix, that's dark. I can't stay in the Lake District. I know you've decided to put the past in the past, but I don't want an Alpha who will abuse their power." She looks determined, and I know she won't budge on this. I feel guilty for being the one who told her what my mum did.

"Alice—"

"No, don't 'Alice' me. Your mum broke the law, Nix. She Alpha Ordered her own son into getting married, and I'll keep your secret, but I can't live under her thumb when I know the truth." I don't argue with her because I know there's no point. Before I can respond, though, the front door slams shut loudly, and I wince.

Cee doesn't come into the living room right away; he clatters in the kitchen. His lack of a greeting doesn't bode well for me. This probably makes me a terrible person, but I'm kind of hoping Alice's presence will keep him at a simmer rather than boiling over.

"Babe, there's leftovers in the fridge for you," I shout, testing the waters. He appears in the doorway, and his eyes look ablaze with fury.

"Keep your leftovers. I hope you fuckin' choke on them, *Phoenix!*" I visibly flinch at the use of my full name, which is never a good sign, and he stomps back into the kitchen.

"I should probably leave the two of you to talk," Alice says, petting Magnus' head and getting up from the floor.

"Don't leave on my account, Alice. Doesn't sound like there's anythin' Phoenix and I could talk about that you don't already know more about than *I* do," Cee spits, reappearing again. He's a pacer when he's mad, and I get the impression he doesn't feel the downstairs of our house is sufficient room for this endeavour.

Shit, I knew, deep down, I just knew this would bite me in the arse one day.

"Leave while you still can," I mouth at Alice, who quickly makes her way upstairs to grab her stuff.

I take a deep breath to try and steady myself. The only thing I can do is tell him the whole truth and hope he can forgive me. He promised he didn't have a foot out of the door anymore, but I'm still worried it wouldn't take much for him to leave.

I say a quick goodbye to Alice and find Cee in the kitchen, time to face the music. He's leaning against the kitchen counter, a tight grip on the granite worktop.

"Babe, can we sit down and talk? I don't want to fight with you," I say, desperately trying to reason with him. I can't go back to the way things were in the spring.

"Would you have gone through with it otherwise?" Cee asks, and he's seething, pacing back and forth across the small kitchen.

"The marriage? Of course not."

"I thought…I really thought. Fuck. How could you keep this from me?"

"At first, I physically couldn't tell you. And then after, it seemed cruel to, when it wouldn't really change anything." I try to keep my voice calm, like I'm trying not to spook a cornered animal. I see some of the fight leave him, and his shoulders droop; he looks deflated, which is somehow worse.

"I really believed you when you told me you loved me."

"Huh? I *do* love you, babe; I've loved you for five years. I've never loved anyone else. This doesn't change how I feel about you at all."

"So you love me, but you wouldn't have married me?" He sounds so broken, and I don't understand why. I get him being pissed at me for keeping this from him, but I don't see why it's making him question my feelings for him. My feelings for him have never wavered, not once.

"I don't understand why you think that. I told you years ago I wanted to marry you, that never changed. It broke my fucking heart when we got married, knowing you didn't want to be there." I've never told him that before. How horrific it is to finally marry the love of your life while knowing they wished they were anywhere else but there. His brow scrunches up in confusion—him and me both.

"You aren't makin' any sense! You literally just said you wouldn't have married me if your mum hadn't Ordered it." His voice is raised, and he sounds exasperated, which, now I'm catching on, is understandable.

I'm an idiot...

"Oh fuck. No. Baby, I'm sorry, I'm so sorry. I didn't mean to make you think that." I try to bring him into my chest to hug him, but he grips my arms and keeps me away. "My mum didn't Alpha Order me to marry *you*. She Ordered me to marry Niamh." I see the moment the revelation sinks in, and he looks up at me through teary eyes. His bottom lip trembles slightly, and I hate that even for a second, he thought I hadn't married him of my own free will.

"Nobody made you marry me?" His voice is quiet, barely more than a whisper.

"Nobody. And I know it wasn't how we planned to get married, but I have never regretted a single day I've been able to call you my husband," I tell him, and this time, when I try to hug him, he lets me. I press my lips to his forehead and inhale his scent. How can I ever be surprised by his fiery temper when he's always smelled like a storm brewing.

I pull Cee towards the living room, but when I take a seat on the sofa, he sits on the far end with his knees pulled up to his chest. Cee's five foot ten and muscly from a labour-intensive job, but he looks small and vulnerable curled up in the corner. It makes my chest ache. I want to reach out and comfort him, but he's chosen space, so I know I need to respect that.

"You still should have told me," he says in a quiet but firm voice.

"You're right, I should have." I go on to explain why I'd chosen not to, not wanting to break up my family. I explain how even after me and Alice looked through every book we could get our hands on, we couldn't find a way out of it. He looks even more surprised when I tell him how we sought out Noah to see if there was a spell to undo it.

"You let me believe you'd given up on us. I thought I wasn't enough for you."

My stomach drops at his words. I really hate myself right now.

"I'm so sorry. I *hate* that I made you feel that way. But I hope you believe me when I tell you that in my whole life, I've never wanted anyone but you. I love you so much, and I know it's my fault you doubted that, but I will show you every single day until we're old and wrinkly and can't get it up anymore." He lets out a small wet laugh but then looks cross with himself for it. "Please come here. We've been through too much for this to be the thing that ruins us. Please come here and let me hold you?" My voice is needy, but I can't bring myself to care. There's a knot of anxiety in my stomach threatening to make my dinner reappear, and I know it won't settle until he's back in my arms. Cee shakes his head, and a tear slips from his dark lashes, rolling down his cheek.

"I need to process this, and I can't just wrap myself up in you to put a temporary plaster on it. The year we were apart was the worst year of my life." His breath hitches, and guilt sits in my stomach like a heavy stone. "I was so depressed some days I didn't even make it into work, Phoenix. And now you're tellin' me all of that was for nothin'? There was no good reason we weren't together durin' that time."

"I tried to reach out to you. You wouldn't speak to me, wouldn't answer the phone, ignored all my texts," I try to reason with him.

"If I'd answered the phone, would you have told me the truth?"

"I don't know. Maybe," I say, trying to be as honest with him as possible. I never intended to tell him, but sometimes I think I would have eventually if it was the only way to get him back.

"Fuck. Somehow, it's worse to know that." He gets up from the sofa and wipes his wet cheek with his sleeve.

"Are you going to bed?"

"No, I'm goin' for a run. I need some space to think and clear my head." The pit in my stomach grows a stem that tangles in my throat until I'm choking on it.

"You're not going to leave me, are you?" I ask, hating how pathetic I sound. I can't lose him over this.

I only just got him back.

"You're my husband," he replies, but that doesn't really answer my question.

TWENTY-EIGHT
October 2022

PHOENIX CAMPBELL

After Cee leaves, I can't seem to settle. Even once I've loaded and set the dishwasher off, wiped down all the sides, and changed Magnus' litter, he's still not home. I may as well go and feel sorry for myself in bed where it's comfortable. I make a little 'psp psp' noise at Magnus for him to follow me up to bed, but the traitor looks at me as if to say he'll come upstairs when *his* person comes home.

I really hope he does come home.

I wouldn't put it past him to run all the way to Niamh and Will's, just to get space from me. Logically, I know none of this is Will's fault, but even the idea of Connor going to Will for comfort and telling him what a shitty husband I am, makes me want to peel my own skin off.

I climb into the shower to kill some more time. Unfortunately, standing under the hot spray of water with nothing but my own thoughts is not the distraction I was hoping for. Maybe if I scrub hard enough, I can wash this entire night away—if only.

My skin has gone pink from the scalding water, so I steal some of Cee's moisturiser and rub it into my arms and chest. I throw on some boxers before I climb onto the bed and bury my face into Cee's pillow. His scent

TWENTY-EIGHT

is strong on it, and the smell is both comforting and makes my chest ache that he's not lying in the bed next to me.

What if I've really fucked it up this time? He managed to forgive me when he thought I had actually agreed to marry his sister, only to find out I'd kept the truth from him all this time. I'm not sure I'd forgive me if I were in his shoes. I should have listened to Jasper and come clean sooner. He should have heard the truth directly from me, not from overhearing a conversation with Alice.

With my spiralling thoughts circling the drain, I accept I won't be getting much sleep tonight. I grab my phone and stick on a podcast, curling up on Cee's side of the bed because it smells of him. I really hope he comes home soon so I can make this right.

I must have dozed off eventually. But when I wake up, I realise something is desperately wrong. My eyes are streaming when I open them.

They're streaming because the room is filled with smoke.

Thick, lung-clogging smoke.

My brain is screaming at my muscles to move, to flee, to escape, to do anything except lie here, motionless. Adrenaline pumps through my veins, but my body is frozen in place. I can't move a muscle. It's strange how quickly I accept my fate; all I can hope for right now is that if I die in this fire, Connor isn't the one to find me.

The horrible sensation dredges up an old memory I had long forgotten. I was only a child, maybe eight years old at the time. I had woken up in the middle of the night, unable to move a muscle or make a noise. Silent tears soaked my cheeks as I hoped and wished my dad would come and find me and make the awful feeling of being locked in my mind go away.

The next morning, when I had reawoken, this time to the sun shining through the gaps in my jungle-themed curtains, it felt like nothing more than a bad dream. The nightmare had faded into the recesses of my mind, and this was the first time I'd thought of that night since.

This feels almost the same but different. It's worse somehow that I can open my eyes and look around the room, but my muscles are frozen in place.

In my periphery, the flames are spreading along the carpet, licking at the hem of the curtains, hundreds of fiery tongues eating through the fabric rapidly. Too rapidly. My eyes close instinctively, the thick, relentless smoke making them red-raw.

If I'm lucky, the smoke will kill me before the fire does. Bile rises up my oesophagus at the thought of being awake when the flames engulf me. I've never considered myself to be particularly morbid, rarely dwelling on how I might eventually die. In contrast, I now find myself evaluating and ranking what kind of death would be preferable over another. In the face of being burned alive, I can confirm I would take most of the alternatives right about now.

Except maybe a death involving a deadly spider—I really hate spiders.

With nothing to do but lie here and wait for it all to be over, my overactive brain won't switch off. I find myself praying the authorities discover my body before he does. Nobody should have to find their loved one's charred remains in the bed they shared together.

Part of me regrets that we argued earlier, and he's pissed off with me, but that's why I'm alone while he's out running off his bad temper. So I've also never been so grateful for his short fuse because although it won't be fun to die here by myself, it would be a hundred times worse to watch him suffer by my side. He'll be furious with me for dying before him, but I'm grateful he'll have a long life ahead of him.

When I reopen my eyes, the curtains are fully ablaze. The bedroom window makes a loud cracking noise, shattering from the intense heat. I try to take deep breaths, inhaling as much of the smoke as I can, willing it to end my life before the fire does. My chest rattles when I cough, and my eyes burn and water furiously.

Closing my eyes once more, I decide it's probably best to keep them that way. All I can do is wait and see what takes me first—the smoke or the flames.

CONNOR KELLY

Karma is real, and she's a fucking bitch.

I was so smug and self-righteous about how graciously I'd forgiven Fee, and now it turns out I'm the arsehole!

Okay, maybe not that graciously, but still, I'd gotten there in the end.

However, now it seems I might have avoided both of us spending over a year, heartbroken, if only I'd answered my fucking phone.

But also, no, fuck him. He could have found a way to tell me.

Realistically, my resolve to stay angry over this won't last very long. Once I go home and Fee wraps his big, sexy arms around me, I'll melt faster than an English snowman. So I'm running all the way to Kettlewell to at least give the pretence I'm not going to forgive this easily. I used to be so good at holding grudges, great even; this one feels like water slipping through my fingers too quickly to hold onto.

I can't quite decide if that makes me more stubborn or less so.

A rabbit darts suddenly in my periphery, and giving into my instincts, I chase it. I'm not going to kill it; just spook it a little. When I was younger, my mum used to tell me off for chasing prey animals, but I won't actually catch it. The rabbit disappears down into a burrow, so I slow down. It's late, must be past midnight, and the ground feels cold under my paws.

Slightly further on from Kettlewell is Starbottom, which never fails to amuse me, even when I'm determined to be a mardy bastard. I huff a laugh at the sign and debate whether I should turn back and go home. Fee has to be up early for work tomorrow, and I know he won't sleep properly until I get home, so that makes the decision for me.

Am I growing up? Look at me being a fucking adult for once.

The truth is that as much as I have a penchant for stewing in my own anger, I don't really want to stay mad at Fee over this. Between losing my mum as a kid and Archie just last week, I know first-hand how much we aren't guaranteed time with the people we love. With my mind a bit clearer from my run, I can see how the whole thing was just an almighty clusterfuck.

Fee did what he felt he had to do. And with the information I had, I did what I felt I needed to do. Realising I really don't want to squander any more time being bitter about the past, I hightail it back home.

Barely over halfway home, as I'm skirting around the edge of Grimwith Reservoir, a sharp pain like a bolt of lightning shoots through my chest. Looking down at myself, I half expect to see blood, but the air is completely still, and to look at me, nothing is wrong.

But everything is wrong.

A phantom hand wraps around my heart, squeezing it painfully in a vice-like grip. My head starts to pound. I search my mind for my pack bond with Fee, and the feeling of sheer terror hits me like a bullet train through the bond. My stomach swoops, adrenaline coursing through me faster than I thought possible. With no time to waste, I choke down the panic and set off sprinting for home at breakneck speed.

My mind is racing with all the different possibilities of what could be wrong. I keep searching the bond for more information, but nothing comes. All I know is he's in danger, and I mean mortal danger. Even with every muscle in my body straining at the speed I'm running, it's still not fast enough. *Not you, too, Fee. I can't lose you too.*

My mind keeps playing over our last conversation. If I wasn't so determined to get back to him, I'd bash my own head in for my stupidity. All he asked of me when I left the house tonight was reassurance I would come back, and my response was fucking manipulative. Finding out the truth had hurt me, so I hurt him back. I'd wanted him to agonise a little, worry I might leave. I need Fee to be okay just so he can punch me in the face for being such a raging arsehole.

Ten minutes from home, and the smell hits me.

Smoke.

I've never felt this much dread and fear in my life, and my limbs are screaming at me from the exertion, but I push on even harder. All the while desperately hoping the smoke isn't coming from our home, and knowing it almost certainly is.

My worst nightmares are confirmed when I make it up the last hill towards our cottage and choke on the thick black smoke the wind is blowing towards me. My heart is in my throat when our house finally comes into view.

No.

No, no, no, no, no. It can't be.

In the front garden, Magnus is mewling, and I've never been so glad that while I was desperately keeping busy to distract myself after Archie's death, I fitted a catflap in the front door. My relief at seeing Magnus is short-lived when I realise there's no sign of Fee out here. The little cottage we've called home these past six months is engulfed in flames. I know there's a good chance I'm already too late, but I have to try and save him.

I stay in my wolf form because I'll heal faster this way, and I make a run for the front door, my hefty weight knocking it off its hinges. The smoke billows out, and the heat is stifling. I can't see a thing as I try to navigate my way through the house from memory alone.

Unable to shout out Fee's name, I howl loudly, hoping for some sign of life. It's unlikely Fee would have ended up trapped in the house if he'd been downstairs, so I make my way to the first floor as quickly as possible.

Breathing becomes harder and harder as I inhale the thick smoke, choking on the fumes. Trying to keep my body as low to the ground as possible, I aim for our bedroom. The wooden door splinters as I barge through, and I finally dare to open my eyes again.

Fee is lying utterly motionless on the bed. The curtains are completely ablaze, and the bedsheets are already alight. His skin is pink and shiny from the obscene temperature, and I'm petrified I'm already too late.

Then the smell hits me. It's not just smoke in here.

I can smell burned flesh—Fee's burned flesh.

I swallow the vomit that rises up my throat and focus on how I'm going to get him out of here.

Shifting quickly, I punch my fist through the window, which already has a crack in it from the extreme heat. Thankfully, it shatters easily. I turn Fee onto his side and shift back. In one swift movement that will possibly kill us both, I bite down onto his shoulder for purchase and dive out of the window.

Making sure to land on my back so I'm cushioning his fall, several of my ribs crack at the impact. For the time being, the adrenaline coursing through my veins is enough to mask most of the pain.

I shift back again and carry Fee's limp body further from the house as debris keeps landing all around us.

"Fee, love, I need you to wake up, okay? You need to wake up and shift so you can heal." I jostle him in my arms. Pressing two fingers to his neck,

TWENTY-EIGHT

I can feel a pulse. It's faint, but it's still there, and I need him to hang on in there.

He's so badly burned; his usually beautiful olive skin is covered in blisters, and the wounds are deep. I dread to think of what the smoke damage has done to his lungs. I don't think he'll heal quickly enough in his human form. He needs to shift, but he can't if he remains unconscious.

Once I lay him back down on the ground out of further harm's way, I really begin to panic. This can't be how our story ends; we were meant to become crotchety old men together. I refuse to be a twenty-five-year-old widower.

"Fee, you need to wake up. You don't get to leave me behind, okay? When we go, we go together, and it's not going to be today, so you need to fucking wake up!" I'm yelling in his face with tear-stained cheeks, but it's no use.

"Phoenix Campbell, I'm Ordering you to shift right now!"

My own voice reverberates around my skull in a way I hardly recognise. It's familiar but not a sound that has ever come from me before.

It's a voice I grew up with. It's the authoritative voice of my father.

Not only that, it's an Order.

An Alpha Order.

TWENTY-NINE
OCTOBER 2022

PHOENIX CAMPBELL

The faint sound of voices slowly stirs me awake. I try to swallow, but my throat feels like it's been scraped raw with razor blades. My eyelids are heavy, and I squint at the light in the room. It's not even that bright, but it feels intrusive and makes my eyes sting. When I try to speak, only a rasping noise comes out, and even that makes me wince in pain.

"Fee? Oh my god. Thank fuck, you're awake. He's gonna be okay now, isn't he?" Cee seems to be half speaking to me and half talking to someone else I haven't spotted yet.

"Yeah, he should be out of the woods." A deep male voice replies. It's vaguely familiar, but I can't place who it belongs to at present.

"Here, have a sip of water," Cee passes me a cup with a straw and pushes it to my lips. I take a few gentle sips, and the cool water feels blissful going down my inflamed throat. I'm so parched I feel as though I could down several pints of water, but Cee pulls the straw away before I can guzzle it and tells me to see how it settles first.

As my eyes adjust to the unfamiliar room, I take in Cee as he perches on the edge of the bed. He looks as bad as I feel. His bloodshot eyes have dark shadows underneath them; he looks exhausted, like he hasn't slept for days.

It's funny how when you see someone frequently, you don't really notice them getting older, but now I'm really looking, I can see how much the boy I met almost five and a half years ago has gone, and how much I love the man he has become.

"What's happened? Where are we?" I croak out, my voice still raspy despite the glass of water.

"There was a fire... You were unconscious upstairs, and I managed to get you out, but we don't know how long you were trapped inside before I got there. You were badly burned, and your lungs were in bad shape from all the smoke inhalation."

What. The. Fuck. A fire? How would our house end up on fire? Why didn't I get myself out? This doesn't make any sense.

"I'm so sorry, Fee. It's all my fault." I scrunch my face up in confusion.

"What do you mean? How is it your fault? Did you set our house on fire?" I ask, knowing full well he absolutely would not have, and there will be some absurd reason he's decided to shoulder the blame for some sort of freak accident.

"No, of course I didn't set our house on fire," he huffs.

"Then it really doesn't sound like it was your fault. What do we know?" I ask him.

He looks over his shoulder to the doorway, and when I turn my head, I spot Noah standing there. It was his voice I must have heard when I woke up; that makes sense now. He steps into the room so I don't have to strain my neck to look at him.

"Once the firefighters got the fire under control, Oliver and I took a look inside to try and find the cause because nobody could find where the fire originated. Neither could we, but when we went up into your bedroom, I found a hex bag under your bed. I've sent it off to Orla to take a proper look, but our best guess so far is that's what prevented you from waking up and escaping." Noah's tone is sombre as he explains, who could possibly want me to die in a fire? Cee leans forward and cups my cheek with his palm, kissing my forehead gently.

"The important thing is you're gonna be fine. Oliver and Noah will figure out the rest, and then we'll deal with it. You should try and rest some more, okay?" I nod, somewhat bewildered by all this information, but my brain is foggy. Every time I try to reach for a thought or a detail, it's like wading through thick mud.

"Thanks, Noah," I croak out before a horrible cough burns through my chest painfully. Noah dips his chin and leaves the room; his faint footsteps fade as he walks down some stairs.

"You look like you need some rest, too. How long have I been out?" I rasp.

"Three days. Longest three days of my life, honestly," he replies. I doubt he slept a wink during that time; he must be shattered. When I shift over slightly and peel back the cover I'm under, he joins me on the bed. We lay side by side, and he brings my face to his chest, enveloping me in his arms.

"I need you to know that I will *never* leave you, and I'm so sorry I let you worry about that for even a moment. When I think about those moments when we weren't sure if you'd make it, I kept thinking I needed you to know I didn't mean the stupid words I said. And I love you, and I'll never stop loving you. And also, I have to die before you do because I'm never doing this again, okay?" His breath hitches, and he swallows loudly, choking down his emotions. My memories of the argument that night are blurry at the moment, but I know in my gut he was never really going anywhere.

"Okay, babe, you can go first," I tell him, making a promise I can't possibly keep, nor do I really want to. Ideally, the two of us will go *The Notebook* style, curled up in bed, and peacefully die in each other's arms. It's unlikely, but I think we're owed some luck at this point.

When I press my lips to kiss the hollow of his throat, he lets out a deep breath, and some of the tension leaves his body. Throwing a leg over his hip, I pull him in close and let the steady beat of his heart lull me back to sleep.

When I next wake up, I'm sprawled on top of Cee like a koala, and he's awake, mindlessly running his fingers through my hair. I've no idea how long I slept, but I feel so much better. When I swallow, I'm still thirsty, but it doesn't hurt my throat anymore, and when I take a deep inhale, my chest no longer rattles.

Something snags in my mind when I scent the air. I'm mostly just appalled that Cee let me sleep on top of him when I'm pretty ripe right now, but there's something else. What the hell is that? Shuffling up on Cee's chest, I scent his neck, sensing a foreign new smell on him.

Why does he smell like that?

"Stop sniffing me," he says grumpily.

"Why do you smell different?" I ask, feeling suspicious, but I'm not entirely sure of what. He doesn't smell of another wolf. He still smells like Connor even; it's just there's a new scent layer, and I can't pinpoint what it is.

"Um... we can talk about it later."

Well, that's an ominous response.

"How are you feeling? Do you want some water? A shower?" The subject change is not subtle, but I do want both of those things.

"Water please, then shower, and then there's a lot of blanks you need to fill in." Cee sighs in defeat, clearly not looking forward to that part but begrudgingly agrees.

The hot water pelting me in the shower feels amazing on my skin. I scrub my hands down my face and immerse myself under the large tropical shower head. There are several patches of skin on my arms and legs that are a light pink colour; the burns must have been horrendous for my skin to still be healing this many days later. I don't think it's really hit me yet; how close I came to dying.

Choosing not to dwell on those thoughts, I take a good look around the room. It's a beautiful mixture of old and modern. Stunning hardwood floors with what appears to be brand-new bathroom appliances installed. The walls are white, but the bath and shower are against a wall of green subway tiles, contrasting nicely. I assume the place is Noah's, but it's certainly not his place in Edinburgh, that's for sure.

"Who's house is this?" I ask, curiosity getting the better of me.

"Can we add this to the talk for after the shower?" Cee replies from where he's perched on the toilet lid while I scrub every inch of my skin. He claimed it was in case I suddenly felt faint, but I'm feeling fully healed now, and I suspect it has more to do with him not wanting me to be out of his sight after what happened.

As much as almost dying in a fire sucks, I don't remember a thing, and I have to keep in mind that if I was in Cee's shoes, I'd be a total mess right now. He pulled me from our burning home, unconscious and covered in burns. He didn't even know if I was alive; that must have been terrifying for him.

"Oh shit, what about Magnus? Is Magnus okay? He got out, right?" I blurt, spitting out a mouthful of toothpaste down the shower drain after suddenly remembering our fur baby, and feeling awful I didn't think to ask sooner.

"He's fine; he's downstairs," Cee reassures me. A smile tugs at his mouth because he adores that little black cat. He takes the toothbrush from me and pops it in a cup by the sink. After I've rinsed off all the suds from the shampoo and conditioner, I turn off the shower, and Cee hands me a large, fluffy white towel to dry off.

Back in the bedroom, Cee pulls out some jogging bottoms, a t-shirt, and socks for me to wear.

When I step out of the bedroom onto the landing, I'm blown away. The bedroom and ensuite are on a mezzanine looking out onto a large open-plan home below. It's simple and minimalist, but every single detail looks thought out, and it's beautiful. At the other end of the house are floor-to-ceiling windows that look out onto rolling hills. Every single detail of this place is breathtaking and unlike anything I've ever seen before. Yet, there's also something so familiar about it.

As I make my way down the stairs, Cee follows and walks into the kitchen to put the kettle on. I perch on one of the bar stools pulled up to a kitchen island, and stare at my surroundings. When Cee turns to face me, something in his expression is self-conscious, but I can't really fathom why.

CONNOR KELLY

"This place is stunning, where's Noah?" Fee asks.

"He's gone home."

"This isn't his place?" I take a deep breath and then blow it out in a rush before answering.

"This is *our* place." His eyes go wide as he scans the space again.

"Um, babe, how much smoke did *you* inhale in that fire? Because this is not our place." He sounds incredulous, and I can't really blame him. I'm suddenly questioning my decision to keep this a secret all this time.

"You know that secret work project I wouldn't tell you anythin' about? Well, this is that," I say to him, gesticulating at our surroundings.

"I'm going to need you to fill in a lot more gaps."

"Firepower. Trend. Blog." His brown eyes stretch wide like saucers as the recognition sets in. He opens his mouth to speak and closes it again several times. "I came here in early May. I'm not sure why. I think I just wanted the nostalgia trip, and I saw a for sale sign on the land. When I got in touch, they said the barn and roughly five acres of land, includin' the woods, were for sale, with plannin' permission already granted for a barn conversion. I'd sold my half of the business to Mikey, and I still had the money from my mum's life insurance sittin' there, so I made them an offer. The sale only officially went through in July, but we were able to put an agreement in place for me to start work on it." I realise I've been staring at a spot on the floor as I explain, so I lift my gaze up to see Fee's reaction. He's just sitting there, slow-blinking at me with his eyebrows almost at his hairline.

"You did this? This is really our place?" he asks, and I nod. He gets up from the stool he's been sitting on and walks towards me. His hands tightly cup my face as he presses his lips to mine. "I can't believe you did this," he mumbles against my mouth, and I smile in relief that I obviously didn't fuck this up.

"Couldn't exactly have anyone else shaggin' in our barn, could we?" I say before returning the kiss. His tongue sweeps inside my mouth, tasting me before he pulls away and looks down into my eyes. He licks his bottom lip and gives me a questioning look.

TWENTY-NINE

"That smell from before; you taste different. What's going on?" In fairness, I think I would react far worse if Fee suddenly smelled and tasted different. I gulp, knowing when I tell him this, it will change everything.

"When I pulled you from the fire, you were in your human form. Your pulse was weak, and you were so badly burned." I scrunch my eyes closed, desperately trying to keep the images at bay. "You weren't healin' quickly enough. You couldn't shift because you were unconscious, and I kept beggin' you to shift. It's like my brain knew it was the only way to save you, and it triggered my Alpha gene. You woke up for a second and shifted, but the Alpha Order I gave you... It changed me." I look up into his eyes, trying to show him how much I never wanted this for us. Fee and I have always been equals, and I hate how this changes things, but I wouldn't take it back. "I didn't mean to, but I can't be sorry because it saved you, and I will always do whatever it takes to save you."

Fee looks surprised, not that I blame him. Since he woke up, I've bombarded him with huge life-changing information, and he's taken it all in stride so far. I'm not sure what I expected, but a bellow of laughter was not it.

"I won't lie; there's a small part of me that thinks I'm in a coma or something somewhere, and this is all a dream," he says once he's gathered himself. "But in all seriousness, there's nobody I would rather have as my Alpha than you, my bossy little bottom." He chuckles again at the ridiculousness of all of this.

"We're still equals," I try to tell him, but he interrupts me with a quick kiss.

"We aren't, but that's okay. In our pack, you're my Alpha now, and I'll always defer to you. But in our marriage, we're still just me and you. I know you won't ever abuse this power. I trust you."

Fee's words are a balm. I don't know how he does that, but he always seems to know exactly what to say to soothe all of my concerns at once. Until this point, I'd been so focused on Fee healing I hadn't even realised how worried I was about how he'd take this news, but I should have known better. Fee has always been my steady rock; reliable, consistent, and always so measured.

Over the years, there have been times when I doubted if Fee felt as strongly for me as I did him, but I know that's my own insecurities. Now, with all the facts laid bare, I can see clearly how much Fee's love for me *never* faltered. Even in the year I wouldn't speak to him, he always tried to reach out, letting me know in his own way that he hadn't forgotten me.

He kisses me again—leisurely—like we have all the time in the world, and I guess we do. His warm tongue laps at the seam of my lips, seeking permission to taste me fully. I gladly oblige and open my mouth for him. As his tongue meets mine, my skin heats all over with a rush of want and need. As his big hands grip my face tighter, his fingers dig into the back of my neck, and I moan into his mouth at how good it feels.

Fee's hands travel down my body, and in one quick motion, he grabs the backs of my thighs and lifts me so I'm sitting on the kitchen counter. I'm marginally higher than him now, and he presses kisses adoringly along my jaw and down my neck, nipping and sucking at my tender, sensitive skin.

"I'm not going to do it today, but one day soon, I'm going to finally sink my teeth into this spot right here," he licks the delicate skin where my shoulder and neck connect. "And everyone will know that you belong to me. Everyone will know what I've known for years: that you're my mate and that you're mine." He speaks the last part quietly into my ear before sucking my earlobe into his mouth, grazing his teeth on it as he lets it go. I groan as my cock thickens behind my jeans, and I arch towards him, seeking friction that isn't there.

Fee's thumb rubs gently on the sliver of skin he's exposed above my jeans, and he presses his hand up underneath my t-shirt, tweaking my already stiff nipple between his finger and thumb. The sensation makes me gasp, loving the fine line between pain and pleasure that Fee always manages to keep me balanced on.

Reaching behind his head to tug his t-shirt off, I'm once again blown away with relief at seeing his beautiful, smooth skin that hardly shows any signs of the horrific burns that marred it just a few days ago.

Leaning down, I pepper kisses along his collarbone in appreciation of having him before me—whole and well. When his arms lift again to remove my t-shirt, I lean into his underarm and inhale deeply; he smells fresh and clean from his shower, but the earthy lavender scent that's all him—is an aphrodisiac like no other.

Since I became an Alpha, I've found myself frequently overwhelmed with the need to smell him. I want to rub myself all over him until our scents are so blended you can't even tell where he ends, and I begin.

Fee pulls on my hips, and I wrap my legs around his waist. He carries me into the living room as though I'm not an eighty-kilogram man before gently lowering me to the rug next to the sofa.

Our lips are fused together, and I suck on his tongue, enjoying the rumbling sound he lets out in response. When he undoes the button on my jeans, I lift my hips so he can tug them off.

Starting at the inside of my ankle, Fee peppers kisses along my leg. When he reaches my inner thigh, he grazes his teeth on the soft skin there, and I whimper in response. Ignoring my erection that's tenting my boxers, he continues up my body, kissing and licking up my stomach until he takes my nipple into his mouth and sucks, swirling his tongue around the hard bud. I try to buck my hips to demand his attention where I want it, but Fee drops his weight between my thighs, pinning me to the rug.

Fee comes willingly when I tug on his face, needing his lips against my own. Needing to taste him and savour the feel of him so alive under my fingertips. His tongue sweeps into my mouth, and he grinds his hips. The feel of his stiff cock pressing into me is incredible, but I want more. I reach into his joggers and take him in my hand, excitement and want bubbles beneath my skin as I anticipate having him inside me.

When he pulls away momentarily to remove the rest of his clothes, I quickly take off my boxers and give my cock a few tugs to provide a morsel of relief.

"Roll onto your stomach, baby," he asks, and I don't hesitate to oblige.

I groan as he massages his thumbs into the backs of my thighs. When he pulls my cheeks apart and gently blows onto my hole, I can't help but flush despite the number of times we've done this. This feels different, though; there's no rush, no fear of being caught. He's making love to me in the home I made for us. I have to fight the urge to run away and hide, feeling undeserving of how he's worshipping my body like I'm his most prized possession.

The tip of his tongue teases my rim, and as much as part of me wants to beg him to hurry up and fuck me, I force myself to be patient. To enjoy the moment and the feel of my husband's hands and mouth all over me. He licks and sucks at my hole before pushing the tip of his thumb inside.

"Lube?" he asks.

"Wallet. Jeans pocket," I pant.

I can hear some shuffling and the tear of a packet before slippery fingers tease at my entrance. I'm relaxed from his ministrations, and he slides two fingers in and out of me with ease.

He moves to lie on his side next to me, his thigh pressing down on mine, and I turn to face him so I can taste his lips as he preps me. It's slow and indulgent, and I can feel the fear and tension of the last few days leaving my body with every soft kiss and touch.

"You're being unusually patient today," he says against my mouth.

"I'm tryin' to be good. I wanna be good for you," I whisper and then moan as he adds a third finger.

"Baby, you're always good for me. I love you exactly as you are."

"In that case, I am very, very ready, so get inside me, like, right now. Please?" He laughs, and when he removes his fingers from me, he swats me on the arse, causing me to yelp.

I turn over onto my back and watch as he uses the rest of the lube packet to coat his cock and then adds some more to my rim.

His wavy chestnut hair is still damp and tousled from the shower. His brown, soulful eyes are eclipsed by his blown-out pupils, and almost a week's worth of stubble makes him look rugged, like a lumberjack. He's absolutely breathtaking. And he's mine. My mate, my husband, my forever. These are the thoughts that circle my brain on a loop as he turns me on my side and lies down behind me. I bring my knee up, and a whimper escapes my lips as the head of his cock nudges my entrance.

Fee's big strong arm wraps across my chest and pulls me tight against him. I take a deep breath and bear down; between the world's longest prep and plenty of lube, he pushes inside smoothly. I can feel the stretch, but it's satisfying, and I welcome the fullness.

"Good?" he asks once his hips are flush with my arse.

"So good. Take me apart, Fee. I'm all yours."

He tugs my chin far enough to lean forward and kiss me. He kisses me like his life depends on it until he finally begins to move.

Fee takes his time, gliding almost all the way out before slowly pushing back in again. The way the head of his cock grazes against my prostate with each thrust is like sweet torture. I reach back to try and grip his hip, encouraging him to move faster, but instead, he stills inside me.

"Nuh-uh. You're being a good boy, remember? Letting me have my way." I scowl, but he can't see. I move my hand from his hip to stroke myself.

Thankfully, I don't have to wait long before he speeds up, thrusting harder and harder. His fingertips dig into my hips and stomach as leverage to fuck into me at a relentless pace, and this, *this* is what I needed. I needed him to make me forget the terror of the fire, the horrific burns that littered his beautiful skin. To consume me with the scent of damp earth and lavender. For his sweat to drip onto my body and mix with mine. To fuse us together and remind me that he's here and he's not going anywhere.

"Fuck. I love you so much; you can't ever leave me," I tell him, and he slows.

"I'm not going anywhere, baby. I'm right here. Feel?" He turns me to face him and kisses my palm before pressing it over his heart. The *thud thud thud* is reassuring under my hand, and the quick, steady beat says 'I'm alive'.

Pressing firmly against his chest, I roll him onto his back and straddle him. Lining his cock up with my hole, I sink down onto him before welding my lips back to his.

As I ride him, undulating up and down his length, he strokes my aching cock at the perfect pace. My orgasm builds slowly, like an exquisite ache in my groin that grows and grows until my balls draw up and it's about to crest.

"You're such a good Alpha, such a good boy. Come for me," he whispers, and I erupt at his words. My cum spurts out of me and paints his stomach; he's a perfect work of art. My whole body shakes and tremors from the magnitude of my release.

Fee grips me and then pistons up, hard and fast, while never taking his eyes off me. It doesn't take long before he swears, plunges deep inside me, and his cock throbs as his cum floods my arse.

We're both panting, and I drop my weight onto his solid body, blanketing him as I slowly return to earth.

We kiss each other; it's languid and full of gratitude for what we still have. What we grew, destroyed, and nurtured back to health.

Eventually, Fee's softening cock begins to slip out of me. His finger strokes and rubs at my used rim, gently pushing his cum back inside as it leaks out.

"Enjoying yourself back there, caveman?" I ask, playful but still drunk and spaced out from my orgasm.

"Mm," he says before planting a kiss on my collarbone. "I wish we had a butt plug so I could keep it trapped inside you," he mutters into my skin. His big brown eyes are as soft as ever, and his cheeks pinken like he didn't quite mean to say that out loud.

I smile at him, and my heart aches with how much love I feel in this moment. Aches at what I almost lost—not only a few days ago. A whole year of him I didn't get to witness, and I promise myself—never again.

All the tension that's made a home in my bones and muscles these last few years finally ebbs away. I can breathe full breaths again. Let myself fall because I know he'll be there to catch me.

I don't know what's coming; I don't know why someone tried to kill my husband, and I certainly don't know how to be an Alpha of a pack. But I do know I'll be tackling every moment of it with Fee by my side, and

I don't have the words for how fucking content and happy that makes me.

THIRTY
November 2022

CONNOR KELLY

My noise-cancelling headphones block out most of the background noise on the plane, and a member of the cabin crew is demonstrating how to put on a seatbelt.

Last week, Noah got a phone call from our great-grandmother, Orla, requesting both of us to come and visit at our earliest convenience. Given she's ninety-eight, we figured we probably shouldn't put it off.

Aside from a few summers as a teenager, I've never spent much time with Noah because he was raised in Northern Ireland while I was raised in England. We never visited for any considerable length of time until after Mum died, and Da would leave us with my maternal grandparents for a chunk of the school holidays. Raising three teenagers on your own with an entire pack to look out for, let alone a pack at war, wasn't an easy feat.

Me: Is Alice with you yet? x

Fee: Yes, my babysitter is here but you should withhold the tip because she drinks like a fish. Very irresponsible ;)

> **Me:** You and Alice are going to make me go grey prematurely. Setting off now so I'll text when we land. Love you x

> **Fee:** Mmm I think I could be into the silver daddy look :p Have a safe flight, love you too x

After I've put my phone on flight mode, I shuffle to try to get comfy. However, this tiny tin can of a plane was not designed for two fully grown men to sit next to each other. Mercifully, the journey is short, but I already know I'm going to get a cramp in my legs.

Twenty minutes into the flight, I glare at where Noah's leg is bouncing against mine. Thankfully, he spots my annoyed expression and places a hand on his knee, stilling it. Noah took the flight with me instead of teleporting so I wouldn't be travelling alone, but when he starts fiddling with the air conditioning nozzles overhead, I wish he'd just met me there.

He eventually settles down, pulling his phone out. I'm bored, so I peek at what he's doing on there, just scrolling through some messages, but when he spots me looking, he quickly locks the screen and places it in the pocket in front of him.

> **Me:** Just landed. Have you and Alice done the perimeter checks?

Ever since the fire in our old house, I've been justifiably paranoid. Noah put up some wards around the perimeter of the land we own, as well as some additional ones for the new house. I only agreed to come on this trip to see Orla on the condition that Alice stay with Fee while I'm away.

Now I'm Alpha, I find myself avoiding anything that takes me off the Yorkshire territory. I've been twitchy as fuck ever since taking off from Leeds and Bradford.

As we stand in the car park waiting for the lady from the car hire station to return with a set of keys, I get increasingly agitated the longer Fee doesn't reply to my text. Noah rolls his eyes at me but doesn't say anything. I'm about to try and call him when I finally get a response.

> **Fee:** Yep, we just got back. All clear babe xx

I let out a sigh of relief.

"Here are your keys; it's the blue Ford Focus just over there." She points to the parked car in question. "If you could take a quick look at the vehicle and then sign here to confirm it's in the condition as stated, please?" Noah nods and grabs the keys. Once we've completed the paperwork, we get on our way to Mourne.

Noah drives since he grew up here and is familiar with the route. We landed in Belfast so it's only an hour and a half drive to Orla's house.

I fiddle with the stereo so I can connect it to my phone and put on a random indie playlist.

"Thank fuck," Noah says.

"Huh?"

"When I was stuck in a car with PC Plod a few months ago, he played the Archers!"

"I didn't even know the Archers was still going."

"Neither did I. He must be their only listener this side of retirement." Noah sounds utterly disgusted and I snort a laugh.

When we set off, it was a grey, drizzly day, but the closer we get to Orla's, the brighter it's beginning to look. The sun shining on the autumn leaves decorates the landscape in stunning shades of oranges and reds. I forget sometimes how beautiful it is here.

"Do you ever miss living here?" I ask. Noah lived with Orla from around the age of four, so this is very much his stomping ground.

"Not especially. I miss Orla sometimes. There's not much around here if you're not a shifter." The loneliness leaks from his voice, and guilt settles like a pit in my stomach. I'd never for a second considered what it must be like to be surrounded by a pack but always an outsider. With the exception of Orla, his entire family is made up of wolf shifters.

We sit in silence after that. Which is common around Noah, but this silence has a weight to it.

Noah parks on the street and leads the way as we walk down the stone path through Olra's wildly overgrown garden. He steps inside without knocking, and I follow behind.

It's been almost seven years since I last visited Orla, and her home is as remarkable as I remember it. It always creeped me out how every step I'd take in the house would cause the floorboards to creak, yet Orla moved around the place silently. It seems Noah learned some of her tricks because he steps through the house ahead of me like a ghost.

It's strange being here with Noah because where I've always been a guest, this is the home he grew up in. After our conversation on the drive over, I can't help but wonder what his life was like here. My da never really explained how Noah ended up living with Orla. Shortly after I was born, my Uncle Rowan—Noah's da—left our pack and joined the Limerick pack. And for some reason, he didn't take Noah with him. Nobody knows who Noah's mother is, as far as I'm aware, so Orla took him in. I suppose it was the best place for him, given he's a witch and not a shifter like his da. Still, I can't imagine either of my parents letting anyone else raise me.

We find Orla grinding some herbs that smell suspiciously of weed with a pestle and mortar at her dainty wooden kitchen table. She grins mischievously when she spots us. Noah bends down to kiss her on the cheek in greeting before taking a seat next to her.

"Come over here and give me a hug, Connor," she says, and I oblige. "Gosh, you really do have your mammy's eyes, don't you?" She sounds a little wistful. It's something both Niamh and I have heard all our lives, so I nod and smile. "Go on, take a seat while I finish up with this." I take one of the empty seats at the table.

"Why are we here?" Noah asks bluntly. It would sound rude coming from anyone else, but he just tends to cut out any preamble, and Orla must be more than used to it by now.

"Some things have been set in motion, and some other things need to come to pass in order for us all to stay on the right path," Orla replies cryptically.

"What's been set in motion?" I ask.

"You have, my dear." My eyebrows scrunch together in confusion. "There were thousands of paths, but then you became an Alpha, and now there are less than a hundred paths. Out of the remaining paths, only two see you reach your thirtieth birthday."

My mouth gapes open.

How can that possibly be?

I became an Alpha to save Phoenix; how can it lead to my almost certain untimely death? A really terrible part of me is hoping Orla's a bit senile and doesn't know what she's talking about; she's almost a hundred after all. Noah's facial expression remains as stoic as ever, giving nothing away.

"Where do *I* come into this?" he asks, narrowing his eyes at her.

"I'm gonna tell ya right now, son, you're not gonna like what I tell ya," Orla replies, but Noah doesn't say a word, waiting for her to go on. "You have to become the pack witch for Connor."

There is a pregnant pause before Noah finally responds.

"Connor, can you give us a minute?" His voice is as cold as ice. I'm still shocked by what Orla said, so I just nod and numbly make my way outside for some fresh air.

When I pull my phone out to check the time, I see a text from Fee, attaching a selfie of him, Alice and Magnus sitting on the sofa eating popcorn. Even with a smug smirk on his face, he looks cute, so I save the photo into an album of pictures he's sent me over the years.

During our time apart, I must have deleted and restored this album literally hundreds of times. Periodically, I'd get smashed and scroll through the photos just to make myself even sadder. Regardless, now things are good between us, I'm glad I kept all of these. Scrolling through the photos, looking at little pockets of our shared history, only sharpens my resolve to refuse to die before I'm thirty. We still have too much life to live together.

Noah's voice is raised inside the house, and moments later, he storms out and stomps past me.

"Where are you going?" I call out after him, but he ignores me and keeps going.

"He'll be back. Come inside and have a cuppa while we wait," Orla says cheerily from the doorway, where she silently appears.

Orla moves so gracefully around her kitchen as she boils some water, you'd have no idea of her age.

"He's always been hot-tempered, a lot like you from what I hear." I blush because she's not wrong. It's odd, though, because I always thought Noah seemed quite closed off. He hardly seems to react to anything.

"Thanks," I say, accepting the cup of tea she hands me.

"Fancy a joint while we wait?" Orla asks, waving a rolled-up spliff in the air. I let out a huff of laughter, but fuck it, how many people have the opportunity to get high with their ancient great-grandmother.

"Sure. May as well if I've only got a two-path chance to live another four years."

"Don't worry, Noah will do the right thing, and I have a feeling once the decision is made, there will be plenty more paths again. You and your Phoenix bird will get many more years together, I am sure," she says, and I'm slightly more reassured. I take a pull on the joint and chuckle at the mental image of Phoenix as a bird.

Olra and I sit companionably, passing the joint back and forth as she tells me stories of my mum as a child. I've heard them all before, but there's still something comforting about them. After she died, it was a few years before Da would even talk about her. He and Mum were mates, and he was so destroyed that it sometimes felt as though he might pine away and follow her into the afterlife like a heartsick swan.

"There we go. I knew my boy would make the right choice," Olra says, seemingly out of the blue. A few minutes later, Noah walks through the door and glares at her.

"Get it over with then," he says through gritted teeth, his jaw pulsating with tension, but Orla just smiles at him knowingly. She briefly leaves the room and returns with a rather crude-looking knife. Are there any rituals that don't entail slicing me open?

"Left hands, palms up," she says to the both of us, and we do as requested. Without any preamble, she slices a shallow cut across my palm, right where the scar from the binding ceremony is, and then does the same to Noah's. The knife is sharper than it looks and leaves only a brief sting. "Quickly, before his hand heals itself," she says to Noah, who grips my left hand with his own, causing our blood to mix.

"I vow my life to your pack and any Alpha who succeeds you. I vow to put the best interest of the pack before my own and will put your life before mine. I will be your witch, to utilise in the manner you see fit to ensure the safety, well-being, and future of the pack. That is my oath."

When I pull my hand away, the blood is gone, but the silvery scar remains. Even brighter, somehow. The blood in my veins is thrumming with magic, like electricity flowing through me. I've never been told exactly what it entails to be a pack witch, and I had no idea it was an actual blood oath. It's difficult to tell how much I'm still buzzed from the weed and how much it's the magic Noah transferred into me.

An hour or so later, we get up to leave. Noah still hasn't said a word and mutters goodbye under his breath as we leave the house.

"Get back here right now, Noah," Orla says firmly. Noah's back straightens abruptly, and he turns around to come back. "How would you feel if that's how you said goodbye, and I died tomorrow?"

"Are you goin' to die tomorrow?" he asks, arching an eyebrow at her.

"It's unlikely, but stranger things have happened. Tell me you love me and be on your way." Orla turns her cheek for him to kiss it, and he mutters what sounds like 'love you' and then stalks off back to where he parked the car earlier. Right before he gets inside, I swear I hear him say, 'manipulative old hag,' and I hope for his sake Orla's hearing is a lot worse than mine.

"You'll be pleased to know you have many more paths ahead of you, my dear Connor. Just don't make the mistakes your forefathers made." I nod, not that I'm entirely sure what she means by that, but agreeing seems like the right thing to do. When I reach down to hug her goodbye, she whispers, "And make sure you look after my boy," before letting me go. Glancing over my shoulder at where Noah is sitting in the car, I tell her I will before joining him so we can make our way back home.

THIRTY

While I'm itching to return to Fee, to return to the land that makes my blood sing, I'm apprehensive, too. I don't think it's a coincidence that Archie was killed and our home was set on fire, trapping Fee inside. There's a reason he almost died the same way the Yorkshire pack were killed fifty years ago. And why, without Noah becoming my pack witch, did it almost guarantee my death?

'You aren't safe here'. That's what that witch's note said. I assumed the note was about Archie after what happened to him. But maybe it was meant for all of us?

THIRTY-ONE
June 2023

PHOENIX CAMPBELL

"How many weddings is too many weddings?" Cee asks from where he's standing in front of the mirror, butchering his bowtie.

"Well, the first one was legal, the second was for show, and I'd say the third one is going to be *just right*." I wink at him and then spin him to face me so I can tie his bowtie properly.

"Alright, Goldilocks. Let's agree this is most definitely the last, though." I smile and peck a kiss on his lips once I'm finished.

With so much tension and resentment shadowing our official weddings last year, we wanted a do-over on our own terms. A chance to have the wedding we had talked about and planned over the years we were together.

"Go time, boys," Niamh shouts from outside our bedroom door.

"Why am I so nervous? Fuck, we've been married for over a year, this is ridiculous." Cee wipes a bead of sweat from his temple.

"Come on, husband," I say, reaching out for him with my hand. Our fingers intertwine, and we both take a deep breath as we leave the room.

With Connor still being paranoid that someone is going to try and kill me, we're having our third and final wedding on our land, within the safety of Noah's wards. We've hired a marquee for the reception, and Niamh and Will have done a beautiful job arranging the seating, flowers, and an archway for the ceremony.

We don't have tons of guests; both of our families, as well as close friends from our old packs, are here, along with a few people from the Eastwood pack. Alice stands under the archway, ready to lead the ceremony. She joined our pack in December, and as the only person who knew us together when we were younger, it seems fitting. Niamh and Jasper are on either side of her as best man and woman. When the music begins, Cee and I slowly walk down the makeshift aisle for our very last, *I do.*

"As this is a somewhat less official wedding, the grooms have opted to write their own vows, which they will now read out," Alice says, and I take a large gulp of air. I'm sorely regretting agreeing to go first. I clear my throat a little too loudly and wince.

"As some of you know, and some of you don't know, I met Connor six years ago today. I was minding my own business, enjoying a late night swim, when this big dark grey wolf appeared, rudely interrupting me." Several of our guests laugh, and Cee rolls his eyes.

"The moment you appeared, it felt like coming home, only to a home I'd never been to before. I knew the moment the breeze blew your scent towards me that this was it. That you were my home and I'd met my mate. You've been the focal point of my world ever since.

"I promise to always see you, Connor Kelly, for all that you are. I see how you show your love quietly in a million different ways and how you fiercely protect the people you care about. I know that to be loved by you is a privilege and one I promise to never take for granted. I promise to love you and always be a place of safety for you to call home."

Cee's eyes are glassy, his throat bobs, and a single tear escapes, tracking down his cheek. Reaching for his face, I wipe it away with the pad of my thumb.

"Fuck, I swore I wasn't gonna cry today," Cee says, scolding himself. "Or swear." A few of our guests laugh, but I spot Cee's dad in the front row, crying freely. There's an empty seat next to him we reserved in honour of Cee's mum. Connor's parents were mated, and I can't imagine what it must have been like for him to lose her so suddenly.

Cee takes a few deep breaths and squares his shoulders before speaking. "I'm regrettin' lettin' you go first because we both know you've always been better at expressin' your feelings than I have, so that's a tough act to follow." He lets out a small huff.

"I was fortunate that for the first twelve years of my life, I got to witness true love. Every single day. My parents were mated from the age of eighteen, and I got to see what it looks like to love someone steadfastly through good days and bad.

"For a long time, I felt as though our love story had a big hole in it. That the year we spent apart would always mean we were a before and an after, but the truth is that even absent from each other's lives, you loved me unwaveringly. You loved me even when I made myself a hard person to love. And I loved you despite my best efforts not to." Our guests let out a chuckle at that.

"So my promise to you is that I will always put my love for you first. I promise to do everythin' I can to make sure you never doubt it. I promise to weather every storm with you, side by side. I promise to love you fiercely until the day I die because, yes, I refuse to let you go before me." He sniffles and laughs wetly. I can feel my own cheeks are utterly saturated with tears, and I'm speechless.

Before Alice even has a chance to say the next part, my hands are on either side of his face, and I press my lips to his. He melts into me, and when I pull away and look down into his bright, sparkling green eyes, my heart settles.

I don't know what the future will bring, but I'm not worried about us. The past six years have only been the beginning of what I know will be our very own epic love story, a love story with no holes in it.

"I'd say 'and you may now kiss,' but you went off script and did that already," Alice says. "So I'm just going to declare you—for the third and *final* time—husband and husband. Let's all go eat, drink and dance until our feet hurt!"

CONNOR KELLY

After the meal, all our guests sit around their tables, drinking wine and chatting away. The atmosphere in the room is so full of joy; it's palpable. I felt a bit foolish when I suggested to Fee we have a do-over wedding. We'd spent so many years discussing and planning it that I felt kind of cheated when we ended up getting married under such shitty circumstances, but this feels right.

Fee nudges me with his elbow, "I think this is the part where we're supposed to do the rounds and make small talk," he says quietly into my ear.

"Ugh. I hate small talk. You love it; why don't you do this part?" I suggest, hopefully, but he just laughs. He stands, reaching his hand out towards me, and I join him begrudgingly, interlacing our fingers as Fee tugs me towards a nearby table.

Apparently getting the worst over with first, we make our way to Fee's family table. Things seem more tense than usual, but they're mostly focused on Henry, who is enthusiastically bashing the table with two spoons.

Why is it so unnecessarily awkward to talk to a table of people who are sitting down while you're standing? It's as though I've suddenly grown extra limbs I don't know what to do with. While Fee says hello to his family, I stand there like a spare part with a fake smile on my face. I promised him I wouldn't make a scene and I'd be civil. However, the anger that still courses through my veins when I think of his mum, Alpha Ordering him to marry Niamh, makes it challenging.

My defences go up when I spot Jasper glaring angrily over at my family's table. At first, I think he's aiming dagger eyes at Noah, but when I glance at Sam, who's to his left, his eyes are wide and faintly bloodshot, but he's staring right back. Jade also seems to spot the bizarrely intense exchange between her husband and my brother, but she glances away sadly before returning her attention to Henry.

"Am I okay to take Henry to the house for a nap?" she asks Fee as she lifts him from his high chair.

"Yes, of course. The house should be unlocked, and his carry cot is set up in the guest room," Fee replies and then glances at Jasper, who doesn't seem to have even noticed that his wife and son have left the table. Fee scrunches his brows at me in question, but I just shrug.

Not going to touch that with a barge pole.

Once we've made our way around all the tables, Fee heads across the dance floor to where the DJ is setting up the music for the evening. Before anyone can grab me to make more incessant small talk, I duck out to use the temporary toilets situated behind the marquee.

I get to enjoy a brief moment of quiet solitude while I take a piss in the urinal, but it doesn't last long before Sam comes bursting through the door.

"Hey, little bro." His words are slurred, and I don't think I've ever seen him this drunk.

"Someone's been enjoyin' the free bar a bit too much, I see." I smirk at him as I turn around and zip up my fly.

"You and Phoenix are mates, right?" Sam asks, jarring me with the sudden subject change.

"Um. We haven't made that part official yet, but yes. Why?"

"How did you do it?"

"Do what?"

"The year when you were apart, how did you manage to stay away? Didn't your skin itch to be near him?"

"I mean, you saw me that year, Sam. I was a hot mess." I try to laugh it off and hope he changes the subject because I still get a horrible feeling in my gut whenever I dwell too much on the year we spent apart. He lets out a weighted sigh. "Why? What's up?"

"Nothin'. Doesn't matter. Probably gonna die alone, is all." When I look more closely at my usually serious and sensible older brother, I can see in his eyes he hasn't slept well in a long while. He's never been one to drink heavily, and at five pm, he already smells like a brewery.

"Come on, let's get you some water and maybe a coffee; the night is young." I wrap an arm around his shoulders to help steady him, and we make our way back over to the marquee.

Fee catches me the second we're back inside.

"Babe, it's almost time for our first dance," he tells me. He's bouncing on the balls of his feet, and his voice is laced with excitement.

"Gimme me two secs." Glancing around the room, I try to locate my sister but can't see her. When I lug Sam over to the bar to ask for some water and coffee, Jasper is there ordering a drink.

"Hey, Jasper, you couldn't do me a favour, could you? It's time for the first dance, and I need someone to help Sam sober up a bit. Could you make sure he drinks these?" I ask, knowing he can't exactly say no since it's my wedding day and all. He looks panicked, and his eyes dart around the room as if someone will jump in and save him from this very small favour. He's out of luck on this occasion.

"Jasper won't help me. Jasper hates me. He prolly wishes I was dead so e'rythin would be simple," Sam mumbles and I'm not entirely sure what he's talking about. Jasper rolls his eyes and wraps his arm around Sam so I'm no longer propping him up.

"Jesus. I don't hate you, and I don't wish you were dead. Here, drink this." He says, holding the glass of water with a straw up to Sam's lips. Content that responsibility for my very intoxicated brother has been palmed off onto someone else, I go in search of my husband.

I find Fee chatting to Alice and Benjy on the edge of the dance floor and sneak up behind him. Wrapping my arms around his waist, I have to go on my tiptoes to prop my chin on his shoulder.

"Ready for our first dance?" I ask. He turns his face and pecks a chaste kiss on my lips.

"So ready." His enthusiasm is infectious, and I know the grin on my face must be a mile wide. Fee gestures to the DJ, who finishes Valerie by Amy Winehouse and then announces through the microphone that it's time for our first dance as husband and husband.

Fee takes my hand and pulls me along behind him to the centre of the now-empty dance floor. When 'Turn' by the Wombats starts playing through the speakers, I can't help but laugh. I told Fee he could choose the song, and he'd wanted it to be a surprise. Fee's smiling like the cat who got the cream. He puts his hands on my waist and squeezes gently. I wrap my arms around his neck, and we dance and sway to the music.

As The Wombats sing about running with the wolf pack when your legs are tired, Fee spins me out and back in again before dipping me low for a kiss. It's hard to kiss him back while I'm smiling so wide, but I wouldn't change a thing. Several of our guests begin to join us on the dance floor, including Niamh and Will, who appear to be doing some kind of salsa.

After dancing for a while, Fee and I go in search of some refreshments. He then takes a seat on a chair that's on the edge of the dancefloor but near enough to the door so we can get the benefit of the cool, night air. He tugs me down onto his lap; I'm generally not one for PDA, but I reckon I can make an exception on my own wedding day.

We take a moment to enjoy watching our friends and family dancing and having fun together, and my heart could burst from being so full. I'm relieved to see Sam and Niamh dancing, and he's looking considerably more sober than earlier in the evening.

In the far corner of the dance floor, I'm surprised to spot Will with Calvin; I didn't think they really knew each other. Their differences should look comical, but they complement each other. Will's slim build, porcelain skin and bouncy blonde hair contrast with Calvin, who must be close to six foot five with brown skin and his tight black curls cut short. Where Will's energy radiates sunshine and combustible energy, Calvin is calm and steady, and he's looking at Will adoringly. It might be nothing, but seeing a spark of potential for Will makes me unbelievably happy. He sacrificed so much for me when he married my sister, and I owe him so much.

When 'Just you and I' by Tom Walker starts playing, Fee taps my thigh gently so I stand up. We rejoin the dance floor, which is quieter now. Mostly couples swaying gently as the pace of the music slows down. We dance together in the centre of the room with our friends and family around us, but I don't see anyone but him.

"Truth or Dare?" Fee whispers into my ear, sending a little shiver down my spine.

"Truth," I reply, smiling at him.

"Hmmm, do you have a boyfriend or girlfriend?" I can't help but laugh, the memories from that fateful night under the waterfall invading my mind.

"Well, no girlfriend, because I don't generally swing that way. But I do have a husband," I reply, trying to keep a straight face but failing.

"Oh, that's a shame."

"Truth or Dare?" I ask.

"Truth."

"Have you ever thought about kissing me?"

"Mm. Only every day for the past six years. Truth or dare?"

"Dare." His eyes sparkle with mischief when I reply.

"I dare you to kiss your husband how you always pictured it."

And I do.

Cupping his face in my palms and angling his head down to meet mine, I press my lips to his. I softly lick his bottom lip with my tongue, and he makes a contented rumbling sound in his chest.

I breathe in his soothing scent, damp earth and lavender.

He smells like *home* and *all mine*.

EPILOGUE

CONNOR KELLY

We had to wait until Fee's school had broken up for the summer before we could take off on our honeymoon. We've just arrived at our hotel in Nidri, Greece. This is our first holiday together, and I'm ridiculously excited. Our hotel room has a small balcony that looks out onto the Ionian Sea. Fee collapses onto the king-size bed behind me, groaning loudly.

"Holy shit. This is comfy," he declares.

"Oi. Go wash all the travel off before you start rubbin' yourself all over the bed."

"I think I might need you to join me in the shower; there's a patch in the middle of my back I can't quite reach," he says, smirking at me.

"How can I say no to such a generous offer to wash your back," I deadpan, but he just waggles his eyebrows at me.

The large bathroom with a huge tropical shower was a major selling point when booking this hotel. It's not often you find a shower big enough to fit two fully grown men comfortably inside. I lather up Fee's loofah with the complimentary body wash. It smells much more expensive than the stuff we have at home, and I slowly scrub it all over his body. I purposefully neglect his very rigid cock, paying all my attention to everywhere else.

When I gently pull one of his cheeks to one side and brush my finger over his hole, he moans, pushing back. I only tease him, though, not applying any pressure. Despite Fee's best efforts with the infamous dildo, he's still not big on being on the receiving end of butt stuff. However, if he's in the right mood and particularly horny, he does enjoy an exploratory finger.

"My turn," I whisper into his ear. His mouth opens wide, and he stares down at his erection incredulously.

"You're going to leave me like this?"

"Patience, grasshopper." I laugh at his affronted expression.

He gets to work lathering me with soap, and I relax and enjoy the feel of his hands roaming around my body. His thumb brushes over my hard nipple, making my cock begin to swell. When we're both thoroughly clean, we rinse off and then head back to the bedroom in the fluffy white hotel robes.

I sit in the middle of the bed with my back against the headboard while Fee scrubs his hair dry with a towel. The fastening of his robe has come loose, so I have a good view of his naked body. Sometimes, I have to literally pinch myself that this is all real. Phoenix Campbell is my husband, and we're disgustingly happy. Like give myself a toothache; we're so sickly sweet, happy. We still bicker the same as we always have, but mostly over stupid shit, like who left a wet towel on the floor—it's always him, obviously.

Fee crawls towards me on the bed, his robe wide open and straddles my thighs. His semi presses against mine, and we watch as they get harder at the contact. Quickly hopping off the bed to go into the bathroom, he returns with a bottle of lube from our toiletry bag.

Reclaiming his spot on my lap, he pours a generous amount of it onto our erections before taking us both in his hand. His grip is perfectly firm and I instinctively lift my hips into his fist. He takes my lips in a fierce kiss, his tongue seeking mine out and groans into my mouth. Fee grinds his hips, rubbing his slick cock against mine, and I can tell he's close already. Tightening his grip on us, he increases the pace, and we're both panting.

"Shit, I'm so close. Gonna come," he blurts out a moment before his release spills over my hand, dick and stomach. I take over from him, grabbing my own cock and jerking myself hard and fast until my orgasm barrels into me. All my muscles tense at once before I go boneless. Fee swirls a finger through the mix of our cum on my stomach, making a satisfied 'mm' sound at the sight.

After a quick wash and a post-orgasm nap, we get ready to head out for dinner. We only brought one big suitcase to share because, at this point, our wardrobe has merged. With the exception of a few tailored items, it's a free-for-all. Fee puts on a pale pink linen shirt with some navy blue tailored shorts, and I go with a white polo and dark green shorts. He's looking at me as though he's already imagining stripping me of my clothes, so I shove him out the door before he gets any ideas. My stomach is growling something fierce.

It's eight pm when we finally step outside the hotel, but it's still stiflingly hot. It's a nice change from the wet British summer we left behind. We walk hand in hand to where there's a row of restaurants, looking out onto the port filled with fancy-looking yachts.

A bustling seafood restaurant called Basillico, with outside seating, catches our eye. We both order the catch of the day with a Greek salad, roasted potatoes, and tzatziki. While waiting for the food to arrive, the waiter brings out a basket of fresh bread with olive oil and vinegar and a jug of white wine. Fee immediately dives into the bread while I pour the wine.

He groans obscenely, making me somewhat inappropriately turned on at the dinner table. We haven't eaten anything since the awful plane food, and I'm ravenous, so I pinch some bread from the basket before he eats it all.

"I can't believe we're actually on our honeymoon," Fee says, taking in our surroundings.

"If anyone earned a honeymoon, it's us." I chuckle.

My phone pings with a text from my cousin, Noah.

> **Noah:** FYI someone tried to breach the wards but they weren't successful and they're still intact. Enjoy your hol.

My hands begin to sweat as I read the message. Enjoy your hol? If one day I found out Noah was actually a robot, I wouldn't be surprised. 'By the way, the person who almost killed your husband might have just tried to get onto your property, but have a nice day.'

"What's wrong?" Fee asks, clearly noticing my concern.

"Nothin' that can't wait until we're home." I plaster a smile on my face, and it must be convincing because he changes the subject quickly. There's no need for us both to worry when there isn't anything we can do about it from here. It's just a jarring reminder that once these two weeks are up, there's a lot still to deal with back home. I guess we better make the most of our break from reality, then.

"You excited to learn to windsurf?" Fee asks, grinning widely.

In a few days, we're hiring a car to drive over to Vassiliki; it's approximately a half-hour drive from here. Fee used to go on regular family holidays to Greece, and he loves windsurfing and sailing. It's times like this that really highlight the different social classes we were raised in.

"I think these lessons will be the biggest test of our relationship so far."

"I'm an excellent instructor, I'll have you know. I taught Jade because she was ready to murder Jas when he tried." I smile because I know he's just excited to show me a part of himself I haven't seen before.

"I can't wait."

We made it through a full day of Fee teaching me to windsurf relatively unscathed. It was a lot of fun, and we both slept like the dead that night. Today, we're making the most of the hire car and driving to Porto Katsiki. Fee is behind the wheel, enthusiastically singing along to a Greek song on the radio, undeterred by the fact he doesn't know the words.

There isn't a cloud in the sky. It's a scorching day at around thirty-seven degrees, and I'm excited to get to the beach for more of a breeze. As we turn the next corner, Fee slows down and has to stop because the road is completely filled with… goats. We look at each other like, 'What do we do now?'. They have big bells on their necks and make an absolute racket as they walk across the road. Fortunately, we don't have to wait long until a middle-aged man appears and begins herding them off the road. We both laugh at how ridiculous it looks and then continue on our way to the beach.

The car park at the top is thankfully not too busy. We have to walk down some steep steps to get to the beach. It's worth it, though, for the stunning backdrop of the huge cliff face. The sand is so fine; it's almost white as it reflects the bright sunlight, contrasting with the clear turquoise waters of the Ionian Sea.

Fee picks out a spot not too far from the water, and we put our towels and cooler box down. We both go for a swim right away to cool off. Fee grabs a snorkelling mask we brought and goes off in search of underwater sea life while I head back to our towels to read my book. I lie on my front in case I pop a boner because this book has some top-tier spice. Fee will likely reap the benefits later.

I'm fully immersed in the story when Fee returns, lying on top of me and getting me all wet.

"Ugh. You're so annoyin'." He continues to rub his wet head all over my back.

"I'm just helping you stay cool."

"Thanks," I deadpan.

"You need to come join me in the water, I found a starfish." This is what happens when you marry a golden retriever type. You don't get to read in peace on the beach; you have to go and look at the weird shit they find. I knew who I was marrying, though, so I put my Kindle into the bag before joining him in the sea to go in search of his starfish.

PHOENIX CAMPBELL

The past two weeks have been an absolute dream come true. We've been out on the water nearly every single day, eaten our body weight in gyros and had more orgasms than is probably healthy, like I think if I come again, nothing but a puff of air will come out.

I'm kind of bummed that tonight is our last night, but I'm also excited for all of our holidays to come. We have a whole lifetime together, and I can't wait to see the world with Cee by my side.

For our final dinner, we went to a restaurant slightly further inland called Taverna Dimitris and had moussaka and saganaki as we watched the sunset. It was the perfect evening.

EPILOGUE

Sitting on the bed naked, I'm scrolling through random shit on my phone when Cee wanders out of the bathroom. He's wearing nothing but tight-fitting black boxer briefs and playing nervously with his fingers.

"What's up?" I ask curiously. He comes over and sits in the middle of the bed cross-legged, facing me.

"So, I've been thinkin' about this for a while, and since it's our last night, I thought it would be maybe a good time?" His intonation suggests it's a question but I've no idea what on earth he's actually asking. Nerves flutter in my stomach in anticipation.

"A good time for what?"

"Uhm. To mate?" I'm simultaneously relieved and elated. I've known Cee was my mate since the day I met him, and we've talked about it a few times over the years but never got as far as planning to do it. My teeth ache at the mere suggestion.

"You're sure?" I ask, needing to double-check. He nods.

"Yeah, I'm sure. I really want us to do this." My heart swells at his admission. For humans, getting married is often considered the biggest commitment, but that can always be undone. You can't undo a mating bite. It's a hundred percent for life. Even if one of you dies, your mating bite will remain.

"I love you so much, baby. There's nothing I'd love more than to be your mate—officially," I tell him, and he beams at me. "Come here," I say, making grabby hands at him.

Cee crawls onto my lap and kisses me enthusiastically. He tastes minty from his toothpaste and I want to breathe him in. Grabbing his hips, I flip us so he's on his back and I can rest between his thighs.

We make out lazily at first, leisurely tasting each other and enjoying the fact we have nothing to do and nowhere else to be but right here in each other's arms. Cee's cock starts to thicken in his briefs, and it presses against my stomach. Sitting up, I tug his boxers down; he lifts his hips to help me, and I chuck them over my shoulder. Reaching down, I stroke him without much pressure and several beads of precum leak from the tip.

I shuffle down so I'm lying on my stomach between his legs, darting my tongue out to taste him. When I glance up, his eyes are blown out with desire. I lick a stripe from his balls up to the tip before taking him into my mouth. I suck on him torturously slowly, wanting him to be a babbling mess by the time I sink my teeth into his neck. His hand roams over his chest, and he pinches one of his nipples, moaning loudly as he writhes on the bed.

I suck each of his balls into my mouth and swirl my tongue around them, just the way he likes and revel in the sweet sounds I pull from him. Pushing his knees back toward his chest, I expose his hole to me. Cee holds onto the back of his thighs to keep himself exactly where I want him. My tongue gently laps at his rim, softening him up. He tastes like heaven—musky and all Connor. I flatten my tongue over his tight pucker and lick him until he's pushing back into my face, begging me for more.

Relaxing back on my haunches, I reach for the lube and coat my fingers. I love watching the way his hole swallows my index finger as I pump it in and out of him.

"More, please. I need more," Cee babbles, and I gladly oblige, adding a second finger and crooking them. He moans loudly when I hit the right spot.

Planting his feet back on the bed, he starts riding my fingers as he languidly tugs on his throbbing cock at the same time. I could probably come from watching him do this. When Cee lets loose and gives in, chasing his pleasure, it turns me on like nothing else.

"Jesus, babe. You have no idea how hot you look right now," I pant.

"Fuck me. Please. Need you to fuck me, or I'm gonna die." I laugh a little at his dramatics, but I coat my cock in lube and stroke myself a few times before I line myself up with his entrance.

As always, he's tight when I push through the first ring of muscle, but then he breathes out and welcomes me inside his body. I have to take a few steadying breaths to stave off the orgasm that's building surprisingly quickly, considering I've already come three times today.

I move slowly at first, pulling almost all the way out before sliding back in. I take my time because I want to remember this moment, the moment when we aren't just fucking, but joining our souls together forever.

There were brief moments when Cee first became an Alpha that I worried he wouldn't want this dynamic between us anymore, that the Alpha in him would demand I submit to him. However, he's always taken pleasure in relinquishing some of the control when we're in bed together.

He hooks his ankles behind my back and pulls me into him, encouraging me to fuck him harder and faster. Grabbing the headboard above his head, I let loose. Pounding into him hard, and our moans echo through the room.

Right when I can tell we're both on the edge, Cee tilts his head to the side, bearing his neck to me. The significance of the moment steals my breath. Because I know I'm the only person he will *ever* expose his neck to this way. The only person he'll ever be this vulnerable for.

Alpha's do not submit. But he'll do it for me in these intimate moments we share. Right before I topple over the precipice, I bury my face into Cee's neck and bite down hard. Seconds later, he does the same to me, and we're both frozen in time.

At first, it's just the coppery taste of blood on my tongue. Then, the electricity of the lightning that seems to be constantly flowing through Cee's veins sparks on my tongue. When I swallow the taste of him down my throat, his essence mixes with mine, and I feel whole. Like a part of me I didn't even know was missing has suddenly been found.

As time resumes, as if the earth didn't just tilt on its axis, we both find our release. My cum marks him on the inside as he spills into the non-existent space between our bodies. I'm not entirely sure what I expected from the mating bond, but I feel both settled and forever changed.

"Holy shit," we say at the same time, and I collapse in a sweaty heap on top of him, both of us panting heavily. When my brain eventually comes back online, I sit up slightly and look at where I sank my teeth into him. Running my fingertip over the pink teeth marks, I watch in awe as the wound heals to become a silvery scar. A mark that will never leave his body or mine.

My mate.

I don't ever want to leave this moment. Bathing in his taste and scent.

Lightning, heather, *home* and *all mine*.

Forever.

COMING NEXT...

Stay tuned for the continuation of the story with Noah and Oliver as they investigate Archie's murder and Connor and Phoenix's house fire in book two of The Northern Shifters series.

ACKNOWLEDGEMENTS

Getting this book from the first draft to something publishable took a lot of help, so I have a lot of people to thank.

Thank you to Siobhan for reading the monstrosity that was my first draft. Bless you.

My sister, Beth, who not only read the first draft but patiently helped me work through several plot holes. Your gentle encouragement throughout got me to the end.

My mum, who also read my first draft, cheered me on throughout and raised me in a home surrounded by books, for which I am forever grateful.

Rianne, for going on this writing journey with me. Writing our books side by side got me to the finish line. Writing can be quite a lonely experience, but doing this together helped hold me accountable, made it more fun, and I don't think I would have made it through every hurdle if we hadn't been doing it together. Thank you for the solidarity and for working through I don't even know how many plot holes with me. We've both learned so much this past year, and I'm so proud of us. Who would have thought back when we were spending our evenings dancing to Charming Man that in 2024, we'd both have written and published a book. We did the thing!

Imi, who read not only my first draft but also the fifth. Your endless support and willingness to answer my millions of questions helped me maintain a smidge of my sanity. I'm sorry for spamming you with endless graphics for my Instagram posts and probably twenty different versions of my front cover. Your advice legitimately made it all a *lot* better. I'm so grateful, and I'm so glad we became besties again.

My sister, Joy, who read my fifth draft in a day and gave me such positive feedback and encouragement at a time when I was feeling like I had bitten off more than I could chew. I have a screenshot of your messages that day that I look at often to keep me going. You've been my cheerleader on the sidelines all the way through and it has meant the world.

Mieke, who gave me invaluable feedback and encouragement, especially during the moments when I felt like it was all terrible. You lifted me up when I needed it. Answered millions of questions about grammar and punctuation. Hyped me up at every turn and I'm so lucky to call you my friend.

Kane, for answering every invasive question I had to ensure the intimate scenes in my book between two men were authentic and for being the most hopeless romantic I've ever known. Never change.

My dad, who is never allowed to read this book, but answered every question I had about grammar, punctuation and word choices.

Natasha, my oldest friend who made the perfect witch. You've been in my corner for pretty much every moment of my entire life, and this was no different. Thank you for always being my rock.

Alexis, who sent me a video and annotated images to show me exactly how Connor might injure himself in a wood shop.

My beta readers: Maya Jean, thank you not only for giving me the kindest feedback about my writing but also for answering my endless questions about the self-publishing process. You've been so generous with your time and advice; you've helped me avoid so many mistakes and I am so so grateful. Jen, your feedback was so thorough and comprehensive and undoubtedly made my book so much better. I cannot recommend you highly enough as a beta reader. And finally, Chelsea, you told me things I didn't want to hear at first; you even convinced me to write a whole extra chapter and then some, but my book is so much better for it. Also, it turned out to be one of my favourite chapters to write in the whole book. Thank you for being the feral rat that you are.

Darin (@wellnessartist), thank you for being so incredibly talented and bringing my vision to life with the most stunning cover artwork I could have imagined.

Last but certainly not least, thank you to the author friends and bookstagrammer friends I've made along the way. I love this community so much, and I'm endlessly blown away by the support and enthusiasm from everyone within it. My queer little heart is so incredibly full.

ABOUT THE AUTHOR

Having been an avid reader her whole life, Emory got back into writing in early 2023. She began writing the first draft of Star-crossed Betas in June of the same year, and the story spilled out of her onto paper in just seven weeks.

It didn't take long for Emory to realise that there were more love stories to be told and a larger mystery at hand, so it became book one of a four-part series.

In the rare moments Emory isn't writing or editing, she can usually be found reading with her cat, Buffy. Or, in better weather, out walking in the beautiful Yorkshire scenery that provided the perfect backdrop for her books.

Add Emory Winters on socials:

Website: emorywinters.com

Join Emory's Facebook group: https://www.facebook.com/share/9kK4nmRrkYoR44fx/

Add on Facebook: https://www.facebook.com/author.emorywinters/

Follow on Instagram: https://www.instagram.com/emory.winters/

Follow on TikTok: https://www.tiktok.com/@emory.winters?is_from_webapp=1&sender_device=pc

CONTENT WARNINGS

Below is a list of content warnings:
- Sleep paralysis;

- House fire;

- Severe burn marks;

- Historical death of a parent—off-page;

- Death/ dead body (broken neck);

- Cut with a knife/bloodletting as part of a ritual;

- Panic attack;

- Recreational cannabis use;

- Pregnancy (of a side character);

- Death threat made against a pregnant side character.

Milton Keynes UK
Ingram Content Group UK Ltd.
UKHW040038310724
446348UK00003B/180